JORDAN DANE

NO ONE HEARD HER SCREAM

AVON

An Imprint of HarperCollinsPublishers

**To John—You are the cornerstone
for every hero I will ever write.**

AVON BOOKS
An Imprint of HarperCollins*Publishers*
10 East 53rd Street
New York, New York 10022-5299

Acknowledgments

This passion to write has been with me for as long as I can remember. There are people who have supported my efforts and contributed in many ways. First and foremost, my beloved husband and plot partner, John, has put up with my wild hours and the idiosyncrasies of a crazed author channeling characters. My family, particularly my father and mother, gave their unflinching support and plenty of fodder for fiction. They tell me if they had known I'd be an author, they would've worked harder at being better parents. Better parents? I can't imagine a reality where that would even be possible.

Thanks to those who helped shape the voice I am still cultivating—Dana Taylor, Beth Daigre, Katie Kuhne, Cindy Sorenson, and Tina "Godiva" Novinski-Radcliffe. And special thanks to Grace Kirkwood, who helped forge this story with a keen reader's eye. Glad you answered the phone all those years ago when a wannabe author called to research your corner of the world. And to other generous author mentors—Merline Lovelace and Mel Odom— I couldn't have done this without you. There were times I firmly believed you hung out in cyberspace solely to respond to my emails.

And with every story, an amazing amount of research takes place—the fun part of the job. For things I may have embellished for the sake of fiction, no one is accountable except me. But for everything I got right, special gratitude to author and former homicide detective John Foxjohn, who shed light on law enforcement in Texas. On San Antonio, my resident experts Kathryn and Ignactio Torres, Jr., played a vital role. And much appreciation to the police department of the City of Edmond, Oklahoma, for the training I received as part of the Citizen's Police Academy, a terrific program conducted by Lieutenant Cleo Land, my "LT."

I also want to recognize those professional organizations that provide great resources for new writers: Romance Writers of America, my beloved Outlaws at the OK RWA, Sisters in Crime, RWA Kiss of Death Online Chapter, Mystery Writers of America, and the International Thriller Writers. And a special thanks to all the hardworking staff at Avon Books—sales, publicity, art department, copy editors, and anyone who contributed to the process. If it takes a village to package a book, then let me extend my never-ending gratitude to Avon's Village People.

And my dream to be published had plenty to do with the intervention of an angel, *New York Times* bestseller Sharon Sala, who read this story and believed in me enough to stick her sweet neck out. Angels do walk the earth and I have living proof. Special thanks to my stylish and savvy ally in the trenches, my agent, Meredith Bernstein. And to my glorious and brilliant editor, Lucia Macro—this wouldn't have happened without you believing in my future. You are my dream catcher.

PROLOGUE

Somewhere in her heart, Danielle Montgomery knew this was wrong, and her guilt had a face. *Momma's face*. Memories of her mother flashed in her head with a steady and persistent rhythm.

"I swear, it's the Catholic guilt," she said to herself. She took a deep breath and fiddled with the senior class ring on her finger. "What's the use of regular confession if a girl has nothing new to say?"

She held a wrist up to the dim glow of a streetlamp and looked at her watch. Twenty minutes late. Had she misunderstood his instructions? In the back of her mind, a bigger question plagued her. Why had she promised to meet him like this?

He was a stranger who'd hit on her at the beach. The attention of a college boy, especially in front of her classmates, made her feel special. She'd been a sucker for his gorgeous blue eyes, but she had a notion Momma wouldn't have been so impressed. Maybe that was the whole point. Now Danielle paced by the side entrance to the club, flicking ashes from a cigarette, another rebellious rite of passage Momma wouldn't approve.

Then the feeling came again—the feeling of being watched. Stronger this time.

Her eyes strafed the alley behind her, narrow and murky with shadows. Nothing. She looked up to a handful of darkened windows. Someone might be checking her out, some pervert in the dark. *Now you're being paranoid, Dani.*

She drew a frazzled breath and took another drag off her cigarette, blowing smoke rings in the air. With the music thumping behind the metal door, she stared up into the night sky, thick with stars. A clear night. And the flickering points of light beat to the rhythm of the music. The bar rocked, just as he promised. But being underage, she had no hope of getting inside without his help. As she watched the smoke rings drift apart, another thought occurred to her.

"Can't believe this. No way the jerk ditched me."

Frustration wedged a lump in her throat. She tossed her cigarette butt and kicked a broken beer bottle with the toe of her shoe, hearing it clink across the asphalt. She'd left her girlfriends back at the hotel, promising a full report if they covered for her with the chaperones. At this rate, unless she embellished the truth, there'd be nothing to say. So much for becoming the new legend at St. Joseph's High, back in San Antonio.

Unwilling to give up on her plans, she fanned herself with a hand. "Damn it. I bet my mascara is runny. Probably have friggin' raccoon eyes."

Muggy hot air clung to her skin and fused with perspiration to make her perfume smell stale. And worse, a tinge of sunburn radiated off her skin, intensifying the heat. Strands of her blond hair felt heavy and damp, clinging to her bare shoulders and back. Even without a mirror, she knew her hair had gone flat. The humidity and salty air off the ocean had done their usual damage. She'd spent two hours getting ready. Now, none of it mattered.

"Damn it, Brandon. Where are you?"

She thought about catching a cab back to the hotel, but in the pale light, she glanced down at her new clothes. She wanted him to see her in this outfit. Tight jeans would get his attention and the blue halter top accentuated the color of her eyes.

All of a sudden, a sound came from the entrance to the alley, the drone of an engine and the crunch of tires. She looked up. Headlights blinded her. She squinted and raised a hand to block the glare. A dark van.

"Brandon?" she called. Her voice cracked. "Is that you?"

No answer. The driver got out and slammed the van door behind him. With the streetlight behind him, his face remained in shadow. Something was very wrong.

"He couldn't make it, sweet thing." Low and sinister, the man's voice skittered across her skin like spiders. "Will I do?"

Her breath caught in her throat. Danielle dropped her purse and turned to run. Maybe he'd settle for money. No such luck. From behind, she heard heavy footsteps, gaining on her. But as her scream pierced the night air, another man emerged from the darkness ahead, lunging at her. She tried to run by him, but he grabbed her arm, almost wrenched it out of its socket.

"Nooo!" she shrieked.

The man spun her around. Now, with no other choice, Danielle balled her fists, ready to fight. She kicked—hard—but nothing fazed him. He backhanded her across the face. The shock jolted her skull, and stars burst deep inside her brain, blinding her. She dropped to the asphalt. Her exposed skin scraped the ground. The heels of her hands and her elbows scuffed bloody and raw.

Can't give up! She fought to stay conscious. *You give up now, you die!*

Two shadows preyed on her, eclipsing the light at the end of the alley. Danielle rolled onto her back, flailing arms and kicking legs at whatever moved. Strong hands gripped her, hard. One clasped her mouth. The weight of a knee to her chest cut off her air. Through her nose, she drew a gasp into burning lungs.

Suddenly, Danielle felt the stab of a needle in her neck. With the sharp pain, fear prickled her scalp, and goose bumps raced across her skin. Her neck burned like acid. A deathlike stillness came when her body fell slack, her arms limp by her sides.

Oh, God. Please. She screamed inside her head, but no sound came from her mouth.

A man's hand suffocated her. As the drug washed through her, once more she caught a glimpse of the night sky. Her eyes fixed upon the stars dotting the heavens, shimmering light. And like an old movie, images of her mother's face flickered in and out of her mind. Momma's lips moved, out of sync, as she spoke. The sound of her voice muffled in the haze until darkness swallowed everything.

Oh, Momma. I'm so sorry. Bittersweet memories played cruel tricks with her mind. But as a tear drained from Danielle's eye, her thoughts drifted apart like smoke rings in the night sky. All she felt was the distant wetness of the drop. With great concentration, she focused on the sensation, picturing the tear as it rolled down her cheek. Buoyancy lifted her body, setting it adrift in a pitch-black void. Soon, the world would cease to exist. Time would come to a dead stop.

And in the darkness, even the memory of Momma's voice wouldn't reach her.

CHAPTER 1

Central Police Station Gymnasium
Downtown San Antonio, five months later

Rebecca Montgomery battered the seventy-pound punching bag in blinding succession, ignoring the price her body would pay. Pain and physical exhaustion dulled the rage and guilt, but nothing would free her from it. *Nothing.*

Her life balanced on a single point in time—poised at a dead stop—resistant to moving forward and incapable of going back. The night her little sister went missing rocked her world, but in the agonizing time that followed, her life changed forever. Becca could never make it right. Not now.

Danielle's body was never found.

She grimaced at the thought and intensified her workout. Not knowing what had happened tore at her, day by day, driven by her own inability to uncover the truth. Horrific thoughts emerged, dark and disturbing. Being a homicide detective prepared her for the worst-case scenario, but in doing so, it robbed her of hope. And for that, Becca hated herself.

Stay focused. Keep moving. Use the pain.

The initial shock of Dani's disappearance morphed into a flood of emotions, from mind-numbing depression to blinding rage when she thought about the injustice. Nothing made the pain go away. She found herself desperate to regain control of her life. Wanting her body to *feel something* and her mind to release the demons.

Becca tightened her jaw until it hurt. *Push through it. You gotta stay strong.*

She welcomed her method of self-inflicted punishment, giving in to its rhythm. Even through elastic wrap and workout gloves, her fists ached with every jab. The bag swayed with each driving blow. The muscles in her legs burned from the early-morning workout.

Circling, Becca picked up the pace and shifted weight to focus her whole body behind each impact. Her lungs heaved like a machine. Bobbing and weaving, she switched the speed and the combination of her punches—left jab, straight right, left hook. With shoulder-length dark hair pulled back, she ignored the loose strands stuck to her cheeks. Sweat trailed off her body and drenched her cotton T-shirt and shorts. Becca had hit the zone.

Within Central Station on South Frio Street, she exercised most mornings in a large facility located in the basement of police headquarters. But her usual workout had taken on more significance. Like the sputtering vapor whistling from a kettle on the boil, Becca needed to vent. And this was a good place to blow off steam.

She'd grown accustomed to the musk of body odor mixed with the persistent smell off the dank walls of the SAPD gymnasium. The steady clacking of weights and the drone of showers had become nothing more than white noise. Male voices echoed behind her, but one finally stood out.

"Hey, Montgomery! You've been shadowin' my case again, and I don't like it."

Silence spread across the gym. All conversation died, and the clank of weights stopped. She didn't have to turn around to know all eyes were on her.

Becca lowered her arms, gasping from the exertion of her penance. Sweat stung her eyes. After yanking off her gloves, she took her time, running scenarios through her mind. *Let it go, Beck.* She reached for a nearby towel and wiped it across her face, draping it over her neck. *Don't let the jerk get to you.* Becca knew what a reasonable person might do, but by the time she turned around, the word "reasonable" vanished from her vocabulary.

"I don't know what you're talking about, Murphy." Her dark eyes took aim like a laser scope on a sniper rifle. "So why don't you mind your own business."

Becca turned her shoulder, but he pulled her around to face him.

"Oh, that's rich, coming from you. You're acting like a damned vigilante, and I'm supposed to mind my own business? Other lives are at risk here."

"I was wondering if you'd noticed that," she said.

Moving closer, she picked lint off his T-shirt and lowered her voice, so not many would hear. "You see, I think you picture this case to be a fast track for your career. You probably figure if you play your cards right, this liaison gig to the FBI might impress the feds. But you know what? Time is swirling down the drain, and you got nothin' on my sister's killer or the other abductions. Good luck impressing *anyone* with that."

"Ooohhh," the men within earshot resounded in unison. Nervous laughter died.

Paul Murphy served as a catalyst to her mounting frustration. All she needed was an excuse to lash out, and he had given it to her. The man didn't know when to quit—a dedicated cop, real determined. Good qualities, except when directed at her. Almost six-foot, the bastard wasn't much taller than she, but he looked like a wall of muscle, broad shoulders and thick neck. A regular fireplug.

"You're a pretty big talker. Maybe you think special treatment is in order, with what happened to your sister and all. But I can't have you stickin' your nose in my business, so knock it off." Murphy stepped closer, close enough for her to see every acne scar. His shoulders and arms glistened with sweat.

Like a chess player, she assessed her next moves. His nose had already been broken once. A second time wouldn't hurt his looks any. She contemplated rearranging his face with a well-placed uppercut, but several of the men drew into a tight circle around him. Although Becca wasn't sure whose side they were on, it didn't matter. Since her sister's case started, she'd made enemies. She'd pushed and pushed until walls were erected, keeping her out of the loop in the investigation that leapt jurisdictional boundaries. So Becca knew—she'd be on her own.

But that didn't stop her from tossing gasoline onto a smoldering fire. She heard the words coming from her mouth, the voice of a stranger.

"I don't expect anything special. I only want you to do your damned job."

"Well, you're gonna have to trust me to do that, Montgomery. Let me do my fuckin' job."

Fists at her sides, she stood her ground, leaving little room to maneuver. The last thing she wanted was to fight one of her own, but she couldn't back down either. Whoever threw the first punch would be the real loser. She knew it, so did Murphy. She could tell by his hesitation. Becca faced a real standoff—two hundred pounds' worth.

"Break it up, you two. That's an order." The bellowing voice of Lieutenant Arturo Santiago forced her to stand down, but she hadn't gotten off the hot seat. "Montgomery, in my office. *Now!* And Murphy? You're next, after you hit the showers. I don't want to call in a HAZMAT team to fumigate after your sorry ass darkens my door."

A lieutenant always knew how to clear a room. Becca took a deep breath, trying to control the surge of adrenaline through her system.

Murphy shrugged and forced a grin. "Come on, L.T. I'm a ray of sunshine. No fumigatin' required." He backed off with a slight nod and pointed a finger at her. "This is my case, Montgomery. Are we clear?"

"Oh, I think we both know where we stand on the subject, yeah." She tugged into her sweats. "And I'll give your point all the consideration it's due."

Murphy stormed off in a huff, reading her message loud and clear.

Becca hadn't picked the fight, but she'd been prepared to end it. Practically egging Murphy on, she found herself wanting him to throw the first punch. And even more disturbing, she'd been disappointed when the lieutenant intervened. What the hell was wrong with her? She had let Murphy get to her, allowing her pent-up tension to cloud her good judgment. Now she had to deal with the lieutenant in the privacy of his office.

She knew what he wanted to talk about, and it had nothing to do with Murphy's sorry ass.

Lieutenant Santiago's office smelled of coffee and stale smoke, a by-product of the old homicide division, before antismoking legislation. Central Station had been smoke-free for quite a while, but the stench lingered from years past, infused into the walls. No amount of renovation had ever managed to eliminate the odor.

With arms crossed, Becca sat in front of his desk, waiting. She imagined how her conversation with the lieutenant might play out, but none of the scenarios were in her favor.

Play the hand you've been dealt. No fancy moves.

Behind his beige metal desk with walnut veneer top, a clock hung on the wall and marked the passing of time with a steady annoying beat. *Tick, tick, tick.*

All part of the charade. Becca knew the man's game of intimidation, making her wait. So far, she had to admit it had worked pretty well. And the glass walls of the corner office made the room feel like a damned sweatbox, even at this time of day. She wiped a sheen of perspiration off her forehead.

To distract herself from the discomfort, she gazed around the room, taking in the details of the man's many accomplishments. Becca's eyes found a photo of Santiago with his family. At work, the lieutenant maintained a stern grimace, but the man had an infectious smile when he allowed it to show. Deepening age lines gave his face character. His short-cropped dark hair had receded to a crown worn like a laurel wreath around his head.

Shiny plaques of meritorious service, framed photos of him with the mayor, and coaching mementos from a local Little League team reflected his life in service to the community and law enforcement. At one time, such recognition would have meant everything to her. But now, with Danielle gone, it all seemed so pointless.

"Jesus, Dani," she whispered. "Why the hell—?"

Tick, tick . . .

Looking out the picture window to her left, she lost herself in the drama of sunrise. Filtered through a cheap set of venetian blinds, the morning sun pierced heavy cloud cover with spears of brilliant orange, a quiet skirmish. City buses and commuter traffic droned in the background. It reminded her that life carried on, and the world spun on its axis, whether she came along for the ride or not. A humbling notion.

"You take your coffee black, right?"

She jumped at the sound of his voice, an unsettling reaction. Lieutenant Santiago entered the office, holding two cups of coffee. The hot beverage would exacerbate the heat, but she could use the caffeine. Becca reached for the cup as he shut the door.

"Yes, sir." She took a sip, breathing in the aroma from the steam. "Thanks."

"This office can be a bit stifling in the mornings, but I kind of like it."

She drank in silence, waiting for him to start. Knowing the lieutenant, she wouldn't have to wait long.

"What happened? Is it true you've been bird-dogging Murphy's work, conducting your own investigation?"

Becca avoided his stare, looking down into her cup. A lumbering silence filled the space between them, interrupted by the steady beat of the clock. *Tick, tick* . . . The lieutenant knew the answer to his question. And she didn't feel the need to incriminate herself.

"We already talked about this, Rebecca. Your involvement complicates the case. You're too close to it."

She looked up, narrowing her eyes.

"Maybe that's what the investigation needs, sir. A fresh set of eyes. Someone with a stake in this." She set her coffee down on the corner of his desk and crossed her arms. "Murphy is a good cop, but a real simple kind of guy. For him, thinking 'out of the box' is a radical concept, reserved for left-wing liberals, four-eyed geeks, and girlie-men."

Santiago raised an eyebrow and wrestled with his lower lip to avoid smiling.

"So why'd you let him get to you?" The man zeroed in on the heart of the problem. "You were ready to deck him."

She shrugged. "Seemed like a swell idea at the time."

"Not good enough, Rebecca." He leaned forward, elbows on his desk. "Look, I know this has been rough on you, not being more involved in Danielle's case. I can't imagine how I'd feel if something happened to one of my kids."

His face softened in empathy. "Don't force me to stop you, Becca. My heart wouldn't be in it. But you gotta see, there's a bigger picture here. And I can't allow you to jeopardize this investigation."

"But my sister's case is getting lost in the shuffle of these abductions, sir." She pressed, her voice laden with emotion. "I gotta speak for her. I don't see anyone else doin' it."

His face settled into his usual stern expression.

"Need I remind you that the circumstances surrounding Danielle are a little different from the other two victims in this case? Yeah, all three lived here and were abducted from class outings across the country. But that's where the similarities end. Your sister left a trail after Padre Island, Becca."

His raised voice merged with an abrasive creak in his chair. The sound made her skin scramble like hearing fingernails screech across a chalkboard. Lately, her nerves were raw, but her revulsion had more to do with what he said. And the lieutenant added insult to injury by harping on his version of the truth.

"Look, you gotta face facts. Dani used her credit card at two gas stations and a motel. And we had an eyewitness sighting and a video to back this up. It looks like she ran away from home and hooked up with the wrong people."

An unreliable witness and one blurry video did not stack up to much in Becca's book. Even if the young girl in the videotape looked as if she wore Danielle's new clothes, identified by her sister's closest friends, it amounted to circumstantial evidence at best.

"But don't you see, Art? She'd never do that. Sure she had a rebellious streak, but what kid her age doesn't? Hell, you should've seen me."

Becca bolted out of her chair and stalked toward his office window, holding back the anger welling deep in her belly. She'd heard this account before, and it always made her furious, but talking about Dani in the past tense gnawed at her gut like a cancer. It didn't feel right.

"You? A rebel? Hard to imagine," he sniped.

"Sarcasm duly noted, but hear me out." She turned to face him. "I think someone stole her credit card and set up a bogus trail for us to follow. I think they wanted to throw us off what really happened to her."

"And what's your theory on that?"

Tick, tick, tick . . . Becca hated to admit it. She was as clueless as Murphy on what happened to her sister.

At first, Danielle's disappearance looked like the random act of a stray predator. After interviewing Dani's friends and extracting the truth, investigators closed in on a local hot spot. Tire tracks, signs of a struggle, and spots of her sister's blood marked the crime scene. And the college kid she was supposed to meet? He had a damned, rock-solid alibi. So the search for Danielle began. Local law joined forces with a contingent from San Antonio to scour the neighborhood for witnesses. Reward posters and flyers went out. Volunteers and local pilots searched for signs of a body. Radio stations and television news teams blitzed the story. None of the efforts paid off.

In between a few promising leads, many hoaxes were investigated, draining the resources of the police. Eventually, evidence of her credit card use trickled in, the sightings leading the search away from Padre Island. The FBI was brought in when it looked like her trail crossed state lines. Then Becca's worst fear. A motel room splattered with blood—too much blood loss for anyone to survive. At first, she was in denial that the blood belonged to her sister. But the tests came back a match. Dani had died in a cheap motel room. No body found.

Two other abduction cases followed in different states, but with connections to San Antonio. And in the turn of a page, Dani's story became old news. The media moved on.

With Becca relegated to the status of family member, she'd been kept at arm's length from the investigation. Her pushing investigators and double-checking leads had alienated her from the insiders to the case. Censored verbal reports gave her limited information, so she'd resorted to stealing peeks at Murphy's case book. Now that looked like a dead end. The word "powerless" didn't begin to describe how she felt.

And looking into the eyes of her despondent mother on the day they buried Danielle's empty coffin cast Becca into a new brand of hell. A part of her died that day.

"I don't have any theories, not yet." Becca slumped against the window frame. "But if Dani's case is so different from the others, maybe I can conduct my own—"

"You haven't heard a word I've said, have you?" Lieutenant Santiago clenched his jaw, a familiar gesture. "Sit. Now."

His command gave no room for interpretation. This was not an invitation to be declined. Becca heaved a sigh and trudged back to her seat, mustering a rebellious slouch.

"The FBI smells the work of a human trafficking ring with connections to San Antonio. And like flies to a pile of horseshit, they're buzzing over my jurisdiction. I don't need to tell you how *that* makes me feel. Pompous bastards." He furrowed his brow. "With you poking your nose into this, the feds have already raised their objections. Your link to Danielle could pose a problem for the prosecution if they find a connection, especially if a defense attorney gets wind of your involvement with evidence gathering. Do you want that?"

"I don't care about any damned court case, sir. I want justice for Dani."

"And that's the problem. Don't make me out to be the bad guy here. If there's some nut bag abducting and killing young women, it's my job—and yours—to put 'em away." A sad expression etched his face. "Don't make me force you to take time off. You and I both know how you'd spend it. I'd rather keep an eye on you myself."

With his brow furrowed, he leaned across the desk, concern overshadowing his personal disappointment. She owed Lieutenant Santiago so much. The man had been a mentor to her. Interfering in Danielle's case had been a flagrant betrayal of his trust and contrary to her sense of responsibility as a cop. Still, she had no choice. Straightening up in her chair, she waited to hear his version of a compromise.

"Before you hit the showers, get with dispatch. They got a call about skeletal remains found at the old Imperial Theatre, the one that just burned down. For now, I'm assigning you to the Cold Case Squad to handle it. On temporary loan."

"Is this an order, L.T.?"

"Does it need to be?" He matched her tone, ramped up the attitude. He'd lost his patience with the caring father routine. "Look, you've got a chance to give someone else closure here. And you must know how important that is. The pile of bones at the Imperial used to be someone's family. You do your job, I'll do what I can to keep you apprised of Murphy's progress myself. Deal?"

Becca crossed her arms and leaned against the

doorframe, staring at him. He had played the guilt card like a master, no way for her to trump it. She cocked her head and crooked a corner of her mouth, watching as he basked in his victory.

He returned her smile. "If you need anything, or just want to talk, let me know."

"Thanks, L.T. I'll remember that."

Becca left his office and headed for dispatch, her mind working on what to do next. Lieutenant Santiago had been right about one thing. Closure was important. It would be worth *any* sacrifice.

The heat from the sun burned off the morning haze, but an early cool front brought a stiff breeze to jostle the trees. Real Texas weather. A taste of winter might come on the heels of sweltering heat or monsoon rains. This time of year, it paid to be a regular Girl Scout, prepared for anything.

Becca turned off Commerce onto St. Mary's Street and found a parking lot across the street from the Imperial Theatre. She found a spot next to one of the fire department trucks. Once outside her vehicle, Becca tugged at the collar of her white oxford shirt and buttoned the jacket to her navy pantsuit, preparing to go inside. Becca removed her sunglasses, slipped them into the pocket of her jacket, and clipped her ID badge on a lapel. She stared across the street to assess the damage from the front.

Yellow crime-scene tape whipped in the breeze, a flag for curious onlookers. Several people lingered on her side of the street and down a block or two. What they expected to see, she had no idea. For all they knew, it had only been a fire. News of the body had not been released. Still, morbid curiosity drew them like flies to roadkill.

But one man stood out from the rest.

Dressed in a sharp suit and tie, the guy looked like he had stepped off the cover of *Gentlemen's Quarterly* magazine with his swarthy good looks. GQ had mongo bucks written all over him. Wearing dark glasses, he leaned against a deep blue Mercedes S 600 parked along the street, hands in his pants pockets. Even without seeing his eyes, she knew he spotted her, his head turning with interest as she stood on the curb. He didn't look like the typical gawker who hoped to catch a glimpse of some action from the old burned-out building. Not this guy. He was anything but typical. And another facet of him caught her eye. Ever since leaving her Crown Vic, she had become his focus, holding his complete interest.

"The feeling's mutual, gorgeous," she whispered. "But I'm not in the mood."

Becca shifted her gaze to the Imperial. The theater bore a certain dignity, even covered in layers of soot. The fire had consumed much of its striking architecture and intricate detail with no regard for history. Prior to the blaze, she believed the theater had been left derelict. *A real shame.*

Seeing it now from the outside—nothing more than a blackened carcass—provoked her already sullen mood. She read somewhere that the recently declared historic building had been slated for restoration, but the work hadn't begun yet. Now, it never would.

From what she remembered of the theater, Baroque,

Mediterranean, and Spanish Mission influences had inspired the design. Conveying theater patrons to a fanciful villa, arches with ornate columns, tile roof-tops, and a bell tower surrounded the stage. Walls were transformed into steeples with colorful glass windows. Rising above the quaint setting, a vaulted "sky" in deep blue twinkled with endless stars and clouds drifted overhead like mist. On a balcony railing, a rare white peacock perched next to doves caught in midflight, all part of the architect's illusory world.

With a young Danielle in tow, Becca had been in the theater as a teen, the treasured memory of an outing with her late grandmother. The experience had forever left its mark. At the time, she and Dani imagined the Imperial to be a grand palace, home to a legendary king and queen with magical powers. Crystal chandeliers soared high above the plush seats, making the gilded walls glisten in the pale light. She remembered holding her breath when the lights dimmed, eyes wide. With its elaborate bro-cade borders, the velvet curtain rose over the stage. Elegant ballerinas performed *The Nutcracker,* look-ing even more enchanting on the ornate stage. *Pure magic.*

Now all that was gone, and so was Danielle. Her heart ached with profound loss.

Ignoring GQ, still standing by his pricey car, Becca crossed the street and walked through what remained of the front door. After she flashed her badge to the uniform stationed at the entrance, he handed her a protective helmet with Plexiglas visor, standard-issue. She reached into the pocket of her jacket for a fresh pair of latex gloves and made sure she had her casebook, pen, and flashlight.

Inside, a dank smoldering odor filled her nostrils. Water damage fused with the fire's destruction. Squinting, Becca adjusted to the dark interior and hit the switch to her Kel-light. The beam of light stretched into the void, capturing fine particles of dust in its wake—a reminder why the air felt thick and smelled stale. The scorched shell captured her attention, a macabre landscape in black and gray. Past the lobby, an eerie hum drifted through the cavernous space, leading her like a beacon.

She heard voices ahead, the words garbled by the distance and the steady whir coming from a portable power generator. With the electricity out to the building, the generator would allow them to work by floodlights. Crime-scene techs were hard at work, bagging and tagging evidence and taking digital photographs.

But one section of the theater caught her eye. Bright lights flooded a murky and gaping cavity in a stone wall to the right of the stage. A group of men gathered near the opening, their silhouettes casting elongated shadows with every flash of the camera. As she approached, one of the men turned.

"Hey, Becca. Was wondering who'd get the short straw." Team leader for the crime-scene technicians, Sam Hastings grinned as Becca snapped on her latex gloves.

Tall and lanky with curly brown hair receding at his temples, the senior CSI stepped aside for her to get a closer look. Details of his face faded from view as he moved deeper into the shadows.

"Short straws are all I get lately." Skeletal remains were uncommon. Becca crooked her lips into a reasonable facsimile of a smile. "Before I forget, have one of your guys record the crowd outside, especially the suit by the Mercedes. And get his tag."

"Good idea. Firebugs like to watch the aftermath of their handiwork. The guy look suspicious?"

"Let's just say he stands out from the crowd, but I want the license tags and faces of everyone out there." She bent to get a closer look and dropped to a knee.

One of the techs knelt by the masonry and removed another stone, setting it on the floor beside him. A couple of bricks were already bagged. She knew anything could be evidence, including the mortar used. It might give some indication of a time line.

With flashlight in hand, Becca kept her eyes focused on the dark hole. She found herself staring into the hollow eyes of a skull. Its jaw gaped open in a grotesque scream. The smell of old death lingered enough to fill the tomb with a stale earthy stench, nothing more.

"So, tell me something I don't know, Sam."

"Okay." He took a moment to think. "When I was ten, a kid half my size made me cry when he threatened to hit me."

Becca turned toward him, an eyebrow raised.

"Not exactly what I had in mind, but thanks for sharing." She fought a smile. "How did they find the body?"

"Firefighter swingin' a mean ax took out the first bricks, enough to find somethin' staring back."

Once again, Becca glanced over her shoulder. Before she made a smart remark, Sam beat her to the punch, "Hey, if I'd gone the fireman route, I would've had to make a trip home to change my shorts. But I'm your basic jaded CSI guy. Nothing much surprises me anymore."

"I hear ya." Becca shifted focus deep into the hole and noticed something disturbing. "What do we have here? He's got no fingers?"

"Phalanges are the first to go. Over time, small bones drop off," Sam replied. He nudged close to her shoulder and used his flashlight to locate the bone fragments in the bottom of the cramped space. "It's gonna take us a while to remove the skeleton. We'll extricate the rest in one piece if we can."

He changed direction of his beam to reveal the skull and spoke aloud as if he were making a mental checklist.

"We don't get many skeletal remains to ID. We may have to bring in a specialist—a forensic anthropologist—maybe try and reconstruct facial features. We'll collect some mitochondrial DNA and retain it to compare against any known relation to the deceased. That'll be your job to find next of kin."

"My best hope to speed up the ID process will be to check into missing persons. The body had to be buried in this theater while it was under construction or during some kind of renovation. Maybe that'll help narrow the time period for my search. We could get lucky."

She made notes in her casebook. With a grimace, she rested an elbow on her knee, and said, "I came here as a kid to see a ballet once. It really creeps me out to know that while the crowd gave a standing ovation, this guy was buried in the wall near the stage."

"Yeah, back in the day, I heard it was murder to get a front-row seat."

Becca shut her eyes and shook her head. A collective groan rumbled through the techs standing behind her.

"Everyone's a critic." The CSI team leader shrugged.

"Hey, Sam. Wouldn't the smell of the body be detected once it was time for curtain call at the Imperial?"

"Yeah, but construction or renovation work takes time, right? Crews coming in and out. Time for a body to decompose depends on temperature, moisture, and accessibility to insects. In the summer, an exposed human body can be reduced to bones in nine days. Now granted, this type of setup would've taken longer, but it's conceivable only bones attended opening night. No tux required."

With more of the wall removed, he craned his neck and directed his flashlight into the makeshift tomb. "Looks like we're gonna have to rethink the gender thing. Check out those hips."

With a tilt of her head, Becca turned to stare at the senior CSI. "You need to hang out with people who're partial to breathing. In case you haven't noticed, this is a pile of bones. What hips?"

"I used the word 'hips' for your benefit. I didn't think—'Hey, check out that sciatic notch'—would get your attention. Am I right?"

When she scrunched her face, Sam explained and pointed to the lower vertebrae.

"The sciatic notch spreads as a woman gets older, allowing the pelvis to make room for childbirth. If I had to guess, this sacrum and pelvic rim are from a young female. And the partially erupted molars back me up. I'd say the victim was late teens to early twenties at time of death." He pointed a finger to the brow of the skull. "Another thing, check out the forehead. It's almost vertical. Men's tend to slant more, develop a browridge. And with the narrow mandible, definitely female."

"So my 'he' is a 'she'?"

"Yep, looks like it."

When Becca peered deeper into the stone vault, markings caught her eye.

"Hey, what's this?" She inched closer and directed her flashlight to the left. "Oh, God. Are those what I think they are?"

Jagged scratches lined the inside of the stone vault. Layers of them overlapped in no discernible pattern. Thin striations mixed with deeper gouges. She felt the group of men move closer. Silence made the air feel thick and oppressive. Motionless. With her discovery, it became harder for her to breathe. Finally, Sam confirmed what she already suspected. By the solemn tone in his voice, she knew it struck him, too.

"Scratches. Probably from her fingernails. Looks like she was buried alive."

Becca closed her eyes to block the images, a gruesome strobe effect triggered in her mind. Tortured screams. A mouth gasping for air. Sheer panic. She pictured Danielle dying an unthinkable death, walled away in darkness with no one to hear her cries for help.

"No one heard her scream." She hadn't realized she'd spoken the words aloud until Sam consoled her with his reply.

"Until now." He sighed and stared into the hole.

Danielle's face haunted her. As a homicide detective, Becca had witnessed the perverse nature of the human condition, carried to the extreme. But the varying degrees of cruelty one human being inflicted upon another never ceased to amaze her. The day it did would be the day she'd quit. Still, she knew this case would brand her psyche for years to come.

"You all right?" Sam nudged her shoulder, his voice quiet and reassuring.

It took her a long while to answer.

"Yeah. I'll be okay." The words coming from her mouth sounded trite and mechanical, lacking any real conviction.

"Think I found something to cheer you up." He reached into the tomb and navigated through the tight space. After shining a light on what he retrieved, he said, "Maybe a lucky charm."

Sam held a thin necklace with a trinket dangling from it. The metal had been discolored with the years, and dirt clung to the delicate chain.

"What's that?" She narrowed her eyes to get a better look at the jewelry she took from his hand.

Holding the evidence toward the light, she answered her own question. "In the shape of a heart. If this isn't some cheap bauble, it might lead somewhere. Good eye, Hastings."

Sam smiled. "Yeah, my wife says I have an eye for the expensive stuff. It's pretty tarnished, but it doesn't look cheap to me. And if I'm not mistaken, there are small diamond chips on it, too."

Becca stood and handed the necklace back, making another note in her book.

"Who's the arson investigator?" she asked.

"Rick Gallegos is workin' lead. You know him?" When she nodded, he pointed to the far wall. "Try over there."

Before she left, the CSI grabbed her arm and pulled her aside, out of earshot from his crew. Concern lined his face.

"You and your family are in my prayers . . . if there's anything I can do."

She smiled. "With what we do, prayers seem like a Band-Aid on a hemorrhage."

"Don't get me wrong. I come from a long line of scuba-diving Protestants. Most of my family only surface on church holidays. But I found it . . . helps me."

"Thanks, Sam. You're a good friend, but really, I'm all right. I'll be in touch on our Jane Doe."

Complete denial. She heard it in her voice. *'I'm all right,' my ass.* Her life had mired in her sister's tragedy and she knew it. But the murder victim's family needed her to function on all cylinders. They deserved her best.

"Guess prayers can't hurt," she muttered as she walked away. "Maybe God still listens to other people."

Gallegos was one of the best arson investigators with the city. The man had extensive experience and training, with an education in chemicals. He'd also been part of a bomb squad at another police station. With the pairing of Rick Gallegos and Sam Hastings on this investigation, maybe she hadn't drawn the short straw after all.

Rick was her height, with thick dark hair and skin the color of rich mocha. His eyes were almost black, and he possessed a piercing stare, the kind that unnerved the guilty. But for those having the pleasure to work with him, he showed warmth and good humor in his gaze. A diligent investigator and a thorough one. She liked him from the first day they had met, several years ago.

"Hey, Rick." She lowered the beam of her flashlight, leaving his face partially lit. "This case is gonna be tough enough. Glad you're working the fire. How's it coming?"

"Getting close to wrapping up, but I've got something for you to see. Follow me, Becca." He waved a hand and led her through the burned rubble.

He took her toward a back door and into the bright sunshine. Becca shielded her eyes with a hand, but it felt good to be out from under the oppressive darkness of the charred Imperial. Parts of her skin were caked with a layer of dust. Feeling gritty, she ran a hand over her chin, only to find her gloves smeared with soot. No telling what she'd find on her white blouse.

Just great! She'd clean up in the car. It wasn't her day. Becca filled her lungs with fresh air and let Rick talk.

"Arsonists believe fire destroys evidence, but not if an investigator knows what to look for. They forget only the vapor burns, not the liquid part of the fuel. So if any material is saturated with an accelerant, the wetness prevents the cloth from burning, leaving behind evidence for us to connect the dots. If we match the fabric to something on the premises of a suspect, we've got a link to the crime scene."

"So what have you learned so far?"

"I've been examining patterns of burn, the structure of the building itself, the ventilation factors, and what fuel loadings were available. The Imperial was a veritable powder keg waiting for someone to strike a match." He brought her toward a large garbage receptacle set too close to the back wall of the building. "But I found some 'pour patterns' in and around this Dumpster. They look promising."

He squatted near a pile of trash and pointed, continuing with his preliminary findings.

"Incendiary fire. A candle ignited the blaze and served as a time delay. It looks like some type of liquid accelerant was used. More than likely gasoline, but I'll confirm that when I run it through the gas chromatograph. See here? It burned in a way that remained visible after the fire." Rick pointed to the burn pattern, or rather, the absence of burn. "I'm still collecting evidence, enclosing what I find in airtight containers to prevent cross contamination and keep the integrity of the accelerant intact. But so far, this looks like arson, deliberately set."

Arson added a wrinkle of complication, but a thought registered in her mind.

"Guess if the fire hadn't happened, we might never have found our Jane Doe buried in the wall. Whoever set the blaze may help us find justice for our murder victim. At least we have a shot at it. Kind of an interesting turn of fate, I'd say."

The irony appealed to her. Becca handed her helmet to the fire investigator.

"I'll leave the stylish headgear with you. Send me a copy of your findings. And thanks, Rick."

"Will do." He nodded and headed back into the building.

Normally, the owner of the Imperial Theatre would be considered a strong suspect for a fire caused by arson. As a rule, the fraudulent act was committed to collect insurance money, especially if the policy amount exceeded the value of the real estate. That fit the bill for the Imperial in its current state of disrepair. But if the property owner had anything to do with the body buried in the theater, an arson fire would be the last thing the owner would want. An arson investigation would only shed light on a very deep, dark secret.

The pieces to this puzzle didn't make sense—yet. But there was nothing like a good mystery. No matter how her investigation proceeded, the owner of the Imperial Theatre would be high on her interview list.

Becca jotted some more notations into her casebook and walked around the building, still thinking about the murdered woman. When she rounded the corner at the front of the theater, she caught sight of her mystery man's Mercedes, but he wasn't in sight. For an instant, she felt—

"Disappointed, Beck? Get over yourself. With my luck, I'll find him in one of the mug books back at headquarters, with priors as long as my arm." She heaved a sigh.

Reaching into her jacket pocket, she retrieved her car keys and walked across the street. After unlocking her car door, she noticed movement near the corner of the Imperial. Becca recognized the man, even under his designer shades. But instead of crossing the street toward his expensive ride, the guy headed in the opposite way, as if he had somewhere else to be. Doubts crept into her mind. Maybe the Mercedes wasn't his.

No way! The man definitely fit the ride.

"So what are you up to, GQ?" She pursed her lips and thought for a moment, giving in to her impulse to follow. With enough people around, she could blend in and tail him from her side of the street. Mostly, Becca was too damned curious to let him walk away. She slipped on her sunglasses. On instinct, she felt for her Glock, lodged in a holster at the small of her back.

Speaking to her weapon, Becca muttered, "Let's you and me take a stroll, shall we?"

CHAPTER 2

The man walked with purpose, hands in his pockets. A sexy swagger. If she'd known the name of his tailor, Becca would have sent a thank-you note. His suit accentuated every asset the man had. Her target moved with a certain power and grace she always associated with a Grade A male. Yet with his head lowered in boyish charm, his body was a contradiction. Navigating the streets with eyes looking down, he seemed to know where he was going. A man on a mission. His face stern, he looked preoccupied and deep in thought. And although people noticed him, they avoided eye contact, maybe sensing a trace of danger. Eye candy tinged with risk.

Becca felt it, too. Gut instincts as a cop . . . and as a woman.

The guy never turned her way. When he slowed and sat down at a small table in front of a sidewalk café, she ducked into a bookstore on her side of the street. With her nose in a book, Becca stood by a large window, maintaining surveillance. GQ placed his order. Before long, the waiter brought two hot beverages. He expected someone to join him.

"This could be interesting," she muttered.

Raising the book to cover her face, she peeked over the top of her sunglasses. In a simple gesture, her well-dressed target raised a hand and waved. His guest had arrived. Becca looked up and down the street, waiting to spot the newcomer to the scene. No one stood out. But he waved again. This time, with a faint smile on his face.

Eyes wide, she almost dropped her book. *What the hell?* She glanced over her shoulder. No one stood behind. *Is he waving at me?*

When she turned back, he had removed his sunglasses and stared at her, a definite invitation—or a challenge. Her face heated with embarrassment, but in no time, her blush dissolved into anger at being caught. Becca jammed the book back on the shelf and took a deep breath.

"Don't let him get to you, Beck. And don't underestimate him again."

Outside the bookstore, she stood on the curb, waiting for the traffic light to change. GQ hadn't moved. Sprawled at the small wrought-iron table for two, he had his arms crossed over his ample chest, looking plenty smug.

With the breezy day, no sane person would have chosen a seat outside. So without a doubt, the mystery man and Becca would have their privacy. She gritted her teeth, determined not to give in to his notso-subtle game of intimidation. Hiding behind her sunglasses, she glared at him as the light changed. He reminded her of an old tomcat about to play with his next meal.

Becca took her time crossing the intersection. What would she say? After all, she'd been caught in the act of following him. Scenarios played out in her mind, but as she approached, he made the first move.

A low masculine voice with a faint Hispanic accent.

"I've taken the liberty of ordering your favorite. Cappuccino with cinnamon, I believe." He stood and pulled the seat out for her. "You looked like you could use a break."

She removed her sunglasses and sat down, eyes focused on the man taking the seat across from her.

"You knew I'd—" Of course, he knew she would follow him. *Damn it!* "And I suppose if you know my java preferences, you obviously know my—"

He never let her finish.

"Your name, Detective Montgomery?" He grinned, showing a subtle display of dimples. "At the risk of sounding like a stalker, the answer is yes. Or do you prefer Rebecca?"

No amount of charm or cappuccino tempered her shock.

And still, he pressed his advantage. With a downright lethal smile, he leaned toward her, close enough for her to get a whiff of his distinctive cologne. His intimacy and the small table did a number on her head. In her mind, the busy street and all its noise faded to nothing. All she saw were those eyes—dark, sensual, and honey brown. They commanded her complete attention. Becca tried to turn away but found it impossible. The man stared straight through her—unnerving and mesmerizing at the same time. With the palpable connection between them, she wondered if he felt it, too.

Becca had to break his spell. She shoved the cappuccino aside and matched his posture, elbows on the table.

"You have me at a disadvantage. I don't know your name. You in a sharing mood?" She tilted her head and waited.

"A resourceful woman like you? You'll find out soon enough."

The cagey bastard sure liked hoarding his secrets. She had to gain control of this conversation, fast.

"I noticed you hanging out in front of the Imperial earlier."

"Is this a crime, Rebecca?" A slow lazy smile, dark eyes riveted on hers. "If so, you won't catch me doing it again. After all, I am a law-abiding citizen."

He took his first sip of coffee. Becca found herself fixated on his lips, full and expressive. *Oh, hell!* This man could be connected to the arson fire. *Focus, Beck. Keep your wits, woman.* She sat back in her chair and forced a smile.

"I think the operative word is 'catch.' You seem to have eyes in the back of your head."

Her mind worked overtime as she kept up her end of the conversation. Becca made a mental tally of his appearance, for purely professional reasons. Well over six feet tall with a lean athletic build, around 180 pounds. But when her imagination drifted to picturing that body up close and personal, under silk sheets, she forced herself back into cop mode and continued with her inventory of the man.

Full head of black hair, well-groomed. And he smelled so damned good.

She grimaced at her lack of focus and continued with the tough job of taking stock. Manicured nails. Expensive threads. A small scar over his right eye—a thin white line against an olive complexion—gave his face character. And it might prove to be a distinguishing mark to ID him. But his most memorable feature—his eyes—she'd recognize anywhere.

If those eyes lurked in a mug book or in a database, she'd know them on sight. Deep brown honey melting under a July sun. Was that an eye color?

"You look like a guy with an agenda. What were you doing at the theater?" She tried the direct approach.

"I was there to represent the interests of my . . . benefactor. At one time, he had an affiliation with the old theater. That is all." He sipped his coffee, a slow deliberate move. "Looks like your investigator found evidence of arson."

"You guessing, or do you know this for a fact?"

"A pretty good guess, I'm afraid."

Putting two and two together, she now understood why he'd been across the street, near the corner by the theater. He'd spied on them as they inspected the Dumpster in the back parking lot of the Imperial. Knowing he'd deny it, she tried a different tack.

"So this benefactor and his so-called affiliation, did he once own the property?" When the man answered with only a sly smile, she tried again. "Okay, let's try something a little more simple. Does your benefactor have a name?"

"All in good time, Rebecca. I have faith in your ability to detect such things." He cocked his head, not taking his eyes off her. "But I have to warn you. My benefactor is a very dangerous man."

"Is that a threat?"

"No, consider it a warning. More of a professional courtesy."

She narrowed her eyes and stared at him, trying to determine any hint of sarcasm. He looked dead serious.

"Aren't you taking a chance by warning the cop working the case? If he's so dangerous, why cross him?"

"Guess I like living on the edge." His expression grew more solemn. Eyes down, he toyed with his coffee cup. "And he doesn't own me . . . yet."

She reached across and rubbed her fingers on the sleeve of his expensive suit. "Oh, I don't know. Looks like he's made a hefty down payment on his investment."

For a brief moment, he torqued his jaw and looked up. She'd hit a nerve.

"Just make sure you bring your A-game with this guy. He's powerful and as nasty as they come."

"Don't you worry about my A-game, Slick." She raised her chin in challenge. "I always bring it."

"Oh, really." With eyes focused on her lips, he picked up a napkin.

In a surprising gesture, he leaned closer and reached for her, a pale blue linen in his hand. Becca pulled back at first, shocked by his bold move. But as he wiped her chin, with an unexpected gentleness, she gave in to the intimacy and relaxed.

Way to go, Beck. Real classy. All this time, she put up a front of bravado with black smudge on her face, a remnant from the fire. And he kept a straight face, not mentioning it.

With a raised eyebrow, he showed her the dirty napkin—proof of her A-game.

"Thanks." She barely looked him in the eye. "Guess it's been a long day."

After a strained moment, Becca noticed he hadn't backed away. She found him staring. And once again, she sensed a strong connection. As close as he was to her, anyone along the street might have assumed they were lovers. Becca imagined she felt his breath on her skin, and yet his touch seemed so natural—as if they'd met in another life.

A stirring, unforgettable moment.

But without warning, he broke the bond, sternness back in his expression. A gust of wind blew her hair, and, in a snap, her connection to him faltered. He sat back in his seat and let awkward silence build between them. It reminded her they were strangers who had run out of things to say.

"Like I said, you'll need an A-game, even if you have to borrow one."

"Look, Slick, I've got an investigation to conduct. And as much as I've enjoyed our little one-sided rendezvous, I've got things to do."

After taking a sip of his coffee, he looked across the table at her cup.

"But you haven't touched your cappuccino."

"I only drink with friends."

The gloves were off. No sense allowing him to monopolize her dance card. She had better things to do.

"So why this cryptic little game, Slick? You won't share your name or the identity of your so-called benefactor, yet you're chock-full of professional courtesies. Surely you have better things to do with your time than waste mine."

After a faint sad smile, the man slipped on his sunglasses, preparing to leave.

"I wanted to meet you. To find out why a homicide detective gets assigned to a fire investigation."

Finally, all his cards were on the table, a well-played hand thus far. But now, he was fishing. He knew she worked homicide but had no idea about the body found in the old theater. *Interesting*. It appeared she still held a card up her sleeve.

And latex gloves in her pocket.

"Well, imagine that. I guess there're things you don't know." As she spoke, Becca slipped on one of her gloves under the table. "But a resourceful man, such as yourself, will find out soon enough. I have faith in your abilities."

She reached across the table for his coffee cup with her gloved hand and without ceremony, dumped what remained of his java onto the sidewalk by their table. Her sudden move drew a flicker of indignation in his eyes, one that quickly faded.

"Two sets of fingerprints on this cup, yours and the waiter's. Thanks for making my job so easy."

Becca stood, cup in hand, not waiting for him to make the next move. With a low intimate voice, she leaned over the table, her face inches from his. Close enough to see through his expensive shades.

"And that bulge I detect? You'd better be damned glad to see me . . . *and* have a permit to carry that weapon. If not, you'll find the next time we meet, I won't be shy about using my handcuffs."

For the first time, the guy looked as if she had caught him off guard. But the instant was gone in the flick of his eyelash.

"Shy doesn't suit you." He stood and smiled. Cockiness had been replaced by an element of sadness in his expression. Yet in a seductive gesture, he leaned toward her. Reacting on pure instinct, she closed her eyes and focused on the moment. The warmth off his skin and his subtle cologne triggered her imagination.

Becca's heart stopped. Instead of the kiss she expected, his soft whisper teased her ear.

"I would have been disappointed if you hadn't made a move for my prints. I look forward to seeing you again, Rebecca."

After setting a hundred-dollar bill on the table, he turned and walked away, back the way he had come. She watched until he melded with the foot traffic on the street, her heart still pounding with the rush of his intimacy.

After a long moment, Becca gave in to a smile as she gazed down at the coffee cup—*her clever coup.* She would enjoy discovering the name of her mystery man and the identity of his benefactor. And she'd have a front-row seat to gauge their reactions when she sprang the news of a dead body found at the Imperial. *That should melt GQ's cool façade.*

He'd done his homework. Now, time for Becca to do hers.

A half-eaten burrito, wrapped in foil, lay atop Becca's desk. The smell of refried beans and old coffee filled her nostrils, almost a distraction. But nothing would divert her attention. She was a woman on a mission. Even though Dani was never far from her thoughts, it felt good to be working a case again.

Most detective work was a painstaking grind, picking apart every detail until a thread of motive could be followed and backed by irrefutable evidence. But it all began with the identification of the victim. So to start her thread, Becca jumped online to retrieve what information she could. She determined the time period for the original theater fabrication and the subsequent renovation through the public record filings for construction permits. This gave her a time frame within which to perform an extensive search of the archives for old missing persons cases. With her investigation narrowed by time period and females by age, she came down to five cases.

One of those had been declared a hoax. The young woman had eloped with an older man. Case closed. Two had turned into murder cases when the bodies were later found. One of those was still open. That left two cases. Becca made a note of the case numbers and submitted an electronic request to have the records pulled. Cases older than five years were archived in the bowels of the County Courthouse, not stored with the newer Evidence Unit on South Frio Street. It would take time to locate the boxes.

While she waited, Becca knew how to fill her time. GQ's dark eyes spurred her on. He had a name, and she'd find it. After leaving the sidewalk bistro, she walked the man's coffee cup back to the theater. A CSI tech bagged it and would process it for prints. And she obtained the recording of the rabble of onlookers outside the theater. She watched it several times, committing each face to memory. Yet she had to shake her head when she noticed that her mystery man had done a vanishing act. *Cagey bastard.*

"Guess you don't care for the limelight."

Luckily, the tech doing the recording backed up his work with a detailed listing of the license plates with the makes and models of all vehicles—GQ's license plate among them. She ran his tag through the Department of Motor Vehicles. According to DMV, the car was registered to Global Enterprises, a corporation she knew nothing about. She ran a check of the name against local businesses. Still nothing.

"Not what I expected," she muttered as she sat back in her desk chair.

But before she redirected her attention, Becca returned her focus to the ownership history of the Imperial Theatre.

"Let's see what's floating out in cyberspace." Moving to the edge of her seat, she popped her knuckles like a concert pianist.

Nearly oblivious to the ringing phones, conversations, and people traffic through the bullpen of the homicide division, she sat at her metal desk, fingers tapping her keyboard. She knew her first step would be the property ownership records. If she found the owner of the Imperial, she could zero in on her mystery man—killing two buzzards with one stone. In most cases, she would have hit pay dirt searching the county tax assessor's records, but nothing doing. Her research only produced the name of a nonprofit organization dedicated to the preservation and restoration of historic buildings for cultural use. She had to dig deeper, back to the original owner.

On a lark, she keyed the Imperial Theatre and San Antonio into an Internet search engine.

"Thank God and Al Gore for the Internet." She smiled, bathed in the pale light off her computer monitor. She scored 360,000 records.

Becca tried a couple of other queries and a more advanced search to fine-tune the hits. Eventually, her persistence paid off.

"Bingo."

An old newspaper archive contained an article announcing the dedication of the Imperial as a historic building, complete with photographs taken at the front of the structure. A bright sunny day. With a twinge of déjà vu, Becca remembered reading the article when it was first published. Less than a year ago, the mayor and the elite of San Antonio had gathered for the occasion. Even though the photo held many smiling faces in the foreground, one set of dark eyes lurked in the shadows of the theater entrance, behind the key players. And he looked anything but happy.

No name for her mystery man in the caption, but

she was one step closer to identifying him. Becca searched the article for any name construed as a benefactor "affiliated" with the property.

"Gotcha. I'd say ownership constitutes an affiliation, wouldn't you, Mr. Crypto?" Her success produced a smile that faded when she read the name of the theater owner aloud. "Hunter Cavanaugh. Thanks for the warning, Slick. When you said he was powerful and nasty, you weren't kidding."

Cavanaugh had a reputation. Good and bad. On the surface, he appeared to be a high-powered member of the community with far-reaching political ties. She had no idea the extent of those connections. Somehow, Cavanaugh had parlayed old family money into an international conglomerate focused on the travel industry. *A sudden turn of good fortune?* Becca stared at the archived photo displayed on the computer monitor, looking at the eyes of Hunter Cavanaugh.

"I'm not a big fan of coincidence."

Since Cavanaugh donated the theater to a nonprofit charity, shifting title to another organization, her insurance fraud angle bit the dust. Of course, she had to confirm the details, but the man wasn't exactly hurting for cash either.

This time, Becca did a search on Global Enterprises and the name Cavanaugh. She scored numerous hits, printing out press releases, financial documents, and newspaper articles on a merger between Cavanaugh's travel company and Global Enterprises, almost three years ago.

"What do we have here?"

She knitted her brow and lowered her chin, staring at her computer screen. Once again, a familiar face skulked in the background of another newspaper photo. Eyes she would know anywhere. Only this time, Cavanaugh was nowhere in sight. Another suit posed in the foreground.

"You sure get around, Slick."

After skimming the article, she printed the material and reread the pages. On the surface, the New-York-based Global Enterprises invested in resorts abroad, with some domestic locations. On paper, the merger made sense. But when the article told of how the corporate head, Joseph Rivera, had been accused of racketeering, Becca smelled money laundering. Rivera's case had been dismissed on a technicality, no doubt through the efforts of high-priced legal help. The name Rivera didn't ring a bell, but after reading the story, she came to one conclusion. GQ had connections to the mob. With his ties to the heavy hitters of New York as well as to Cavanaugh, her gut told her he might be pulling double duty. Could he be working for more than one boss?

At first, Becca saw Cavanaugh's link to mob money as one of the reasons his travel business diversified and flourished. But from what she knew about Cavanaugh, the man had too big an ego. He wouldn't stand for a spy operating in his midst or welcome any interference from an outside source in the form of someone he deemed lower on the food chain. Cavanaugh might be fueling the engines of the Mafia train with GQ on board for the ride, doing his dirty work. That kind of combo was dangerous enough, but she didn't want to get caught in the middle of a turf war. Something didn't add up.

The news story made her stomach lurch for another reason. A personal one. How could she have been so wrong about her mystery man? She had sensed the danger but overlooked it, finding something redeeming in his eyes. She had to admit it. A more powerful urge had overruled her better judgment. The man rattled her, touched her in a way she had never experienced. If he stood in her way, could she ignore her personal feelings to do her job?

"Only one way to find out." Becca heaved a sigh. When her desk phone rang, she answered, "Montgomery."

"Hey, Rebecca." She recognized the voice of Sam Hastings, her CSI guy. "Those fingerprints on the coffee cup? We ran 'em against NCIC without any luck, but through AFIS, we got a hit off firearms registration. Your boy's name is Diego Galvan and he's got a permit to carry concealed in Texas."

The FBI's National Crime Information Center contained computerized criminal justice information, available to law enforcement twenty-four/seven. And the state's Automated Fingerprint Indexing System had been created to store fingerprints from a myriad of sources, from the private to public sector. AFIS also linked with a national repository system maintained by the FBI, allowing law enforcement to perform national criminal record searches—all in the spirit of cooperation. But not every state participated in the effort. So even with the high-tech assistance, criminals still fell through the crack in this multijurisdictional computerized world. Becca made a note of Galvan's name in her casebook.

"I'll send over my findings. Anything else you need on this?" Sam asked.

As Becca listened, her request for the archived missing persons cases arrived. Two boxes were shoved onto a corner of her desk. After adding her initials to a receipt log, she smiled and waved to the delivery kid, keeping up her end of the conversation.

"No. Thanks for the quick turnaround. I'll do a little more digging on my own. Later."

Now she had a name. Becca would cross-check it against other data sources to get a better picture of the man. She knew her search for Diego Galvan should take a backseat to the old case files, but it had become personal—and she knew it. Instead of going through the boxes right away, she got back on her computer, hoping to find greater insight into her mystery man. An hour later, she was no closer to answers.

"Damn it!" Another blind alley in her research into Galvan's background.

Becca justified the search as part of the case, but in her heart, she knew the truth. His dark eyes haunted her, dared her to dig deeper. The more Galvan eluded her, the more she dug, letting her stubborn streak get the better of her.

A New Jersey driver's license and two credit cards went back six years or so. Prior to that, he was a ghost. Becca peeled away layer after layer, and still she couldn't get a glimpse of any pertinent history. His tax records might reveal something, but that would take time to retrieve and a warrant signed by a federal judge. For a *person of interest*, she didn't have enough reason to justify the intrusion into his background, so she remained focused on the data at hand. No traffic citations or warrants outstanding. She had already learned that his current vehicle was registered in the name of Global Enterprises, but so was his insurance. Nothing to trace there. And to add to her frustration, for every record she uncovered, Becca found a different post office box.

The guy lived in plain sight but off the grid.

"You're good, Diego. Real good. Did Cavanaugh finance your disappearing act or someone else? Top-notch stuff."

After running his prints without a hit, Becca had been stymied. His lack of a criminal record surprised her the most. She felt certain he had spent some quality time at the gray bar hotel, maybe under a different name. A jaded cop's instincts. But she came up empty.

"You haven't beaten me yet, Galvan," she muttered. "But I've almost got enough to pay a call on your benefactor, Hunter Cavanaugh."

Still, a persistent question lingered in her mind. What was the purpose of Diego Galvan's warning against Cavanaugh? He had known who she was and staged the whole thing, right down to her late-afternoon addiction to cappuccino with cinnamon. A part of her hoped he might make an interesting ally, if it came to it. But she knew better than to be so gullible. In her line of work, trust had to be earned.

Heading north on I–10, Diego Galvan watched the late-afternoon sun glisten on the surface of a man-made lake at the gated entrance to The Dominion, a prestigious residential area located northwest of San Antonio. Mist from a shooting fountain cast a rainbow across a bridge made of Cantera stone. A beautiful setting, but one he'd grown to resent. Seeing it meant he was twenty minutes from the private estate of Hunter Cavanaugh. He tightened his jaw as his stomach churned. No matter how idyllic the scene, he reacted with his usual conditioned reflex, like one of Pavlov's dogs at the ring of a bell.

Get over it. You asked for this gig.

On the last leg of the trip, vast ranchlands stretched across the interstate, bordered by mesquite trees, sagebrush, and miles of barbed wire. Cattle lolled by flowing creeks, with abandoned hay bales weathering in the sun—the hill country of Texas in all its glory. But as a hawk made lazy swirls in a cloudless sky, held aloft by an updraft, Diego found himself envious of the bird's freedom. It reminded him of the police detective who'd seen through his subterfuge.

He knew by his outward appearance, most people would see affluence and success. The carefully orchestrated façade, conjured up by Cavanaugh, reflected more on him than Diego. Yet the colorful plumage of the rooster hadn't fooled Detective Rebecca Montgomery. Although he'd been pleased by her intellect, her honest insight had been an embarrassment. And he was to blame for that.

"Very perceptive, Rebecca." Saying her name aloud summoned a memory of her face—spirited eyes, flawless skin, and lips that aroused his blood even now.

Don't go there, Galvan. The woman deserves better.

Jaw tight and eyes glued on the road ahead, Diego gripped the steering wheel of the Mercedes. He had taken the long way home, needing time to think. Rebecca's words stung like tequila poured into a gaping wound with a lime-and-salt chaser. If she hadn't been dead-on with her assessment, he might have laughed it off.

"Looks like he's made a hefty down payment on his investment," she had said.

The attractive detective sized him up as a man who could be bought. Diego couldn't argue the point. Her sentiments reflected the dread in his *own* gut. The wealth surrounding him had taken some time to get used to. But now, the attached strings weighed heavy—an anchor around his neck. Somewhere along the way, he had turned a blind eye to his conscience, in complete denial of how much he'd changed over the years. Every day, a darker side of him emerged—and he had yet to draw the line. He'd convinced himself he couldn't afford to. So much had changed, Diego wasn't sure he could find his way back from the precipice. His only way out might involve a treacherous leap.

He turned onto Citadel Drive, minutes from the elaborate front gates of the Cavanaugh estate. A mantle of oak trees gave an air of timelessness to the shaded driveway dappled by the sun. His cell phone rang as he picked up speed. Diego reached into the pocket of his suit and glanced at the display.

With a grimace, he answered. "Galvan."

"I expected a report before now." Low and intimate, the voice of Hunter Cavanaugh raised the hair on the back of his neck. "Where are you?"

He thought for a moment and said what came to mind.

"I get paid to be thorough . . . not to report to you every five minutes like some mindless sycophant." One day, Diego knew his sarcasm would get him killed. And it would probably be at the hands of the man on the other end of the line. With reluctance, he responded to the question. "I'll be there in five minutes."

Dead silence. Finally, a raspy whisper came through the cell phone.

"Why do you continually try my patience? One of these days, I might surprise you and grant your death wish, Diego."

"If you put me out of my misery, people might think you've grown soft."

The breathing on the other end of the line changed. A low, menacing noise turned into full-blown laughter, devoid of any real humor. Diego pictured the older man's face, aristocratic features tainted by fierce eyes of ice blue.

"You still amuse me, but don't take that for granted." The contempt was hard to miss. "I want a full report when you get here."

The line went dead.

"What the hell are you thinking, Galvan?" he muttered, dropping the cell phone onto the passenger seat.

A death wish? An astute observation. For him to deal with Cavanaugh, a death wish made the job interesting, like playing catch using a live grenade. Yet, at some point, his insane game would come to an abrupt end. Diego could accept the consequences with only *his* life on the line. But Detective Rebecca Montgomery posed a problem.

She'd confront Cavanaugh on the arson fire, no wiser than dangling a red bandanna in front of a deranged bull. The man would fix his sights and not let go, toying with her for mere sport. No matter how gutsy and smart she might be, the detective would have her hands full trying to outwit him. His vast resources and unrivaled cruelty would give Cavanaugh the advantage. Diego had seen him in action too many times.

With the growing demands of his job, Diego found his life tough enough, but Rebecca could bring down his makeshift house of cards. At first glance, the woman didn't have the savvy to play on Cavanaugh's turf. But what she lacked in expertise, she more than made up for with nerve and determination. Gut instinct told him Rebecca wouldn't back off. He'd seen the conviction in her eyes.

Would he stick his neck out for her? Taking on that kind of responsibility might tip the scales of his balancing game, force him to make a move off dead center. The risk might get him killed.

"Don't get stupid. Not now." Diego swore under his breath as he turned onto the cobblestone drive of Cavanaugh's stronghold—his gilded cage.

Becca spent the late afternoon behind her desk, dredging up the tragic past of two young women still missing. Their lives had taken a perverse detour—severed from their families by a faceless evil. She understood the enduring pain of their loved ones.

Not knowing was the worst.

Taken from the archived evidence boxes, photographs of the victims provided by the families morphed into Dani's face. Her eyes. Her smile. An unfulfilled future. For an instant, Becca even thought she smelled her sister's perfume, lingering in the air, triggering a haunting and pervasive guilt. She shut her eyes tight, holding back the tears that were never far from the surface.

Keep digging. Becca took a deep breath and plunged into the boxes for more. Her instincts told her the answer might be at the next turn of a page. A young woman, buried in a very dark place, had died alone with only a futile scream to break the silence that marked her passing from this life. Putting a name to the bones at the Medical Examiner's was step one to finding her killer.

Yet something in the photograph of Isabel Marquez drew her attention time and time again. And in the quiet of the late afternoon, she almost heard the girl whispering—*Look again, or you'll miss it.* She held up the high school class photo once more—a pretty young girl captured forever in a happier time, with a mischievous grin and eyes graced by innocence. Although her thoughts turned to Danielle, Becca wanted to remember the face of Isabel—as if it would be possible for her to forget.

"Wait a minute. I knew that name sounded familiar."

Finally, it clicked. The word "coincidence" raised a red flag. She'd seen the name of Marquez earlier in the day.

Becca remembered something from the list of license tags taken by a CSI tech outside the destroyed theater. Standing hunched over her desk, she rummaged through the accumulating piles of paper, searching for the report she received earlier. As she suspected, the name of Marquez was on the list—a red Ford F–150 truck registered to Rudy Marquez. After a quick look in the case file, she learned that Isabel's father had been deceased at the time she went missing, but her mother and two brothers filed the initial report. Rudy was one of Isabel's brothers.

To place a face with the name, she replayed the CSI video, hoping to get a fix on the owner of the truck. Of all the people gathered outside the Imperial The-atre, one set of eyes reflected a different level of inter-est than the rest of the rabble. And she knew, without confirmation, she'd found Rudy Marquez amidst the gawkers, standing by a red truck.

"That's gotta be you," she whispered. "What are you up to?"

Becca felt certain it wasn't idle curiosity that had drawn the man to the theater, but so much remained unexplained. Did Rudy Marquez know anything about the dead body found at the Imperial? And was there any connection to Hunter Cavanaugh, the onetime owner of the property—a man dangerous enough for the mysterious Diego Galvan to risk his own neck to warn her?

Questions flooded her mind. But when she picked up the school photo of Isabel again, she knew she had a solid lead. Her eye caught another reason to make the trip to see Marquez.

"Well, I'll be damned. Right under my nose all along." After a nibble on the corner of her mouth, she smiled. "Thanks, Isabel."

CHAPTER 3

Becca headed west on General McMullen, a bustling six-lane thoroughfare. A place where men still stood on busy street corners hawking newspapers, taking their lives in their hands to peddle bad news. Businesses along the way were mostly converted houses painted in vivid reds, yellows, and electric blues. In the light of day, the paint colors could do some serious damage to perfectly good eyeballs if a person stared too long. Now, with the sun on a downward spiral, the boulevard would soon blaze in neon and the night shift rabble would scurry from their hiding places like cockroaches on party patrol.

Under the heading of surreal, churches wedged between bars, tattoo parlors, hooker hot spots, and tarot card readers—an eclectic hodgepodge of vice and redemption offered up in a single locale. Yet despite the rough nature of the neighborhood, a steady vitality pulsed through the district like blood coursing through an artery.

Before she hit the intersection of Castroville Road, Becca turned her Crown Vic down a side street near

Taqueria Vallarta, one of her favorite places to grab
a bite. The restaurant served killer barbacoa in fresh
corn tortillas, a traditional weekend treat. And if
Jose Cuervo took unfair advantage of her the night
before, a mega bowl of menudo would do the trick.
The breakfast of champions. In "the hood," you
couldn't beat the aromas. The dinner hour and her
stomach growled in response. But as hungry as she
was, Becca had too much on her mind to stop.

After turning onto San Bernardo Street, she spotted the red F–150 of Rudy Marquez and pulled in
behind the vehicle. Glittering in the waning sun,
rosary beads hung from the rearview mirror of the
truck, a common display in town, but the man was
nowhere in sight. Before she got out, Becca scanned
the neighborhood and confirmed the street address.
House numbers reflected off a rusted white mailbox
that listed to one side, its concrete base uprooted.
She'd found the place.

The Marquez family lived in a dingy white clap-
board house with window frames and front door
painted in a bright blue, the paint peeling in spots.
A dismal pit the size of a matchbox. Even though
wrought iron covered every window and door of the
house—no doubt meant as a deterrent to crime—the
run-down condition of the property should have been
enough to discourage a criminal looking for a quick
score. What could these people possess that would
be worth stealing? But she knew better. Criminals
preyed on the poor, who lacked the resources to do
anything about it. So much went unreported.

Becca heaved a sigh and got out of her car, shifting

her thoughts to how she would conduct her interview with Marquez. Until she got a sense of Rudy's part in all this, she had to play her cards right.

A chain-link fence bordered patches of green in front of the Marquez place. Weeds and dandelions had locked horns with what remained of the St. Augustine grass. Yard work and house repairs were low on the family's list of priorities. They had enough on their minds. With casebook and pen in hand, Becca stepped inside the cyclone fence and clanked the gate shut behind her.

Yellow ribbons made of plastic fluttered in the breeze, tied to a scrawny mesquite tree. A reminder of the family's loss. A stone shrine stood near the cement front stoop with a ceramic statue of the Virgin Mary gazing down, arms outstretched. Placed under rocks to hold them in place, laminated photos of Isabel had weathered and were lying at the foot of the sculpture—a sad memorial.

For a long moment, Becca stared at the grotto, wanting to pray. But the words wouldn't come.

"Can I help you?" A thick Hispanic accent.

As she turned, the glare of sunset hit her sight line, blaze orange on a last-ditch assault. Becca squinted and raised a hand to block the light. From what she saw, the silhouette of a man stood inside the screen door, his face in shadow. She reached for her badge and held it up.

"My name is Detective Rebecca Montgomery. I'd like to ask you a few questions."

"Is this about Isabel?" The man's face came out from the dark.

Becca stopped, taken back by the sight. He had an uncanny resemblance to the missing girl. Yet the white collar had been a complete surprise. Standing in the threshold of the Marquez house stood a priest.

"Are you a family member, Father?"

Intense dark eyes framed by a full head of black hair, dark skin, medium height and build. Although she saw the family resemblance, this man's stern expression hardened the Marquez likeness, gave it an edge.

"Yes, I'm Victor Marquez. Isabel is . . . my sister."

The priest struggled with whether to use the present tense. She knew the feeling. He didn't open the screen door, only stared out the mesh, using it as a fragile barrier against what would come next.

Becca knew the look, had seen it many times before as a detective delivering bad news. Now after what happened to her own sister, she knew firsthand how dread mixed with the strange sensation of relief for it to be over. A gut-wrenching contradiction. Even though the priest set his jaw and steeled himself for what she would say, his eyes couldn't hide the pain. Becca raised her chin and took a deep breath as she walked up the steps to the front door. She had to be the cop now, not the victim. *Don't read too much into this, Beck. He's not your personal mirror. Stay objective.* Easier said than done.

"Do you mind if I come in?"

For a moment, she didn't know if he would allow it. Eventually, he did.

Sparse furnishings, but the place looked clean. A faint hint of pine cleaner played second fiddle to the pungent aroma of roasted jalapeños and bell pepper,

someone making salsa. Scented candles burned near
the entry. Another shrine for Isabel dominated the
tiny living room. Keepsakes and photos of the missing
Marquez girl were cast in the pale glow of flickering
red votive candles. Isabel had been elevated to saint-
hood by her family. Becca understood the sentiment.
In death, the imperfections of the victim were forgotten. The priest noticed her attention to the memorial.

"My mother tells me the constant reminder helps
her cope." His words were punctuated with a sigh.

"But you don't think so."

He shrugged. "Why are you here, Detective?"

Before Becca answered, an older woman entered the
room from the kitchen, wearing a blue house frock
and a faded green apron, wiping her hands with a
rag. Petite and rail thin, Hortense Marquez looked as
if she'd been crying. Her eyes still brimmed with the
sheen of tears. She wore a yellow bandanna wrapped
around her head, and curly wisps of gray hair poked
out from under it. Grief etched her face, making the
woman appear older than her years. And despite the
memorial of hope she'd set up in her living room, de-
spair had found a home in this woman's eyes. Becca
knew the look all too well.

"This is my mother. Please excuse us."

After a quiet exchange in Spanish with the priest,
the woman forced a smile and nodded before she left
the room. But not before she gave Becca one final look,
one she'd seen from her own mother's eyes. Although
Becca knew only enough Spanish to be dangerous,
no words were necessary. For the things that really
mattered in life, there were no language barriers.

Once they were alone, the priest gestured for her to take a seat.

"Was there some reason you didn't tell her I was with the SAPD?" she asked as she sat on a green floral love seat, armrests frayed on the corners.

"Her English is not good. No sense in alarming her until I know . . . something for sure." Father Victor took a seat across from her, a wooden chair that had seen better days.

"I'm investigating your sister's disappearance."

Before she went on, the priest interrupted. "Investigating? It's been almost seven years. Why have the police taken an interest now?"

Suspicion narrowed his eyes. Father Victor had set aside his religious affiliation to become brother to Isabel, the patience and generosity of his profession forgotten.

"I know this must be difficult, but—"

"Know? How could you know?" He lashed out, his face wracked with grief. But when he looked into Becca's eyes, he stopped himself. "I suppose you see a lot of families like this."

"Unfortunately, that's true, but it's still not the same as going through it." Becca met his gaze. She wanted to stop, not go any further. Maybe it was his white collar. Or maybe she saw herself in him, like a mirror. "My baby sister, Danielle. She was taken . . . and killed. We never found her body."

The priest stared at her in disbelief. They sat in silence. The quiet gave Becca a strange comfort. She looked away to give him time to recover. Or maybe she needed the time. But when she looked up, the priest's eyes glistened with tears. The sudden display of sympathy caught Becca by surprise.

He reached for her hand, his fingers clutching hers. Becca flinched at his gesture. She hadn't been touched in a very long time.

"But if you never found her body, how could you know for sure?" he asked.

How could you know? His words brought back a flood of doubts. Her acceptance of Dani's death had never felt real. She gave it lip service, but in the end, she didn't believe it herself. Not without a body. Becca felt an old familiar wall erecting. The tiny living room closed in on her. She gritted her teeth and pulled her hand away. Becca couldn't deal with his pity.

"We . . . I know, Father."

She squeezed the casebook in her hand. Although closure for the Marquez family had its inescapable merits, she didn't want to be the one to rob this family of hope. Still, she had a job to do. Her usual mantra.

But as the flickering red votive candles of Isabel's shrine taunted her, a disturbing thought took hold. Had she really given up on Dani so easily? An empty casket. The headstone. Becca believed she'd done the right thing to give her mother closure, but now it all felt like such a betrayal. She avoided the priest's stare and took a deep breath.

"Are you all right, Detective?"

"Yes, I'm fine." She cleared her throat to shake off the emotion. No sense in prolonging this. "We've found some remains that may be your sister's. I'll need a sample of the family's DNA to help with the identification."

Father Victor shut his eyes and lowered his head, a quiet prayer. At least the man had his faith to give him strength. She gave him a moment, gazing around the room. Her eyes found a Marquez family photo hung on a nearby wall. In his priest garb, Victor stood behind his mother with Rudy and Isabel at her side, a picture taken at a happier time. It reminded Becca of another photograph. The one she'd brought with her from evidence.

"I'm so sorry for what your family has gone through," she added in a quiet tone. "Father Victor, can you tell me anything about the necklace your sister is wearing here?"

Becca showed him a photograph from her casebook, evidence from the archived box on the Marquez missing person case. Earlier, she had recognized the gold jewelry in the photo as being the same item recovered from the bones at the theater.

"I remember this. The Isabel I knew never could have afforded such a necklace." He clenched his jaw and held the picture in his hand, his eyes glazed over by the past. "She told me she bought it for herself, but I never believed that. At the time, I heard she was dating an older man, someone with money. But she would never talk about it. Not with me."

"If she didn't talk to you about it, Father, who *did* she talk to? How could you know about the older man if she wasn't the one who told you?"

"It's been so long ago. I forgot."

By his expression, Becca could tell she'd surprised him by her question. And his answer had been too abrupt. Coupled with the shift in his eyes, he looked like a man concocting a story. After the priest handed back the school photo, he shifted in his chair, a guarded posture. Another sign of his reluctance. Becca tried a different approach.

"The piece looks like a unique design. Can you tell me anything more about the heart charm?"

"I'm afraid I can't help you with that." With a fingernail, Father Victor picked at a chip in the armrest of his chair, avoiding her eyes. Another stall and another dead end.

"Well, who *could* help me?" When he didn't answer right away, she tried another avenue. Becca had to get him talking again. "Did you all grow up in this house, Father?"

"Yes, we did." A faint smile. "My mother did the best she could raising us after my father died."

"Tight quarters. And only one bathroom?" After he nodded, Becca smiled. "That could test the strength of a family, for sure."

"It wasn't so bad after I moved out. St. Mary's Seminary in Houston. The archdiocese gave me a scholarship."

"Good opportunity for you, but I bet Isabel and Rudy still fought over the bathroom even after you left. Typical brother-sister stuff, huh?"

"Oh, no. It wasn't like that. Isabel and Rudy got along great. They were inseparable, really. They shared—" He stopped himself.

"So Isabel and Rudy were close?" she asked.

The memory opened fresh wounds for the priest. Becca witnessed a dark haze spread across his face.

"Maybe Isabel confided in Rudy about the necklace

and who might have given it to her. Do you know what she told him, Father?"

"How would I know that? I didn't even live here anymore. I can't help you, Detective. I have no idea what they talked about."

"Maybe Rudy can help me. Where is he now?"

"He's at work, but no telling when he'll be home. Is this really necessary?"

"How does he get to work, Father?" she persisted. She kept up the questions, hoping to distract him. And her constant use of his title was deliberate, reminding him of his calling.

"He drives himself, normally."

The man hadn't lied. The word "normally" was a smoke screen. *Normally*, a very clever one, but not today. Not when she knew about the truck outside.

"Why all the questions about my brother?"

And why all the resistance, Father? she wanted to ask. But if she did, his limited cooperation would dry up in a hurry. Evasive didn't begin to describe how Father Victor had reacted to her questions about Rudy.

"Excuse me, Father, but what kind of vehicle does he drive?"

She painted him in a corner to see if he'd lie about the truck. He took a long moment to think. His moment of truth, or not. But by the defeated look in his eye, she knew there was no point to continue along this line of questioning.

"You know, Father, it won't take me any time to run a DMV check on the red F–150 parked in front. You want to save me some time?"

"Why would you assume that truck belongs to my brother?"

Suspicion edged his face, but by his contrite tone, she knew the man was more on the defense than the offense. Becca was still in control. Yet for her to admit she knew for certain the truck belonged to the cleric's brother, she might tip her hand on Rudy's trip to the Imperial. And she wasn't ready to do that.

"Call it a hunch. Your mother doesn't look like the F–150 type, in red no less. Is the truck yours, Father?" She had no idea if Roman Catholic priests owned vehicles or not.

"No. I came in a few days ago. Rudy lets me borrow his truck when I'm in town. My parish, St. John's, is in Houston."

"So how did Rudy get to work today?"

It took him a long moment to respond. He knew she had gotten the better of him again.

"I drove him," he replied. Before she asked another question, he pressed, "Detective, what are you after? If all you want is to talk about that necklace and get a DNA sample, I can help you. There's no need to dredge up the past with my brother."

Tough cookie. A priest with street smarts and a stubborn streak to boot. Father Victor was not making this easy. Being the oldest, he slipped into his big brother role with ease. When it came to Rudy, the man put up one helluva roadblock. But after taking a deep breath, the priest softened his expression and tried another approach.

"Look. Tomorrow I promise to bring my brother by your precinct. We'll cooperate with the DNA testing, but I'd like to be present while you speak to Rudy. As kids, he and Isabel were very close. I'm afraid this will break his heart. Can you understand that, Detective Montgomery? I'm trying to protect my family. What's left of it."

Becca handed the priest her business card.

"When would be a convenient time to talk to your brother?"

"I'll bring him by after work, around six if that's not too late."

"That's fine. Just ask for me." Becca wanted him on her side. "You want closure for your family, don't you, Father?"

Without looking up from her business card, he nodded.

"Please . . . help me do that." She leaned forward, resisting the urge to touch him. "It must be hard for you, not living here."

For an instant, pain tinged his expression. The conversation had turned personal again.

"I came in for my sister's birthday. It was yesterday." He couldn't look her in the eye. Instead, Victor stared at Isabel's shrine, his eyes mesmerized by the flickering candles. "We still celebrate her special day. My mother even wraps a gift, saving each one for when Isabel . . ." He steepled his fingers and pinched the bridge of his nose, slouching back in his chair with eyes closed. "It's been hard for all of us. I stayed with my mother today after I drove my brother to work early this morning."

Danielle's birthday wasn't for another couple of months. Becca wondered what she and her mother would do to mark the occasion. The thought twisted her gut into a knot until she replayed what he had said in her mind.

"Out of curiosity, what kind of work does Rudy do?"

"He's a mason, works for various subcontractors. The construction business in San Antonio is quite healthy. He does okay."

"Those guys work hard. He must have a pretty long day. What are his usual hours?"

"Dawn to dusk this time of year."

If Rudy was at work by dawn and without his truck, who had been outside the Imperial Theatre midmorning? Was Victor telling the truth about his hours, or protecting his brother once again?

Okay, she had to admit it. The brothers looked so much alike that Becca didn't know if she'd made a mistake in assuming the crime-scene videotape had been of Rudy in front of the theater. But maybe the DMV records influenced that decision. Thinking back, she recalled a man stood by the truck in worn jeans, a sweatshirt, and a jacket, sans the white collar of a priest in uniform. She would have remembered a priest. Doubts leached into her brain.

Which one had been outside the Imperial?

"Well, I won't take up any more of your time, Father." Becca stood. "The sooner we get things resolved, the better. Maybe you and I can find our answers, bring Isabel home once and for all."

"And maybe some questions are better left unanswered." Before she replied, he gestured for the door and walked her out. "See you tomorrow, Detective."

Becca walked down the short sidewalk to the gate, resisting the urge to look over her shoulder. She felt the priest's eyes at her back. All she wanted was to shed light on a despicable crime, but this interview drilled another point home. She needed to learn much more about Isabel and Rudy. And after meeting Victor, new questions stirred in her mind. The priest knew more than he said.

Her investigation had taken a 180-degree turn.

PASEO DEL RIO (THE RIVERWALK)
DOWNTOWN SAN ANTONIO

Staring out the window of her small condo on the Riverwalk, Becca took a swig of lukewarm beer, ignoring the flat taste. Her eyes took in every detail, yet nothing registered in her mind. The trip to the Marquez house had struck a personal chord, setting her into a deep funk. Becca ran fingers through her dark hair and pulled down the sleeves to her SAPD sweats.

Even though Father Victor Marquez looked anything but happy, the priest still had his family to protect. He ran interference for both his brother Rudy and their mother, a tight bond.

In sharp contrast, Becca had closed down to deal with her grief, shutting herself off from anyone who got too close—especially after Momma did the same. Before the abduction that ended Danielle's life, Becca would have bet good money on the underlying strength of her family. But in the end, the tie to her grieving mother had been as fragile as glass. Maybe they were too much alike. She remembered her last visit with Momma, hearing the words that broke her heart.

"Get out. Leave me alone, damn it!" Her mother screamed, her face red and swollen with rage, her breath bitter from alcohol. "Who are you to preach to me about needin' anyone but yourself? My baby is dead. I got nothin'."

Like a sucker punch to the belly, Momma's words struck deep, even as Becca stared out her window, reliving the past.

"You got me, Momma," she whispered. "For what it's worth, you still have me."

All she had tried to do that day was get her mother into rehab and counseling. Her drinking had gotten out of control. With the therapy, they could have taken it together. But Momma wanted no part of it.

When her mother drank, her rage took over. First, the focus was little day-to-day stuff. But as time and grief wore on, her anger shifted to Dani's killers, the useless police investigation, with the final stages centering on herself—the kind of mother she had turned out to be. The failure.

But eventually, Momma's rage took on a bitterness, all pointed at Becca. And that hurt the most.

Sure she could rationalize and say her mother hadn't really meant her cruel words, but an element of truth filtered through. When she dared to look into her personal failings, Becca discovered she had no one to trust, no one to share how she felt. A harsh reality check. Her job and her ambition had always been enough, until now. Momma had a point.

"God, I hate this. When will it ever stop?"

Becca took a deep breath, stifling the lump wedged in her throat. The unending hurt had left her bone weary. She hadn't realized she'd been crying. Trembling fingers wiped away the tears.

She glanced back at the clock on the far wall. Almost midnight. The sounds outside her window died down to a muffled thump, a jazz band nearing last call. And the dregs of city traffic, coming from the streets of Crockett and Presa, had been reduced to a vague notion carried on the breeze. Despite the surge of emotions welling inside her, the familiar cacophony gave her a strange comfort.

Her home was nothing to brag about, but it had become a safe haven, of sorts. Martha Stewart wouldn't be knocking on her door looking for housekeeping tips. But her condo had been an amazing return on her investment, inheritance money from her grandmother. On a cop's salary, she couldn't touch the locale.

For most people, the noise might have made it difficult to sleep. Yet Becca found the steady clamor of downtown to be soothing—up until Danielle first went missing. Now it didn't matter much. She and sleep had parted ways. Irreconcilable differences.

Becca wiped her cheeks with a sleeve of her sweatshirt and stretched her back. The muscles between her shoulder blades felt stiff, and her thighs were sore, the result of her early-morning workout, self-inflicted abuse. After grabbing a fresh beer from the fridge, she walked toward her fire escape window, heading for her nightly ritual. Raising the window, Becca ducked through and stepped onto the first landing, cold beer in hand. Her skin erupted in goose bumps when her bare feet hit the cool cement.

She made a short climb up the fire escape and over the parapet wall to her rooftop garden, an oasis she maintained to preserve her own sanity. Rather than flick on the festive white Christmas lights she had strung across the ornamental garden, tonight Becca preferred the anonymity of the dark. She pulled up a lawn chair and rested her elbows on the brick ledge, gazing to the river below. Becca took a sip of her Corona, feeling the chill rush through her. She shut her eyes and listened to the sounds of the city.

Adrift on the cool breeze was the faint smell of the river. The earthy essence of stale humidity mixed with the lingering aroma of fajitas, a gift from the Casa Rio Restaurant. She opened her eyes to glance toward the river bend. At this hour, festive lights shimmered along the water and made a dramatic silhouette of the weeping bowers of cypress trees. From a nearby club, a muffled voice on a microphone announced last call, and the jazz band began its final short set. She knew the drill and listened to every note, letting time sift through her fingers like sand.

But as her gaze drifted toward the music, something peculiar caught her eye, triggering her cop instincts into high gear. A lone man stood at the crest of a stone bridge over the river, his body silhouetted by a pale light. Becca craned her neck to get a better view. Squinting, she tried to catch a look at his face. Her mind played tricks.

It made no sense, yet she pictured Diego's handsome face in her mind.

"Come on, Beck. No way," she muttered.

From her perch, foot traffic this time of night always drew her attention, but this man stood still, almost a fixture. He melded with the footbridge as if he were part of the stonework. She almost missed him.

But suddenly, he moved.

He held something in his hand, raising it to his face in a sweeping gesture. Even though his features were shrouded in darkness, the object caught the light before he tossed it into the water. She leaned forward, hoping to catch a glimpse of what he'd thrown. It floated on the water's surface, buoyant, not heavy enough to sink. A bulb of white caught in the lazy current of the river. As it drifted by her vantage point, under the reflection from a security light, she recognized it.

A single white rose.

The flower bobbed on the water. Faint ripples skimmed the surface, undulating with every movement of the rose. Becca furrowed her brow and peered through the shadows toward the bridge, searching for him. Nothing. She stood and leaned over the parapet wall, straining to see under the heavy bower of trees. Up the river and down.

He was nowhere in sight. Gone. How did he disappear so fast? *Damn it!*

Becca's heart picked up the pace to match the jazz band downriver, pounding for all the wrong reasons. Her face flushed. She searched every shadow, yet eventually gave up on finding him. Clenching her jaw, she wrapped her arms across her chest to ward off the chill of the night breeze. The wind rustled the trees of her garden, stirring a memory. Becca pictured Diego's lips, his strong jawline, and she remembered the gentle touch of his large hands when he wiped the smudge off her chin. But most of all, his dark eyes haunted her.

"You better put him out of your head, Beck. The man's trouble."

No doubt, it had only been her imagination that willed the stranger to be him. A heaping dose of wishful thinking and a couple of Coronas hadn't hurt either.

"Last call." She raised the bottle of beer to her lips and downed the rest.

With empty bottle in hand, Becca navigated the steps down, her mind preoccupied with the image of the man on the bridge. As she turned to her window near the landing, Becca caught a glimpse of something. Her eyes fixed on it.

"What the hell?" A breath jammed in her throat.

Another white rose lay on the cement near the open window to her condo.

On pure instinct, she pressed her back against the outside wall, hiding in the shadows. Becca didn't want to be silhouetted by the light coming from her living room, making herself a target. Her eyes searched the darkness, squinting to regain her night vision. After a long moment, she felt certain her mystery man had skipped.

Exercising caution, she inched her way toward the window and peered in. Everything was like she left it, but had he been inside? She hadn't been gone long, but damn it, the man was a ghost. *A blasted ghost!*

And he had the gall to leave a calling card, one that would lurk in her memory for nights to come. Either he knew her routine, or he'd waited for the right opportunity.

Why? None of this made sense.

He could have come and gone without her knowing it. Instead, he chose to leave a rose and made a show of calling her attention to it—a very deliberate act. A romantic gesture tinged with an element of danger. The man had some kind of personal agenda involving her, but she had no clue what it could be. Not yet.

Becca knew she'd see Diego tomorrow when she called on Hunter Cavanaugh. Maybe that thought played on her subconscious more than she realized. Or maybe her loneliness had triggered the illusion of romance—driven by her need to be touched by someone. Either way, she had to be careful. She knew nothing about his past, only that Diego Galvan had unsavory connections to the mob and traveled in dangerous circles. Their worlds could not be farther apart—cop and criminal. Tainted and forbidden fruit, that's all he represented to her. No way she'd allow anything to happen between them.

Becca crawled back through the window. After a quick search of the premises, gun in hand, she found nothing out of the ordinary. She locked up for the night, flicking off lights as she went. One last time, Becca stood in the dark by the window, scanning every shadow along the river.

"Who the hell are you, Diego?" she whispered. "And what do you want from me?"

CHAPTER 4

Barefoot and dressed in jeans and black T-shirt, Diego sat in the kitchen before dawn, a morning ritual he'd cultivated since taking up residence at Cavanaugh's estate. He preferred to be alone with his newspaper and coffee, before the onslaught of the chef and his kitchen crew. Diego lived amidst the pampering, but he fended for himself, keeping Cavanaugh and his staff at bay. No one knew his comings and goings, by design.

And this morning, although he held the newspaper in his hand, Diego hadn't retained a single word. An image from last night replayed in his mind, over and over.

Drawn to the Riverwalk, he had stood in the shadows, watching her. That's all he intended to do. But Rebecca held him there, spellbound from the first tear. He still pictured her staring out the window, a beautiful face tainted by sadness.

And all he wanted to do was hold her.

Clearly, the woman could handle herself, so why had he been so hell-bent on taking her in his arms? Diego knew the answer, had avoided it like a scourge.

He'd been alone for so long, maybe he'd mistaken her need of comfort for his own. And that thought scared the hell out of him. The isolation of his work, of his life, had sowed a seed of restlessness. He no longer accepted the way things were. And the seed had sprouted, threatening to take root.

The white roses had been plucked from a vendor's cart, an afterthought, the only way he could touch her and still keep his distance. But judging by her reaction, when she shoved her back against the wall in fear, he should have resisted the urge. He hadn't intended to frighten her with the gesture.

But what the hell *had* he intended? That first day. He should never have made contact with her outside the Imperial. Big mistake. Now he was behaving like an idiot. He had no right to meddle in her personal life. Someone like Rebecca would never—

Intruding on his thoughts, a hulking presence blocked the overhead light, casting a shadow on his day and the sports section. The ugly face of Matt Brogan looked down at him.

"Where were you last night?"

"Out." Diego found single syllables worked best.

"Not good enough."

Brogan, the bully. A shaved, meaty head atop broad shoulders with no neck. So early in the morning, and the man wore a suit. Diego had never seen him without one. For all he knew, he wore the damned thing to bed, tie and all. But no matter how expensive the label, Brogan wore designer duds like they came off the rack. That about sized the man up. And those were his good points.

He didn't like Brogan's advantage over him, so he got up and moved, using the pretense of refilling his coffee mug. Brogan stood a head higher and out-weighed him by fifty pounds, easy. Diego preferred to keep his distance, choosing a spot across a food preparation island to stand and sip his coffee. Besides, the hanging pots and pans blocked his view of the man's fleshy face. A side benefit.

"Who died and made you hall monitor, Brogan? You're just pissed 'cause I ditched you. You had no business following me, especially when you're no good at it."

Brogan had been dropped on his head as a child. At least, that's what Diego preferred to believe. Brain damage explained a lot. No sane mother would've raised a child using Brogan as a prototype.

"You don't know nothin' 'bout my business," he blustered, ready to pick a fight as usual. "As far as I'm concerned, you're some kinda outsider 'round here. You're nothin' but a damned watchdog with a fancy pedigree forced on us by Rivera and Global Enterprises. And those New York boys don't know squat about our operations in Texas unless the old man tells 'em. The way I see it, Rivera needs us a helluva lot more than we need you. So don't push your luck, mutt."

"The merger with Global is working as it should be, for now. And I'm here to see that both sides live up to the agreement. But you cause a blip on Castengra's radar screen, and you'll see how much he needs you. Hell, even worse, I wouldn't want to be the guy that topples this house of cards for Cavanaugh. But maybe you're man enough to take both of them on."

"You threatenin' me?"

Diego shrugged. "Actually, I'm conducting a scientific study on the correlation between abnormally high levels of machismo and stupidity. I think you'd make a perfect test subject."

Brogan tightened his jaw and clenched his fists. But after a long moment, the arrogance evaporated from his face.

"Hey, I'm only lookin' out for boss man's interests, even if the old man is too blind to see through your lone wolf act. You been spendin' too much time off the reservation. Don't think it's gone unnoticed."

Diego laughed and placed a hand over his heart in mock sincerity, trying to downplay his behavior. He didn't need the suspicion.

"Can't a man have a love life without you knowing about it?" He shrugged and shook his head, making light of it all. "But I tell you, I'm touched. I had no idea you were such a concerned citizen, looking out for the welfare of others. All this time I thought you only cared for *número uno*. I see now I was wrong. Can you forgive me, *mi amigo*?"

"Cut the bullshit. I don't trust you, Galvan."

The man stepped closer, his eyes no bigger than slits. Diego had seen the look before, but usually rodents didn't come as big as Brogan.

"You're hiding somethin', Mex. And it's only a matter of time before I catch you runnin' crossways of the old man. Then you're mine."

Diego lowered his voice, his eyes on Brogan. "A wise man would turn and walk away."

Brogan sneered. "Yeah, but which one of us is *that* smart?"

"If you have to ask—" Diego shrugged. In a surprise move, he turned to go, catching Brogan's reaction from the corner of his eye.

"Hey! Don't you turn your back on me, you son of a bitch."

The bigger man torqued his jaw and lowered his chin. He dodged the food prep island and lunged for Diego, yanking at his shirt to throw him off-balance. Brogan punched him in the jaw, making the first move.

That's all Diego needed. All his frustrations bubbled to the surface.

In seconds, Brogan's assault would land another fist to Diego's face. He couldn't let him get the upper hand. He stiff-armed the grip Brogan had on his shirt and broke free, dodging the second blow. Ducking under the punch, Diego let the man's weight propel him forward, prodded by a shove of his own. And a well-placed kick to the man's ass sent him sprawling. Brogan hit the floor, hard.

"Uumpphh."

The man stumbled to his feet, seething from his abrupt encounter with masonry. He came up bleeding. His lip cut.

"It's not too late for you to apologize." Diego knew his caustic remark would lead to round two. He wasn't disappointed.

In tight quarters, Brogan came at him again, shoulder lowered like a linebacker. He pinned Diego to the kitchen counter, grappling him in a bear hug. He saw stars with the exertion. The edge of the tile counter cut into his back. He had to make a move, fast. A man as big as Brogan could do some serious damage. Diego let his instincts take over. He shoved the man's head back and punched Brogan's nose. Once. Twice. On his third attempt to break free, Diego felt the man's cartilage give way.

Brogan cried out in pain and released his grip on Diego. With eyes watering, the man bent over in agony, hands to his face.

"Shit, you broke my—"

Before Brogan got his bearings and tried something else, Diego shoved him back and swept his legs out from under him, toppling him to the floor. He held the man down, pinning his throat with an arm to cut off his air, a powerful persuader.

Brogan had tested Diego on other occasions, picking his spots. So far, the results had been the same. He never learned from his mistakes, but Diego couldn't let his guard down for a second. He had to stay sharp. And on top of it all, he suspected Brogan had his own agenda. The man wouldn't hesitate to kill if he got the chance. That made his counterpart very dangerous. Within Cavanaugh's organization, Matt Brogan had earned his number one ranking.

Diego reminded himself of this fact as he watched Brogan's face turn purple. He still cinched the man's throat in a viselike squeeze. In a generous concession, he eased up on his chokehold. And Brogan collapsed to the floor, sucking air into his lungs.

That gave Diego time to assess the damage as he stepped back. Blood spattered the man's tie and white shirt. A trickle came out his nose and smeared through the sheen of sweat on his skin. His lower lip was cut and swollen, fatter than usual. Seeing Brogan this way had one bonus. Up 'til now, Diego couldn't imagine the man any uglier. Now, he could.

"You're done marking my territory. Quit pissing on my turf."

Brogan clenched his jaw but never said a word. No sign of gratitude. The man took another gasping breath and pulled himself up from the floor, unable to look Diego in the eye.

It was over, or so Diego thought.

Diego turned to leave, but as he got near the doorway, he heard the hiss of metal. He turned back around to see Brogan threatening him with a butcher knife. The man taunted him, daring him to come closer.

"Come on. We ain't done yet."

Diego had no choice but to prove the bastard wrong. He reached for a ten-piece knife set on a nearby butcher block, taking the four-inch paring and the five-inch serrated utility knives from their slots. He flipped one of the knives in his hand end over end, grabbing it by the blade tip.

High-carbon steel, good balance. This would do.

Diego took aim. Without hesitation, he launched the knife. It happened so fast, Brogan had no time to react. His jaw dropped and his eyes grew wide. The paring knife whizzed by his head and landed with a thump on the kitchen cabinet behind him. And in case he hadn't gotten the message, Diego hurled a second knife. This time, he nicked the man's ear to drive his point home.

"Aaarrggghh. Damn it. Okay, okay, knock it off." Brogan cupped a meaty hand over his ear and reached for a dish towel with the other. The kitchen staff would have a mess to clean before they heated the griddle and flipped eggs.

"I'm done talking. And I don't want to have this conversation again. We clear?"

Although Brogan nodded in agreement, Diego knew it wasn't over—not by a long shot. As he headed up the back stairs to his quarters, leaving Brogan to lick his wounds, Diego knew he hadn't done himself any favors.

Next time, Matt Brogan would come at him with a short fuse and a taste for getting even.

Cavanaugh's seductive henchman had plagued Becca's thoughts all night. If she intended to keep Diego Galvan at a distance, her libido never got the e-mail. She hadn't slept a wink. All too soon, her alarm clock buzzed, a demonic grating sound. She had allowed enough time for her usual workout at the gym. But this morning, she had hit the snooze bar and yanked the covers over her head instead. One of those days. If a positive attitude measured up to a tank of gas, she'd be running on empty.

Now, in the harsh light of day, Becca drove to the Cavanaugh estate in a daze, no better prepared for the appointment she had made. Dosed up with caffeine, she hovered at cruising altitude, primed and pumped to see Hunter Cavanaugh and Diego Galvan.

Primed and pumped? *Who the hell was she kidding?*

Becca turned off Citadel Drive onto the estate and stopped to show ID to a security guard. Cavanaugh expected her. The impressive front gate and pristine grounds zipped by without notice. Too much on her mind. But as she drew closer, butterflies the size of vultures battered her insides.

The main house loomed ahead, a massive sprawling mansion of Mediterranean design. A cobblestone drive circled an imposing fountain with colorful flowers at its base. Vivid red awnings encased an ornate front door and custom windows across the façade. And a terra-cotta roofline accentuated stucco walls with imported stonework to match, a distinctive Italian influence.

Becca parked her Crown Vic short of the front door, feeling unworthy to block the main entrance. With one last look in the rearview mirror, she checked her hair and makeup and took a whiff of the white rose pinned to the lapel of her charcoal gray pantsuit jacket. Normally, the floral boutonnière would be too natty for her taste, but she wanted to send a clear message to Galvan. His midnight FTD service hadn't intimidated her in the least.

Yeah, right, if you didn't count the whole sleepless night thing.

A stern-faced butler answered the front door, looking like a member of the Addams family. The man sported a major combover of gray hair, his eyes the color of pewter. But heaping insult on top of injury, the butler's suit looked like it cost more than a month's salary for a civil servant. So far, her day had warped into a peachy keen affair.

"Right this way, Detective. Mr. Cavanaugh is expecting you."

As Becca listened to the high-pitched strains of a violin, she followed the butler through a magnificent rotunda. Her shoes echoed on the tile floor in the foyer, staccato time. With the butler keeping his eyes straight ahead, she walked behind him, sneaking a peek at every detail. Becca had never seen anything so lavish.

Subtle recessed lighting reflected anteroom walls of muted green. Marble columns, veined in black and gold, supported archways of carved ivory. Beyond the dim light of the foyer, a mahogany-and-beveled-glass doorway marked the entrance to the salon. As a focal point, inside the entrance to the chamber, a crystal chandelier hung low over a massive center table braced by gilt lions. Hunter Cavanaugh had extravagant taste. It must feel good to be king.

After Becca crossed the threshold, she heard a man's voice from across the room.

"Please . . . join me, Detective Montgomery."

In a lavish chair covered in leopard skin and framed in curves of bronze and black, an older man in his fifties sat with chin raised, like royalty holding court. She recognized Hunter Cavanaugh from her research. With a backdrop of gilded walls, his pale skin and white blond hair gave him the appearance of a statue, his pale blue eyes a stark contrast. Cavanaugh wore a crisp white shirt and black slacks, with a vintage smoking jacket in blood red. The guy either had a flair for drama, or he had a thing for Vincent Price.

Diego Galvan stood by his side. It took all her discipline to ignore him.

"These are my associates." Cavanaugh gestured with a hand. "This is Mr. Diego Galvan."

"A pleasure to meet you, Detective."

What the hell? Diego acted as if they had never met. A complete departure from the other day. But more to the point, it didn't look as if he had told Cavanaugh about their little encounter outside the Imperial, an even bigger curiosity. That and the bruise on his jaw. The man could even make a bruise look sexy.

Diego smiled, warm and genuine, the cockiness gone. Yet his eyes shot her a clear message—*play along, Rebecca.* How generous did she feel? And why would he assume she'd cooperate? But when she returned his smile, he added a wink, meant for her alone. It stopped her cold. Her smile dissolved into an awkward businesslike nod, a move that amused him.

Despite the clandestine greeting and his subtle flirtation, she couldn't help but notice. Diego looked elegant in his gray suit and black cashmere turtleneck, the picture of confidence and style. Bruise or no bruise. *Why does he have to look and smell so good, damn it?*

Cavanaugh's voice intruded, "And this is Mr. Matt Brogan."

If Diego had all the qualities of a charming and intelligent Dr. Jekyll, Matt Brogan had to be his alter ego, Mr. Hyde. The guy's face looked like it had spent some quality time pressed to a George Foreman grill. Streaks of red skin appeared swollen to the touch.

And his ear had a major gash in it. Brogan nodded, no real greeting. And he barely made eye contact.

A falling-out among thieves? Apparently, Diego had won the argument. A tiny voice in Becca's head told her to keep her mouth shut about his raw appearance, but her host noticed her reaction.

Cavanaugh raised an eyebrow, a glint of amusement in his eyes. He crooked his lips into a smile. "It seems Mr. Brogan had a dispute with the chef this morning." He leaned toward her and whispered, as if the man in question stood out of earshot. "I'm afraid his kitchen privileges have been suspended."

Cavanaugh stood and walked to a console table. "May I pour you some coffee?"

A silver coffee service had been arranged. An elaborate setup.

"Yes, sir. I'd love some."

Cavanaugh poured two cups and gestured for her to sit on a velvet divan, midnight blue with gold piping. He brought the coffee over and served her. The whole idea was to get him to feel comfortable with her—not a difficult task if she set her mind to it. But today, with this man, Becca would have to force the mindless banter.

"You are a striking woman, Detective Rebecca Montgomery. But I suppose you hear that a lot."

"Oh, I don't know. I find a man says just about anything to a woman with a gun." She smiled. "But in my line of work, it's hard to gauge sincerity without a lie detector."

"Well, unfortunately, I've found honesty is a rare commodity these days. Wouldn't you agree?"

His face remained stoic, unreadable. But he coerced a smile from her again. Cavanaugh had either
seen through her strained cordiality or the man had
informed her that he rarely told the truth.

"I must say you were a little cryptic on the phone.
What is this about, Detective?"

"I do appreciate you seeing me like this, Mr. Cavanaugh. I'd like to ask you a few questions about the
Imperial Theatre."

"I was disturbed to hear it burned down. Pity. But
I'm afraid I no longer own the building. Sometime
back, I donated it to charity as a historical site." He
smiled and sipped his coffee.

"Yes, I remember reading about that in the paper a
year or so ago. As a young girl, I visited the theater.
Magnificent original architecture. Who handled the
last renovation design work?"

For an instant, she glanced toward Diego.
Becca hadn't intended to do it, but like a compass
compelled to point north, she caught herself
drawn to the man. Diego narrowed his eyes, seeing
through her subterfuge. Idle chitchat had never
been her forte.

"Hans Muller, a local architect. He gained national
recognition for that renovation project, I'm proud
to say." And with a wink, he added, "For specialty
work, I hire it done."

You hire out specialty work, as in murder? Becca
got the distinct impression Cavanaugh was toying
with her. The man was in his element, feeling cock-
sure. Could he be hinting at a truth only he knew,
daring her to find it? And were Diego and "No Neck

Boy" nothing more than hired thugs? Becca's gut twisted, her cop instincts on the blitz.

After a sip of her coffee, she asked, "And did Muller handle all the renovation work?"

"Yes, he did. Of course." He leaned toward her. "Why all the interest in architecture, Detective?"

"Actually, I loved that old building. When, specifically, did you relinquish ownership of it, sir?"

He gave her a date she already knew. Becca kept her eyes on him, watching for a change in body language. Up until now, they had chatted, idle conversation to establish a "baseline" of his normal behavior. Enough time for her to get a read on his mannerisms, his voice, his thought processes. Now she'd hit him with the real reason for her visit.

"I'm sorry to say that we are investigating more than a fire at the Imperial. It seems that seven years ago, a body was buried in a wall during the last renovation."

"What? I don't understand."

"Skeletal remains were found after the fire, Mr. Cavanaugh. And I'm sure you'd like to get to the bottom of this as much as I would."

Slick as black ice, the man tried to suppress his reaction, but Becca caught something all the same. His eyes were jumpy, like a suspect's. With a man like Cavanaugh, the best she might get is a slip-up on his part, a careless word that would give her a clue to chase. But the man salvaged his composure in two seconds flat.

"How dreadful," he said. "Do you happen to know the identity of this poor individual?"

"We're working on it. But in the meantime, when was the last time you saw this young woman?"

Becca handed Isabel's photo to Cavanaugh. The way she posed the question, she made it appear as if Cavanaugh already knew the girl. A deliberate ploy.

"Sorry, can't help you. I don't recognize her at all."

Cavanaugh waved a hand and gestured for his men to come over. "No Neck" shook his head and shrugged. A cold response. He hadn't even glanced at the photo of Isabel for more than two seconds. Becca suspected the guy would react the same way if someone asked if he were lactose intolerant. Talk about a poker face. A dead girl would hold no more significance to this whack job than that bloated feeling after eating dairy.

But Diego had been a different story. He stared at her, his eyes narrowed in question, suggesting a hint of concern and compassion. *Well, what do ya know?* Becca took a deep breath, resisting the urge to read too much into this man. With her life being a complete wreck, she couldn't deal with a potential disappointment named Diego Galvan.

"Do you suspect it is this young woman's body in the theater, Detective?"

"Too soon to tell, sir."

"Well, certainly, I'm sympathetic, but what does this have to do with me?" Cavanaugh asked.

Becca hated that question. Had heard it many times before. She took a deep breath and held back her resentment. Murder was a crime against humanity, a depraved act that diminished mankind as a whole.

But Cavanaugh viewed the world with him at its center. End of story. She would get nowhere explaining her belief to a man like him.

"I have to investigate all the angles. And you owned the property at the time." She set her coffee cup down on its saucer. "What motive would someone have to select your theater for a body dump?"

"I have no idea." He answered way too fast.

No outrage. No questions. The man didn't even seem curious. In her experience, an innocent person might mull over the question, maybe speculate on an answer. But someone with something to hide would answer without thinking, like Cavanaugh. She decided to try a different tactic.

"Play along with me here, Mr. Cavanaugh. 'Cause I tell you, I can use all the help I can get on a case this old. Why would someone kill and leave a body buried in a wall of your theater?" she pressed.

If she read him right, Cavanaugh looked like a man who relished being in charge. Stroking his intellect seemed like a natural choice. Given the man's ego, he might have the audacity to reveal certain elements of the truth, throwing them in her face. A man like Cavanaugh might believe he was above the law and smarter than the police. It wasn't up to Becca to prove him wrong. Her only objective, at this point, was to keep him talking. If she was any judge of character, his ego would do the rest.

But from the corner of her eye, she saw Diego shift his weight. Becca resisted the urge to look over. His deliberate move triggered his words of warning about his "benefactor." They replayed in her head.

Just make sure you bring your A-game with this guy. He's powerful and as nasty as they come. Suddenly, her lowly Columbo routine didn't feel adequate for the challenge.

When she looked at Cavanaugh, the man smiled, ingratiating and perverse. Her skin crawled at the sight.

"Hypothetically speaking, you say?" the man asked. When she nodded, Cavanaugh gazed across the room and made a good show of playing along. "Well, let's presume this unnamed body is the beautiful young woman in the photograph, shall we?"

He waited for her to acknowledge his clever deduction before he continued, "Perhaps it was a crime of passion, the stuff of Edgar Allan Poe. A jilted lover buries her alive, the sound of her beating heart still resounding in his ear. What better place for high drama than an old theater?"

"With all due respect, Mr. Cavanaugh, I didn't say the victim was buried alive. But please go on. Your thoughts interest me."

He fell silent for an instant, considering her observation.

"No, I guess you didn't." He smirked. "But Poe wouldn't have had it any other way."

Cavanaugh raised his chin and spoke in a raspy whisper.

"I didn't know the girl, but perhaps she wasn't entirely innocent. Maybe this girl had a secret life no one knew about. Is that the type of speculation you mean?"

For an awkward moment, he turned his gaze on

her like a weapon. She blinked. The intensity of his ice blue eyes took her breath. And even though he asked questions, his conjecture sounded an awful lot like statements of fact.

Witnessing her uneasiness, Cavanaugh leaned toward her, closing the gap of her comfort zone. His voice low and intimate, he brushed a finger across the petal of the white rose on her lapel.

"An older man can offer a younger woman so many things. Maybe unwittingly, she became the moth to a very dangerous flame."

Becca held her ground, not backing off. *Breathe, damn it.* She returned his unblinking stare, resisting the urge to bolt. Her creep barometer had hit the red zone. Yesterday, Father Victor suggested Isabel had a relationship with an older man, one who had money.

Was Becca staring into the eyes of a killer? She swallowed and forced a smile.

"That's very good. If this whole wealthy playboy thing doesn't work out, I could put in a good word for you down at the SAPD." To regain her composure, Becca took a sip of coffee before she continued. "The recent fire may prove to be arson. Any theories on that?"

"Arson? Well, there's your answer," he offered.

"How so?"

"Whoever set the fire no doubt knew about the body. Don't you see? Otherwise, it would be too much coincidence. Your arsonist may well be the killer."

"Interesting theory, sir."

Cavanaugh looked like a man who had delivered the only line he had in a stage play. Smug and theatrical. Surely Diego had told the man about the possibility of arson at the Imperial. If he did, Cavanaugh had plenty of time to conjure up his great insight, his theory to place blame on a faceless firebug.

Becca had thought of this angle before. But why would someone wait seven years to pin a murder on Cavanaugh? Could the body have been intended to act like a time bomb, waiting to blow up in the man's face at the worst possible time? Why now? Too many questions without answers.

"Do you know of anyone who would frame you for this murder, sir? Set you up to take the fall?"

"A man in my position has made enemies to be sure, but I can't think of anyone who would do this, no."

Yeah, right. From what she gathered, Cavanaugh had jump-started his family business on a foundation of mob money. And he hired "muscle" to ensure his protection. Yet he sat before her—innocence personified. Time for her to rock the yacht.

"Your travel company merged a few years ago with Global Enterprises. And since that time, your business has flourished. Any possibility of—"

Cavanaugh interrupted. "What would cause you to look into the merger of my company?" The man's eye twitched. A subtle gesture. But the tightening of his jawline had been more pronounced. Becca hit a nerve.

Throughout most of the interview, she struggled to maintain control, with Cavanaugh playing the part of grand master of their mental tug-of-war. Yet with the topic of Global Enterprises on the table, Cavanaugh clammed up, pretended to be insulted by her line of questioning. His cooperation came to a grinding halt. Becca had discovered his trigger—an Achilles' heel. *Score one for the visiting team.*

"At this stage of my investigation, I have to look at anything and everything, Mr. Cavanaugh."

His composure had vanished. "If you are asking if someone within my corporation would do this, the answer is no, Detective." Cavanaugh set his coffee cup down and stood. "This conversation is over. Anything else I can do for you?"

Becca had been dismissed.

"No, sir. That will do for now. You've been very helpful." She stood and reached for her casebook to retrieve a business card. "If you think of anything else, please contact me."

Although Cavanaugh took her card, he never glanced at it. The man had no intention of picking up where they'd left off. The next move would be hers.

"Diego will see you to the front door," the man ordered.

As Cavanaugh left the room, gesturing for Brogan to follow him, Becca caught a distinct reaction from Diego. His double take gave him away. Cavanaugh's directive had surprised him. And he didn't appreciate being odd man out.

"I can find my own way out. After all, I am a detective," she teased. And in her best Hispanic accent, she added, "I can detect such things."

Diego looked distracted and totally missed her impersonation of him. The man watched Cavanaugh leave the room with Brogan and his beady-eyed stare that only a coiled rattler would understand.

"Why didn't you—?"

Before she finished her thought, Diego flashed her an intense look coupled with a subtle shake of his head, cautioning her to keep quiet.

"No trouble, Detective. It will be my pleasure to escort you out."

They walked in silence, his hand touching the small of her back. Although she tried to ignore his gesture, the feel of his fingers on her body kindled a surge of adrenaline she couldn't control. Toe-curling stuff. With cheeks flushed, she set her jaw. No way she would acknowledge his effect on her.

"This estate has eyes and ears," he whispered out of the corner of his mouth, not looking her way.

Becca knew the clack of her heels on the tile floor would make audio surveillance difficult, but video was another story. So she kept her eyes straight ahead and her voice low.

"We gotta talk," she muttered.

"Not here," he whispered. When they got to the front door, Diego reached for the knob and opened it. In a louder voice, he added, "Good day, Detective."

Diego Galvan looked edgy, his unflappable façade a distant memory. And his dark eyes darted back the way they'd come, his jaw taut with tension. Something had caused him to lose his cool. She had to admit that seeing him like this did a number on her head. But her head was the least of her problems. Her body had a mind of its own.

Diego stood close enough for her to feel the warmth off his skin, mixed with his subtle cologne—a potent combination. Although the man tried to maintain his distance, his eyes conveyed another message altogether. They held a sense of danger mixed with an ironclad humanity, an intriguing labyrinth she had to explore.

Becca narrowed her eyes, resisting the urge to ask him how and when he would contact her. Instead, she walked out the front door, taking her first step toward trust. Besides, playing a little cloak-and-dagger with gorgeous eyes wouldn't ruin the rest of her day. Diego looked like a man who wanted to talk. A perfect match.

She wanted to hear whatever he had to say . . . to a point.

Becca merged the Crown Vic into traffic on I–10 with a lot on her mind. Diego's words of warning about Cavanaugh were dead on the money. The man gave her a serious case of the creeps, triggering a gut reaction that the affluent pillar of the community hid something, especially where Global Enterprises was concerned. But as she replayed the interview with Cavanaugh in her head, her cell phone rang.

"Montgomery."

"Becca? Where are you?"

She recognized the voice of Lieutenant Arturo Santiago.

"I'm on I–10, heading back downtown. Why?"

"I wanted you to hear this from me, before the media gets ahold of it."

His words gripped her heart. A grave tone to his voice. It drew her back to the day she first heard about a bloody motel room. This couldn't be good.

"Sounds ominous. What's up?"

"There's been another abduction, in Austin near the U.T. campus. A couple of days ago."

Another young life ruined, a family torn apart. The news wrenched her gut. Danielle's sweet face flashed in front of her eyes. Becca clenched her jaw and gripped the steering wheel, hard. She tried to regain her composure, stay focused.

"Same MO?" She hated the edge to her voice. The need. "Is there a connection, Art?"

"No, the MO is different. Broad daylight this time, no nightclub involved. And the girl was a college kid, some foreign exchange student from Japan. The FBI clued Murphy in on this one. We wouldn't have seen it as connected except for one thing."

"Yeah, what's that?"

The man hadn't heard her. He kept on talking.

"We're not gonna leak this detail to the press, Becca. This one we keep."

"Art, spit it out. I gotta know."

"Your sister's senior class ring was found in a van they dumped, wedged in a crack."

The news stole her breath, bringing a sudden rush of tears to her eyes. The innocence of a graduation that would never be collided with the horror of Danielle's violent death in a blood-splattered motel room. A cruel jolt. It took every ounce of concentration to keep her car between the painted lines. No way she'd be frozen out on this one. Not now.

"By itself, this doesn't mean much. It's only her ring, judging by the initials on the inside of the band. We have no context, no time frame. The ring ties this vehicle to the FBI's case, that's all."

"But it's something, Art," she pleaded, softening her tone. "Something of Dani's."

"Look, I know what you're thinking, but I gotta tell ya," Santiago added, "I got a new guy from the FBI down here today. He's buttoning things up tight. You're not gonna . . ."

Becca didn't let him finish.

"I want in, Art. One way or another, I *want* in." She insisted, not waiting for Lieutenant Santiago's response.

Becca ended the call and tossed the cell onto the seat next to her. She hit the gas pedal. No way Santiago would bar her from the investigation now.

CHAPTER 5

"Detective Montgomery is going to be a problem, one I will place in your hands."

Hunter Cavanaugh collapsed into his black leather desk chair, the start of a headache pulsing at his temples. The study smelled of brandy and cigar smoke, with the underlying musty odor of old books. The combined pungency gnarled his stomach, intensified by the reversal of fortune to his morning. Cavanaugh sat behind his desk and stared straight through Brogan, his mind on other things.

"And let's keep this our little secret. Diego is not to find out. The last thing I need is for Rivera to hear about my little . . . hobby."

"But this body in the theater, they won't find a connection."

"Does that really matter?" He didn't feel like explaining himself to Brogan. "Being under a cop's scrutiny is never a good thing."

The pretty detective piqued his interest when he thought she was investigating the fire at the Imperial Theatre. Diego had given him a heads-up on the blaze being arson. Professional courtesy, the man had said. And when Detective Montgomery walked into the room, he felt like a kid waking up Christmas morning—a new toy caught his eye. Yet in no time, she doused him with a harsh reality. And she didn't look like the kind of woman who knew how to play outside the rules.

"I'm afraid the detective has no idea how to have fun."

"We could teach her." Brogan's face squeezed into a grin like a compressed accordion.

"Yes, I suppose we can." Cavanaugh crooked a corner of his mouth, a fleeting gesture. "But this couldn't come at a worse time."

"What do you need me to do . . . exactly?"

Although Brogan lacked imagination, he made up for his shortcoming with a genuine enthusiasm to execute a direct order. A quality Cavanaugh appreciated in a subordinate.

"To start, let's consolidate the merchandise. You know what to do. I can't have the police nosing around my affairs."

Cavanaugh recognized the necessity for shoring up his defenses, but he resented his need to do so.

"How far do you want me to go . . . with the detective?"

He saw the glint in Brogan's dark eyes and marveled at what little it took to amuse him. Despite Brogan's eagerness, Cavanaugh wondered if he could entrust his well-being to such a man. He took a deep breath.

"I have some ideas on the subject. Pour a brandy for both of us, Mr. Brogan. Let's talk."

*   *   *

Becca had to slow her steps as she trekked down the corridor to Lieutenant Santiago's office. Gauging by the play of light from a window, she knew his door was open. When she rounded the corner and stepped inside, Santiago looked up, his expression stern. But he wasn't alone.

"Detective Montgomery. Please come in and close the door." Santiago gestured for her to sit. She shut the door but remained standing.

Paul Murphy, dressed in a dark gray suit, white shirt, and his favorite red power tie, turned from the window as she entered the office. He leaned against the sill, arms crossed. Murphy stared at her, his expression blank. That surprised her. Normally, the man wore his smugness like an extra layer of skin. Arrogance fit him like a glove.

But the balding man to Murphy's left captured her attention. Tall and lanky, the older man wore his suit as if he were a human coat hanger. An unflattering cut couldn't be blamed for the guy's inability to fill it out. His dark eyes looked like two lumps of coal set amidst the deep wrinkles creasing his face. She got the distinct impression the lines were not caused by his stellar sense of humor. Becca extended her hand to force an introduction.

"I don't believe we've met. My name's Detective Rebecca . . ."

"I know who you are, Detective. Please take a seat." He didn't reach for her hand.

"This is Mike Draper with the FBI's Criminal Investigative Division out of DC."

Santiago made the one-sided introduction for her benefit. Without a word, Draper glared at her lieutenant, a look intended as a directive to get started. And Santiago complied, without so much as an insolent scowl.

"Draper has some questions for you. I expect your cooperation." Santiago turned his gaze to the man standing near the window.

"Your investigation on the arson fire and the bones found at the theater. Brief me on the case and the meeting you had with Hunter Cavanaugh this morning," Draper commanded.

"Sir, I can do that, but I'd rather talk about my sister's . . ."

"Your sister's investigation is off-limits to you. Now tell me about this case and Cavanaugh's involvement," the man insisted.

Becca tried to read him, but the fed didn't allow it. Something was going down, and she wouldn't be a part of it. She took a seat in the chair nearest her. Becca stared at the men who would deny her and made a deliberate choice. She was damned tired of playing by their rules.

"Not much to report yet, sir. I've got an appointment with the Medical Examiner this afternoon. No ID on the victim. As you know, nothing much can happen until we get that identification."

"Tell me about your meeting with Cavanaugh. What transpired?"

"We had coffee, sir," she replied. In a roomful of interrogators, she had to remain calm, an open book. "Cavanaugh seemed surprised to hear about the skeletal remains found after the fire. I don't think he's going to be much help. He's not even the owner of record for the property anymore. It's some kind of historical site."

If Santiago had gotten a complaint from Cavanaugh, her lieutenant would know she had lied about not knowing the identity of the victim. Her lie by omission. He gave no sign of that, so she stuck with her makeshift game plan. Becca had grown accustomed to treading on thin ice.

"Is that all, Detective Montgomery?" Draper persisted. "Do you suspect Hunter Cavanaugh of any wrongdoing on this case of yours?"

How much did this man know? If he or Murphy had dug around, they might know she had requested two archived boxes on missing persons. Would they call her bluff? To throw these men off their game, she decided to go on the offensive. After all, they had hit her broadside. Time to return the favor.

"At present, I don't have any reason to suspect Cavanaugh of anything." She hadn't really lied. "But I have some questions for you, sir."

Becca leaned forward in her chair, placing an elbow on Santiago's desk, her eyes fixed on the fed. She didn't wait for Draper's permission to go on.

"Just now, you called the Imperial an arson fire. The final report isn't out yet. Why would you call it arson? And how did you hear about my visit to Cavanaugh this morning? I hadn't mentioned it to anyone. What's really going on here?"

Draper tightened his jaw and narrowed his eyes. For a second, she saw his flinch of surprise, but the man recovered quickly. Even Santiago and Murphy reacted. She saw it from the corner of her eye. But hitting the bull's-eye wouldn't win her any prize.

"By the end of shift, you will turn over all your case notes to Murphy. Any files you've started on the fire and the skeletal remains will be his."

"But, sir." She looked at Santiago for help. "Why am I being pulled off this case? I don't understand . . ."

Her lieutenant took back control of the meeting.

"You'll be reassigned. But until then, I'd like you to consider taking some vacation time, like we talked about the other day." Santiago sat back in his chair, his eyes unwavering. "You mentioned taking time to help your mother. I think that's a great idea."

Becca felt like she had stepped through a portal to another dimension, an alternative universe. Only the other day, her lieutenant told her time off was not an option. He wanted her close at hand, to watch her. But today, he doled out vacation days like party favors. Something was definitely up, and Arturo Santiago wanted her to play along. She knew the man, sensed his message. But above all, Becca trusted him.

She looked over to Murphy and shrugged.

"You'll have my files by the end of today." Glancing back to Santiago, she asked, "Anything else, sir?"

"No, that will be all. Thanks for your cooperation, Detective."

And just like that, she was out. Becca avoided looking at Draper and Murphy as she stood. She opened the door and walked out of Santiago's office without a sideways glance. The urge to slug them both would be way too strong. She headed down the hallway, gnashing her teeth until her jaw ached.

Thinking back to her earlier cell phone conversation with Santiago, the man had bucked the system to share the news on Danielle's case. No doubt the chief would have reprimanded him if Draper had found out. Maybe she still had Santiago on her side.

"Thanks, L.T. But you and I aren't done yet. Not by a long shot."

Becca bounded up the stairs to her desk on the fourth floor, in no mood to ride the elevator with other people. She had until the end of the day to turn over her files and case notes. Murphy would get a sanitized version, one to back up the story she told Draper. She owed her lieutenant that much. In the meantime, Becca had a Medical Examiner waiting and the Marquez brothers coming at shift end. And if that wasn't enough to keep her busy, Isabel's background needed a thorough search.

Her investigation at the Imperial had gotten the attention of the FBI. She suspected the abducted girls and Danielle's case were somehow linked to all of this. The fed had all but confirmed that with his line of questioning. The arrogant bastard.

At the heart of it, she pictured Hunter Cavanaugh. Mike Draper didn't give a damn about Isabel. A seven-year-old murder of a local girl would have no sex appeal for a fed. But a wealthy guy with an international travel business and connections to the mob would lure Draper like a bottom-grubbing catfish to stink bait. A high-profile case that might cross borders.

"This is about you, Cavanaugh. I know it."

After today, Becca would be forced to take time off. Although she'd be cut off from the action, being on vacation would allow her to keep her badge and gun. A clever move on Santiago's part. Through it all, her lieutenant had proven himself a loyal friend. Maybe he'd keep her connected to the case within the SAPD.

But having someone on the inside of Cavanaugh's organization would be a real coup. Becca made up her mind. She would recruit Diego Galvan for the honor, even if she had to play hardball to get him.

"Sorry, Galvan. The gloves are off. Don't expect me to play nice."

BEXAR COUNTY MEDICAL EXAMINER'S OFFICE
LOUIS PASTEUR DRIVE

The skeletal remains found at the Imperial Theatre had been steam cleaned and arranged in order on a light table. The bones were stark ivory white with a section of the skull cut out. A macabre jigsaw puzzle. And with all other lights in the room dimmed, the light table cast an eerie glow on the faces of crime-scene investigator Sam Hastings and the Medical Examiner, Charles Leibowitz.

The ME was a short, pudgy man with thinning white hair. His eyes bulged out from their sockets with puffy bags of skin beneath them. Shadows traced his full cheeks, masking their true size. Both men had pale green surgical gowns draped over their clothes, with latex gloves on their hands, same as she wore. Even with the added layers, she felt the constant chill in the room through her clothes.

"Well, the age, gender, and height are in line with what we know of the Marquez girl, but you say we'll have the family's DNA to match the mitochondria?" Leibowitz asked.

"Yeah, probably after six," Becca replied, bending over to look closer at the cutaway of the skull. "Tell me about this fracture here? An odd shape. Kind of a wedge."

"Blunt force trauma. The indentation is pronounced enough to indicate some kind of hammer. Something with a long, narrow head and slight curvature. See here?" The Medical Examiner pointed with a gloved finger. "The edge of the break in bone hinges downward. That indicates the bone was fresh and elastic when the injury took place. The fracture lines radiate out from there. But the blow wasn't a solid, dead-on strike. The impression is deeper here, but barely noticeable on this end. More of a glancing blow."

"But Sam, remember the scratches on the wall where we found her?" Becca turned toward the crime-scene investigator. "I thought she was buried alive."

Sam opened his mouth to speak, but Leibowitz beat him to the punch.

"Oh, this blow wouldn't have killed her," the ME explained. "I believe the cause of death will be determined more in the context of how you found her, Detective."

"Let me translate for Charlie," Sam intervened with a grin. "Buried alive in a vault without much air and no food or water is a pretty good indicator she didn't die of natural causes or a crack on the head. And the scratches on the wall and condition of her fingernails paint a grim picture. Charlie's right on the head trauma thing. She wouldn't have died from it."

"So the killer knocked her unconscious and bricked her into the wall, knowing she was still alive?" she asked.

"We may never know the killer's intention here, unless we get it in a confession. A head wound like that? There would have been a lot of blood given all the blood vessels in the scalp. Maybe whoever did it thought she was dead." Sam gave his opinion, one that would never end up in an official report.

"And back to the weapon. What kind of hammer, Sam?"

"Since we only have a partial impression, I'm gonna have to do some comparisons before I commit to anything. Unlike the good doctor here, I'm a hard-working stiff." Sam Hastings crooked his lips into a smile, a gesture that quickly faded. "Stiff? Can't believe I used that word in this place."

Becca raised an eyebrow. "I don't remember seeing any fabric in the hole where we found the bones. Any theories on that?"

"There's an outside chance the body was buried without clothing, but more than likely, the fabric deteriorated over time. You figured this girl went missing seven years ago, right?" When she nodded, he continued, "And we found evidence of rodent activity in the vault. That suggests another factor to the decay of fabric. Scavenging critters can break down the material pretty quick."

"Lovely. I hate rats." She winced.

"Especially the two-legged variety." Sam smirked. "Anyway, that's all we've got for now."

"Call me when you have something more definitive, huh? On my cell?"

"Yeah, sure thing. Charlie and I have some more work to do here, taking an inventory and measurement of the bones and their conditions. But I'll let you know what I find out."

Becca should have told them she was off the case, but something stopped her. She might get mileage out of keeping that fact a secret.

But another thing ate at her craw. Murphy had every opportunity to attend this meeting with the ME, but he never showed an interest. If the bones on the table belonged to Isabel Marquez, Becca had a feeling the case would get shoved onto a back burner. Whatever they had on Cavanaugh would take precedence. Isabel's killer might never be identified. Becca couldn't let that happen. After meeting the Marquez family, she owed them the truth.

Shrugging out of her surgical gown and stripping off the latex gloves, she headed for the door.

"I'll get the DNA sample to you ASAP. Later, guys."

Becca dumped her surgical gown and latex gloves into a receptacle outside the autopsy room. She had a lot of ground to cover before she'd be ready for the Marquez brothers.

CENTRAL STATION
DOWNTOWN SAN ANTONIO

The room adjacent to interrogation room number 5 was dark, but not empty. Through the two-way mirror, a pale light shone, giving shape to Becca's silhouette. She stood in the dark with arms crossed, watching the Marquez brothers wait for her to show up in the next room. A crime-scene tech had already swabbed both men for DNA testing. Now she let time do its work. Both looked anxious, each in his own way. Their voices were muffled on the intercom speaker.

"Don't volunteer anything. If you have any doubts, don't answer. Just look at me, and I'll tell you what to do."

Dressed in his priest vesture, Victor sat rigid in his chair. His tone low and forceful. He talked out of the corner of his mouth, not really looking at his brother.

"I don't need you here, Victor. You should have let me drive myself."

Rudy rolled his eyes and slumped deeper into his chair, but the priest ignored his objection.

"Don't worry. If we need a lawyer, I know someone who may do it for free."

"You get what you pay for, bro."

The priest didn't reply. He shut his eyes for an instant and took a deep breath. Victor raised his chin and maintained his stoic expression, hoping to assure his younger brother he could handle the situation. But by Rudy's actions, Becca saw he hadn't bought into Victor's overtures. The guy avoided looking at the priest and fidgeted in his seat. His eyes darted to the closed door every few minutes.

Despite his nervousness, Rudy's dark brown eyes appeared childlike. An undeniable innocent quality to them. He looked most like Isabel in that sense. Dressed in his work clothes of faded blue jeans and a black Spurs basketball T-shirt, Rudy looked like he'd barely had time to wash his face and hands. His clothes had a layer of dust and grime, the pattern only broken by the darker markings of sweat. Shorter than Victor and very slender, Rudy had the appearance of a boy in a man's body.

But Becca couldn't let her first impressions of Rudy sway her judgment as a cop. Her instincts told her this family was holding something back. Now she'd push them to uncover the truth. Becca walked through the door of interrogation room 5.

"Sorry to keep you waiting." She dropped her casebook on the table in front of the Marquez brothers. "I appreciate your cooperation, Father."

Becca extended her hand to Rudy. "My name is Detective Rebecca Montgomery."

After a long moment, he eventually returned her gesture.

"Rudy . . . Rudy Marquez."

His eyes avoided hers. He raised a hand to his mouth and chewed on a thumbnail. Becca sat in front of him. She leaned forward with her elbows on the table, forcing him to look at her.

"Your brother tells me you and Isabel were very close. So I'm going to need your help, Rudy." She paused, making sure she held his attention. "Tell me what she was like. Tell me about your Isabel."

Her request surprised him. Eyes wide, he looked up and sat straight in his chair. Nearly a minute ticked by before he spoke, his voice almost a whisper.

"When she was little, Isabel wanted to please Mama so much. She was a good girl." He stared across the room, not focusing on anything in particular. The past had caught up with him. "When I think of her, I remember Isabel putting her hand in mine when we walked to school, and not just at the crosswalks. She used to tell me how I made her feel safe."

That memory took its toll. Tears welled in his eyes, a contradiction to the sad smile on his face. "She needed me then."

He quit talking. Silence overwhelmed the room. And Father Victor didn't fill the void. The priest swallowed hard, watching Rudy.

"But at some point, little girls grow up," Becca prompted. A flash of Danielle's sweet face wedged a knot in her throat. "Little girls learn to live their own lives."

A tear slid down his face. Rudy never looked up. "Yes, they grow up. And they learn about ugliness from despicable men with no honor."

Father Victor turned his head in surprise. "Please, Rudy . . ."

"You never want to hear about this, Victor. Yet here, you drag me in front of this stranger to talk about it. Why is that? So you can act surprised, like you never knew? So you can remain the saint?" Rudy's voice rose in anger. He glared at his brother. "You were gone. I was left to deal with it alone."

"Deal with what, Rudy?" Becca asked. "Tell me about Isabel."

"Don't do this, *mi hermano*. Please." Father Victor clutched Rudy's arm, pulling his brother closer. "Hasn't our family suffered enough? Hasn't Mama been through enough pain?"

Rudy yanked his arm free and turned his back on Victor.

"About a week before she went missing, I saw Isabel get into some kind of Mercedes, a block down from our house. She was with another girl, Sonja Garza. It was kind of dark, but I recognized the Garza girl. When I asked Isabel about it, she lied. She told me the car belonged to Sonja's boyfriend."

"But you didn't believe her?" she asked. After Rudy shook his head, Becca persisted, "Why didn't you believe her, Rudy?"

He leaned forward, resting his elbows on the table. He looked tired. After a moment, Rudy wiped both hands over his face. "I followed the car, that's why. Out I–10 to some rich guy's place. I didn't like her sneaking around like that. It wasn't right."

"Did you ever actually see the man driving the car?" she asked.

"It was Hunter Cavanaugh."

Hearing Rudy say Cavanaugh's name surprised Becca. She tried not to let it show.

"How did you know it was Cavanaugh, Rudy? Had you ever seen him before?"

He hesitated. Anger replaced the accusation in his eyes.

"Oh, I get it. You don't believe me. You wanna protect that son of a bitch." He stood and paced the floor behind his chair, running a hand through his thick dark hair. "The dude's old enough to be my old man. A guy like that only wants one thing from a young girl like Isabel."

"So you actually saw him?" Becca needed confirmation. "You said it was dark."

"I saw good enough. I recognized the car. He came out to the Imperial Theatre sometimes, during the renovation. I saw him there." Rudy sat back down, on an edge of the chair.

"You worked the renovation at the Imperial?" she asked.

She'd know the answer soon enough. Becca had requested the billable personnel listing taken off the architectural firm's invoices from the subcontractor on the renovation. And she had requested the personnel records for the subcontractor for a comparison, but none of the information had come in yet.

"I think we've told you enough, Detective." Father Victor stood and reached for Rudy's arm, pulling him to his feet. "Go talk to this Hunter Cavanaugh but leave my brother out of it."

Yet despite Victor's plea, Rudy wasn't ready to quit. He leaned across the table and pointed a finger at her.

"Cavanaugh bought her that damned necklace. The one you were asking about, the gold heart. I'm sure of it."

"You don't sound sure, Rudy. Sounds like you're guessing." Becca stood and stepped closer to Marquez. "Tell me about the last time you saw Isabel."

His eyes grew wide. He stopped himself and swallowed. As Rudy opened his mouth to speak, Victor intervened.

"That's it. No more." The priest rattled off in Spanish, too fast for Becca to keep up. Whatever he told Rudy, it was enough to shut him up. "Please, Detective, stop this. If you want to speak to either of us again, it will be through an attorney. Now I'd like to take Rudy home. Mama is expecting us for dinner. Are we free to go?"

Father Victor's voice wavered. And his eyes no longer looked confident. He clung to his brother, hoping she'd let him claim his small victory. Eventually, Becca nodded and watched them leave the room. After they shut the door behind them, she sat down, alone with her thoughts.

Not once did Father Victor or Rudy ask about Isabel, where her body had been found. She had deliberately held back the information to see if they would. One of them had been at the Imperial after the fire. Becca had a sinking feeling if she told them where Isabel's body had been found, she wouldn't be telling them anything new. *Damn it!*

She replayed the interview in her mind and made notes in her casebook. When she was done, Becca pulled the cell phone from her jacket pocket.

On the second ring, Hastings answered the call.

"Hey, Sam. When you're looking for that hammer, check into masonry tools first, will ya?"

"Any particular reason to start there?"

"Just a hunch. Let me know what you find out."

Becca ended the call, deep in thought. Rudy worked on the renovation project at the Imperial, probably as a mason, his usual gig. Suspicion twisted her gut, her professional instincts grappling with the love she felt for a dead sister.

Becca shut her eyes, letting her training take over. She would follow the evidence, even if it led to someplace she didn't want to go.

CHAPTER 6

Becca opened the front door to her condo and tossed her keys and purse onto the kitchen counter. She didn't flip on any lights. Instead, she opened a cabinet and took out a bottle of Glenmorangie single malt scotch whiskey, pouring a small glass. She resisted the urge to call Santiago. It was late. After her forced vacation, she'd have plenty of time to make contact. So, without changing clothes, she collapsed on her sofa and stared out the windows from the unlighted room.

Dim lights from the Riverwalk bled through the glass. A kaleidoscope of pastel dappled her carpet and walls, mixed with murky shadows. Stirred by the faint breeze outside, branches of cypress made the colors undulate in the dark and across her body. Hypnotic.

She took a swig of scotch. It shocked her system and burned her throat. But once its heat radiated through her chest and down her arms, she melted into the cushions of her couch.

The noise from the city throbbed, a dull pulse, out-of-sync. Becca shut her eyes and let the events of the day close in, the faces of Danielle and Isabel clouding her mind. Alone in the dark, she felt grief the most. It emanated from deep inside, leaving her no place to hide. By the time she opened her eyes, tears streaked her face. Her skin prickled where the tears had strayed, the air starting to dry them. She finished her scotch and went for more, but when Becca stood, a glimpse of white caught her eye.

A white rose lay on the brick outside her window, its green leaves stirred in the breeze. And another had been dropped on the fire escape steps, at eye level, so she wouldn't miss it. For an instant, her heart leapt in her chest.

"Diego," she whispered.

A part of her felt too fragile to withstand his influence. But an even greater part willed him to be on the rooftop, waiting for her. Becca walked to her kitchen and took another dose of liquid courage, grimacing with the potency of the scotch. At the window, she took a deep breath and raised the pane. No amount of self-control would rein in the feeling. Her heart pounded in her rib cage.

Becca picked up the first rose and ducked through the window onto the landing. More flowers lay on the steps, leading her to the roof. Her eyes trailed the roses to the top. The white lights of her rooftop garden replaced the stars in the night sky, shimmering points of light. He must have turned them on, another invitation.

But Becca had a plan for Diego Galvan. And it had nothing to do with a starlit night and roses.

*   *   *

Diego stood on the edge of the light near a parapet wall, feeling more at home in the shadows of Rebecca's garden. Sand and small pebbles crunched under his boots in this section. Clay Saltillo tile pavers covered the rest of the rooftop decking. He ran his fingertips along the greenhouse. Had she constructed it herself? He understood her need to have such a place, admired her for it.

He cocked his head to one side when he heard the window slide open below. Rebecca was home. Diego turned to face the steps to the roof and waited, but the beat of his heart ramped up a notch, an unnerving reaction.

You're acting like a damned kid, Galvan. Get a grip. He pulled open his brown leather jacket and shoved his hands into the pockets of his jeans, trying to appear casual. When she peered over the wall, he walked toward her and spoke up.

"I hope you don't mind. I made myself at home."

He offered his hand to help her over the brick wall—a well-intentioned and chivalrous gesture. But Diego couldn't help himself. He watched her move. Not even the conservative pantsuit hid her tight athletic body. If she looked at him now, Rebecca might be afraid of what she would see reflected in his eyes. He cleared his throat and glanced away.

"For a guy who lurks in the shadows, you do like a grand entrance. I'll give you that. Thanks for the roses . . . again."

When she touched his hand, a jolt of electricity shot through his system. He tried to downplay his reaction to her, but the exercise would be pointless. He had seen it before, in her eyes. In his mind and his heart, Diego knew the truth. This woman saw through his detached façade, making him feel raw and exposed. And in doing so, she forced him to remember the man he used to be. She shed light on every dark corner of his being, making him feel . . . redeemable.

"I tried your front door, but you weren't home. This was . . . Plan B."

The faint breeze tousled her hair, the strands cascading the light. She stood close enough for him to smell a fragrance on her skin, a subtle floral scent. Provocative and feminine. And he smelled alcohol. Rebecca had been drinking. But Diego stopped breathing altogether when he looked into her eyes. Steely defiance and a quiet restraint defined them, an intoxicating blend.

She held his hand, clutching his fingers even after she had made it over the wall. He took in every detail of her face, committing it to memory, knowing the moment would not last. Perfection so fleeting.

"Glad you stuck with Plan B," she replied, a fragile smile on her face and expectation in her eyes. "We have to talk."

Yes, talk. About what? Words failed him. His brain failed him. He only wanted one thing—to kiss those lips.

Diego memorized the line of her lips, the soft skin glistening in the moonlight. With his free hand, he traced a finger along her jaw, lost and completely seduced. And she surprised him by permitting his brash move. Encouraged by this, he leaned closer, lowering his lips to hers. He pulled her to him, knowing he took a liberty. The heat of her body felt so good next to his, every curve fit. He couldn't stop himself.

But she could.

"No, please . . ." Even though she placed a hand to his chest, her eyes carried a very different message. "I need to . . ."

"What do you want, Rebecca?" he whispered.

She hesitated, her gaze dropping to his lips. He clung to the hope she would change her mind and kiss *him* instead. But Rebecca only took a deep breath and pulled away from his arms. And his emptiness returned.

She crossed her arms, looking cold. And her lips trembled. Diego shrugged out of his jacket and placed it on her shoulders. She smiled at his gesture.

"Thank you, but you don't have to . . ."

She tried to hand the jacket back, but Diego raised his hands in protest.

"No, I insist." He jammed his hands into his jeans, ignoring the breeze filtering through the weave of his turtleneck sweater. "I suppose you want to know about Cavanaugh."

"Yes, what's going on between you two? You kept our little coffee break to yourself. Why is that?"

The truth. It should have been an easy thing to share with someone like Rebecca. But Diego had grown accustomed to his secrets. He wouldn't risk exposing them, not even for her. What part of the truth would he share? He'd have to tread a very thin line.

"I don't tell Cavanaugh everything. It is a game we play."

Diego circled the spot where she stood, not taking his eyes off her. A slow, calculated maneuver. But the woman didn't give an inch. She turned with him, matching his intensity.

"Not good enough, Slick. You don't strike me as the type of guy who wings it. That was a deliberate move on your part. Now answer the question."

"I'll answer your question if you tell me why you were crying the other night, by the window." When she wavered, Diego flashed a lazy smile. "You see? It's hard to take that first step, isn't it? The trust factor." His amusement faded, replaced by his intense stare. "Then I will go first."

It took him a moment to find the words. He knew how he felt, but saying such things aloud did not come easy.

"Sometimes it feels like I've lived my whole life doing things for someone else. Meeting you? That was for me. I didn't want Cavanaugh to share any piece of that. It meant too much."

He stepped closer and brushed back a strand of her hair. Graced by moonlight, the magic of this woman touched him, more than he wanted to admit.

"You have an undeniable strength in you, Rebecca. I can see it in your eyes. But it's the complete vulnerability I find most intriguing. And that, you cannot hide. Not from me."

The urge to kiss her took hold. More powerful this time.

Diego pulled her toward him, cradling the back of her head in his hand, his fingers laced through her hair. Without hesitation, he pressed his lips to hers, taking what he had no right to take. At first, she flinched in resistance. But when Rebecca's arms reached for him, her hands found the skin under his sweater, and his belly grew taut. Blood jolted through his system, on fire, fueling his arousal. He parted her lips with his tongue, and she returned his hunger, her fingers clutching his back. The sounds of the city faded—replaced by their breathless urgency. He wanted her . . . needed her.

"Oh, God, please. I can't do this," she gasped. "I'm so sorry."

She pulled her lips from his, but collapsed against his body, clinging to him. With his chest heaving, he held her in his arms, his eyes shut tight.

"No, it's me. I should be the one to apologize."

Regret filled him. He had pushed too hard, expected too much. Eyes still closed, he lowered his forehead to hers, breathing in her scent. Heat radiated off his skin. Not even the night air tempered the rush. She backed away, unable to look him in the eye. Rebecca turned her back on him, letting the clamor of the city build a wall between them.

"If you want me to go . . ." he offered.

"No. Please . . . stay." Rebecca faced him now, standing in a murky fringe of light. "Before I say what's on my mind, I do want to answer your question, about why I was crying the other night. Trust doesn't come easy for me either."

She sat on the brick ledge, staring down river. Diego edged closer, standing at a respectful distance.

"Not too long ago, I lost someone. Someone I loved very much." Rebecca's voice sounded hollow and distant. "I'd been so focused on my career, I let what was really important slip through my fingers. And now, I can't get those precious moments back with her. She's dead, and there's nothing I can do to change it."

Her words resonated with him. His personal life had taken a backseat all too often. And there were days when the bitterness of regret was all he tasted. He knelt by her side, not taking his eyes from her.

"Is that why this case is so important to you? The young girl discovered at the theater?"

"I'm sure that's part of it." She fell silent for a long moment and fixed her gaze on him. Her eyes narrowed in suspicion. "I never mentioned the age of this person. Why is it you know so much about me, Diego? Are you telling me you know about my sister, Danielle?"

He stood and shook his head. "Your sister?"

"Don't play dumb, Galvan. It doesn't suit you." She rose to her feet and handed him the jacket he had loaned her, a stern expression on her face. "Well, you've made this easier than I thought it would be."

She stood toe-to-toe with him, hands on her hips.

"I had an interesting conversation with the FBI today. They seem to be reading my mail."

He raised his chin and narrowed his eyes. "Well, you know what they say. Big Brother is watching."

"It's more than that, Slick. The feds are calling the fire at the Imperial arson even before the official report, kind of like you did the first day we met." She cocked her head. "And they knew about my interview with Cavanaugh right after I left the estate when I hadn't told anyone about it. But I've got a theory on all this."

"Oh?" He turned his back on her, avoiding her glare.

"I think the feds have someone on the inside of Cavanaugh's organization. Maybe someone under deep cover."

He clenched his jaw and shut his eyes for an instant, then turned to face her.

"I don't see how that's possible. Cavanaugh wouldn't take anyone into his confidence without a background check with references. He's known for that. No way someone in law enforcement could get inside. I know the man."

"Not unless this person had connections with someone Cavanaugh respected . . . or feared. Rivera got you inside, didn't he?"

"You don't know what you're talking about. You're fishing." He stared at the moon and took a deep breath.

"Maybe. But I think I've got the right bait." She tugged at the sleeve of his sweater and stroked his arm, forcing him to look at her again. Her voice softened. "Come on, Diego. Why else would you be here, connected to Cavanaugh? You're not like him or Brogan. I can feel it. Please tell me the truth."

Diego didn't want any secrets between them, but he had no choice. The FBI had taken away his options and suspended his life for their own agenda. *The bastards*. For all intents and purposes, Draper held a gun to his head, and Joseph Rivera would pay the price if Diego reneged on his end of the bargain. He wouldn't risk it, not even if his stonewalling cost him Rebecca's trust.

"Don't kid yourself about who I am. I understand men like Cavanaugh and Brogan. You don't know anything about me."

"Well, you're right about that. Why is it when I run a background check on you, I get nothing? Casper the Ghost has more substance than you, my friend."

"I have my reasons, none of which concern you."

"Yeah, but you're making it my business. You keep turning up when I least expect you. One way or another, you're plugged in to the FBI, and you're an insider to Cavanaugh. I don't have to understand why. All I need is for you to take on a partner. The way I see it, you don't have a choice."

"You don't know what you're asking. Stay out of this, Rebecca."

"You want to push me? Call my bluff. See what happens."

"Is that a threat?"

"Take it anyway you want, Diego, if that's your real name. If you don't play by *my* rules, I'll expose you to Cavanaugh. At this point, I have nothing to lose."

"You would do that? Risk my life, maybe others?" She couldn't look him in the eye and gave no indication she would answer, so he added, "From where I stand, you're not much better than Cavanaugh. You have no idea what you're doing."

"Then explain it to me," she shrugged. When he kept his silence, she went on, "Thought so. To hell with mutual trust, huh? Look, all you have to do is keep me in the loop. And I may need you to do things for me, without a big debate."

"If Cavanaugh thinks I'm working with the SAPD, that loop you talk about will be around my neck."

"Then you'll have to keep your guard up. That should be second nature to a guy like you."

A guy like me? She definitely had him pegged. And he couldn't exactly belabor the point. He was the one with a membership card to two criminal organizations, secret handshake and all.

"Nice to see you hold me in such high regard."

He had warned Draper not to pull Rebecca off the case, but Diego was in no position to take on the FBI. He had no clout. Now the egotistical fed would get her fired if the man knew she was trying to blackmail his prize informant into cooperating. Diego wouldn't let it happen. Rebecca was a good detective and didn't deserve the added grief.

But he wouldn't let Joseph Rivera down either. The way he looked at it, one more secret to keep wouldn't break the bank. So he had a new partner, one he had to protect from Cavanaugh *and* the FBI.

Besides, trusting someone else would be his first step back to a normal life. He'd been an undercover persona non grata for such a long time, he didn't know if he had it in him. But for Rebecca, he would be willing to try.

Diego only hoped he wasn't pinning a bull's-eye on his own back.

"I need time to think. I'll give you my decision tomorrow." Diego turned to leave.

Yeah, right. Like you have a choice, she fumed. His posturing left her frustrated. He hadn't admitted to being an undercover fed, but he hadn't denied it either. In Galvan's world, secrets were never in short supply.

But as he grabbed the fire escape rail and swung a leg over the wall to straddle it, Becca's eyes strayed to areas of Diego's body she wouldn't have the nerve to stare at with him watching. She pictured him without a stitch of clothes. And the vivid image brought a rush of blood to her cheeks . . . and elsewhere. In every way, this man would be a handful.

"Don't think too much, Galvan. If I don't hear from you, I'm moving on to my version of a Plan B. And I guarantee, you won't like it."

She followed him to the edge, crossing her arms, chin raised. Becca had to make him believe she intended to go through with this. But before Diego started down the steps, he fixed his dark eyes on her. This time, he didn't bother to hide his appetite. The lust in his eyes mesmerized her.

"Threats don't work with me. But I've always found a little honey goes a long way."

He pulled her to his chest, wrapping her in his strong embrace. Diego plunged his tongue into her mouth and teased her with the promise of unrestrained sex. Nothing delicate about *this* kiss. A moan of pleasure rumbled in his chest and resonated through her body, making her light-headed and weak in the knees. A powerful quiver raced across her skin. But all too suddenly, the kiss was over, leaving her empty and wanting more.

Eyes wide, she couldn't move. Her feet were planted like a damned geranium in a heavy clay pot.

"Until tomorrow, Rebecca."

His chest heaving, Diego stroked a finger across her cheek with yearning in his eyes and a kindhearted smile on his handsome face.

"And I do understand the importance of family, more than you know," he whispered.

The gentle tone in his voice and his affectionate touch on her cheek lingered long after he had gone down the fire escape. Becca leaned against the wall and watched him go. In the wake of his heated kiss, Diego's sudden tenderness touched her heart. She wanted to take everything back.

Blackmail was no way to start a relationship.

But speaking aloud would only break the spell. Becca touched her lips, trying to hold on to the fevered sensation of his kiss, the urgency of it. And despite her threats, the man maintained his dignity.

She hadn't deserved his generosity, but she'd take it—especially if it meant justice for Danielle and Isabel.

Across the river, a man stood in the shadows of another rooftop, pulling the binoculars down from his battered face. Following the detective home from the police station to find out where she lived had paid off in spades. Matt Brogan couldn't believe his stroke of good luck.

"Well, I'll be damned." He grinned. Wicked thoughts of retribution dominated his mind. "Why the hell are you so fuckin' cozy with a cop you only met this morning, Galvan?"

He couldn't help it. A chuckle rolled through his

chest, giving voice to the smirk on his face. The gesture made his bruises ache and his broken nose throb—a merciless reminder of the humiliation he had suffered at the hands of Diego Galvan.

But no more.

He would finally have the upper hand with the Mex. Brogan had tried to catch Galvan off the estate by following him, to see where he went after hours. But he'd been caught every time and ridiculed afterward by the slick SOB. He should have thought of this before. All he needed was the right bait. Brogan couldn't wait to see the look on Cavanaugh's face when he reported this. The old man would be pleased. He might even earn points with Rivera, uncovering his boy playing tonsil hockey with a cop from the SAPD.

Matt Brogan would enjoy killing Diego Galvan, a slow, agonizing death—a gift to the boss man and a show of respect to the Rivera clan. All in one package. And with any luck, Cavanaugh would reward him for a job well done by giving him the sexy cop. He grew hard just thinking about it.

"I told you it would only be a matter of time, Mex. Now you're mine."

CHAPTER 7

CAVANAUGH ESTATE
AN HOUR LATER

He had a sickening feeling in the pit of his stomach. Overnight, the universe must have realigned and his luck turned—and not in a good way. A dark premonition weighed heavy.

After a quick finger comb of his ashen hair, Hunter Cavanaugh pulled at the sash of his black silk robe, as he stood at the top of the grand staircase. Only minutes earlier, a servant had awakened him, rapping on his bedroom door. An urgent matter. Now he looked down into the foyer, awash in pale light. Brogan paced near the entry. The man's heavy footfalls echoed on imported tile, an ominous noise at this hour.

With a hand gliding down the banister, he took a step at a time, his descent cautious. Nothing good ever came in the middle of the night. He made his facial expression a blank slate.

"This had better be important."

Brogan stopped and turned, his face a mix of dread and a peculiar smugness.

"I followed the detective like you said," he blurted out.

Before the man continued, Cavanaugh waved a hand to stop him.

"Let's talk in the study. I'm sure privacy is in order."

Brogan followed him, close on his heels. When Cavanaugh crossed the threshold of the study, he flipped on an overhead light and dimmed it. He turned his head, and ordered, "Close the door behind you."

Cavanaugh poured himself a cognac and took a sip before he settled behind his desk. He did not offer any to Brogan, not until he heard what the man had to say. Brogan sat on the edge of a black leather chair, leaning forward to place an elbow on the corner of Cavanaugh's desk. A gesture he found presumptuous and rude.

Without waiting, Brogan continued his report.

"That detective, I followed her like you said. She lives down on the river in a condo. But when I set up my surveillance across from her windows, I found out she had a visitor."

Brogan raised an eyebrow and nodded, a grin on his face. The man waited without another word. After a long moment, Cavanaugh spoke up.

"Tell me, Mr. Brogan, how long have you and I worked together?" His question threw Brogan.

The man narrowed his eyes and answered. "Almost ten years, sir."

"Yes, and in all that time, have you ever known me to play guessing games with you?" Cavanaugh asked.

"No, sir, guess not. I mean, no sir." Brogan swallowed. His smirk faded for only a second, but it came back with a flourish. "But you never woulda guessed in a million years. Turns out that sexy cop had a visitor waiting on her rooftop. And he didn't look to be a stranger, no sir."

"Out with it, man," Cavanaugh demanded, letting his anger seep to the surface.

"Diego Galvan. Rivera's boy and the hot cop, they got a thing going on."

His words lingered in the air like exhaust fumes. Cavanaugh had a hard time catching his breath.

"What?" His heart leapt in his chest. Blood rushed to his face.

"Yep, they were goin' at it, hot and heavy. He even shelled out some bucks to buy her flowers. Looks like the Mex has been doin' her for a long time. And I know how you feel about coincidences, sir. I never trusted the bastard."

Cavanaugh shut his eyes tight. Conversations he had with Galvan replayed in his head over and over. Had he seen it coming? Rivera assured him, Galvan was a player, someone he trusted with his life. *No, this can't be happening.* Brogan rattled on, but Cavanaugh blocked out his ramblings. His chest heaved. The pulse of his heart thudded in his ears, his weakness mocking him.

"Are you quite sure it was Galvan?" He opened his eyes and glared at Brogan, letting the ice blue of his eyes reinforce his message. "Because if this is some vendetta between you two—and you bring down Rivera on my head and ruin everything—you will wish your mother had never spread her legs to conceive you."

Brogan's eyes grew wide, his Adam's apple bobbed.

"I swear, boss. I ain't lyin'. I was as surprised as you. Sure, I hate the guy. But I was only thinkin' of you when I saw that high-and-mighty Mex betrayin' you. Honest to God." The man waved a hand over his chest in the sign of the cross. Brogan had conveniently found religion.

The gesture, coupled with Brogan's justifications, almost made Cavanaugh laugh aloud. Almost. Cavanaugh tossed back the rest of his cognac and let the liquor burn. He had to think.

"Please, boss. Let me kill him for you. I swear I'll do it right, slow and hard."

"That would give us both satisfaction, indeed, but I can't let you do that. Not yet."

Brogan couldn't hide the look of shock on his face. Cavanaugh raised a hand so the man wouldn't interrupt his thoughts.

"This is a game for shrewdness, Mr. Brogan. I'm afraid you are ill equipped."

He knew the man hadn't understood his insult. Cavanaugh never would have conducted such a battle of wits with Galvan. His disappointment in this sudden turn of events swelled inside him. He'd had high hopes for Diego. He had intended to test his loyalty for Rivera and determine how far he'd have to go to sway the younger man to work for him instead.

Now those hopes were crushed, beyond salvage. And Diego Galvan's life would soon follow the same course. Diego's death wish would become his self-fulfilling prophecy.

"I hadn't intended to play such a game, but the choice is no longer mine. Now I must stay one step ahead." Cavanaugh sat back in his leather chair and swiveled as he thought, his fingers steepled in front of him. "I would like to assume Rivera is not a party to this betrayal. He has as much to lose if Galvan is working with the police. But you see, Mr. Brogan, I can't be sure of that."

Cavanaugh stood and walked to the console table to his right, deep in thought. He refilled his crystal snifter with cognac and filled another glass. When he returned, he placed a cognac in front of Brogan. The man had the audacity to finish the glass in one gulp, wiping his lips with the back of his hand. Cavanaugh ignored his lack of refinement.

"Galvan has no knowledge of my sideline business." Cavanaugh cringed at how close he had come to cutting Diego in on his little endeavor. After tightening his jaw, he continued, "And this body found at the theater is only a recent occurrence, hardly significant enough for the local police to point a finger my way. None of this makes sense, but I must play it safe and move while I still can."

He sipped his cognac, staring straight through Brogan. He reached across his desk and retrieved a pricey Cuban cigar from his humidor. After cutting the cap with his double-bladed guillotine cutter, he lit the cigar and rotated it between his fingers. The puffs of rich smoke filled the air.

"I'll find a way to compromise Galvan, place him at the center of it all." He smiled at the thought. "Rivera must not suspect my involvement. And if the police are using Diego as an informant, they might be embarrassed to find that their mole is part of a very nasty business."

A plan took shape in his mind as cigar smoke made lazy spirals above his head.

"Either way, I'll have to cut my losses now. Time to liquidate the inventory. Unfortunately, my little hobby has come to an abrupt end. Did you and your men consolidate the merchandise as I asked?"

"Yes, sir. Just like you said."

Brogan licked his lips and glanced over to the cognac decanter. Cavanaugh knew what he wanted and waved him permission to refill his glass. The man filled it to the rim and brought over the decanter, making himself at home.

"I'm afraid that as disappointed as I am to find out about Diego, my business associate Mr. Rivera shall be mortified to learn of Galvan's betrayal. After all, the man recommended him so highly. Rivera might have to make it up to me . . . somehow."

Cavanaugh's low chuckle reverberated through the chamber, disrupting the stillness of the study.

"All I ask, when the time comes, you let me do it." Brogan smirked. "I gotta take the Mex out, my way."

Cavanaugh crooked his lips into a smile. "Agreed."

"And after this is all over, I want the cop, too."

In the dim light of the study, Cavanaugh studied Brogan. The man's dark eyes glinted with an underlying madness. And he took great pleasure in killing, his undeniable skill.

"You take pride in your work, don't you, Mr. Brogan?" Cavanaugh grinned.

"Yes, sir, I do."

"And who am I to deny you such fun? Detective Montgomery is yours when this is behind us. And for that, I would like a ringside seat."

Cavanaugh sat back in his chair, listening to Brogan cackle. He sucked on the end of his cigar and blew smoke into the rafters of his study. *Premonition be damned.* Perhaps this turn of events would prove to be favorable after all.

MI TIERRA'S CAFÉ Y PANADERÍA AT MARKET SQUARE
MORNING

Becca had specific instructions to meet Lieutenant Santiago in the back of Mi Tierra's, in the room with the huge 3-D mural on the wall. The sweet smell of baked goods lingered in the air as she walked by lighted display cases brimming with an array of pastries and Mexican candy. The hostess had called her number. A young girl dressed in a white lacy blouse and colorful print skirt ushered Becca through the narrow aisles. Waitstaff and busboys darted across her path, a mad game of restaurant dodgeball.

A sea of Christmas lights and tinsel draped from the ceiling, a festival year-round. All the glitz and glitter came from an absurd collection of Christmas paraphernalia and rainbow-colored lightbulbs, the café's trademark decor. And the vibrant sound of a Mariachi band resounded through the sprawling restaurant, a refrain of "*Cielito Lindo*." A high-pitched violin blended with a heart-thumping trumpet. And strong vocals were heard over the heavy strum of guitars as the musicians strolled from table to table.

Santiago had picked the place on purpose, knowing audio surveillance would be impossible. It didn't hurt to be cautious.

Dressed in jeans and a University of Texas sweatshirt with her dark hair in a ponytail, Becca had walked from her condo, arriving early. She ordered coffee and waited for Santiago. But another man had plagued her mind since last night. She stared into her coffee cup, thinking of Diego. In replaying their time together, she found something he said had lingered.

If Cavanaugh thinks I'm working with the SAPD, that loop you talk about will be around my neck.

At first, she didn't know why this stood out in her mind. Yet she kept coming back to it. Finally, it struck her. Sure Diego would be worried about Cavanaugh, but why had he not expressed the same concern about Rivera? Galvan should have been worried about both men, equally. She had missed something big but couldn't put her finger on it.

"Damn it," she muttered under her breath.

"Is the coffee that bad?" The lieutenant's voice pulled her back. The man grabbed the chair across from her and sat. "So, how's vacation?" Arturo Santiago grinned, a welcome sight.

"Yeah, burning vacation days. Remind me to thank you when I'm feeling more generous." She returned his smile. "Actually, I owe you one. Big-time."

"Good to know," he replied.

Santiago called the waitress over, and they ordered. Two machacado plates. Eggs mixed with shredded beef jerky, tomatoes, onions, jalapeños, and served with refried beans and fresh homemade tortillas. Becca's empty stomach grumbled, drowned out by a chorus of "*La Bamba*," a favorite request with the tourists.

"So tell me. Why did I get kicked off the Marquez case? It wouldn't have anything to do with Cavanaugh, would it?" She leaned her elbows on the table and narrowed her eyes.

"Everything to do with him. As you know, Draper suspects the man might be the one behind the missing girls, a human-trafficking slant." Santiago munched on chips and salsa. "But they don't have much so far. Cavanaugh is a clever bastard, and it's not an easy crime to prosecute."

Becca didn't hide her look of shock. "Draper thinks the guy is using his travel business for the sex trade? That's a push, isn't it?"

"It's a theory. But human trafficking goes beyond the sex angle. It's modern-day slavery, with forced labor in factories, restaurants, or agricultural work. It can even hit closer to home with someone's nanny or housekeeper, a forced marriage, or even trafficking in human organs for transplantation. A heart going to the highest bidder under the radar of authorities. It's the third largest and fastest growing criminal industry in the world, and Cavanaugh may have brought it to our doorstep. No telling what the guy's into." Santiago shook his head in disgust.

"You'd think it would be a business with a lot of risk to it."

"What risk? These bastards prey on vulnerable populations like runaways, abused kids, and the poor. Who are *they* gonna complain to? Traffickers turn a quick profit with virtually no overhead. And their coin is earned over a longer period of time, using the same victim, unlike drugs that can be depleted." He slouched back in his chair, a distant look on his face. "And with the international borders, it makes it more difficult to detect and prosecute."

"Hell, I would guess prosecution doesn't stack up to much compared to the income potential." She let his anger influence her own. "Prosecution is no kind of deterrent. And I bet a large well-funded group like Cavanaugh's organization can wield political power, too. Extortion and violence can convince a lot of people to turn their heads the other way."

She let the idea sink in before she continued, "I wonder how long this has been going on? Maybe Isabel . . ."

"Who?" he asked.

"Oh, sorry." She shrugged. "I kept a little information from Draper. The bones in the theater? I may have a name. Isabel Marquez, but no firm ID yet."

"I knew you had something up your sleeve. You caved too easy." He took a sip of coffee, hiding a smile.

"And I think I know how Draper found out about

my interview with Cavanaugh." She pulled off a piece of a flour tortilla and ate it.

"Go ahead. Say it." He grinned. "I knew you'd figure it out."

"He's got someone on the inside, doesn't he? A fed." Becca smiled when Santiago shrugged, but she didn't share any more information about Diego. Her foray into blackmail would remain her little secret.

"Yeah, but his guy's not a fed. Supposedly, Draper turned someone already in place, made him an informant. The feds can play real dirty when they need to. He's got something on this guy, but Draper's pretty tight-lipped about the whole thing. I had to pull strings to get that much."

The waitress brought their plates and refilled their coffee. Becca had been hungry, but the thought of Cavanaugh being involved in sex slavery turned her stomach. Had Isabel Marquez been one of his early victims? And when Danielle's sweet face emerged in her mind, she shut her eyes tight and lowered her head to stifle the image of Dani being involved in such cruelty. Her sister's last days were hard to imagine, even for a jaded cop. Had Cavanaugh been the purse strings behind Danielle's abduction?

"What's the matter, Becca?" He set his fork down on the side of his plate. "You okay?"

"Human trafficking. What if Dani . . ."

"Don't go borrowing trouble. You don't know what happened to Danielle. Her case was different from the other girls, but whatever happened to her . . . it's over now." His face reflected the pain in her heart. "You've got to find some closure, Becca. I'm worried about you."

"I know, Art. And I appreciate your concern, but I have to get through this my own way . . . my own time. Please understand."

"I do. I hate seeing you go through it, that's all."

To get the focus off her, she changed the subject. She briefed him on Joe Rivera and the Global Enterprises connection to Cavanaugh.

"What about Rivera? Do you think he's involved in the trafficking with the merger of his company?" she asked, poking through her eggs with a fork.

Her stomach twisted into a knot as she waited for his reply. If both Rivera and Cavanaugh were guilty of such a despicable crime, maybe Diego had played a part, too. And even if Draper turned Diego, planning to use him as an informant and a witness to indict the bigger fish, it didn't let him off the hook. Diego's bargain with the FBI wouldn't exonerate him from his part in such a heinous crime. The thought shocked her. How could she be so wrong about him?

"Art? I think the Marquez case is linked to Cavanaugh in some way. His connection to young girls could span many years. Maybe Isabel was an early victim." She wiped her mouth with a napkin. "I don't have any hard evidence yet, but my gut is sending me hinky vibes."

"My gut does that, too, but I call it gas," he teased.

"Thanks for the image burned into my brain, but hear me out. I think Draper and Murphy will drop the Marquez case to go after Cavanaugh on the bigger, more visible arrest. They may not notice I'm still working it. And this case may shed some light on Cavanaugh from another direction. What do you think?"

"Sounds logical. What are your plans?"

"Rudy Marquez, Isabel's brother, told me he saw his sister get into a Mercedes one night, along with a friend of hers. Sonja Garza. He followed them to Cavanaugh's estate."

"No kidding. Could be a connection worth exploring, Becca."

"Yeah, I thought so, too. I'll track down Sonja Garza later today."

"Before I forget." He reached into the inside pocket of his suit jacket and pulled out a thick white envelope. "You received a couple of faxes. I thought they might have something to do with your theater case. I made copies for you but gave the originals to Murphy."

"Yeah, I'm sure he was thrilled."

Becca opened the envelope and looked at the contents. She had contacted Hans Muller's architectural firm and the subcontractor on the first renovation of the theater, asking for the roster of personnel on the job. The work coincided with the time frame of Isabel's disappearance. She spotted Rudy Marquez's name on the subcontractor's listing easily enough, but the architectural firm's statement would require some review. The billing of time had more detail. She wanted the invoicing for comparison against the subcontractor's payroll records. Becca shoved the documents back into the envelope and set it on the table by her plate.

"Personnel records. I'll have to check them out. Thanks." She took her last bite of refried beans and set her fork down. Santiago had wiped his plate clean. "So tell me, Art. Why did you decide to help me?"

The waitress slipped the check on their table and refilled their coffee cups. Santiago waited for the girl to finish and leave before he answered Becca's question.

"Draper is an arrogant ass, and he's pissing on my jurisdiction. And you? You're one of mine. End of story." He shrugged. "And if he's got an informant on the inside, I don't want you getting wrapped up in the middle."

Santiago stared at her for a moment, but after a while, he rolled his eyes and grinned.

"You're probably gonna ignore my sage advice, so do me a favor. Don't fly solo on this one, Becca. If you need backup, call me. And just for grins, let's pretend I'm your supervisor. Keep me informed, will ya?"

Without waiting for her reply, Santiago reached across the table and tossed her the check. "By the way, the tab's on you."

"Thanks, Art. Remember this at my next evaluation. A raise would be nice."

Before he took off, Santiago stood and fixed his eyes on her.

"Without knowing more about this inside informant, I'd proceed with extreme caution. He might self-destruct in Draper's face. And with the stakes being so high, killing may become a part of the equation. Watch your back."

Becca nodded and gave him a mock salute, pretending a show of humor she didn't feel.

"Draper won't keep me apprised of every detail, only the big-ticket items if I press him. So I don't know how much help I'll be, but I'll do my best," he added.

"You've already been a big help. Thanks, L.T. Nice to know you're on my side."

She watched Santiago leave, but his words remained in her mind. *Watch your back.*

In light of what she learned from the lieutenant, maybe her coercion of Galvan had been hasty, guided more by her libido. Would she heed Santiago's warning, or would she trust her own judgment of a man with soulful dark eyes and a gentle touch?

Lieutenant Santiago could play the role of cavalry if she got herself painted into a dark and dangerous corner, but she still needed a wingman, someone on the inside of the investigation.

The next time she met him, Becca would have to decide if she trusted Diego Galvan.

Texas weather earned its notoriety for sudden change. Leaden clouds lumbered in for the late afternoon, with the rumble of thunder heard in the distance. The wind kicked up, not to be outdone.

As she got out of her car, Becca looked toward the darkening horizon, hoping she'd be done before the onslaught of rain. Rush-hour traffic in San Antonio was tough enough, but an abrupt downpour would make it impossible. She had upgraded from sweatshirt and jeans to a rust-colored skirt and blazer, her gun at the small of her back in a holster. But given the weather, she might not have made the right choice. Becca turned her attention to an address she came to find and headed toward the building.

Sonja Garza lived in a modest apartment down from Ingram Park Mall off the Loop 410 frontage road. The drone of traffic from the freeway groused in the background, a steady murmur. Gang signs had been spray-painted in black on the mailbox units, utility boxes, and a brick wall at the entrance to the parking lot. No one bothered to clean them up. They'd only reappear.

Sparse shrubs and small patches of lawn were the only real color to the bland setting of white brick with a layer of dirt at its base and beige paint peeled by the sun. And if the drab, unkempt appearance to the complex didn't tell the tale, by the looks of the cars in the parking lot, rent must be cheap.

With the smell of rain heavy in the air, Becca walked up the wrought-iron steps to the second floor, one of the units in the back of the parking lot. She knocked on the door marked 203.

A young woman, with straight dark hair to her shoulders, answered the door. High cheekbones and a narrow chin with thin lips of glossy pink. Her almond-shaped eyes were outlined in smudged black, a bit much for daytime. The slender young woman wore faded blue jeans and a T-shirt in black under an oversized blue plaid shirt rolled at the sleeves. A black leather wristband. She had a pseudogrunge goth style that gave her an edge.

"Sonja Garza?"

"Yes." She narrowed her eyes and stood her ground at the door, playing the role of gatekeeper. Becca showed her badge.

"My name is Detective Rebecca Montgomery with the San Antonio Police Department. I'd like to ask you some questions about Isabel Marquez."

"Isabel?" she asked. Sonja looked as if she didn't know the name, but her questioning expression eventually faded to dread. "I was on my way out."

"This will only take a minute," Becca insisted.

It took a long moment for Sonja to shrug and back away from the doorway.

"Come on in . . . for a minute." She tightened her jaw, and her posture tensed as Becca stepped through the door. "I'm not sure how much I can help, Detective Montgomery."

The apartment was not very big. From the front door, Becca got a good picture of the whole place. A small living room and galley-style kitchen with one bedroom and bathroom to the rear. Chipped and uneven harvest gold linoleum butted up against dated brown shag carpet, with forgettable furnishings to match. The stale odor of cigarettes, grease, and cheap perfume lingered in the air. Dirty dishes lay in the sink alongside empty takeout Chinese cartons, a feast for the flies buzzing the room.

Hard to believe Sonja Garza was only a few years younger than Becca. Different choices, another road taken. Depressing.

When she noticed Becca canvassing the room, Sonja rolled her eyes, and said, "Maid doesn't come until tomorrow."

Becca was afraid to sit down, but if she wanted to encourage Sonja's candor, she had to help the woman relax.

"Yeah, same with mine." Becca smiled. "Hard to find good help these days."

Sonja returned a quick grin and joined her on the sofa. She sat on the edge of the couch, looking like she'd rather be sitting in a dentist's chair, getting drilled for cavities.

"Do you work, Sonja?"

The young woman avoided her eyes. "No. Not right now. I got fired a week ago from a warehouse job, night shift. Alejandro Meat Packing. Guess now I have time for travel."

Becca ignored her sarcasm. "How well did you know Isabel?"

"We went to high school together. Knew a lot of the same people. Hung out sometimes," she replied, nodding like a bobblehead doll.

Underneath the makeup, Becca saw the young girl Sonja might have been in high school. But the years had taken their toll, aged her through the eyes. An old soul.

"Is there something new? Has Isabel been found?"

"I'm looking into her missing persons case. When was the last time you saw her?"

"We, umm . . ." Sonja stalled and avoided eye contact. She crossed her legs and picked at the chipping polish on a fingernail, her stubby nails polished in black. "I can't remember. It's been too long ago."

She had no preconceived notions about Sonja, but she hadn't expected to get the cold shoulder from a friend of Isabel's. Her evasive demeanor struck a chord. Becca searched for a way to get her talking.

"Someone told me you and Isabel were friends. What did you used to do together?"

"I don't see how me telling you about two kids shopping at North Star Mall is gonna help your investigation."

When Sonja's attitude flared, Becca kept her cool. Not an easy trick.

"Your insights might give me a better picture of Isabel. What can you tell me about her?"

"What do you want to know exactly?"

Answering a question with a question—not a good sign. Becca sat back, letting the young woman know she intended to stay a while. The rain started to pour outside. In no time, it battered the front window in waves. The sound only added unnecessary tension to a room filled with it.

"Oh, I don't know. Basic questions like, who were some of her friends? Where did she like to hang out? Did she have any enemies? Was she dating anyone in particular? Things a friend should know."

Becca couldn't help the edge to her voice. She was tired of playing games. But her new approach garnered the same resistance. Sonja glared in silence.

"You're not being very helpful, Ms. Garza. That makes me wonder why." Becca prepared to take the gloves off. She needed answers, and Sonja looked like a girl who could provide them but chose not to.

"Do I need a lawyer?"

She leaned forward, her eyes fixed on Sonja. "Not if you have nothing to hide."

When the woman kept her silence, Becca added, "You want to take a ride downtown, make this official? Because I'll be more than happy to oblige. You've probably got your lawyer on speed dial. He can meet us."

She shut her eyes and shook her head. "Look, before Isabel disappeared, we grew apart and things changed between us."

As she talked, Sonja stood and walked into the kitchen to light a cigarette. She blew the smoke into the air with force.

"How so?" Becca asked.

"She . . . changed. She wasn't the person I thought, that's all." She shrugged, a hand stuffed into a pocket while the other held her cigarette.

"You gotta give me more than that, Sonja," Becca pressed. "Before she disappeared, when was the last time you saw her?"

"Months, I'd say." Her answer came without hesitation, punctuated by another shrug, the gesture du jour. Her improved memory did not go unnoticed by Becca, along with her contradiction of Rudy Marquez's story about the Mercedes.

Sonja paced her small living room. She took a quick look out her front window, peeking at the rain through dingy venetian blinds. An animal trapped in a tight cage of her own making. With the growing darkness outside, the room melded into shadow, a blessing as far as Becca was concerned. But eventually, Sonja flicked on a lamp, the pale yellow struggling to make a difference. Ignoring the deluge, the woman turned and flicked ashes to the floor, a question on her mind.

"Why are you here, talking to me? I mean, it's not like me and Isabel were best friends."

Time to turn up the heat. She stood and joined Sonja at the window. A crack of thunder made Becca's heart race, but she kept her face stern.

"I have an eyewitness who saw you get into a Mercedes with Isabel the week before she disappeared. So if you lie to me, I'll know it. Now tell me what happened."

Becca held her gaze rock steady and climbed into the girl's space, her discomfort zone. Sonja only flinched for an instant, but the attitude came back with gusto. She raised her chin in defiance. But soon, her eyes glistened with the onset of tears. The sudden change took Becca by surprise, a tough girl taken down a peg.

"A Mercedes? I don't know anyone with that kind of car. Not then, not now. What's this about, Detective?" A tear slid down her face. Without hesitation, Sonja wiped it away. "Look, I'm telling you the truth. I don't know anything about Isabel and a Mercedes."

Becca hung tough. She wasn't done with her bluff.

"And your boyfriend, the one with expensive taste in cars? I suppose he never drove a high-priced ride like that."

"I don't know who you've been talking to, but I never had a boyfriend with that much jack. Look at me . . . at this dump. Does that make sense to you?"

Sonja's shoulders took on the image of profound defeat. She retreated to the sofa and slumped into it. The girl had a point. Had Rudy lied to her abo

Cavanaugh's connection to Isabel? Why would he do that?

"Back then, I dated some, but no one in particular. I wasn't exactly considered outgoing as a kid. I don't understand. What has this got to do with Isabel?"

Her hardened expression melted into genuine concern. She looked lost. Becca joined her on the couch as the rain pelted the windowpane behind her.

"I'm trying to establish a time line prior to her disappearance. What did you and Isabel argue about?"

"What argument?"

"You said you grew apart, but that usually translates to an argument of some kind." Becca smiled. "My sister and I used to . . ." She stopped herself. "Tell me what happened between the two of you."

"There's nothing to tell, except . . ." No eye contact, but a dark trail colored her cheeks, makeup mixed with tears.

"I'm listening." Becca edged nearer.

"Look. Isabel and I were friends until she . . ." Sonja took a deep drag off her cigarette and blew the smoke into the air. With slender fingers, she swiped her face again. "Her mom is real sweet. I don't want her mother to find out."

"Find out what?"

Sonja leaned forward and stubbed out her cigarette onto a dirty plate. She collapsed back onto the sofa. With pain in her eyes, she began, "You gotta understand. Kids like us don't see a lot of cash. The money was tempting. I thought about going to college even. A real pipe dream for suckers, huh?" Bitter regret tainted her voice.

"Cash for doing what?"

"I don't want to get into trouble." She looked away, tears flowing. "No one can know."

Becca reached for her hand, a gesture she couldn't resist. "Talk to me, Sonja. Tell me what happened." Becca used her first name, a deliberate move.

A roll of thunder outside muffled quiet sobs. Sonja pulled her hand away, looking frail and thin. She crossed her arms over her chest, withdrawing into the past.

"Did someone try to recruit you into prostitution, Sonja?"

Becca took a chance by prompting her, not exactly following interview protocol. To get at the truth, she nudged Sonja and gambled on the prostitution angle. After a long moment, the young woman nodded and wiped her face with a sleeve, her eyes and cheeks red.

"Who?" Becca inched closer. "Who did this to you?"

She expected to hear Hunter Cavanaugh's name. Becca held her breath and fixed her eyes on the girl, waiting.

Time stopped. Sonja drew a ragged breath and whispered her secret in shame.

"Isabel Marquez."

Lightning flashed across the blinds, trailed by a loud crack of thunder. A stunned Becca never heard the sound.

CHAPTER 8

"I never did it. I couldn't," Sonja Garza confided as she stood, her arms wrapped around herself. "No one knows. I was so ashamed I even thought about it. That's why I lied to you before. Denial is so much easier than admitting it to myself. And I always believed Isabel would twist what happened, to get back at me if I said anything."

The young woman walked toward the window and peeked through the blinds.

"I never wanted Isabel's family to find out," she added. "What good would that do? They've suffered too much already. I didn't want to be the one who told."

Becca knew what she meant. She'd seen the family's pain imprinted in the eyes of Hortense Marquez. And the brothers each carried his own burden.

"You won't tell them, will you?" Sonja turned her head and looked back over her shoulder. "I don't think they could handle it."

"Not sure I'll be able to keep a promise like that. Depends on how the investigation goes." Becca heard the compassion in Sonja's voice and wanted to reflect the same. "What happened? Tell me about Isabel."

A low rumble of thunder and light filtered through the blinds, then vanished, casting the room back into shadows. The meager light from the lamp strained against the gloom, but at least the storm had lost its loud bluster. Sonja turned from the window and leaned against a wall. Her eyes stared straight through Becca. The past eclipsed a dreary afternoon.

"She started hanging out with different people." Her voice was almost a whisper, choked by regret. "We grew apart, especially after she pushed so hard to get me to—"

Sonja stopped and lowered her head. Becca distracted her with another question.

"Who did she hang out with . . . exactly?"

She thought for a long moment, then answered, "I never knew. And there were the rumors."

"Rumors about what?" Becca asked.

She joined Becca on the sofa and gripped a pillow to her chest.

"Isabel came from a poor family, but all of a sudden, she flashed cash and wore expensive jewelry. I hated math in school, but even I knew how to add two and two."

"She wore a gold necklace. You know anything about it?"

"A gold necklace?" Sonja's brow furrowed.

"Shaped like a heart with small diamonds on it," Becca clarified.

Sonja swallowed hard, a look of surprise on her face. Eventually, she shook her head.

"No, I don't know anything about it. I think I saw it on her once or twice. She may have worn it for a class photo. But I never knew where she got it."

"Come on. You mean you weren't even curious enough to ask about it? If I saw my friend wearing a necklace like that, I'd want to know where she got it."

"You have to understand, Detective. We weren't talking much by then. She was such a stranger . . . and anything like that only reminded me how she earned it."

Her tears flowed again, more tragic in light of the distinct rhythm of the rain. A gentle patter doused the pane, lingering in the wake of the storm. She reached for Sonja's thin shoulder and stroked it with her fingertips, a reminder she wasn't alone. This time, Sonja didn't pull away.

As Becca looked across the small room, she saw the afternoon sun gain strength in spurts through the venetian blinds. The storm had subsided. She took solace in nature's cooperation and hoped Sonja would, too.

"I'm sorry to dredge up the past. I do understand how hard this must be," Becca commiserated.

"I feel like such a baby." Sonja sobbed, her words garbled. "I haven't cried like this since those days . . . about Isabel."

"It's hard to lose someone. Especially like this."

"Can I ask you something, Detective?" Sonja wiped her eyes and looked up. "Ever since you walked in here, I've wanted to ask. You look familiar, like maybe I've seen you on TV. Is that possible?"

Becca had gotten this question before and always dismissed it without an answer. But with Sonja, she wanted to be truthful, to a degree. It felt like the thing to do.

"A while back, I lost my sister, Danielle. She was abducted and . . . My mother and I were interviewed by the news media."

"Oh God, now I remember. Danielle Montgomery, sure. I must have seen that." Sonja cupped a hand to her mouth in surprise. "Did you ever find your sister?"

Becca swallowed and brushed back a strand of hair behind her ear before she answered.

"No. She's dead." She didn't want to shed light on the details. She'd already said too much.

"I'm so sorry. Isabel's case must be hard for you." Sonja looked her in the eye.

For a moment, Becca felt a connection to a kindred spirit in her tragedy. But a sharp feeling of vulnerability closed in, and all she wanted to do was leave the depressing little apartment. The rain had eased enough to make a run for her car. Becca handed Sonja her business card and walked to the door.

"If you think of anything else, please contact me. Anytime." She forced a smile and touched Sonja's arm. "And thanks for your candor. It couldn't have been easy."

The younger woman only nodded. No smile. In truth, none of this had been easy, for either of them.

Becca walked out the door and headed for her car, under the steady drizzle. The face of Isabel Marquez flooded her mind. Up until now, she had built a perception about her murder victim. Being a recruiter for a prostitution ring had not been part of the equation. Sonja's revelation shocked her. It shouldn't have. Becca should have stayed objective and open to anything, allowing the evidence to lead the way.

Why hadn't she allowed her training and experience to guide her?

Becca unlocked her car and slid inside, starting it with a turn of the key in the ignition. She drove through the apartment complex and pulled onto the frontage road, with her wiper blades beating to a slow steady rhythm. The rain and traffic sounds were no more than white noise. In the aftermath of the storm, drivers jockeyed for position and made the drive home slow. It gave her time to think . . . about things she'd been avoiding.

The Marquez case took a backseat to the issues she had on her mind. It wasn't the murder investigation that challenged her most. It was how the case affected her, forced her to take a long, hard look at herself.

Her personal life had been the source of her weakness. Everything sprang from there. One by one, her failures emerged for a closer look, persistent like the unchanging rain. At the root of it all, she had lost her family—a link she thought would be impossible to break, indestructible. Becca blamed herself for the fragile tie. And with her sister dead and her relationship to Momma strained and virtually nonexistent, she compounded the blunder with another grand mistake. She let Diego Galvan get under her skin without really questioning his motives. The skeptical side to her nature had been stifled when she needed it most. Why?

But with the question barely out there for examination, she knew the answer. Her need to stay connected to another living soul had been the driving force. She'd become a master at erecting walls to keep others out, and the task had grown exhausting. Becca knew it and understood the need, yet she had broken down the barrier for Diego. She had reached out to a stranger—a man who might not have her best interests at heart. The move didn't strike her as savvy. She only hoped the word "self-destructive" wouldn't describe it best.

Her mind surged with questions about Diego Galvan.

How much did he actually know about her? Had Diego taken advantage of her vulnerability on purpose, for his own personal agenda? Yes, he could have learned about Danielle from recognizing her on TV as Sonja had. But his link to the FBI as an informant made more sense as the source of his great insight.

In the end, none of it mattered. She had allowed it to happen. Diego had gained a foothold in her heart, trust or no trust. Becca prepped the ground herself, making it fertile for whatever would sprout from their union. How far would she let him go? Diego might want more than she had to give.

"You are such a fool, Becca," she muttered.

At a stoplight, she ran fingers across her damp hair, looking at herself in the rearview mirror. The eyes of a stranger stared back, until the mirror shifted to another image. Her sister trickled from her memory, and Becca saw remnants of Danielle in her own face.

That's when she knew. She'd screwed up.

Her professional judgment on the Marquez case had been clouded by her obsession—a fixation to find answers in Dani's death. As a result, she had tainted the Marquez investigation, right down to the way she'd conducted her interviews.

Were Isabel's and Danielle's cases linked at all, or did she merely want them to be—need them to be? Was it easier to blame someone like Hunter Cavanaugh than to admit she might never find Danielle's killer—her own failure? She gritted her teeth as she made a right turn toward home.

THE RIVERWALK
DOWNTOWN, SAN ANTONIO

Becca stared out the window of her condo onto the river below. The rain had cleared the usual crowds of tourists. Stone walkways and big-leafed foliage were slick with sheen, making everything appear lush. And as the sun dipped below the horizon, it cast a fire against the lingering storm clouds. Orange and gray streaked the sky over the rooftops of the city.

She glanced at her watch. After six. Within the half hour, it would be dark, given the added cloud cover. The day had passed, and she still hadn't heard from Diego.

After coming through her front door more than an hour ago, Becca half expected to see a white rose placed near her window by the fire escape. The move had become his signature in her mind. Despite her effort to quell the expectation, she found her heart racing at the thought of him waiting on her rooftop again. With his hair damp and his body slick with rain, Becca would envy the raindrops as they slid down his warm skin. But no roses heralded his presence. Her disappointment made her anxious and moody.

Despite the doubts she had about Diego's motives, having him around made her feel like she wasn't alone. A completely insane notion.

"I gotta get a grip on this thing."

Dressed in her SAPD navy sweats and a white T-shirt, she headed for her kitchen and poured a glass of Chardonnay. Before she brought the wineglass to her lips, the phone rang. Her cell phone. She grabbed it off her kitchen counter and flipped it open.

"Montgomery."

"Hey, Becca. Sam Hastings."

She recognized the voice of her CSI guy.

"You're working late. What's up?"

"I think I have a murder weapon on the Imperial Theatre case. Your hunch saved me some time. I got a match."

"To a mason's hammer?" she asked.

"Yep. The murder weapon was similar to other hammers, but it had a more angular head, a specific structure. The trauma to the skull is consistent with a twenty-ounce mason hammer. Now it's up to you to put the weapon into context."

"Yeah . . ." Her head spun with the implication that Rudy Marquez might have had something to do with his sister's death. "Thanks, Sam. Now go home and make your wife happy."

"Definitely, my pleasure." He hung up after a soft chuckle.

For a moment, she stood in the kitchen with motive scenarios gyrating through her head. Eventually, it came to her. She remembered the payroll records and the architectural billing the lieutenant had given her that morning. The white envelope. Earlier in the day, she'd tossed the faxed information onto her coffee table in the living room.

Becca rounded the corner of her kitchen and sat on her sofa. She spread the papers out to compare the two documents. As she expected to find, the name of Rudy Marquez had been on the payroll of the subcontractor, listed as a mason apprentice. Seven years ago, around the time Isabel went missing, Rudy would have been a teenager. No more than eighteen or nineteen tops. Becca drilled through the more de-tailed listing used to support the billings on the reno-vation charged to the architectural firm. She ran her finger down the list, not wanting to miss any detail. She found Rudy's name on page four, but another name stopped her cold.

"No way. There's got to be some kind of mis-take."

She rummaged through the papers and compared the two faxes again. One name had been omitted off the subcontractor's payroll, but was clearly listed on the invoice to the architect.

"Well, I'll be damned."

Victor Marquez. The priest had been in the semi-nary during that time, but had apparently worked the renovation at the Imperial Theatre on occasion.

"Why didn't you say anything about this, Victor? You kept your mouth shut and let Rudy take the spotlight."

Why did the subcontractor not list Victor as an outright worker on the payroll, yet bill his hours on the project to the architect? With his part-time status, had they paid him under the table?

But a bigger questioned loomed in her mind.

If the investigation turned up the heat on Rudy, his older brother Victor could divert attention and share the limelight. With both brothers appearing guilty, reasonable doubt might set them both free. Had the priest planned to protect his little brother in the only way possible? Would the priest let things go that far?

From what she had seen of Isabel's mother, the woman might not withstand such pain. Becca couldn't imagine Victor putting his mother through the turmoil. But it wasn't up to Becca to interpret the facts, only to follow the evidence to an irrefutable conclusion—not a long list of "what ifs." Finding a plausible and substantiated motive would be key.

Her list of suspects had grown by one more— a man wearing the white collar of the Catholic Church. Isabel Marquez might have died because of her involvement with prostitution, killed by person or persons unknown. Or maybe an overly protective brother, who disapproved of her choices, had murdered her. Pick a brother. Becca could make a case for either one doing the deed.

Only hearsay pointed a finger to Hunter Cavanaugh, the desperate accusations of a brother who might have killed his own sister. Sonja had denied Rudy's story about the Mercedes and the trip out to the Cavanaugh estate. But even though Becca's gut told her the wealthy entrepreneur might still be involved, could she trust her instincts where Cavanaugh was concerned?

Becca heard a soft knock. She rose from her couch and went to the door, peering through the peephole.

"Oh, boy. Not sure I can deal with this right now," she whispered. Slowly, she undid the dead bolt and chain and opened the door.

Diego Galvan leaned against the doorframe, a long-stemmed white rose in his hand. Looking good enough to feast on with a shrimp fork and lemon—scratch the lemon—the man wore a brown all-weather coat with boots, jeans, and a cream cable-knit sweater. At that moment, a phrase from the Sci-Fi Channel popped into her head. *Resistance is futile.*

Their eyes met, and his lazy smile greeted her, his dimples embellishing an already perfect moment. Infused with a lyric Hispanic accent, his low, seductive voice titillated her ear.

"Did you miss me, Rebecca?"

CHAPTER 9

"You better be here with good news," she threatened. "I don't have time for mental sparring with you. Gloves or no gloves."

Diego handed Rebecca the rose and stepped inside her place. With a show of reluctance, she took his offering. He wanted to smile, but couldn't.

"You and I working together? Not sure *that* should be considered good news."

He meant it. They were about to play a very dangerous game, one that might get them both killed.

"So you've decided to accept my offer?"

"You act like you proposed some kind of legitimate merger. You blackmailed me. Let's at least start off with some kind of reality check." He yanked off his coat and tossed it over the back of a chair. "What now?"

"You have to fill me in on everything you know so far."

He rolled his eyes and turned toward the window, looking down on the river. Diego jammed his hands into his pockets.

"Look," she persisted. "You gotta give me a reason

to trust you. The way I look at it, you're square in the enemy camp. Show me you're willing to cross sides."

In the reflection of the glass, he saw her posture, defiant, with hands on her hips. Diego knew it would come to this, but Rebecca had no sense of foreplay.

"Can I have a drink first? I'm not a cheap date. I've got my reputation to think about, you know."

He turned in time to catch her surprise at the shift in topic and her faint smile.

"This doesn't have to be an interrogation, does it?" He shrugged. "Besides, I'm hungry."

She pointed a finger. "This is not a date, mister."

"Fine. I'll cook. What do you have in the fridge?" He trudged past her into the kitchen.

Diego did a quick inventory of her pantry and refrigerator, hampered by a steady barrage of objections from Rebecca.

"Look, this is business, not a social occasion. Get out of my stuff."

When he turned, she hit him square in the chest with a pot holder. It flopped to the floor. Diego stared at it, then looked up. "I hope you have a license for a concealed pot holder. If not, I may have to report you to the authorities . . . or the Food Network."

"Go ahead. There's never a cop around when you need one." She crossed her arms and raised an eyebrow, any amusement well disguised.

In truth, all she had to do to stop him cold was look into his eyes. She stood in front of him now. The smell of her skin and the fire in her eyes made him forget what he wanted to say. Eventually, it came back to him.

"Eggs . . . omelet. A basic to the single guy's play-book." He swallowed and cleared his throat. "You feel like breakfast, Rebecca?"

"You don't have to . . ."

He never let her finish. Diego stepped closer and touched the side of her cheek with a finger.

"I know I don't have to. I want to." He smiled. "Now make yourself useful. Pour us some wine . . . and find some music to inspire my culinary skills."

"Something from *Sesame Street*? Or would that be too challenging for you?" she sniped. "Not exactly my taste in music, but I can humor you."

He pointed a finger. "Hey, you can take a cheap shot at me, but lay off Big Bird."

Sesame Street and Big Bird broke the ice. As Diego worked, they talked about the rain, the Riverwalk, and the understated perfection of the eggshell. The subject matter wasn't important. He marveled at how it made him feel to speak of such mundane things, to feel so . . . normal. Diego wanted to remember every second of their time together. He hadn't felt this carefree in years.

"Who taught you how to cook?" she asked, sipping wine as she sat on a chair near the breakfast bar and watched him work from a safe distance.

Diego sautéed vegetables while the eggs cooked in another pan. A fond memory crossed his mind.

"My mother." He grinned and gestured, holding a hand to his neck. "She had it up to here with men who suddenly became invalids in the kitchen. My mother wanted nothing to do with raising one. She used to say, 'You and I are going to redefine the word "machismo," Diego.'"

"I like her. Sounds like you two are close."

"We were. She's dead now. I loved her very much."

"I'm sorry. I didn't mean to . . ."

"It's okay. I brought it up."

Thinking about his mother, Diego felt sadness infuse his soul. Rebecca mirrored how he felt with her sympathetic expression. Given their family situations, they made a fine pair. Diego scooped vegetables into the omelet and topped it with a sprinkle of grated cheese, happy for the distraction. He folded over the eggs and placed the lid on top to allow the cheese to melt.

"Actually, my mother was the reason . . ." He stopped himself and set the spatula down. "It all started with her."

"Okay, now you've got me hooked, but what about Mike Draper? What role did he play?" She retrieved plates from a cabinet and helped set the table. Her eyes never strayed far from him. "I heard you were an informant for the FBI. Is that true?"

"Yes, unfortunately, but not by choice. Look, I don't want secrets between us, Rebecca. Not anymore. Let's eat, and I'll tell you whatever you want to know."

With only a sliver of moon, the heavy cloud cover made the night black as ink. Puddles on the street reflected the shift in light when the clouds parted, but darkness prevailed. Brogan liked the dark. After hitting his remote control, he drove his jet-black Mercedes S550 through the automated gate and headed for the bowels of the old warehouse. On the outside, the place looked abandoned, but Brogan knew better. The broken-down old building housed a very dark secret.

As a warehouse bay door lifted, its metal rattling and creaking, Brogan got a call on his cell. He recognized the number.

"Talk to me."

"Like you said, the Mex is at her place again. Pretty cozy setup."

Brogan recognized the voice of his boy Nickels, the man he'd assigned to handle the surveillance on the cop. He yanked off his tie and undid the top buttons of his shirt.

"You picking up anything on that parabolic mike of yours?" Brogan had insisted on the added surveillance equipment. If the Mex wasn't pounding the cop into her mattress—a move Brogan could understand—he wanted to know what they were talking about.

"So far, I haven't gotten much, boss. They talked about working together and some kind of blackmail, but once she put on the music, my party was over. I'm only picking up a garbled mess now."

"Well, stick with it. Keep track of how long the bastard stays, but no matter what happens, stay with her. I know *that's* tough duty." He grinned. "I'll check in with you later." Brogan disconnected.

Using the cop as bait made it easy to track Galvan's whereabouts, an added bonus. And stalking the sexy cop with the tight little body had side benefits, especially with a good set of binoculars. He hated handing over the assignment to someone else, but Cavanaugh had given him other duties, ones with their own advantages.

Brogan drove into the subterranean level of the building and parked. After he stepped from the car, he shrugged out of his suit jacket and tossed it onto the passenger seat. He rolled up his shirtsleeves and retrieved a flashlight from the backseat. With a slam of the car doors, he flicked on the light and let the beam guide him.

The dank air smelled stale, and a chill lingered after the storm. With minimal electricity serving the building, the concrete vault closed in like a tomb. But the layout gave his men a fortified position to defend. Although from the outside it looked like the only way in, Brogan made sure he had an escape route, a recent addition before they moved in. Not even his men knew about it. He contracted it special. Like in all his other locales, he made sure both entrances were sealed and reinforced.

His cleverness made him smile as he swaggered toward the noise, flashlight in hand.

Only a few well-positioned lightbulbs and the faint sound of a radio marked where his men were in the underground maze of ramps. Without windows, their rathole remained steeped in shadows and never changed. Time meant nothing here.

As he approached, Brogan raised his voice.

"Shut that crap off. This is a no-rap zone. You know how much I hate that shit."

One of his men cut off the radio and emerged from the darkness, with the rest of them not far behind. A single overhead bulb cast a pale light where his man McPhee stood.

"Sorry, boss. It helps pass the time."

"If that's all you can think of to pass the time down here, McPhee, you got some serious problems." Brogan joined the rest of his men in a good laugh. When he lost interest in poking fun at McPhee, Brogan picked through boxes of stale pizza sitting on a crate. He griped, "This place stinks. What's that smell?"

"One of them got sick again. Pretty rank stuff." McPhee shrugged. He lowered his voice, "They're beginning to suspect something's up."

Brogan glanced into the shadows, catching glimpses of young girls huddled together. He heard the rattle of chains. Some of them needed discipline, and had been chained as punishment. A patchwork of blankets covered the concrete floor. And the oldest girls defined their personal space, using wooden crates, old cardboard boxes, and other trash to create temporary walls. They staked out their territories like caged animals, their clothes stuffed into garbage bags around them.

The girls had been moved from place to place, but their new home wasn't fit for pigs. They had no idea this would be the last time they had to worry about their "accommodations." Before the consolidation, the girls worked everything from porn flicks to frat parties. Some had been sold outright through foreign connections. And for a fee, any sex act would be digitally recorded and distributed all over the world. Business had been good, but all that changed. Thanks to the cop and Diego Galvan, Cavanaugh wanted out. And Brogan had been charged with tying up loose ends and terminating the business. He resented the interference, especially from the Mex.

"Boss man wanted them all in one place." Brogan clenched his teeth, but eventually relaxed with a smirk. "Don't worry. This won't last long." After a quick head count of his men, he asked, "Where's Ellis?"

One of the men pointed to the far corner and nudged his head in the direction. Under a dim light, Brogan caught the motion and heard the sounds of flesh slapping flesh. Ellis writhed in the dark, his hips grinding. He had one of the girls pinned beneath him. No wonder McPhee had the radio blaring.

Before all this, there had been rules about roughing up the inventory. Now, all bets were off. Cavanaugh had washed his hands of everything, leaving the girls to the twisted appetites of the men. And Ellis was making up for lost time.

Brogan hated the sudden crimp in cash flow, but with Cavanaugh never coming near the girls, that left him in complete control. The next-best thing. And he had taken full advantage of his new authority and the change in ground rules.

"Check it out, McPhee. Ellis knows how to relieve the boredom. Take notes."

"Good point. The man's a machine." McPhee chuckled and peered into the darkness. "What do you want me to do with the sick one?"

"No time for that right now. First things first." Brogan licked his lips. "Bring me the new one. I got to sample the goods."

Two of his men left the circle. From the dark, Brogan heard a high-pitched shriek and the crying of a young girl. Metal grated against metal. The sounds of her cage echoed in the vault. He felt the blood rush under his skin, making him hard.

"No, please," she cried. Her sobs turned to whimpers.

Like a pack of hyenas, his men fixed their eyes on the new girl taken from the U.T. Austin campus. No one had touched the Japanese exchange student since the abduction. Brogan would have the honor, the only rule remaining.

Tears beaded in her eyes and streaked her pale cheeks. Small and petite with a pretty face marred by fear, she flailed against the grip of his men, a man on each arm. With one hand, Brogan grabbed her dark hair at the back of her neck and yanked her to his chest. With the other, he ran his fingers down her body. His men yowled like animals, encouraging him to make a show of it. He didn't disappoint them.

When he was done, she grimaced with eyes wide. His men now watched in predatory silence. Most of her clothes had been stripped from her body. Exposed, the girl had no idea what would happen next. Brogan smelled her fear. In the stagnant air, the sweat of his exertion rolled down his back, but the fun was only just beginning.

"Please . . . don't hurt me," she pleaded, her voice heavily accented. The girl clutched his chest.

"Oh, come on now, darlin'. You ain't in Kansas anymore. Clickin' little red shoes together won't get you rescued," he laughed. Turning his voice into a whisper, his lips to her ear, he said. "But I'll let you in on a little secret. Now's your chance to convince me that keepin' you alive is a good thing. And you better be mighty willing, and persuasive as hell."

THE RIVERWALK
DOWNTOWN SAN ANTONIO

Well, what do you know? The man knew his way around a kitchen without a road map.

Becca enjoyed another bite of omelet and caught him staring at her. Those dark sensual eyes left her breathless, especially by flickering candlelight. Diego had insisted on the ambience, music and all. The only thing to improve the meal would be service in bed. Her imagination conjured up his dark muscular body under white bed linens, a feast for the eyes and no carbs.

"A penny for your thoughts," he said, taking a sip of wine.

She couldn't help but laugh. "No way. These thoughts are worth a lot more than a copper Lincoln, my friend. Maybe one day I'll clue you in."

He returned her grin. "That might be worth the wait . . . and I'm a patient man."

Becca had no doubt of that.

In between the wine and subtle flirtations, they ate their meal, each knowing the social banter would come to an end. The real reason they were together loomed ahead. For all Diego's patience and restraint, Becca had no such poise. And she dared to let it show.

"It's killing you, isn't it?" he asked. Before she replied, he offered, "Go on. Ask me anything."

"Is Diego Galvan your real name?"

He stared at her a long moment and eventually answered. "Yes. My mother's maiden name to be exact."

"Why the big mystery about your past? Your history only goes back so far."

"The masquerade was for Cavanaugh's benefit, in case he did a background check. I didn't want him to find out how I was connected to Joseph Rivera."

"The mob guy linked to Global Enterprises? You work for him, right?"

"Not exactly." Diego stood and walked toward the window with wineglass in hand. "He's the closest thing I ever had to a father."

Becca slouched back in her chair, dumfounded by an answer she hadn't expected. "I think you'd better explain."

Diego looked over his shoulder, his handsome face solemn. He looked like a man wondering where to start. She waited without a word, letting him find his way.

"Joe adopted me when my mother died of cancer. I was twelve. I never knew my real father and had no other family."

Diego rejoined her at the table, sitting by her side. He stroked her hand with his fingertips, his downcast eyes mesmerized by the past.

"Joe fell in love with my mother, Aurelia. They had plans to get married, but before it happened, she got real sick. Ovarian cancer." Diego squeezed her hand and took a deep breath before he went on. "He spent money, hoping for her remission. But in the end, the cancer won. I would have become a ward of the state without a relative to take me in. By then, Joe and I had become family. He raised me, gave me an education. I would do anything for him."

"I'm so sorry to hear about your mother, Diego." Becca understood his grief. "I guess after she died, Joe introduced you to the family business."

She couldn't keep the judgmental tone from her voice.

"It wasn't like that." His eyes flared for an instant. He sat back in his chair and took his hand from her. "He did everything to keep me out of it. At least until Draper came along."

"Draper? What did he do? How did he turn you into an informant if you weren't involved with Rivera's mob business?"

"He trumped up racketeering charges on Joe, about the time Global Enterprises merged with Cavanaugh's travel company. Draper saw it as his opportunity to infiltrate an organization he suspected of human trafficking. Cavanaugh's. He threatened to send Joe to jail and throw away the key if I didn't cooperate."

Becca remembered reading about the racketeering indictment in a newspaper article, part of her background check on Diego. She thought Rivera had beat the rap. At least that's how the paper reported it. Instead, it appeared the charges had been held over his head with all the subtlety of a guillotine.

"He blackmailed you? Did he really have anything on Rivera?"

"Not really. I don't think Draper took the time to set it all up. He fabricated his evidence and the testimony. You see, Joe is a careful man. He's not a model citizen, mind you. But it would have taken years to gather enough proof to compromise him. Apparently, Draper preferred the fast track."

"Why you? You weren't part of Rivera's organization. Why did Draper pull you in?"

"I didn't have any real family ties, and he knew how much I loved the old man. Draper had Rivera insist on my involvement with the Global Enterprises merger, to get me inside. Cavanaugh never objected. But even with the leg up from Joe, it took me a while to move freely within Cavanaugh's organization."

He stroked his temple like he had a headache, but continued.

"It was easy to cover up my history. We only had to blow enough smoke to destroy the link to my mother and the adoption. I didn't want Cavanaugh to find out. In his world, any vulnerability is a sign of weakness. I agreed to become an informant so Joe wouldn't have jail time hanging over his head. He deserved better."

"The man's neck deep in a criminal organization, Diego. He's not exactly innocent."

"Look, Rebecca. I never saw him that way. And I refuse to pass judgment on a man who gave my mother peace of mind when she needed it. You know how hard it was for a kid to watch his mother die a little each day? Powerless doesn't begin to describe it. I had nothing to give her, only worry."

Becca felt his pain, saw it in his face and heard it in his voice. She reached for his hand with both of hers, his skin warm to her touch. In truth, she found it hard to keep her hands off him. She craved intimacy like an addiction.

"But Joe changed all that. He vowed to take care of me. Not a small thing. When she knew I'd be okay, she accepted her death and made peace with it." Diego took a deep breath and went on. "Making empty promises to a dying woman would have been easy, but Joe lived up to his word, to her and to me. He loved my mother, and for that, I owe him my life."

The importance of family. She understood how he felt all too well. In Diego's world, loyalty had its price. Draper's price. And Diego had been willing to pay it for a man who had shown compassion to his mother when she needed it most. Joseph Rivera could have walked out on his empty promise but chose not to—and Diego had returned the favor. He stood by a man he thought of as his father. As far as she was concerned, Diego Galvan was the only one who didn't have another agenda or something to gain in all this. Becca had nothing but respect for his selfless act of love . . . of duty.

In her mind, the FBI had taken advantage of the situation. Regardless of his motives, Draper parlayed the love between a father and son and gambled on a chance to stop a greater evil. Could his cause be considered noble? Did the end justify the means?

A part of Becca understood Draper's motivation. Playing by conventional rules, law enforcement was often at a disadvantage in the criminal world, a world without boundaries and the confines of law. Only yesterday, she had done the very same thing to Diego, blackmail being the weapon she held to his head, her method of coercion. Would she have gone through with her threats if he resisted? Now, thanks to Diego's sense of fair play, she would never find out. But a harsh reality glared her in the face. In hindsight, Becca was no better than Draper.

And that scared the hell out of her.

"I thought you were some kind of muscle for the mob. An enforcer," she confessed. "What did you do for Rivera before all this started? You look like a guy who can handle himself. Don't tell me you were his CPA. The bean counter geek defense won't fly with me, Slick."

He chuckled. "Not exactly. But I do have a financial background, believe it or not. I look for investment opportunities for Joe. I find ways for him to spend his money."

"Money laundering?" she asked.

"I only look for legitimate business ventures or properties for him to acquire or sell off. Beyond that, I have no idea how his finances are handled. I strictly optimize the hard assets of his net worth."

"You must specialize in hostile takeovers then. Why else would you carry a concealed weapon?" she teased, sort of.

"Now *that*, I can explain. It was Joe's idea. A man should be able to defend himself, he would always say. Considering his career choice, I saw the merit in his point of view." Diego grinned and shook his head. "Joe arranged for my training and made sure I was proficient with weapons. And roughhousing with some of his guys put eyes in the back of my head. Hell, for a while Joe and I trained together, until prosperity made a beeline for his belly."

"Up 'til now, the drills were exercise, a way for me to focus my mind and body. I never thought—" He stopped himself and fixed his eyes on her. "Do you mind if I ask you a question?"

He turned the tables. She cleared her throat and forced a smile. "I think I can handle that."

"Trust is a gift, a two-way street. Do you trust me, Rebecca? If you do, I'd like to hear more about your sister."

Becca swallowed, searching his eyes for a reprieve. None came. He waited for her to fill the silence. She had no idea where to start, so she cut to the heart of the matter, a testimony to her newfound trust in him.

"When she was little, Dani looked up to me. Somewhere along the way, I lost that. I took her love for granted and shoved it aside like it never mattered. I was too busy." Becca stood and headed for the couch, wine bottle and glass in hand. With her prompting, Diego followed. "Now I wish I had my time with her back. She died, and I never got a second chance to make things right between us."

"If you had that second chance, what would you do differently?"

"I would have centered my world on what really mattered . . . my family. Momma and Dani would be top of my list." A tear rolled down her cheek. Staring into the shimmering gold of her wine, Becca didn't bother to wipe the tear away. "I feel so lost without them. My mother is dead inside, paralyzed with grief, and I can't find a way back into her life. She doesn't need me . . . or want me there. I feel so ashamed of my part in this. And now, I can't even find Dani's killer."

"That's hard to do when you've been banned from the investigation. You shouldn't blame yourself." He leaned closer and reached for her hand, kissing her palm with tenderness. The compassion in his eyes touched her heart. "I believe in second chances, Rebecca. And the people we love? We hold them in our hearts. They make us who we are, become part of us."

He grasped her hand and squeezed it, infusing her with his strength. Becca shut her eyes and took a deep breath, comforted by his words. For an instant, she felt the love of her baby sister, even pictured her smiling face. *God, it feels good to be connected again.*

When she opened her eyes, she saw Diego in a new light. How could someone with deception in his heart speak like this? He had let her see inside him, given himself freely. And the foundation of his life had been family, something she envied. Diego made it look easy.

"You are a strong woman, Rebecca. But how you bear the burdens in your life defines that strength. Never be ashamed of your vulnerability. It's as much a part of you as your courage."

He wiped a tear from her face and smiled. "And what about this case you can't ignore? The body of a young girl found in the theater. I can see why it hits close to home, but do you think the murder is connected to Cavanaugh?"

"The evidence suggests other suspects, but my instincts as a cop tell me otherwise. I can't ignore those feelings. Somehow, I think this case is linked to him. I just haven't found the connection yet."

Becca told him about her case, thankful to be off the painful topic of her family. He paid attention to every detail and asked intelligent questions. It felt good to bounce her theories off someone else. It felt good to have a partner.

"If Cavanaugh is involved in trafficking, he's got to have his stash of girls nearby. And I think Matt Brogan is up to his red neck in it." Anger raced across Diego's eyes at the mention of Brogan. "I haven't found any direct evidence, but I've been feeding possible locations to Draper as I find them."

"I can't imagine it would be easy to catch Cavanaugh with his hands in the cookie jar."

"No, the man would distance himself. Brogan is his middleman. I can feel it."

"How have you been finding the locations, the ones you've been feeding Draper?" she asked.

"Any way I can. I rifle through his personal records, both online and hard copy, looking for properties he owns or leases. But lately, he's shut down my sources and changed security codes. His men have been mobilized, mostly at night, but I've got nothing. It's like starting over at ground zero."

"What about your own audio surveillance, phone taps?" she asked. "Draper should have been able to get anything you needed."

"Cavanaugh sweeps the estate at irregular hours and is paranoid as hell. I couldn't risk getting caught planting my own bugs, equipment that might be detected before it did any good. And if the man was foolish enough to incriminate himself on the phone, he has the latest high-tech gear. The phones are encrypted, cells and landlines."

Diego raked fingers through his hair, his frustration showing. He might have resented Draper's interference at the start, but Becca could tell he had found his own motivation to persevere. She respected him for it.

"So far, Draper has nothing. The warehouses and various locations were empty when he got there. We've worked the streets, canvassing for any unusual activity with the girls, and nothing." Diego sighed and shook his head. "If Joe had known Cavanaugh had this thing going on the side, he never would've approved any damned merger. He would've shut the guy down in a hurry. Joe's sick with worry over me and mad as hell the feds got me involved, but I think most of all, he feels guilty about the role he played in putting me here."

"It's got to be hard for Rivera to sit on the sidelines, especially with his son paying the price for his sins." She shifted her weight on the sofa to face him. "So what's next?"

"Desperation. A 'Hail Mary' pass downfield." He shook his head, dimples on full display.

Boyish charm mixed with his seductive qualities, a dangerous combination. Diego moved, his warm thigh touching her leg. Becca liked the feeling. When her cheeks flushed with heat, she didn't pull away. It took all her concentration to listen to what he had to say.

"You see, I found a receipt for some repair work at an old warehouse. Someone added a commercial-sized lock and reinforced the metal on a delivery bay door. It's not much, but I won't know until I check it out."

"What part of town?" she asked. After he gave her the general area, she had to know. "You and Draper going?"

"Yeah, I'm meeting him in an hour. It'll probably be another dead end, but this property? It doesn't show up on Cavanaugh's records, and none of his subsidiary companies are involved. Not a sublease either. As far as I can tell, it's not linked to him at all. The repair raised a red flag with me. I mean, why pay the bill if the property isn't yours, right?"

He finished his wine and set the glass on her coffee table.

"Sounds intriguing. Will you let me know what turns up?" she asked.

"Yeah, sure." Diego stood and reached for her hand to help her up. "Thanks for dinner . . . and everything."

"The next time I feel the urge to have my eggs whipped, I'll know who to call. You make a mean omelet. My regards to the chef." Becca grabbed his coat and walked him to the door. "We're partners now, remember? From here on out, I'm looking out for your backside, Slick."

"Good to know. My ass feels safer already."

For the first time, she felt a twinge of worry for him. Tonight, Draper would be protecting his backside, not her. She should have been okay with Diego being in the company of the big bad FBI, but she only felt useless. A woman forced to take vacation.

"Why hasn't anyone invented bulletproof boxers in Kevlar?" Becca pulled him closer, snuggling into the warmth of his arms.

"Good idea. Maybe Victoria should have a new secret." He lowered his lips to hers, those same full lips she'd eyed all night.

Sensitive to everything Diego, Becca felt his hands on her body and craved more. She filled her senses with him, the aroma of his warm skin, the sweet taste of his lips tinged with wine. This time, she gave in to him, body and soul. Nothing ever felt so right.

Brogan watched as one of his men hauled the Japanese girl away, still crying and barely able to walk. He'd left his mark, as sure as if he had branded her with a hot iron. She wouldn't likely forget him. Wearing only a grin, Brogan walked over to a utility sink and washed up. The musk of sex and fear were heavy in the air.

His men kept a respectful distance until he buttoned his shirt and zipped his pants. He'd done what he came to do.

"Nickels called while you were . . . busy. I answered the call." McPhee reported, handing over Brogan's cell phone. "He said the Mex was on the move, but the cop stayed put. Nickels is still with her."

"That damned Mex is a pain in my ass, but not for long." Brogan clenched his teeth and headed for his car.

"Anything you need me to do, boss?" His man followed.

"Be on the alert until you hear from me. No coming or going tonight, McPhee. Lock this place down tight, you hear me?"

"Yeah, boss. Consider it done."

Brogan hated the idea of Diego on the loose without one of his men keeping track of the bastard, but Cavanaugh had a plan. Brogan would get his time with Diego Galvan soon enough. He got to the Mercedes and started it. The squeal of wheels echoed in the garage. Once he got out into the night air, his cell phone rang. Without checking the display, he punched the button to talk.

"Yeah, Nickels, is that you?"

"No, honey. It's me."

Brogan gripped the steering wheel, his eyes narrowed. It took him a while before he recognized the woman's voice. When it finally registered who was on the line, he almost ended the call. *The bitch.*

"I never figured you for bein' this stupid. You got a lotta nerve callin' my cell."

"Don't hang up, Matt. Not until you hear what I got to say. I have to talk to you in the flesh. You remember what that feels like, don't you, baby?" She slathered sex into her voice like warm lubricant. "You name the time and place, and I'm there."

As spent as he was, Brogan still felt his body react. He hated her for that. She knew how to punch his buttons, even ones he didn't know he had.

Holding the phone to his ear, he stared into the night, his jaw rigid. He drove out the gate with his mind working double time. The psycho bitch had always been crazed. Brogan heaved a sigh and made her wait while he figured out what to do. He had no intention of picking up where they left off years ago, but the urgency in her voice made him reconsider meeting with her.

"I'm all ears, Sonja. But this better be good."

CHAPTER 10

A sleazy motel off Guadalupe Street suited Brogan's purpose. It rented by the hour.

But the place had gone downhill since the last time he saw it, though it was hard to imagine the dump getting any worse. No doubt the beds made a fertile training ground for a forensics team, a real cesspool of DNA. It had been years since he and Sonja met there, but Brogan's choice had nothing to do with sentimentality—and everything to do with coercion. If she dared to meet him, Brogan would make her pay for such stupidity. She had a lot of nerve contacting him after so many years, especially the way he ended it. Who would take such abuse and beg for more?

He rented the room for an hour. Brogan slouched in a chair, smoking a cigarette and imagining all he could do to Sonja in sixty minutes. A box of condoms sat on the nightstand, with a few packets tossed onto the bed. He wanted her to know this meet had its price. One lamp lit the room, a necessity he wished he could do without. No other way to look at this rathole except in the dark.

Cigarette smoke coiled through the air like a writhing snake and disappeared in the shadows. He preferred to watch the trail of smoke. It kept his mind off the huge roach scurrying across the shag carpet. Brogan made no effort to kill it. He figured the critter had more right to be here than he did.

After a soft knock, he slid his gaze from the roach to the door.

"Baby, it's me," she called out.

Brogan recognized Sonja's voice, but didn't answer.

She tried again. "You in there, Matt?" Another knock.

Still, he didn't say a word.

Eventually, the bitch opened the door. It creaked on rusty hinges. A rush of night air and traffic noise intruded from outside. In the doorway and backlit in neon lights, Sonja stood in silhouette. She wore a black spandex dress. The clingy material hugged her body like a second skin, her nipples wearing party hats. She smelled of stale cigarettes and wore the same cheap cologne he always remembered, her dark eyes smeared by too much makeup. Without warning, the past came to stay. His body hardened, straining against his pants.

She shut the door behind her, a strange mix of fear and lust in her eyes. Brogan didn't move at first, never gave her a word of greeting. His eyes strafed her body, inch by inch. He put out his cigarette in an ashtray and stood. Slow and easy, he walked toward her. Sonja backed up a step, but stopped and held her ground. *Stupid girl.*

"You're gonna hurt me, aren't you, baby?" she

whispered when he got close. Her lips trembled, and she forced a weak smile.

But before Brogan answered, Sonja reached for his aching crotch, adding fuel to his fire. Greedily, she rubbed the length of him while pretending to be a dewy-eyed virgin. Reverting to one of her old games, she manipulated him with practiced innocence. Sonja was quite the little actress.

"Punish me, baby . . . like you used to."

With her slut switch turned on, Sonja got to her knees, brushing her nipples against his legs as she worked. Her eyes fixed on his, she unbuckled his belt and unzipped his pants, letting them fall to the floor. She teased him with her tongue and made him rock-hard, her fingers groping the rest of him. The warm wetness of her mouth drove him insane. Brogan clutched at her, his fingers thrust into her hair. He gasped with urgency, his skin raging hot as he yanked the bitch to her feet.

Losing control, Brogan tore at her dress and yanked it over her head, ripping it. His mouth clamped on hers, his tongue down her throat. In a fevered rush, Sonja clawed at him, her nails digging into his back. Her breathless panting blended with his. When she ripped open his shirt, buttons flew. His pants pooled at his ankles, and he kicked them off, along with his shoes, not caring where they landed.

Once again, memories of Sonja assaulted his brain, mingling with the present. Brogan grappled her to his chest, clenching soft mounds of her flesh in his hands, rubbing them with force. Her skin flushed with his brutal brand of foreplay.

"Oh, God . . . easy baby. That's it," she coaxed. "Aarrgh. So good."

When they were both naked, he threw her onto the bed and smothered her with his body. Brogan bit her nipples and made her cry out in a strange combination of pain and ecstasy. He wielded his mouth like a weapon, using his tongue and his hands to subdue her. Every move a skirmish, Sonja writhed under him, her body resonating with moans of pleasure and torment. He knew she liked it rough, but Sonja had only one speed—full throttle.

"No, please. Yes. Oh, yes," she cried out, shuddering under the influence of her first orgasm. "Oh, God . . . feels so . . . Yesss."

The word "easy" had been created for Sonja. The woman could come with a flick of his tongue in her ear. But tonight, Brogan made up his mind Sonja wouldn't have it so easy. Without asking, he flipped her onto her stomach, shoving a pillow under her hips. When she resisted, he pinned her down.

"No, baby. You know I don't like it this way," she protested, turning back to catch a look at him. But he didn't want to see her eyes, not now. Not with what he had in mind.

"Yeah, I do. Believe me, I do." He forced her face into the mattress, a hand to the back of her head. "But that never stopped me before, remember?"

With a sneer, he forced himself between her legs. Prepared to take what he wanted, he slipped on a condom and double-bagged himself to be safe. Until Sonja's demented obsession turned him off, she had been his equal in bed. He never knew a woman to match his sexual appetite. In fact, she had grown more deviant and harder to satisfy. So he learned to take what he wanted when they were together. His needs . . . his perversions. The only way Brogan retained control. Eventually, he called it off, tiring of her never-ending compulsions. Better to quit Sonja than find out he wasn't good enough anymore.

"Please, baby. You don't know what I got to say," she pleaded, her voice muffled. Sonja tried to squirm free, but Brogan wrestled her into submission with an elbow. She argued, "You're gonna thank me later, I swear."

Her panic set in. She bucked under his weight, but Brogan showed no mercy.

"I don't want to wait. I'd rather thank you now. My way," he whispered in her ear. With his teeth, he tugged at her earlobe, tasting blood. "You deserve this . . . and so much more."

From his experience, this crackpot bitch couldn't be trusted, so why start now? Brogan shoved into her and took her down payment on the past, watching as she clutched at the bedspread under the force of his "gratitude."

"Aarrgghhh," she screamed into the pillow. Her body rocked under him. "Stop. It hurts . . . stop!"

For old time's sake, Brogan started real slow. But as his anger mounted, so did he. Sonja tried crawling away, making things worse. He ramped up his abuse until she cried real tears, her face blotchy and red. Her knuckles blanched white, glazed in sweat as he humiliated her.

Sonja would think twice before contacting him again, regardless what she had to tell him.

If Cavanaugh kept his stash of girls here, Diego's heart wrenched with the thought of them held against their will in such a vile pit. The warehouse loomed on the horizon, looking more like an apparition. The bluish haze of moonlight washed over the scene, casting an eerie glow. Kids with too much time on their hands had broken many of the windows, but streetlights reflected off what remained. The mirrored light gave the impression the old building had eyes, luminous and vigilant.

Diego drove to the designated spot alongside the others. After parking his Mercedes, he got out and stripped off his light-colored sweater—no sense making himself a target. Underneath, he wore a black T-shirt. He joined the man in charge of the operation.

"You're late," the FBI agent groused. Mike Draper tossed a Kevlar vest in his direction. "And put this on. You're not getting shot up on my watch."

Diego strapped into the vest and pulled out the latex gloves stuffed into a side pocket.

"What, you not getting enough fiber in your diet?" he theorized with a shrug, ignoring the "stink eye" glare from the fed. "Something came up. We ready to go in?" Snapping on his gloves, Diego fixed his eyes on the warehouse.

Draper would never hear an apology from him for being late. In his opinion, the man's face stayed in a constant state of discontent. His concern for the fed's fiber intake had sound reasoning behind it. Draper stood by Murphy's unmarked police car, dressed in his FBI windbreaker, pacing and barking orders on his com set. SAPD had the place surrounded and waited for his final order to move in. Diego knew the drill.

"Just waiting for you," the man sniped. He hit the switch to his com set. "Green light, Murphy. I repeat, green light. You've got a go."

On the move, Diego reached for his .45-caliber pistol, a model 1911 Colt. He pulled the weapon from its holster at the small of his back. Alongside Draper, he walked toward the front of the old warehouse. Since he was a civilian, others would clear a path.

In the night air, he heard the first wave of Murphy's men calling out, "San Antonio Police. We have a warrant to search the premises. Open up!" When they were met with silence, the cops busted in, a precision maneuver. Beams of light strafed the structure as they rushed in, weapons drawn.

The place looked deserted, like all the rest had been, but something new laced the air. A strong odor of ammonia hung heavy, a by-product from neighborhood crystal meth users. Old mason jars, strips of surgical tubing, and empty bottles of hydrogen peroxide were piled in a corner, next to discarded boxes of time-release Contac and old bottles of rubbing alcohol. Nothing in working order, but the setup was unmistakable. Since the stench of crystal meth lingered and would permeate the walls for a long time, no telling if Cavanaugh would have used the place before or after the cooks had come and gone.

Diego didn't like the looks of it. He couldn't

picture Cavanaugh's operation working out of here. He followed Murphy's men into the dilapidated building. They fanned out to secure the site for an investigative team to do their work. But he felt the oppressive stillness close in.

"Place looks dead," Draper muttered, voicing the concerns Diego had twisting in his gut.

Even though it took a while for the three-story structure to be searched, the "all clear" sign came too soon. If the cops had found any sign of the missing girls, the com set would be full of chatter. No such luck. Diego eased the tension in his muscles and holstered his weapon. Nothing would be happening tonight.

"Damn it," he cursed under his breath.

"Murphy? Get your forensics guys in here. I want every inch of this place scoured for evidence," Draper ordered. He directed his next comment to Diego, "We may still find something."

"If Cavanaugh's got girls stockpiled somewhere, why haven't we found them?" Diego ran fingers through his hair, frustrated as hell. "These girls have suffered enough. They need to be with their families. I hate this."

"All the more reason not to give up now. He's got to make a mistake and we'll be there when he does." Draper holstered his gun. "We knew what we had going in. This shit hole had no direct tie to Cavanaugh."

Diego nodded and heaved a sigh. "It was a long shot, I know." He found it hard to keep the disappointment from his voice.

"You've done your part in this investigation, Galvan. I've got no complaints. We'll process what we get and hope for a break. I'll put a rush on it." Draper walked off with flashlight in hand, leaving Diego standing in the shadows. He'd wait to see what the forensics guys came up with, but his expectations were low.

Diego had hit a dead end. Another failure.

"You act like you don't care what I got to say?" Sonja Garza filched one of Brogan's cigarettes and glared at him as he got dressed. She lay naked on the bed, propped up by pillows.

"Maybe I don't." He smirked, all full of himself. "I got what I came for, all I've ever wanted from you. You ain't much to look at, but you always were a great piece of ass. I'll give you that. Nobody makes me hard like you. But I ain't steppin' back onto your lunatic merry-go-round. No way."

"You used to like it." She blew smoke out her lungs and through her nose. "But I tell ya, I never thought lovin' you could hurt so bad, baby."

He never looked up to see the tears welling in her eyes.

"Get over it. It's not like we never done it that way before. Or are you forgettin' how we met?" Brogan grimaced at the buttons missing from his shirt, then chuckled under his breath. Real smug. "And I'm damned sure not the only one to blaze that trail. You ain't no virgin, honey."

She clenched her jaw and watched him dress. *Nice threads*, she thought. *Real uptown*. Life hadn't dumped on the bastard like it did her after their split. But inside where it counted, Brogan hadn't changed one bit. Every time he opened his pie hole, she remembered his nasty streak. And to prove her point, Brogan kept up his abuse.

"Hey, Sonja, anyone ever say you ride like a bad-tempered mustang with a burr under its saddle? You got a mean buck, girl." He laughed and zipped his pants, barely looking at her. "I could've used some leather rigging to stay on top."

"I see you're spending quality time with the livestock . . . and it shows. Too bad you couldn't last the eight-second count, cowboy. I might have enjoyed it." She dished back his rodeo talk, not giving an inch.

"You are one mean bitch, Sonja." Brogan buckled his belt and glared at her, venom in his eyes. She remembered the look.

"That's why we get along, you and me. Bein' mean is foreplay, remember?"

Sonja talked tough, not letting him know how much she hurt. Her skin rubbed raw, she ached all over. But inside, her blood churned for more. Brogan always did drive her crazy. He never understood why, and maybe she didn't either. In the old days, she used to fantasize about him, day and night. She would have done anything for him . . . and she had. Matt reminded her so much of—

Images of Matt Brogan jumbled with the shadows of her stepdad, coming to her room in the middle of the night. An eight-year-old kid forced to keep secrets. And she never told. *Not ever.* Since then, older men drew her. She sought them out, especially the mean ones. The cycle repeated for a girl who didn't deserve better. She brought it on herself, like her stepdad used to say.

Lewd flashes of her old man's body were never far from the surface—his smell, his nasty fingers, the things he made her do, and the way he grunted when he finished. It all came back in a rush, along with her pathetic need for his approval. The images of every man she had screwed ran together and dominated her brain, her best dreams and her worst nightmares. Sonja could never separate the two.

Until she experienced a glimmer of hope years ago. She always thought if she fixed Brogan, made him love her, the cycle would break. But *that* dream died. Matt booted her out when she needed him most. Afterward, she let depression and self-hatred run roughshod over the rest of her life.

Now Sonja stood and walked toward the man who could have saved her. As she got closer, a chill of fear and desire ran along her skin, her nipples hardened.

"I don't want to make you mad, honey." She trailed her fingers down his chest. He watched her move with interest and stood his ground. Slowly, she made her way around him. "Sure you hurt me . . . didn't listen when I wanted you to stop, but I still would rather be with you than anyone else, Matt."

His ego needed stroking. A chronic condition. But she knew how to work him. Sonja massaged his back through his shirt and moved her hands down to his slim waist. Her arms embraced him from behind. She brushed a hand across his crotch. He was aroused again. Brogan was predictable . . . and so easy to manipulate. If she wanted to engage the only brain he had, all she had to do was unzip it and *Free Willy.*

"We got a history. And I can't stop thinking about you, even now." Sonja stepped around and hugged him, hearing his heart beat in his muscled chest. She used to love the sound. His hard body always turned her on. But Brogan pulled away, his hands on her shoulders, keeping her at a distance. All for show. The hunger in his eyes betrayed him. The big jerk wanted her for another round. And it wouldn't take much to put Brogan over the edge.

"Yeah, we got us a history, all right. I remember holding a knife to your throat and tellin' you to lose my number, but did you listen? No. Your version of our history is whacked, like you."

Brogan never remembered their history like she did. He had his own slant. She did, too.

"Well, maybe I can help you remember the good parts." She shoved him onto the mattress, clothes and all, and straddled his taut belly. He raised himself onto his elbows and made a lame show of protest before she stopped him. "Don't worry, baby. I won't hurt you. You just gotta listen to me. What I got to say is important."

"But I don't trust you, Sonja. Can't get around that."

"Oh, yeah? Well, not too long ago, you trusted my mouth with your prize possession. I think you should reconsider."

He laughed, this time with humor in his eyes. "Guess you got a point. So what is it that's so important?"

"You still runnin' girls, Matt?" Before he answered, she touched a finger to his lips and added, "You don't have to tell me. I know you. Just hear what I got to say." When she had his attention, she kissed his neck and gyrated in his lap, a slow, steady move. "I heard something you ought to know if you're still connected. A cop came to see me the other day, asking about some chick I knew in high school. Isabel Marquez."

"Oh, yeah?" He narrowed his eyes. "Did you get the name of that cop?"

"Detective Rebecca Montgomery." She nibbled on his ear and tugged at his open shirt, whispering, "The cop told me she had a witness linking me and Isabel to a man in a Mercedes. Sound familiar? You still working for that rich guy?"

"What did you say, Sonja?" His voice stern.

"I denied everything. You know I wouldn't rat you out, baby." Sonja sat back and smiled. "I covered for you, Matt. My coming here tonight proves how much I still love you." After unbuckling his belt and unzipping his fly, she stopped. "I would do anything for you."

"Jury is out on that one. She ask about anything else?"

"Yeah, this detective had a sister Danielle who got herself kidnapped and killed by some nasty sons of bitches. I heard about it myself, on the news a while back. Does the name Danielle Montgomery ring a bell?"

With his brow furrowed, he stared through her for a long minute, his eyes glazed over. When he finally fixed on her again, he grinned.

"You know? I think I've missed you after all."
Nudging her up, Brogan shoved his pants down his
thighs, a part of his anatomy standing at full attention. After looking down at himself, he grinned up at
her and handed over a condom. "Take all you want
of this. I'm feeling real generous. And if you do me
good, I got plenty more."

He lay back on the mattress and let her take
charge—the way it had been . . . the way it would be
again. Sonja had to free herself from the past. And
unknowingly, Matt would play his part. He owed
her *that* much. She crooked her lips into a faint smile
and gazed down at him.

Sonja had special plans for Matt Brogan. And step
one had gone off without a hitch.

CHAPTER 11

It took most of the morning for Becca to track down Rudy Marquez. She knew he'd be at work and wanted one-on-one time with him, without having to dodge interference from his brother, Father Victor. All she had was the name of a subcontractor he had worked for years ago. After countless phone calls, she found his current employer and the job site he would be at today. The timing worked. Nearly the lunch hour, the odds were good she might catch him on break.

As she drove, Becca's mind pondered what she remembered about Isabel's brother.

Many questions nagged her, leftovers from her session with him downtown at Central Station. His insinuations directed at Cavanaugh were top of her list. Becca would push him, to see if his finger pointing at Cavanaugh had any merit. Yet she couldn't ignore the murder weapon being consistent with a mason's hammer, a tool of Rudy's trade. And the fact he had an arguable motive to kill his own sister and had worked the renovation project at the Imperial Theatre didn't bode well either. No doubt, Becca had to keep an open mind about Rudy being a viable suspect, but would Cavanaugh make the cut on her "persons of interest" list?

When Becca pulled up to the construction site, a small professional building off Loop 1604, she stayed in her car and scanned the workers for a familiar face. Most sat near the open tailgate of an old blue truck with a worn camper shell, eating their lunches and chatting it up. But Rudy wasn't among them. When she wondered if her trip had been wasted, she spotted a man off by himself, sitting under the shade of an oak tree. She recognized Rudy Marquez and headed his way.

Sitting apart from the others, he wore faded jeans, a white T-shirt under an oversized blue chambray shirt, all of it covered in dust and sweat. His dark hair was mussed and hung over his eyes. Rudy looked lost. A real loner.

She knew how it felt to live in a vacuum—a self-imposed prison. Despite how her heart went out to him, she had to set aside her personal feelings. Becca had made the mistake before, superimposing her own grief onto a young man who might be guilty of murder. She had a job to do. And Isabel deserved justice, even if it came at the expense of her brother.

"I'm not supposed to talk to you," Rudy said, as she walked up.

Sitting on the ground, his back against the tree, he stared at the horizon, barely acknowledging her presence. Although he hadn't greeted her with open arms, at least he hadn't waved an attorney in her face. She took this as a good sign.

"Why not? I'm only trying to find out what happened to Isabel." She knelt beside him, her eyes fixed on Rudy. "Don't you want to know what happened to your sister?"

Becca picked up a clump of caliche and worked it in her fingers while she watched him. The chunk of soil, made white by its lime content, gave the ground a cement quality. With the construction, her jeans and hiking boots would be covered in a layer of its white dust before she left the site. In his own way, Rudy reminded her of caliche. Hard on the outside, but soft and pliable underneath when pressed. At least, in theory. Becca tossed the chunk and wiped her hands, poetic analogies shoved aside.

As she expected, Rudy kept his silence, his eyes dead ahead. His only reaction was the tightening of his jaw. A sign she'd gotten a rise out of him.

"It's just you and me here, talking about Isabel." Becca lowered her voice, made it personal. "Ever since I've taken on this case, Isabel has haunted my thoughts. I can't imagine what you must be going through."

She told Rudy the truth, hoping it would draw him out, make him confide in her. But it all stemmed from raw emotion. After a long moment, Rudy looked into her eyes, a sad, damaged expression on his face. A wounded kid with too much on his shoulders.

"Maybe you do know." Rudy squinted into the sun at her back. "Victor told me about your sister."

When the conversation turned toward her, Becca stopped, unsure how to proceed. Eventually, she decided to take a risk. "Yeah. I bottle it up inside, but that's not the answer. Sometimes . . . sometimes I can't even breathe. The guilt chokes me. You understand what I'm saying. I know you do."

"Guilt?" he asked, turning in her direction. "What guilt do you have?"

"You name it. Guilt I couldn't stop it from happening. Guilt I never found her killer. Guilt I didn't get a chance to tell her how much I loved her. Sound familiar?" She fought the lump wedged in her throat. Becca didn't want to cry. She had to stay focused on the case. "So tell me. Did you ever confront Isabel about her trip out to the estate off I–10? I mean, you were the man of the house, with Victor gone. Did she ever tell you what happened?"

Rudy's lips quivered, and he shut his eyes tight. When he opened them again, he began, "She hated how I pushed her. I only wanted what was best for her, you know? But she didn't see it that way. Isabel wanted to be grown-up, make her own decisions. Me questioning her came off like—" He stopped.

"Like a parent?" she guessed.

"No, like Victor. We never knew our father, but who needed one with *Father Bro* around. When he left home and went off to Houston for seminary school, Isabel and I thought things would be different."

Rudy crossed his legs and fiddled with his lunch sack, one of his knees rocking up and down. Nervous energy with a mind of its own or fidgety guilt, Becca had no idea. Although he sat near her, only a shell of him remained in the present.

"Isabel started to change, spent more time away from home. I saw her that day, getting into a Mercedes, and

I lost it. We had a fight, one of many. So when I asked her about the fancy ride, she shut me out. Hard."

"You said Hunter Cavanaugh had been behind the wheel of the car. You admitted it was dark, remember?" Becca pressed, making sure he understood. "The truth, Rudy. If you and I are going to find out what happened to Isabel, you have to tell me the truth, not what you think happened. Did you actually see him driving the Mercedes?"

Rudy's eyes flared in anger, but he held his tongue. His face twisted as he struggled to recall what had really happened. Finally, he answered, "No. I never actually saw him behind the wheel." His shoulders slumped, and he dropped his chin to his chest. "I only recognized the car, nothing else."

Rudy wadded up his lunch sack and threw it in anger. His eyes brimmed with tears. Becca admired him for his honesty, but she had to keep him focused and talking.

"About the necklace. You said Cavanaugh bought it for her. Was that a guess, too, or do you know something for sure?"

By the time he looked up, a tear drained down his cheek. Rudy searched her eyes for relief, but she had none to give. He had to go through this himself. Becca watched him face his demons and knew what it meant. To cut loose Cavanaugh as the culprit behind Isabel's disappearance meant Rudy had to acknowledge the role he'd played, a gut-wrenching realization.

"She wore it for a class photo once. Putting on airs. I tore into her about it, asking all sorts of questions like a damned cop." He stopped and shrugged. "No offense."

"None taken. Now please . . . go ahead."

"She told me a friend gave it to her, but I didn't believe her. You don't give away something that expensive, I told her. So she changed her story. Someone loaned it to her. I didn't know what to believe." He wiped his face with a sleeve. "After a while, Isabel refused to talk about it. Said I wouldn't listen anyway. You gotta understand. In my neighborhood, good girls don't get gifts like that. Not unless strings are attached, you know?"

Becca didn't know how to reply. She understood his logic but felt his deep regret even more. She might have taken the same tack with Danielle. At least, the old Becca would have. Once Rudy found out about what really happened to Isabel, his worst fears would be vindicated, but that would mean nothing. He'd be empty. His last words with Isabel came from anger, and no amount of justification would heal the wound. He'd have to live with it.

"So as far as you know, Cavanaugh had nothing to do with the necklace. Is that right?"

She had to get him to admit it, own up to it. If Rudy couldn't tie the necklace to Cavanaugh, another part of the puzzle dropped away. She would have nothing substantial on the wealthy entrepreneur.

"Guess so. I never found out who gave her the necklace." Rudy turned away to wipe his face again, his version of reality crumbling. "She never said."

Hunter Cavanaugh looked squeaky clean on Isabel's unconfirmed ride in the Mercedes and the necklace. At least, according to Rudy. But Becca had to shift to a new tactic, and she wasn't looking forward to it. She had to retrace her steps in the investigation, confirming everything. It had to be done. She'd missed something.

"I got the billings for the renovation project on the Imperial Theatre. How often did Victor work the job? His name didn't show up as many times as yours."

Becca worded her question to sound as if she already knew about Victor working the job. Her training officer, Lieutenant Santiago, had taught her the trick. Maybe Rudy would answer without thinking.

"Victor only worked when he was in town, on breaks from seminary school. Our employer threw him a bone now and then. That's all."

"So it looked like they paid him under the table. Bet that helped your family. Pretty generous of your employer, I'd say."

"Yeah. They were good to Victor . . . and me. Guess they thought my brother would put in a good word for them upstairs." Rudy forced a smile. It didn't last long. "But if Victor is so plugged in to God, why did this happen to Isabel?"

Becca grabbed a few stones off the ground and rolled them in her hand, thinking of what to say. Nothing would give him comfort.

"I can't believe God had anything to do with what happened to my sister Danielle. If I did, the world would be a bleak place, without hope." She swallowed hard, searching her own heart. "And I don't want to believe that. I refuse to. You may be tempted to lash out at your big brother in frustration and anger at what happened. But I'm here to tell ya, don't make that mistake. Now's the time to hang on to each other. Believe me, I know. It's too hard to go it alone."

Her eyes welled in tears, but she didn't care.

"I know this is going to be tough, but can you tell me about the last time you saw Isabel, Rudy?" Becca saw his pain, felt it inside. "Believe me, I understand how hard this is. But you've got an open wound in your heart, just like me. It won't heal if you let it fester. Maybe talking about it will help."

As a cop, Becca knew her job and how to manipulate a guilty suspect into confessing. But if Rudy had nothing to do with Isabel's murder, she would use his grief to get what she wanted. Justice came with a price tag, one she'd been willing to pay until now . . . until Rudy Marquez. Using a broken young man to get at the truth challenged her moral barometer.

"I gotta walk. I can't sit anymore." Rudy stood and headed across the asphalt parking lot toward the property next door, an empty lot filled with mesquite trees and underbrush. He never looked back to see if she followed. Maybe he prayed she wouldn't.

But as Becca jogged to catch up, a thought crossed her mind. Rudy was a potential suspect, one she trailed alone toward a vacant lot. Out of habit, she reached for the weapon in the holster at the small of her back. Her eyes glanced back to the men near the truck. None of them looked up. Would they even remember she'd been there at all? Becca turned back around and stared at Rudy's back. How lucky did she feel?

Her nine-millimeter Glock balanced the scales.

"Rudy. Stop right there," she called out. "I'm not in the mood for a hike."

He slowed his steps and started to wander without direction. Even in his own little world, Rudy looked crushed and beaten. Before he made it to the scrubs, he turned back to face her.

"Isabel came to the theater to pick me up from work. My car was in the shop. That girl, Sonja Garza, was with her." Rudy paced and chewed at a thumbnail. He quit and jammed his hands into his pockets, but that didn't last long either. "She was all dressed up in a blue glittery dress, like a woman, you know? She looked so pretty . . . but older."

"Did she have a date?"

"A date?" He laughed, a hollow sound. Rudy rolled his eyes, no doubt avoiding what he really thought. "I have no idea, but Sonja was dressed up, too, some tight black dress. She looked cheap. Isabel told me they had someplace to be. She tried to rush me, but I wasn't done yet. I mean, my God, my job was feeding the family, you know? She never appreciated that."

"So let me guess. You argued with her."

He nodded and chewed at the corner of his mouth. "Bad. We cleared out the place. Guess we got pretty loud."

"I have to ask, Rudy. Did you hurt Isabel?" She kept her eyes on him, waiting for his reaction.

He stopped dead, his eyes wide and glistening. He raised his voice. "No, I swear to God. I wouldn't hurt her. You have to believe me. At least, not the kind of hurt that leaves bruises."

"What does that mean?" Becca asked.

He shrugged with exasperation, hoping he wouldn't have to explain himself, but no such luck.

"I called her all sorts of names. I'm not proud of it, okay? I've had seven years to kick myself in the butt over this. Think how good I'll be years from now." Rudy raked both hands through his hair, his jaw tense. He kicked a rock with his boot. "I left her there. She had plans, and I was only in her way. But I never looked back. I walked home by myself. What an ass!"

Rudy balled his hands into fists and cried aloud. His sobs choked his words.

"S-Something happened to her that d-day because of me being a jerk. And I c-can't forget it. It replays in my h-head . . . over and over. Isabel n-never came home. She never . . ."

Before Becca mulled the implications over in her mind, he turned on her and pointed a finger. "I g-gotta ask you something n-now. And you have to answer, okay?" Without waiting for her, he pressed, "You ran those t-tests on Victor and me . . . for our DNA. It wasn't just to g-get it on f-file, was it? You f-found her, didn't you? You found Isabel."

Tears streaked his face. A different kind of anger took hold. More aggressive. Becca dialed back her voice to make it nonthreatening. Anything might put him over the edge now.

"I haven't gotten the official report yet. I needed your DNA to compare."

"Compare to what?" His voice cracked. He clenched his fist to punctuate his need.

But Becca had no doubt Rudy already knew.

"Where did you find her?" he asked. "Please . . . I gotta know. Tell me where you found Isabel. And how she . . . d-died."

"I will soon. I promise."

His questions surprised her. If Rudy killed Isabel, he would have known where to find her body and how she died. The crazed desperation on his face and the twist in her own gut made her a believer. Either Rudy Marquez deserved an Oscar for his performance, or Becca had to look elsewhere to find Isabel's killer.

His confusion raised another point. If Rudy had no idea where the police found Isabel's body, she had a good idea Victor had been the Marquez brother outside the theater the morning after it burned. How did Father Victor know Isabel's body would be found inside the Imperial? A sense of urgency swept through her. Becca had to find Father Victor.

And she had a feeling Rudy's cooperation wouldn't run in the family.

"Please join me, Diego." Hunter Cavanaugh waved a hand as he sat behind his desk in the study. "I haven't seen you in a while. Days in fact."

"I've been busy. Mr. Rivera has asked for my assistance on a private matter."

Diego walked into the room and didn't notice Matt Brogan until he got to Cavanaugh's desk. The man stood by a far window, hands clasped behind his back, his usual sneer cast over a shoulder. Typical Brogan. A beefy pit bull with an attitude, camouflaged by expensive threads.

"A private matter. Sounds important." Cavanaugh smiled and gestured for Diego to sit. "Anything I can do to facilitate my partner's business opportunities? I would be pleased to help in any way I can."

"No, but thank you for the offer. I will pass your regards on to Mr. Rivera." After unbuttoning his suit jacket, Diego sat and forced a cordial smile. The strained civility between them took effort, and the mounting silence added to the tension. "You look like a man with more to say. What's on your mind, Mr. Cavanaugh?"

"Ah, you never disappoint me, Diego. Direct and to the point. I like that." Cavanaugh raised his chin, and an eyebrow, his hands clasped over his waist. "Tell me about the detective the other day."

The word "detective" stopped Diego's heart. The last thing he wanted was for Cavanaugh to take an interest in Rebecca. "What do you mean?"

"Well, what did you make of her?"

"I didn't have an opinion either way." Diego threw it back at the man to distract him. "Have you heard anything more from her . . . on the arson case?"

"Actually, if my memory serves me, it was a murder investigation. Or did you forget that one minor point?"

"Yes, I suppose you're right." Diego shrugged and pursed his lips. "Why is my opinion of the detective important to you? If she hasn't returned to question you further, maybe her investigation has taken a different path. You may have nothing to worry about."

"My dear boy, I have nothing to worry about regardless." Cavanaugh smiled and leaned back into his leather chair. "Perhaps you're right. The detective is of no consequence. Not anymore."

Diego narrowed his eyes, Cavanaugh's words registering, but the inference unclear. Any reaction on his part might send the wrong message.

"Is that all, Mr. Cavanaugh?" Diego stood to leave, buttoning his suit jacket.

Brogan moved closer, standing behind the chair of his "handler."

"You might find this hard to believe, Diego. You and I have had our differences the last couple of years. But over the course of our working together, I have grown to admire your loyalty. Your discretion is impeccable. The way you look out for the best interests of your employer is admirable. Enviable in fact. You've earned my respect."

Brogan's eyes shifted toward Cavanaugh, his face flinched. The man had no clue what the boss man would say. Diego fought to hide his amusement. In the game of poker, having an unreadable face had merit. An involuntary twitch or a blink would be considered a "tell," giving a player away. Brogan was Cavanaugh's "tell." Diego wondered if the boss man knew it.

"You thought I had a death wish, one you might grant, as I recall. Doesn't sound like a mutual admiration society to me," Diego replied.

"There . . . you see, Mr. Brogan? He speaks his mind freely. Another admirable quality." Cavanaugh laughed aloud, gesturing with enthusiasm. "No, you are far too entertaining, Diego. Killing you would be an absolute waste of a bullet. And I don't say that about many people."

"I see your point," Diego replied, knowing the entire conversation had been lost on Brogan. The man still looked confused. But Cavanaugh grinned, confidence personified.

"I have a proposition for you, Diego. I'll share it over dinner tonight if you are available. Believe me, it will be worth your time. I'll send a limo for you by eight. Meet the driver out front. Curb service."

"Actually, I'd prefer to meet you. Where are we going?"

"The destination is part of the surprise, I'm afraid." His expression remained steely and unreadable. "Compromise is not an option."

"We won't be riding together?"

"Sorry to say, no. I have business to attend to elsewhere . . . prior to our little engagement." Cavanaugh leaned forward in his chair, his pale blue eyes casting a chill. "Join me. Find out what the mystery is all about."

Diego stared at the man, searching his face for something he would never find—the truth. Yet for the sake of the missing girls, he really had no choice. "I'd love to. Count me in."

Finally, Brogan smiled.

CHAPTER 12

DOWNTOWN SAN ANTONIO
3:45 P.M.

Diego pulled into the parking lot of the Wells Fargo Bank on North St. Mary's Street. Without hesitation, he got out and went into the lobby. Not speaking to anyone, he picked up a brochure and sat in a grouping of chairs designated for loans and new accounts. Sitting behind him, off to the right, a man busied himself with a similar activity.

Diego watched the comings and goings of the people in the bank, looking for anything out of the ordinary. The lobby would close soon.

"Can I help you with anythin', sir?" A petite older woman in a gray business suit and a string bolo tie smiled at him, her head cocked to one side. Sprayed in place, her big Texas hair looked more like a silver helmet. And her slick colored lips matched her fingernails.

"No thank you. I'm waiting for someone." Diego looked down at his bank brochure to avoid a second look at the hair.

With her thick Texas accent, the woman kept talking, "I see you've got one of our brochures." She raised both eyebrows and waited, the same smile frozen on her face.

"What?" He shrugged. "You going to charge me for reading it?" The minute he said it, Diego regretted his impatience. He only wanted to get on with business and get out of there. Fortunately, the woman took the high road and ignored his shoddy manners.

"No, silly." She giggled with a hand across her lips. "I just wanted to see if I can explain anything to you. You might have a question."

"If it's in English or Spanish with plenty of pictures, I think I'm good." Diego returned her smile. "Thanks anyway."

"Well, call if you need anythin'. We're fixin' to close up shop, but I'll be right over yonder." She pointed and walked away, her sensible pumps echoing across the lobby floor.

After a long moment, the man near him spoke, without turning his way.

"Nice. I think she likes you, Galvan. I never knew you were such a hit with the blue hairs," Mike Draper said with rare amusement in his voice. "Those Latin good looks are a real magnet."

"Is that why you won't leave me alone?"

Diego fought back a smile, catching Draper's reaction from the corner of his eye. The man almost choked and mumbled under his breath, "Male bonding is overrated."

With a double dose of testosterone added to his already gritty voice, he got down to business. "Talk to me, Galvan. What's going on?"

Diego indulged in a grin and slouched deeper into his chair, raising the brochure for cover.

"I had an interesting conversation with our man a couple of hours ago. He wants to have dinner tonight. A real covert affair. He's got a limo picking me up at the estate by eight. No destination. No details. The man likes surprises."

"Well, I don't. What the hell is this all about?" the FBI man questioned.

"He says he's got a proposition for me, something worth my time. Apparently, I've earned his respect in the loyalty department." Diego cocked his head to the right, his voice low. "If it makes you feel any better, he said killing me would be a waste of a bullet. High praise coming from him."

"So he uses a knife. Dead is dead," Draper argued. "I don't like it. We gotta talk about this."

"Nothing to talk about. If we want to find those missing girls, I'm gonna have to take the risk," he insisted. Whether Draper went along with this or not, it didn't matter. Diego had made up his mind.

A long moment of silence went by with nothing coming from the fed. Diego tightened his jaw and waited. He searched the faces of the few remaining customers in the lobby. No one stood out. No one watched them. A teller shut the main door but stayed to let the stragglers out.

"You've already convinced yourself, I can tell. And I see your point. But you're not going in without surveillance, maybe some high-tech toys."

"The fancy cell phone you gave me is good enough. I'm not getting caught with any 007 spy shit on me. Cavanaugh would kill me on the spot. Tomorrow when I wake up, I don't want to find myself dead. I'd be real disappointed."

"Don't worry. I'll keep our surveillance discreet. But you're playing by my rules. You're not going it alone, Galvan. *¿Comprendo, mi amigo?*"

Diego winced. "Knock off the lousy Spanish, Draper. You've got all the sincerity of an Anglo politician trying too hard for the Hispanic vote. And believe me, we're not friends."

The fed ignored him. "You got anything else?"

Diego's thoughts turned to Rebecca. He didn't want to tell Draper about Cavanaugh's specific interest in her. If her backside needed protecting, he preferred to handle it himself. Literally. He'd struggled over what was best, but in the end, he couldn't rule out the FBI when it came to her safety.

"I got a favor to ask." Diego made eye contact.

"A favor?"

"You owe me, Draper. Don't give me attitude."

"I'm FBI. Attitude is what I do." The man shrugged. "Okay, don't get your boxers in a bunch. What is it?"

"You remember the local cop I was telling you about a while back? The one looking into the arson and murder at the theater?

"Yeah."

"Well, I think Cavanaugh has taken an interest in her. I don't know what it's about, but I think you should put surveillance on her for the time being. Just for a couple of days. Something is going down, I can feel it."

"Is this a hunch of yours, or you got something to back it up?" the fed asked.

"Yeah, call it a hunch."

Draper looked like a suspicious man, but to his credit, he didn't give Diego any more lip.

"Okay, consider it done. I'll have someone on her by this evening. Anything else?"

"No, nothing." Diego got up to leave. "I gotta go."

He tossed the bank brochure onto his vacant seat. When he looked at Draper, the man had a stern expression on his gaunt face and something else on his mind.

"Cavanaugh is dangerous. Nobody knows it more than you. Don't turn your back on him tonight. This smells like a stinkin' trap."

"Yeah." As Diego walked toward the door, he muttered under his breath, "I know."

THE RIVERWALK
4:50 P.M.

The first chance he got, Diego hit a pay phone to call Rebecca on her cell. He had memorized the number she'd given him. And using a pay phone to make contact served his purpose. He didn't want his call to a cop to show up on his billing records.

Rebecca told him to come to her place. She was already home. When he arrived, she greeted him at the door with a fierce kiss.

"A man could get used to this kind of welcome." He held her in his arms and nuzzled her neck. She smelled so damned good.

"That's me. The Welcome Wagon." She groaned when he got to her ear. "Mmmm . . . Oh, yeah."

Diego didn't want to stop, but he worried for Rebecca's safety. With his appointment tonight, he'd be distracted, unable to protect her if she needed it. But he wouldn't tell her about his dinner engagement with Cavanaugh. She had enough on her mind.

He pulled away from her arms with reluctance.

"Earlier today, Cavanaugh said something to concern me . . . about you. We have to talk."

Her eyes narrowed, a questioning look on her face.

"I shouldn't be a blip on his radar screen. Why would he bring up my name?" Rebecca took his hand and led him into the living room. She curled up on the sofa with him by her side. "I've got nothing on him with this case I'm investigating, just my gut. Besides, they've taken me off it officially. What did he say exactly?"

Diego didn't have much on the man either. With Cavanaugh, it was never what he said but how he said it and all the nuances in between. Diego embellished points based on his experiences with Cavanaugh, but mainly, he warned her to be careful. Stressed it.

"The man doesn't make meaningless chatter, Rebecca. If he brought up your name, it's for a reason. Don't underestimate him."

"I'll be careful." Worry lined her face, but her expression softened when she shifted topics. She raised her chin and nibbled on the corner of her lip, an enticing gesture. "Besides, I've got someone new watching my back. I'm not worried."

Not me. Not tonight, he thought. He hoped Draper could handle her surveillance for tonight. Diego forced a smile, shoving doubt from his mind. Besides, Rebecca was smart and could take care of herself. And tonight, he'd have Cavanaugh with him where he could keep an eye out. Diego would be the first to know if Rebecca courted trouble, but in the meantime . . .

"Just do me a favor. Let's keep your shades drawn, and I want you to take extra precautions. Okay?"

While she watched, he closed her blinds and drapes and flipped on a light before rejoining her on the couch.

"Will I see you later?" she asked.

His mind conjured up images of her. He didn't trust himself to remain a gentleman indefinitely. Even now, he stared at her lips, soft and full. And without restraint, his gaze trailed to her breasts.

"Do you want me . . . to?" Diego swallowed, hard. His heart beat against his ribs like a hammer. "It might be late."

"How . . . late?" she whispered, and inched closer. So close, Diego felt the heat off her skin.

Throaty and sensual, Rebecca's voice triggered a deep-rooted yearning in him. Something he hadn't felt in a very long time. When he looked up, he found her eyes probing his body, without the pretense of innocence. He had no doubt she wanted him.

Rebecca didn't wait for his answer. She tugged at his tie and loosened it, her eyes never leaving his. In a slow and deliberate gesture, hand over hand, she pulled it from his neck, an inch at a time. She flung it over her shoulder, not caring where it landed.

"I've always been a 'here and now' kind of girl." Rebecca undid the top button to his shirt. One at a time, button by button, she worked her fingers. He felt cool air on his skin as she opened his shirt. Her slender hand raked fingers through his chest hair.

Following her lead, Diego mirrored her restraint . . . for the moment.

"Oh . . . yeah?" he asked. "How does that work? The 'here and now' thing."

Diego maintained his cool, even with his body raging hot. His lungs gulped air and fueled the flame. Slowly, he trailed a fingertip down her throat. Touching her velvet skin sent a jolt of electricity up his arm and down through his belly. The arousing sensation jabbed at his insides like a roller coaster spiraling downhill after teetering at its crest. Still, he held back, determined not to be the first to break.

When he got to her collar, he took a detour and used the tip of a fingernail to circle a nipple through her blouse. The nub constricted and hardened, making her gasp.

"Oh, God. . . ." Rebecca stifled her reaction—not very convincingly.

Diego smiled and saw her struggle to regain control as an obstacle to overcome. Up until now, she had harnessed her body's natural impulses, waiting for him to make the first real move to a point of no return. A sensual game. But as her chest heaved, Rebecca moved her breasts against his hand. Unable to hold back anymore, she grabbed both his hands and pressed them to her.

"Here and now. Whatever I've got *here* . . . you can have right *now*. That's how it works." Rebecca guided his hands and watched as he took pleasure. No holds barred.

"I don't think I can wait"—she gasped—"for later."

With her foot, she shoved her coffee table aside and pulled him off the sofa, bringing him to his knees on the carpet. Urgency replaced her subtle flirtatious game of shedding clothes a piece at a time. Now, without ceremony, Rebecca tugged at his jacket and unbuckled his pants, a race she didn't have to convince him to play. He did the same for her. So many buttons, hooks, and lace, his larger hands almost failed the test. In a sobering moment, when he triggered the on switch to his brain, Diego remembered.

"I didn't bring anything . . ." he panted, his eyes rolling back in his head. The woman knew how to use her tongue. "I mean, I don't have . . . Oh, God." He shivered, the real good kind.

"A condom?" She finished his thought without stopping. When his concern registered, Rebecca popped her head up with eyes blinking, getting her bearings. "Oh, right."

She raced to a back room as if she were being timed. Rebecca left him sprawled naked on her living room floor amidst the pile of clothes. With effort, he rose onto his elbows, listening to her rummage through cabinets and drawers, the noise peppered by her muffled curses. He shook his head, unable to hide a grin.

When Rebecca returned, Diego couldn't take his eyes off her. All he wanted to do was pick up where they left off, his body making a rally. Naked and glorious, the woman jiggled in all the right spots. And her radiant face showed no sign of being in the least self-conscious. Maybe because she was completely engrossed in the fine print of the condom packet.

"Do these have an expiration date?" Rebecca milked the moment. When she looked up and winked, the gesture tugged at his heart. "Just kidding. I didn't want you to think I do this all the time." She grinned.

Diego laughed out loud. A real belly laugh. It felt so good to let go. He hadn't laughed like this for a very long time.

In a rush, Rebecca knelt by his side again. She held his face in her hands and kissed his lips, her tongue fondling his. The sudden affection stole his breath. He took her in his arms and rolled on top, unable to hold back. Diego always thought of himself as an experienced lover. Yet with Rebecca, it felt like the first time. The thrill of it churned his blood. Fierce desire took hold—a desire to please her—to make her need him as much as he needed her. Unbridled intimacy. The curves of her soft flesh pressed against his muscled skin.

"Oh, Diego . . . yesss." She moaned his name. A honeyed sound he never wanted to forget. It echoed through his mind with all the reverence of a prayer whispered in church.

None of the lovers who had come before mattered. Only Rebecca mattered. She infused him with life. Her life. Every fiber of his being took what she offered. She breathed life back into his soul—a drowning man given a second chance. She opened his ears to a life to which he'd been deaf. For so long, he had been living without hope of a future. He believed it didn't matter. But it did, and Rebecca made him care. She made him want something more. And above all, she made him feel worthy of it.

His tongue explored her body, his hands eager to follow. As he caressed her breast, the nipple hardened in his hand. She wrapped her legs around him and clutched at his back, pulling him to her.

"I want you." She nuzzled his ear. After Rebecca helped him with the condom, her velvet fingers stroking him, he wedged himself between her legs. When she offered her body, he pushed into her dewy cleft, nudging for every quarter inch. As he did, she cried out, "Oh, my . . . Oh my God," she panted.

"Am I hurting you?" He held still, looking down at her. "We don't have to . . ."

She held a finger to his lips, her eyes wide.

"If you stop now, I'll kill you. I've got a gun." Rebecca kissed him hard, running her fingers through his hair. As her eyes glistened with the start of tears, she whispered, "It feels so incredible. Please don't stop. I've never wanted anything more in my entire life, Diego."

To make her point, Rebecca moved her hips, grinding into him.

"Oh, yeah," he groaned. "You've convinced me."

Slow and easy, Diego writhed to the rhythm of her

body, letting her guide his every move. At her urging, he picked up the pace, sweat glistening off the skin of his tanned forearms. Her fevered groans drove him dangerously close to orgasm, but he resisted the driving urge. His hands grasped Rebecca's as he struggled to hold on, his release second to hers. He surged harder, faster.

Finally, Rebecca thrust her hips into him and convulsed deep inside. "Yesss . . . Oh, yes."

Her body clenched at him, a suckling embrace. He had nothing left to resist. Diego arched his back, veins jutting from his neck.

"Aarrgghh. Oh, God . . ." he cried as he spilled into her, wave after wave. "Sweet Rebecca . . ." They climaxed as one, depleted and shuddering.

An overwhelming rush of emotion filled his heart as he gave himself to her, body and soul. No more holding back. Absolute and profound joy. And when he stared down at her face—made more beautiful by their love, if that was even possible—he smiled to see that tears streaked her cheeks. He pictured a velvet white rose under a pastel dawn, its petals covered in dew, and marveled at the sheen of her blushing skin.

Perfect. Simple. Complete.

Thoroughly spent, Diego buried his face in the warmth of her neck, his lips addicted to her. He rolled over and drew her into his arms, letting the stillness of the room settle upon them. Speaking aloud would only break the spell. But as he listened to her heart and felt her breaths against his chest, he finally let it all go. His own tears trickled down his face. And he was not ashamed.

Diego believed in second chances. And in Rebecca's arms, he had found his.

In the wake of Diego's leaving her place, an oppressive stillness lingered, a void where he had once been. He shared his life and his intimacy with her. And now, without him, the stillness had moved to her heart—nestled beside a euphoria she had never known.

"Diego." She whispered his name to hear how it sounded on her lips.

Becca wiped away the steam from her bathroom mirror, unable to do the same with the smile on her face. She pulled a thick white robe around her and brushed her wet hair while images of him ran rampant in her mind.

She basked in the afterglow of Diego Galvan making love to her. Breathing in the last of the steam from her shower, she shut her eyes and replayed it all again—his lips on her body, his hands caressing her breasts, and the feel of him deep inside her. A gentle touch turned to a driving force, culminating with an all-consuming release. And all she wanted was to do it again.

Now, with eyes tight, she indulged herself. Becca reached under her robe and ran fingers over her breasts, imagining the feel of his hands. Heat rose from her belly and rushed to her face. Her heart throbbed at her eardrums from inside. And each breath awakened memories of him, stirring and unforgettable.

"Oh, God . . . this is insane," she gasped. Becca

stopped and opened her eyes. "I can't—" Nothing would equal his raw yet undeniable capacity to caress her body.

Her new lover. Rare and extraordinary.

And what about her tears? She remembered being overwhelmed by the force of her orgasm, but the flood of emotion surrounding it surprised her. In hindsight, she dwelled on that single moment. Why had it affected her so profoundly? Becca knew the rush of feelings had little to do with the amazing sex, although most women would disagree . . . vehemently.

No, for the first time, she had made love to a man with her heart wrapped up in the gift. And shocker of shockers, she let him love her back the same way. No man made love like that without having more at stake than the fleeting gratification of toe-curling, nipple-raising, brain-expanding sex. And for once, the high stakes didn't scare her.

He had promised to meet her late tonight. The thought brought another smile to her face. "This time, it'll be about you, Diego. But I've got a ton of things to do first."

In the waning hours of the afternoon, Becca got ready for her late-night caller with plenty of errands. Now her kitchen was stocked with groceries for the meal she planned, a mix of aphrodisiacs and finger foods to draw attention to her mouth. And she splurged on a playful array of enticements, some old tried-and-trues, many new and different even to her. Things to try together. Becca had no idea what he would like or even if he had food allergies. She laughed at how frivolous her preparations made her feel, like a teenage girl with a heart-stopping crush.

"Oh, Beck. You've got it bad," she chastised herself.

Becca had stocked her bathroom with scented oils and placed more candles around the tub and in the bedroom. It would take forever to light them all. And with a big grin plastered on her face, she concealed condom packets in decorative tins, arranging them throughout her condo within an arm's reach of an inspired moment. She even practiced maneuvering for them, picturing the surprised look on his face when she'd whip one out. Becca hadn't heard his laughter until today, but a girl could get addicted to the sound of it.

Saving the task for last, Becca remade her bed and tossed red rose petals over the comforter. The fragrance filled the room. With the stage set, she brushed a hand across the fresh white linens. She pictured Diego's muscular body under them with a wicked yet playful smile on his handsome face.

"This I gotta see in the flesh."

Becca glanced at her watch. How late is late? she wondered. Now it would be a waiting game, and patience was not her gig. But her cell phone rang to bail her out.

"Hello?" Her voice coy, Becca thought it might be Diego asking to come over.

"Detective Montgomery? This is Sonja Garza." Her timid voice was hard to hear over the traffic noise in the background. "You said I should call . . . you gave me your card."

"Yes, Sonja. I'm here. What's going on?" Becca narrowed her eyes.

Diego had been a brief oasis, an amazing and consuming distraction. He'd been a glimmer of light piercing the shroud of Danielle's abduction and murder. But at the sound of Sonja's voice, the weight of her life and the Marquez murder case came back in a rush like a harsh slap to her face. The cold reality of it sent a chill scurrying across her skin.

Right before Diego called, Becca had spent the afternoon in search of Father Victor Marquez. A visit to the family home only met with Isabel's mother unable to help. The woman didn't speak enough English to answer Becca's questions on the whereabouts of the priest. And Rudy's red truck wasn't parked out front. Neither of the brothers was home. Retracing her steps in the investigation had given legs to her case. And Sonja had been next on her list of follow-ups. She'd been a witness to the argument Rudy had with Isabel around the time the girl went missing. Becca needed her take on the fight and the details of the time line she was building of Isabel's last hours. But the sound of Sonja's voice on the line stirred a twist in her gut. *What now?*

"I want . . . I have to t-tell you something." Sonja sobbed, her words garbled.

"Slow down, Sonja. I can barely hear you." Becca sat on the edge of her mattress, the phone pressed to her ear. She plugged a finger in the other one. "What do you need to tell me?"

"Not on the phone . . . please. You won't understand," she cried. "Can you meet me?"

Sonja had reached out and contacted her. Normally, a good sign. But something tugged at Becca's instincts. Despite her misgivings, she had no choice but to hear the girl out.

"Yeah. Just tell me where and when." Becca listened to the girl's instructions. And again, she glanced at her watch, one thought on her mind.

Late better be late, my love. Duty calls.

CAVANAUGH ESTATE

8:00 P.M.

Dressed in an Armani suit, Diego looked at himself in a hallway mirror to straighten his tie. He knew his outward appearance was the same, but inside he had changed. He fought hard to hide the smile emerging from deep in his soul. Rebecca's influence. A sensation he hoped would be permanent.

But a dark and sinister rumbling tainted his happiness, replaced by the face of Hunter Cavanaugh. He took a deep breath, remembering he had a limousine to catch. Diego turned from the mirror and made his way toward the grand staircase.

Tonight, it could all be over. *One way or the other.*

At the top of the stairs, Diego touched the butt of his .45-caliber Colt, the weapon in its holster at the small of his back. And he felt for the sheath of knives, strapped to his leg. Reassuring old habits. Diego buttoned his suit jacket and walked down toward the foyer, lost in thought.

Cavanaugh might not have an ulterior motive. Maybe the man had been straight up and would tell him everything he'd need to nail his despicable arrogant ass. A man like him didn't deserve fair play. If it went down like that, Draper would lose the permanent grimace etched on his face. The overbearing FBI man might see fit to let his father, Joe Rivera, step out from under the threat of an indictment held over his head. And Diego would reclaim his life—a life with a glimmer of hope, thanks to Rebecca.

Better still, if the missing girls were alive, Cavanaugh might reveal their location. They could be rescued from a living hell. Since Rebecca had told him about her sister, Diego put faces to each girl, even Danielle's. He had forced Draper to give him their case files and photos. He'd studied them, committed each to memory. In his mind, he pictured what they were like before the long arm of a sexual predator stole their lives for money, capitalizing on the depraved weaknesses of others. Big business built on a foundation that human life had no worth. For him, these girls weren't blank canvases anymore. Each had a name, a face, and people who loved them. Even now, candles burned in vigil until they came home.

Diego knew the rest of their lives would be an uphill struggle to heal. But at least they would have their lives back. And in the arms of their families, they wouldn't be alone. He understood the value of hope.

It might work out that way. He preferred not to think of the alternative, but he had no choice, being a realistic guy. Draper said it first. Cavanaugh may be setting up an elaborate trap, complete with a last meal—*how very civil.*

"It is what it is," he muttered under his breath as he walked across the tiled atrium.

The stakes were too high not to take the risk. Diego shut the front door behind him and stood under the elaborate red awning over the entryway outside. As promised, a black stretch limo was parked at the curb, ready to pick him up for his solo ride to Cavanaugh's mystery location. Dressed in the formal uniform of a chauffeur, the driver hustled around the vehicle to open his door, all part of the service.

Diego took a deep breath and got inside. The soundproof vacuum of the interior had the feel of a cocoon when the door slammed shut—giving an eerie quality to the voice that greeted him.

"Glad you decided on comin' to our little shindig. It wouldn't have been the same without you." Matt Brogan grinned. "You bein' the guest of honor, and all."

Diego held firm to his composure. Only the hair raised on the nape of his neck gave him away.

CHAPTER 13

NORTHWEST SAN ANTONIO
8:15 P.M.

Becca had gotten lucky. No doubt about it. And she wasn't one to downplay her stroke of good fortune. She glared into her rearview mirror to make certain the burgundy sedan still tailed her from downtown. A Lexus LS 430. A burned-out headlight made her notice and now helped her spot the vehicle in traffic, several cars back. Becca clenched the steering wheel of her unmarked Crown Vic, her mind racing with scenarios on how to play this. But first, she had to confirm the unwanted surveillance.

Under the ebb and flow of streetlamps, she tried for a glimpse of the driver by changing speed, but the windows on the Lexus were too heavily tinted, a curse for police officers making traffic stops. And forget about a peek at the tags—no, no such luck from this distance.

Heading west on Loop 410, she hit the Ingram Park
Mall area and made her exit. As she eased to a stop,
she kept her eyes on the mirror. Headlights from a
car behind the sedan only showed the driver in dark
silhouette. A man by her guess. At the frontage road
light, she pulled a U-turn under the overpass. The
Lexus followed.

Sonja asked to meet near the Dumpsters in the
south parking lot of the Regal Movie Theatre, Cielo
Vista 18 on Cinema Ridge. The massive complex
was located across the freeway from the mall. Becca
would keep her promise to meet the young woman,
but not before she figured out if paranoia was mess-
ing with her head.

If the guy tailing her had his heart set on a
blockbuster movie, why drive to the burbs to satisfy
his stale popcorn and Goobers addiction? Becca
would know soon enough. If the jerk had other
things on his mind, she wouldn't lead the bastard
straight to Sonja. Hell, if things played out her way,
she might get the chance to ask him herself, up close
and personal.

With fewer cars on the residential side streets, her
pursuer would have to lag farther behind and risk
losing her. A major disadvantage. But Becca had a
problem, too. She'd be easier to track. Timing would
be everything. She'd have to pick her spot and pray
her luck held.

Becca saw the cinema up ahead on top of a ridge,
a sprawling facility. Moviegoers pulled in and out of
the lot. A hive of activity. One of the reasons Sonja
had picked it. Some big movie must have let out. She

glanced at the clock on her dash. Fifteen minutes before the meet time. Becca knew she'd be late.

Avoiding the theater down the street, she made an immediate right and accelerated up Ingram, into an older section of town. Callaghan Road was the next major intersection. Fewer houses lined the streets, making the road darker. Bigger lots with acreage for sale, but not many lights. Better odds for her, she figured. Plus, Becca's car was the only one on the road. She slowed down, waiting to see if her tail drove straight for the theater or followed her down the side street. Becca smiled when the Lexus turned and shut off his one good headlight. A careless move. He had made things way too easy. Now she had no doubt the surveillance was meant for her.

Becca felt the pressure of her Glock in its holster under her jacket. Time to play.

The street elevations in this section of town would serve her purpose. She gunned it over a ridge and searched for the right timing to turn off her headlights. Two could play that game. After cresting a hill, she killed her lights and sped for a dark side street to the right. Her tires squealed as she made the abrupt turn.

Becca turned her Crown Vic around at a cross street and kept her motor running. She waited in the dark, looking like a parked car at the curb. Adrenaline jacked her up, forcing her heart to beat full throttle. The sound of her breathing filled the vacuum of the car. No sign of the Lexus. She licked her lips and leaned forward, chest heaving.

"Where are you, buddy?" she whispered, her voice dry and raspy. "Come on. Don't let me down."

Finally, the sedan drove past the street. Becca hit the gas pedal and gunned it to the corner. When she hit the main drag, she turned right and spotted the Lexus up ahead. She accelerated to close the gap, to read a tag or catch a look at the driver. But as soon as the car got near Callaghan Road, the guy must have spotted her. He spun out, heading east at high speed. No lights.

"Damn it." She only got a partial read on the tag. The rest, she couldn't be sure.

Becca had a decision to make in the blink of an eye. Pursue the bastard or let him go? A high-speed chase in this area of San Antonio had a lower risk than one in a more densely populated residential neighborhood. But if she did this thing, she had no choice but to run Code 3 to act as a warning beacon. The way the Lexus tore through city streets without headlights put innocent bystanders at risk.

Not backing down, Becca floored the Crown Vic in pursuit and hit the switch panel on her dash. At the punch of a button, her headlights flashed, and her siren wailed. The spiraling lights cast eerie shadows onto the mesquite trees, scrub oaks, and barbed-wire fence posts whizzing by.

Suddenly, the Lexus swerved hard left onto a side street, trying to lose her.

"Shit."

She gripped the wheel, leaning into the turn. His car spun out, kicking up gravel in a spray. Rocks pummeled her windshield. Each loud smack sounded like a bullet. In reflex, she shielded her face with a hand. Becca's heart leapt into her throat. Her breaths came in short gasps.

"Now you're just pissing me off."

She gritted her teeth and maneuvered through narrow streets and low-water areas, trying to make up ground. She zipped past low-rent horse stables to her right. Her flashers reflected off the eyes of a curious bay quarter horse. The animal bolted and trotted off for a quieter piece of ground.

"Sorry, big fella."

Suddenly, her Crown Vic hit a pothole and the jolt jarred her teeth. One of her hands popped loose from the wheel. Her seat belt locked and drew tight across her chest, the edge cutting into her neck. Becca tugged to make it release. No luck.

That's when the guy hit a series of S curves and a fork in the road. He never slowed down. His tires screeched at every turn. With only her headlights to guide her, she peered through the shadows up ahead for a way to end this.

"What the hell are you doing?" She had no idea if her question had been directed at the maniac up ahead or herself, the crazed woman behind the wheel of the Crown Vic.

Normally, Becca would call for backup on her radio. But explaining her reason for the high-speed chase would get her butt in a sling, no matter how justified. Santiago might cover for her, but Draper was another matter. He'd have her ass canned and throw away the opener.

The way she saw it, she only had a short window of opportunity. She had to catch the Lexus—fast.

But her luck had run out. The madman had been heading for the lights of the freeway. Now, one of the side streets cut onto the frontage road of Loop 410. With more traffic, too much could go wrong. Unable to make her chase *official,* she had no choice but to back off and kill her pursuit.

"That's it. I'm gone." She couldn't risk it, not anymore. People might get hurt.

But the bastard took advantage of his lead and ran a light. He cut across lanes of traffic to hit the freeway entrance ramp. Becca grimaced as other drivers veered to miss him. Tires skidded to a halt. She let the asshole go, never getting close enough to pull more than a partial tag. After turning into the left lane, she cut her speed and watched the red taillights of the Lexus merge into traffic up the hill. With his headlights back on, he headed east, back the way he came.

"Damn it to hell." She pounded the steering wheel with a fist and groaned in frustration at being so close. "Arrgh."

Becca took a deep breath to slow her heart. She checked out the time on her dash and made a turn back to the movie theater. A quarter to nine. She had no idea if Sonja would wait long, but she'd find out soon enough.

Who had tailed her in the Lexus and why? The pricey car ruled out almost her entire list of suspects— *all except one.*

Cool water. A placid surface as unchanging as glass. Diego pictured the image and tried to maintain his composure as he watched Brogan in silence. His muscles tense like a tight spring, he sat ready to defend himself if it came to that. His dangerous companion stared back with dead eyes, like a coiled rattler in tall grass. Brogan looked content with the absence of conversation as traffic and road noise droned in the background.

The limo headed downtown. Diego kept a vigilant eye on the route they took. He had no way of knowing whether Draper followed, but he was sure the FBI man had his back. The guy had the tenacity of a pit bull and the face to match. But Diego hated not knowing what lay ahead. With their destination being downtown, Rebecca's home turf, he had a growing suspicion she played a part in Cavanaugh's game of intimidation.

After Diego's last glance out the window, Brogan smirked as if he read his mind.

"You don't look like a guy who likes surprises, Mex." Brogan smirked.

"Neither do you." His steely gaze and quick, understated comeback made the man flinch. Brogan's sneer faded.

The limousine maneuvered through the historic arts village of La Villita and pulled up to the curb outside a trendy new restaurant called Fusion on the River. Diego had read about it. Its new and innovative menu combined the melting pot of cultures located in the region. An extravagant fare of continental cuisine blended with the old-world charm and grace of San Antonio. The limo driver let them out, and Diego followed Brogan inside. Hunter Cavanaugh had reserved a private dining room in the rear.

"Gentlemen. Glad you could join me." Cavanaugh

welcomed them with open arms and a glass of wine. "Diego, please take the seat across from me."

An intimate scene. Polished silver on white linen, flickering candles, and fresh-cut flowers created an elegant table setting. Tasteful oil paintings of local artists decked the stucco walls. The restaurant was a maze of small rooms with terraced outside patios carved into the south bank hillside of the San Antonio River.

They placed their order and dined on an array of appetizers, compliments of the house. The owner of the restaurant was an old acquaintance of Hunter's.

"You have admirable taste, Mr. Cavanaugh." Diego gave the man his due as he admired the restaurant. "Is this a special occasion?"

"Yes, you might say that." With his Nordic good looks and aristocratic features, Hunter Cavanaugh commanded the evening with his usual flair for the dramatic. His eloquent voice resonated in the private room. "Sometimes a man must cut his losses and begin afresh. And I am on the verge of being reborn."

"A spiritual awakening, or are you referring to a business venture?" Diego asked. He forced a smile, hiding the knot in his gut. In his most subtle way, Cavanaugh enjoyed twisting the knife. And tonight, Diego knew the man would take his time. He would not be rushed.

His polar opposite, Brogan sprawled in his chair and gulped wine without the slightest interest in conversation. The ambience was wasted on him. The bastard would be in his element if you shoved a cold brew and a TV remote in his hand with a Barca-lounger under his ass. Diego heard the vibrating buzz of the man's cell phone under the table. But Brogan only checked out the phone display, not answering. Glancing at his watch, he looked preoccupied.

"Ah, a spiritual rebirth or a new business venture? An astute question, Diego." Cavanaugh raised a finger and winked. "Over the years of our association with Global Enterprises, I have been impressed by you. And your loyalty to Mr. Rivera is certainly commendable. In similar fashion, Mr. Brogan would do anything for me. And I assure you, he has."

"You seem to be making a point." Diego narrowed his eyes and took a sip of wine. "And I'm content to wait for it."

"Yes." Cavanaugh grinned. "I've noticed. You are a very patient man. In that regard, you and I are very much alike. I, too, value composure . . . especially under stress. And I'm not afraid to make difficult decisions even at the expense of others. Perhaps this is where we part company."

"What do you mean?"

"You talk a good game. And you hold your own in a fight." Cavanaugh glanced at Brogan. The man jerked his head, suddenly paying attention. "On more than one occasion, Mr. Brogan reported for work sporting unexplained bruises or a broken nose, presumably after having a conversation with you. But deep down, Diego, you have a soft heart. Don't try and deny it."

"Why do I get the impression you consider compassion to be a sign of weakness?"

"Because it is, my dear Diego. It is." Cavanaugh smiled, his fierce eyes unwavering.

Brogan leaned his elbows on the table and glared at Diego as if he played a hand in the coy conversation. But when his cell phone sprang to life again, the smug bastard checked the incoming number and excused himself from the table to take the call.

On the surface, Diego was a pristine lake at dawn, but underneath, he churned to know what was happening with Brogan. And worse, Cavanaugh pretended not to notice or even care. Diego had a feeling he wasn't going to enjoy Cavanaugh's brand of after-dinner entertainment.

"I'm waiting to hear about the proposition you have for me."

"All in good time, Diego. All in good time."

An old mustard-colored Ford Fiesta sat at the back of the cinema parking lot, rust eating at its wheel wells and belching puffs of black smoke. The car was running with someone inside. Becca circled the vehicle, getting a good look at the driver. She pulled up facing in the opposite direction on the driver's side and rolled down her window. Sonja had her arm out, flicking ashes from her smoke. Between the exhaust fumes and the cigarettes, her lungs had to be a ticking time bomb.

"I almost left." She chewed at the corner of her mouth. Her eyes darted to her rearview mirror, checking out the empty lot behind them. Real antsy. "How come you were . . ." She stopped in midquestion and tossed her butt. "I got scared, is all."

"Yeah, I'm sorry." Becca had no intention of telling Sonja what had happened. The woman was spooked enough. "But I'm here now. You said you had something to tell me in person. You got my ear."

The high-speed chase had left Becca's nerves frayed. On edge, she kept her foot on the brake and her car running, ready to bolt at a moment's notice. And she gripped her Glock. The weapon was out of its holster and in her lap. The meet left her leery, her senses wired. Under any other circumstances, meeting a first-time snitch, Becca would have asked Sonja to keep her hands visible. But the move might kill any chance she had to get the young woman to open up. Becca had to take a risk.

"The other day . . . at my apartment," Sonja began, her voice choked with emotion. She didn't look Becca in the eye. "I didn't tell you everything. And I may have lied."

Nice opener. Sonja had her attention.

"May have? That's like saying I'm sort of pregnant. What did you lie about?" Without trying to alarm Sonja, Becca kept an eye out for a burgundy Lexus. She scanned the cars parked in the lot for any unusual movement.

"You gotta understand. I was scared. Talking about Isabel after all this time, it brought back the nightmares. I haven't been able to sleep." She clutched her steering wheel and peered through the windshield and into her rearview mirror. Agitated. "Fuck, I don't think I can do this," she muttered, letting her head fall back against her headrest. Her shoulders slumped.

"Oh, no. You got me out in the burbs, Sonja." Becca shook her head and tried a little lame humor to put the girl at ease. "You gotta understand, I don't do burbs. Too many malls and minivans. You can't clam up on me now."

Eyes wide, Sonja stared at her before she ventured a faint smile. The gesture didn't last.

Becca softened her tone, but her eyes made one more pass at the parking lot. "Come on. You want to clear the air, or else you wouldn't have called. Talk to me."

"I lied about . . . the Mercedes." Sonja looked out the corner of her eye, but shut them tight and took a deep breath. "I got into that car . . . with Isabel."

"Tell me what happened, Sonja? And why did you lie about it?"

"You're mad. I can hear it in your voice." Sonja fidgeted in her seat, a hand tight on the wheel. Eyes alert.

"I only want to get at the truth here." Becca softened her tone. "Tell me about the trip you took in the Mercedes. Let's focus on that."

Sonja lit another smoke. After a few drags, she loosened up. "Isabel had arranged everything. We drove out I–10, some rich guy's place. I never paid attention how we got there."

Sonja's latest version of the truth corroborated Rudy's story. Becca had never told her Isabel's brother had followed the Mercedes out I–10 to the Cavanaugh estate. Pieces to the puzzle were fitting into place.

"We never went into the mansion, only stayed in

the back. They had a pool house. Everything was lit up. A real fancy party. Lots of hot older guys in expensive clothes. And plenty of girls, too, dressed real nice. I felt out of place. My dress wasn't the best, but it was all I could afford. I felt so grown-up in it, even though we were kind of young compared to everyone else. But none of the people made us feel like party crashers, you know?"

"The party sounded real friendly."

"Yeah, it was. Those rich people made me feel like a rock star. The guys flirted and got me drinks. Isabel said they were always like that. Real gentlemen."

"Isabel must have been to a few of their parties if she knew that."

Sonja narrowed her eyes, a questioning look on her face. "Yeah, guess so, but I never figured that out until later."

"What happened next?" Becca prompted.

"I started to feel dizzy and sick to my stomach. I thought I had too much to drink, you know? But one of the guys took care of me. He took me into the pool house, let me lie down on a bed."

"But something must have happened. You kept this part from me. Why?"

A dark memory shrouded her face. Sonja tensed her jaw and avoided looking at Becca. "That's because later, I found out . . . I was the big attraction. You see, they had a special room set up, just for me."

Sonja smiled with a look of confusion on her face, a strange, distant gaze. Her cigarette hung between her fingers, burned almost to the stub. Couldn't she feel the heat?

"The guy started to take my clothes off. I told him no, but he only laughed. Other men were in the room. They did things to me. But I couldn't move."

Sonja dropped the butt from her fingers, barely noticing. She looked too numb to move a muscle, mesmerized and haunted by her past. As much as she wanted to console the girl, Becca kept her eyes trained on the parking lot and the empty acreage behind them. She wiped the sweat off her palm, the one holding the Glock.

"After that, it got real fuzzy. All those rich men at the party? Their faces kept coming at me, one after another. Laughing. Pointing. Some of them were naked, sometimes more than one. I can still hear 'em." She cried. "And I have nightmares . . . even now."

Sonja went on, each remembrance worse than the last. A lost soul with rock-bottom self-esteem. No wonder she suffered from nightmares. The shame. The degradation. Becca couldn't imagine a young life being shut down by such cruelty. Each new revelation brought Sonja's tragic world closer. Its oppressive weight made it hard for Becca to breathe.

Danielle must have suffered the same way, only her ordeal ended in a torturous, violent death. Overwhelming grief flooded Becca, sucking the air from her lungs. She couldn't catch her breath. Tears blurred her sight, but Becca fought the urge to cry. She kept her mind focused on the case. On the here and now. On Sonja.

Becca cleared her throat and shoved her personal torment aside so she could function.

"Where was Isabel through all this? Did the same happen to her?" She felt fragile, unsure she wanted to hear the answer to her question. So many lives ruined. No wonder Diego risked his life to stop a man like Cavanaugh.

"I found out later that Isabel left me there." Sonja broke down and cried, her face wincing with each disturbing reminder. "Yeah, some best friend, huh? That's why we didn't hang out after that. I never forgave her. That night ruined the rest of my life. And God, I was so afraid Isabel would tell what happened."

Sonja shifted in her seat and faced Becca to stress her point. "You know what it feels like to live with fear . . . every day? You think others see what happened in your face, like it's tattooed across your forehead. Whenever anyone looked at me sideways, I thought they knew. I lived in constant fear Isabel would tell on me, so I kept my mouth shut."

"You never reported it to the police? You could have pressed charges." Becca knew the answer before Sonja opened her mouth.

"People like me don't talk to cops, lady. Press charges? No fuckin' way." Sonja picked at the torn upholstery of her door panel. When she began again, her voice was faint. "When Isabel went missing, I thought I'd be next. I hid and didn't talk to anyone. But after a while . . ."

"What, Sonja? Tell me."

A new tear slid down her cheek. "It was a relief she was gone. It meant my secret went with her. I didn't have to worry no more." In the pale light, Sonja's face glistened with tears and bitterness. "I couldn't tell you before. I was too ashamed. That's why I lied. Please don't be mad."

A part of Becca had a soft spot for Sonja, but she had lied before. Why would this version be the truth?

"I have a witness who puts you at the Imperial Theatre with Isabel when she had a fight with her brother Rudy. Tell me about it."

Sonja narrowed her eyes and shook her head, like she didn't remember the incident. "I don't know . . ." Then her eyes registered something. "God, that was so long ago. Yeah, I remember she went to this old theater to pick up her brother from work. They had your typical brother-sister argument, and he split. Not much to tell. We were going to a club, so we went. It was no big deal."

"What did they argue about? Do you remember?"

Sonja grimaced and shook her head. "Don't remember, except it had something to do with his job feeding the family and her rushing him so we could party. Guess he didn't like working hard so she could play."

"And that's all you remember about it?"

"Yeah, that's it. Like I said, it was no big deal."

"Is there anything else you want to tell me?"

"Like what?" the woman asked.

Stall tactic. Answering a question with a question. Sonja erected a speed bump in Becca's path toward the truth. What was she hiding now?

"Like who was driving the Mercedes? Did you get a name?"

"Yeah, I got a name. But I have to tell you about the necklace first. It's all connected." Sonja fixed her eyes on Becca. "I know who gave Isabel the necklace, the heart with the diamonds. She got it from an older guy."

Becca's heart sputtered to a stop. She held her breath, again expecting the name of Hunter Cavanaugh to come up. "Who? You know the name of the guy?"

Sonja nodded, her face in shadows. "A guy by the name of Matt Brogan gave it to her. I don't know where he got it or nothin', but Isabel told me he gave it to her. She was real proud of it, you know?"

"And he's the guy who drove you to the party? The one with the Mercedes?"

"Yeah, he's the one."

Matt Brogan? Becca remembered him. She had met the guy at Cavanaugh's and made a note of his name in her casebook. Now her mind flooded with speculations. Becca wouldn't have considered Brogan an older man, but to a teenager seven years ago, he might come off that way. Plus, the guy had the money to afford the necklace and drive a Mercedes. And with his link to Hunter Cavanaugh, a man under FBI surveillance for human trafficking, the pieces to Becca's mystery were falling into place.

Was Cavanaugh back on her list of suspects, or was Brogan operating on his own? From what she remembered, Brogan gave off a nasty vibe. A real cold fish. Could he be operating a prostitution ring under the nose of his rich boss, or was Cavanaugh giving the orders?

No matter which way things turned out, Diego had to be told. This put a whole new slant on his human-trafficking angle. All Becca wanted to do was see Diego . . . to talk to him . . . to be with him. He had become her oasis in the dismal wasteland of this case.

"But you gotta promise me," Sonja pleaded. "Don't tell Brogan I was the one who told. He'd kill me if he found out."

"You think Matt Brogan still remembers you? I mean, seven years is a long time ago."

"Oh, believe me. He remembers how we met, and the bastard knows who I am."

"How can you be sure?"

Sonja took her time answering. She lit another cigarette, gathering up the courage for one last push of her story. Becca witnessed the toll it took. The young woman swallowed hard, her breathing coming in short gasps like she was hyperventilating. Sonja ran a hand through her hair and cleared her throat.

"The party ended, but not for me. Matt Brogan kept me for himself and some of his . . . men. The things he made me do . . . and without the drugs? I remembered everything." She wiped her face with a sleeve, her mascara smeared. "He threatened to kill me if I ever told."

Sonja looked like she wanted to throw up. Even in the shadows, her face looked ghostly white, and her lips trembled. When she lifted the cigarette for another drag, she stopped and spoke in a shaky voice.

"I learned the hard way. Matt Brogan is a sadist, as vicious and cruel as they come. And he may be the one who killed Isabel."

CHAPTER 14

FUSION ON THE RIVER RESTAURANT
10:50 P.M.

Once more, Brogan excused himself from dinner with a phone call. This time, he never returned. Diego pretended not to notice his absence, but it weighed heavy on his mind. And he felt certain Cavanaugh recognized his discreet signs of anxiety, despite his efforts to hide them.

Diego picked at his meal, forcing himself to eat, smile, and carry on a conversation. In sharp contrast, his host looked very much at ease. He challenged Diego's intellect with discussions of local politics and the business climate both domestic and abroad. And the man even speculated about the long-term impacts of the energy crisis on the travel industry. Normally, Cavanaugh had no patience with idle chitchat, but tonight, he reveled in it, with a shrewd smirk on his face.

By the time coffee was served, Diego's neck was knotted with tension. His eyes darted for the door or out the window, his concentration long gone. They were practically the only customers in the place, but with Cavanaugh's connections to the owner, the man took advantage of his pull.

Could he trust Draper to watch over Rebecca? Remembrances of his afternoon with her haunted him, along with the distinct feeling it may have been for the last time. A premonition or the product of an overactive imagination, he had no idea. Either way, his wariness betrayed him to the man who latched onto another's weakness with a stranglehold.

"You look distracted, Diego." Cavanaugh's pale blue eyes looked glacial. "Anything I can do to help?"

Smug didn't begin to describe Cavanaugh's face. He beamed with a mix of contempt and self-importance, setting Diego's temper on edge. He had grown tired of playing by the man's rules. Up until now, biding his time had allowed him to operate under Cavanaugh's nose without notice. And over the last couple of years, he had a sense Cavanaugh had grown accustomed to his being around, the closest he might get to trust from the man.

But during the last week, something had changed. Cavanaugh scrutinized him with the same interest he had in the beginning. A lab rat before the start of a grand experiment. But once the rat served its purpose, it got tossed out belly-up and stiff as a board. Diego glanced down at remnants of their cheese course and understood where the rat analogy came from, but it didn't make him feel any more in control. He ventured a change in direction.

"If this dinner was a game of football, I'd have to penalize Brogan for delay of game," Diego observed. "Do you have any idea where he slithered off to?"

"I'm not a fan of sports metaphors, but I do commend your rather late offensive maneuvering. Mr. Brogan has duties to attend to. Orders of mine, to be precise. Why?"

Cavanaugh stressed the words "orders of mine" and dared him to ask his meaning. But a frontal assault would only feed the man's ego. Diego needed a different approach.

"No reason. I thought he might like a doggy bag." Diego smiled at Cavanaugh's surprised reaction when he didn't rise to the baited question. "On paper, the merger with Global Enterprises has been mutually beneficial, wouldn't you agree?" he asked, watching Cavanaugh cock his head in question.

"Yes. I believe you know how I feel about your generous employer. I would like to think we have a rather lucrative future together. And I certainly enjoy the infusion of cash into my international travel enterprise. Why do you ask?"

"You should know I did the original financial analysis of the merger and brokered the deal to Mr. Rivera. But in the end, I recommended against it. I was overruled and assigned to direct the transition period. Mr. Rivera wanted his resident skeptic to be satisfied."

"And are you?" the man asked.

"In short, no. I get the sense you don't trust me as

the business liaison between our two . . . organizations. You appear to keep certain aspects of your affairs to yourself. Unexplained trips and undisclosed meetings with certain clients. If we are building a relationship for future endeavors, I believe a more solid base of trust should be mandatory."

"I agree, but I had no idea how strongly you felt on the subject. Interesting." Cavanaugh sipped his coffee and peered over the cup.

"If you don't have faith in me, I fail to see how this business opportunity with Mr. Rivera can be optimized to the fullest. I intend to discuss the matter with him, in fact."

"Bravo, Diego." Cavanaugh sat back in his chair, a broad grin on his face. Soulless eyes flickered with a touch of humor. "Get a man's attention by trying to snatch his wallet. I suppose dinner should be on you."

"Is that all you've got to say?"

"Can you be discreet, Diego?" The man leaned over the table. Before he replied, Cavanaugh waved his hand, and added, "Forget I asked that. Of course you can. After all, you are a loyal man. You would never do anything to harm Mr. Rivera or myself. Isn't that right?"

Diego narrowed his eyes and kept his silence. His jaw tensed.

Cavanaugh smiled. "Before you bring anything to Mr. Rivera's attention, I have something you must see firsthand. A business opportunity I have savored for a long time. Low overhead, bountiful yet expendable inventory, and exceedingly profitable. I feel certain your employer would have a keen interest in my endeavors, but on a more global scale. I had only waited to present this opportunity when the time was . . . right. I hope you forgive me for my timing. As I've said on many occasions, I value trust and loyalty as much as your Mr. Rivera."

"I appreciate your candor, Mr. Cavanaugh . . . and the opportunity for my employer." Diego raised his chin, unsure how to proceed. Maybe the man had arranged the dinner for a real purpose. For the sake of the missing girls, he had to play this out. "Please forgive me if I jumped to the wrong conclusion. I'm interested in seeing your new business venture. Care to share any details in advance?"

"No, I'd prefer to wait. Your honest first impression might help me gauge your employer's reaction. But before we go, I'd like a snifter of cognac. Waiter?" Cavanaugh waved his hand for service. "Anything for you, Diego?"

"No, nothing." He couldn't hide the edge in his voice. A headache brewed at the base of his skull. The man was stalling. Yet with Brogan gone, Diego had no choice but to stick with Cavanaugh, his life-line to the night's event. Otherwise, he'd be stranded without the price of admission.

"You may as well order a drink. I'm waiting on a call from Mr. Brogan. He left to make sure everything is set for your visit and that the inventory is secure and in good working order." Cavanaugh smiled. "As soon as he contacts me, I intend to show you the extent of my trust in you. A show of good faith. And I'm sure Mr. Rivera will be very pleased with the outcome of our dinner engagement. Nothing like a little unfinished business for dessert, savoring the best for last. Wouldn't you agree?"

Diego had nothing to say . . . and everything to lose.

THE RIVERWALK
10:45 P.M.

Becca walked through her front door and flipped on lights, still rapt in Sonja's story. Matt Brogan had known Isabel and Sonja when the girls were in high school. He had a history with them. But if that were the case, why didn't he show any sign of recognition when she handed over Isabel's school photo the day she first interviewed Cavanaugh? Granted, the bastard would have been a moron to raise his hand and admit he knew Isabel. After all, in Sonja's latest version of the truth, Brogan had a direct tie to Isabel— prostitution and the rape of a young girl, maybe even murder.

"I'll take Sleazeball Perverts for $200, Alex." She sighed, too drained to deal with Sonja's mind games any longer. "And why don't you throw in what's behind door number three while you're at it."

She felt an ache in her shoulders as she set her gun, keys, and cell phone on the kitchen counter. Isabel's past was murky with innuendo and supposition. She wanted to see the girl as her brothers Rudy and Victor saw her. In her gut, she imagined Isabel to be more like Danielle, innocent of the seedy underbelly of this world and in need of saving. But with every step in her investigation, Becca unraveled a new side to the girl, each darker than the last. And still, none of them fit in her mind, not completely anyway.

She poured herself a glass of scotch and glanced toward her window out of habit. Before the glass touched her lips, she put it down. The drapes were drawn. If Diego left the gift of a white rose, she had to take a peek outside to see it. Becca walked to her window and peered out. A white rose lay on her outside windowsill. Her heart pinged off her rib cage. A thrill of expectation mixed with a sudden tingle radiating over her skin. The ticklish sensation made her smile.

"Diego," she whispered.

In the quiet of her living room, she loved the way his name sounded like a melody she would hear years from now and always associate with this feeling. Saying his name would trigger the way she felt right now. And a silly grin would not be far behind.

"Ah, girl." Becca looked down at her clothes and shrugged in a fleeting display of frustration with the timing of it all.

Jeans, sneaks, and a white cotton shirt under a sweater vest with a wool sport coat. Urban and trendy, yes. Sexy and alluring, no. Not exactly the attire she had in mind for their evening together, but it couldn't be helped. Being practical and impatient, Becca wouldn't make Diego wait so she could change clothes. She prided herself on being a low-maintenance woman.

Becca opened her window and stepped outside, the first rose in her hand. But as she looked up to the rooftop, where she expected to see her garden lights burning kilowatts, it was dark. And no other roses trailed up the steps.

"What the hell—?" She turned and looked the other way. His path of white roses went down the stairs of the fire escape instead. With a crooked grin, she shook her head. "What are you up to, Diego?"

One by one, she picked up the flowers as she made her way down the steps. When the path became obscure, with the roses near a hedge line, Becca raised an eyebrow. They led to the Riverwalk level and down a walkway toward a nearby pub.

"Silly, boy. You could have quaffed your thirst at my place for free." She grinned and shook her head.

With her mind set on picking up the next rose, Becca never saw it coming. As she crossed a narrow alleyway between her condo and the next building, an arm grabbed her around the middle and yanked her into the dark passageway. A crushing grip over her mouth.

She jerked her body—hard—and screamed through the hand. Raking her nails across skin, she tried to pry the fingers from her mouth. Her feet kicked the air, flailing for a way to strike. A man. He raised her off the ground, not giving her a chance to gain a foothold. It all happened too fast.

Deeper and deeper he dragged her into the dark alley. Becca needed time. She needed someone to notice her desperate moves, hear her strangled call for help. She dug in her heels and kicked, straining against his grip. But the man had no trouble carrying her. A second man emerged from the dark and lifted her legs. *Why wasn't the alley security light on?* Becca remembered the light. It should have been burning. When she heard the crunch of shattered glass under-foot, she realized the overhead bulb had been broken. She'd been set up, roses and all. *Who knew about Diego's roses?* Her heart sank, along with her re-maining hope. Swallowed up by shadows, Becca had no chance of being noticed now.

The sound of her screams still raged in her head. But she was losing her fight.

Suddenly, she felt the jab of a needle in the soft flesh of her neck. It burned as it seethed under her skin. Becca had no time left. Struggling for air, she lost her ability to scream. Her lungs were on fire. Her body fell limp and heavy. To orient herself, Becca tried to focus on the lights of the Riverwalk or cypress branches under the night sky, but she couldn't see details anymore. They blurred together, like the voices. People laughing and talking came in and out of her awareness. More of a dream. Eventually, the muffled voices dwindled to nothing more than white noise.

Fading in and out of consciousness, Becca remem-bered hands on her body and being wrapped in heavy, smothering material. A moldy smell nearly suffocated her. They lifted her body, but Becca's arms and legs were deadweight, leaden and unable to move.

Sounds and flashes of light swirled around her, flickering in and out like a candle in the wind. Her mind wavered in the twilight between awareness and dreams, captive to the drugs in her system. A cruel and torturous state of limbo. Was she truly awake or only hallucinating?

Becca fought to hold her own . . . to stay on the right side of reality. But now, she had no idea where that might be. Before the blackness won, her mind drifted to a distant time. She welcomed the soft light and the soothing quiet of it.

She pictured Danielle's sweet face and imagined the fragrance of her warm skin. Sisters sharing a bed and napping together on a hot afternoon when they were kids so long ago. A fan whirred quietly in the background and blew cool air across their skin, back and forth. Danielle never woke up. Strands of her hair wafted in the breeze off the fan. Her eyelids flicked and fluttered with a dream, in contrast to the steady rhythm of her breaths. And Becca watched her sleep from two sets of eyes—as a young girl lying at her sister's side and as the woman she had become.

The odd vision filled her with an overwhelming peace. But out of context, Diego stood over them, smiling down as if he knew everything would be okay. Seeing him there, a profound serenity washed through Becca. He looked so beautiful in the afternoon light. So still . . . and rock-solid.

She wanted to reach for his hand—and whisper his name—but nothing would come.

CHAPTER 15

DOWNTOWN SAN ANTONIO

"What? Say again." Draper squinted as he turned on the lamp, the cell phone to his ear. He yanked the covers off him and sat up in bed. His downtown hotel room came into focus, but his mind hadn't fully grasped the situation.

"That surveillance we had on Rebecca Montgomery? Our men are on the move. I just got the call," the man said. "It happened too fast. Our guys weren't in a position to stop it."

He recognized the voice of Paul Murphy, the SAPD member of his team.

"What happened? Start from the beginning." Draper stumbled to the bathroom to take a leak.

"We staked out her place, down on the river. She wasn't home, so we waited." Murphy sighed into the phone, catching his breath. "Becca got home around . . ."

He heard Murphy flip through papers, looking for details that didn't matter in the grand scheme of things. "A quarter to ten. We had a two-man team, one in front, the other in back. For whatever reason, Becca crawled out her fire escape window. I still don't understand why."

"In the absence of a three-alarm fire in the building, do you think she saw our guys? Maybe she tried to ditch 'em by going out the fire escape," Draper theorized as he shook himself and flushed. After performing a one-handed wash maneuver, he looked at himself in the mirror and ran his free hand through his graying hair, what was left of it. An ugly skinny bastard stared back, same as always.

"No, I don't think so. Our guys said her leaving had something to do with flowers, sir. But it doesn't make any sense to me."

"I hear ya, son. Women don't exactly come with logical instructions and a free set of kitchen knives. Making sense is not in their playbook. What else?"

"Like I said, she was picking . . . flowers. But some guy grabbed her from behind. He pulled her into an alley near her condo." Murphy's anxiety for his fellow officer gave an edge to his voice. The man was still short of breath. "I had a cop in plain clothes near a footbridge across the river, looking into the back of her place. By the time this all went down, he radioed for help from his partner on the street level in front, but they lost her."

Murphy cursed under his breath. "Damn it. This was supposed to be a babe-sitting job. I don't know what happened."

"Stay focused. Where is she now?"

"That's just it. We're not one hundred percent sure. The cop out front had seen some movers who'd been there for an hour or so before all this happened. No company name on the outside of their truck. But he got pulled off to search for Becca. Him and his partner made it inside her place through the open window off the fire escape, but she wasn't there. Her gun, cell phone, and keys were on a kitchen counter."

Murphy had fucked up a simple surveillance operation. But things could have been far worse. If the timing had been off even a fraction, the sons of bitches who kidnapped Rebecca might have panicked and made it a hostage situation in downtown San Antonio. A shoot-out, for cryin' out loud.

Yet another potential outcome plagued him on a personal level. If these alleged kidnappers were linked to Cavanaugh, as he suspected, his operation would have been blown. And most probably, Galvan's life would have been forfeited. Draper felt like an asshole for thinking only of his case, but he had invested too much time to have it wiped out by some local wannabe fed. Hell, Galvan was already in the hot seat, hanging with Cavanaugh. Draper didn't need another complication.

He blocked the thought from his head and listened to Murphy give his report.

"By the time my team got done searching, they remembered the movers and the small truck and hauled ass to the street level again. They were almost too late. The truck had already pulled from the curb. They only had enough time to scramble to their car and follow."

"Movers in the middle of the night? Does that make sense to you, Murphy? 'Cause if it does, you can tear up your federal employment application."

"No, sir. It didn't. That's why my guys are tailing the truck, as we speak. What now?"

"Like my daddy always used to say, get on her and stay on her, son. This might be our only chance to nail that rat bastard Cavanaugh. Let's get more cars tailing the truck so we don't unzip our fly and let 'em know we're there. And gather up the rest of our team. I got a feeling this is it. We won't get another chance."

"But if they have Becca, we can pull the truck over right now. We've got probable cause to do the search, sir."

"There's a big picture, Murphy. You're thinking too small. Just do as I say." Squirming out of his pajama bottoms with cell phone in hand, Draper bellowed, "And get over here to pick me up. I'll be in front of the hotel in five."

It took a while for the cop to respond, but once he did, Draper heard the dissent in his voice. The man didn't agree with his order.

"Already on my way, sir. Make it three."

Draper ended the call, his mind firing on all cylinders. In a rush, he ransacked his room for clothes, throwing on whatever he found.

He made a big leap in logic to assume Cavanaugh had ordered the kidnapping of a local cop, but it made sense given Diego's earlier warning. Gutsy and stubborn Rebecca Montgomery had wanted in on his case. Now she was . . . *the hard way.* He hoped she would live to appreciate the irony.

And for Diego's part in all this. His simple *favor* on a *hunch* had turned out to be anything but simple. His prized informant had to know more than he let on at the bank. Diego's sudden concern for a cop he only just met was too much coincidence.

But no matter how it happened, Draper didn't care. It all might end tonight with something more than the foothill of circumstantial evidence Diego had gathered so far. He was so close, he tasted it. Cavanaugh had taken a huge risk. No doubt, the man had something special in mind for Rebecca. And with an ego the size of Texas, the son of a bitch would be front and center when it all went down. Draper knew it.

Dressed and armed, he raced from his room with his blood hot from the thrill of the hunt. Cavanaugh was going down, no matter what he had to do to make it happen.

Nearly Midnight

A smothering stench assaulted Becca's nose. Numb with cold, she lay on a hard surface, her shoulder blades and a hipbone ached from the clumsy position of her body. And she couldn't move, not even to open her eyes. Despite the foul air, she focused on her breathing. And she forced her brain to work at recognizing the staggering smell. It gave her something to concentrate on besides the pain. Dank mold mixed with the heavy musk of body odor, but the rank fumes of a broken sewer overpowered the mélange.

Little by little, she pierced the veil of fog in her mind. Minutes seemed like hours, but eventually, Becca became aware of her body convulsing. Tremors ripped through her muscles unchecked. Drugs still affected her system, and the chill off the floor didn't help.

With great effort, she pried her eyes open. At least, she thought they were. Everything looked dark. No shapes. No light. Only inky black. Becca had no way of knowing where she was or if she was truly awake. She tried to swallow, but her mouth felt like cotton. Her tongue was thick and swollen.

As the haze lifted, the room took shape. An eddy in gray surged with shadows. And a stabbing light centered above her head. She tried to raise a hand to shield her eyes, but her arm flopped to her side, limp. Her wrist banged against something solid, a sharp crack to her bone.

"Arrgh . . . mmm." She heard the sound, unsure it came from her.

Becca's eyes burned, stinging with tears. She forced them open. A blinding white light filled the space. It hurt her eyes, like staring into a scorching desert sun. Unrelenting and without mercy. That's when she heard the echo of footsteps. The sound skittered off walls and came at her from all sides. A slow terror welled inside, roiling from the pit of her stomach. Still, she couldn't focus. Even as her heart thrashed against her ribs, she fought to wake up. To move. To run. But nothing.

"You awake, darlin'." A man's voice, low and gritty.

His body eclipsed the intensity of the burning white light. His shadow brought the chill back to her skin. Becca felt a finger across her cheek, and she flinched. His hand grabbed her chin and shook it. She blinked and forced her eyelids open to keep the image of the man in her brain.

"Come on. We only gave you a light dose. I don't have all night. And neither do you."

His laughter jolted her awake. The man's face spiraled from the haze, coming to a screeching halt in front of her eyes. Matt Brogan. Becca pulled from his hand and shoved away, clumsy like a drunk on a weekend bender.

"You and me got some catching up to do." He grinned. "I know we don't hardly know each other, but I got a real nice surprise if you're good."

"Wh . . . Where . . . this place." She fought for each word.

"You don't need to know that. All you gotta do is . . . be nice and do what I say. Then we can talk about my surprise. You like the roses I sent you? The Mex isn't the only one who can buy his way into your pants."

His revelation jolted her brain. Brogan knew about her and Diego? That meant Cavanaugh did, too. Becca sucked air into her lungs to regain her senses. Diego was in trouble.

Before she could move, Brogan reached for her. In her dazed mind, his fingers undulated like a nest of slithering snakes. Becca jerked her head back, but he only laughed again and forced himself on her. Brogan's hand gripped her neck. When he had her attention, he let go and trailed down her body. He fondled her breasts with his fleshy hand. But when she raised her chin in defiance, without more of a reaction, Brogan pressed his luck and squeezed her nipple . . . hard. She gritted her teeth but didn't cry out. Becca had no intention of giving the man what he wanted.

"Oh, I can see you and me are gonna get along just fine." He grinned, a sickening dead look in his eyes. "I like a challenge. And *rough* is my favorite indoor sport."

Becca let him grope her body through her clothes, staring him down as best she could. Nauseated, she wanted to throw up, but resisted the urge. Eventually, Brogan backed off, taking his short victory lap. He walked into the shadows with a swagger, chuckling under his breath. She knew she hadn't seen the last of him.

Becca's mind raced with how she would play this guy. Scenarios competed in her head. And as her brain cleared, she searched the room for any advantage. In the shadows, she saw movement. Dim lights glowed in the distance, but with her eyesight still blurred, she couldn't make anything out. She heard voices, men and women. And the rattle of chains clanged against metal and dragged heavy on the floor. Who were all these people? And why were they in the dark? And the smell . . . how could they live like this? She pictured a rabble of homeless street people living in a sewer.

But the sound that chilled her to the bone was the quietest of them all. Sobbing cries. Real agony festered bone deep like cancer. A vague whimper gained urgency. And Becca heard Brogan's gruff voice, cursing. Chains dragged along the ground, and a large shadowy shape lumbered toward her. A group or just one man, she had no idea. When Brogan came into the pale circle of light, he yanked at the arm of a thin girl. Her blond hair was matted and covered in filth, head down.

From what Becca remembered of Diego's investigation into Cavanaugh and human trafficking, she began to understand what she was witnessing, playing out before her eyes. This was what Diego and Draper had been searching for. Cavanaugh's elusive stronghold. The bastard held abused young girls against their will, degrading and sexually assaulting them for money, all in the name of business enterprise. Becca couldn't stand it anymore. She heaved the contents of her stomach, bracing her arms under her where she sat. Nausea came, wave after wave, until she ached with the exertion. She tasted raw bile in her throat and smelled it in her nostrils—along with a mounting fear for her own safety, wallowing deep in her belly.

When she looked up, Brogan stood over her, the sickly girl still at his side. Becca squinted into the light, the blonde's face coming into focus.

"I believe you two know each other." Brogan grinned and shoved the girl to the floor in front of her.

Becca came face-to-face with the blond groveling on the floor. She appeared too damaged and beaten to look her in the eye. But when she did, Becca swallowed her heart. Eyes wide and jaw open in shock, Becca stared into the face of her sister, Danielle.

"Oh my God." Every fiber of her being shook. "Dani?"

Brogan laughed. "What? You look like you seen a ghost." His sickening cackle filled the chamber.

But Becca blocked him out to concentrate. Was this another hallucination? A cruel hoax? God wouldn't be so heartless. She wanted to believe that, but the delusion of the girl lingered amidst the carnage of this place, a persistent manifestation. With shaky fingers, she reached out to touch her gaunt face. In an instant, Becca knew. Her eyes brimmed with tears.

Dani's wide blue eyes stared back. Damaged and lost, but they belonged to her sister. Dirt smudges and tears streaked her sweet face. Her lips quivered, and she mouthed words Becca couldn't hear. She cradled Dani's cheeks in her trembling hands.

Everything around Becca faded to nothing. Her sister collapsed into her arms, still disoriented and confused by the whole encounter, unsure who Becca was but thankful for the tenderness. Her body rail-thin and fragile, Dani would break if Becca pressed too hard.

"Oh, God, Dani . . ." Becca cried, and clutched her little sister to her chest. "Is it really you? Please, God. Oh, honey, is it you? It's Becca. Don't you recognize me?"

"Becca?" she whimpered, her voice raspy and spent. "I thought I'd never . . ." She broke down, choked with emotion.

"Momma and I thought you were dead. The police found your blood in that motel room . . . so much of it."

"Momma?" Dani gripped her harder. "Where's Momma?"

"She's . . . okay, honey. She misses you." Becca could see Dani didn't comprehend it all. The motel room. The excessive blood, looking like a murder scene. Trying to explain would only confuse her more. But before Becca could reassure Dani, Brogan interrupted.

"The blood was my idea," he boasted. "We took it from her over a period of time, collected enough to fake a real slaughterhouse. Once the media got ahold of her credit card trail and the bloody motel room, things died down, and it was business as usual for us."

"Us? This is Hunter Cavanaugh's organization, right?"

"Like you don't already know. Galvan has been feeding you intel for a while now. What's he gettin' in return, huh?" He yanked Danielle's hair and pulled her from Becca's arms. Her sister's cries tore open her gut.

Dani grimaced, her face twisted in pain. She had little strength to resist his manhandling. Not anymore.

"The other day when I heard you two were sisters, I knew a family reunion was the way to go. I'm kind of an old softy, like that," he bragged, chest out.

"The other day . . . when you heard?" Becca asked.

Brogan hadn't let on he recognized her when she visited the Cavanaugh estate. He could have discovered her connection to Danielle only recently and put two and two together, but the man didn't look like he excelled at math. No, Matt Brogan had no appreciation for the subtlety of mind games. He came at you headfirst and shoulder down. Someone told him about it and helped him figure out the puzzle. Although she had her own thoughts on the subject, she wanted to keep Brogan talking. The more he yapped, the less likely he'd mess with Dani.

"Who told you about Danielle and me?"

"Let's just say an old friend thought I should know."

Before Becca got her head wrapped around his answer, two men grabbed her from behind. They yanked her up to stand on wobbly legs. On the edge of the light, they pinned her against a railing. Becca heard the sound of duct tape, and her arms and legs were strapped to the metal bars.

"Don't tape her mouth." Brogan grinned at Becca, giving an order to his men. "I want to hear her scream when she sees what I'm gonna do."

She watched in horror as Dani cowered at Brogan's feet, under the light. He stroked the girl's head and grinned, his face distorted by shadows like a grotesque mask. A gruesome stage play was about to be played out.

"Don't hurt her, you bastard!" Becca screamed, struggling to break free. "I'll kill you!"

Anger sparked in her brain. She felt blood rush to her face, and stars spun across her eyes. In the dark, Becca raged with a survivor's instincts, protective of Danielle. She knew Brogan intended to play a game using her sister in center ring while Becca watched, torture inflicted on them both.

Her mind raced with schemes. Psychological tactics and her training in interrogations flooded her thoughts now. How would she work this? She had no margin for error. Danielle was expendable to Brogan. In the shape she was in, she had no value. If Becca didn't do this right, she could witness the murder of her sister before her very eyes—an ordeal more horrific than her nightmares over the past months. Neither of them had much chance of walking out of here alive. But even if it meant sacrificing her own life, Becca would pay the price for a second chance to save Danielle.

Don't go there, Becca. Ain't gonna happen. She shoved the negativity out of her mind. Trussed up like a turkey before the slaughter, Becca didn't have many options. All she had left was her brain and her mouth. It would have to do.

Becca had lost Danielle once. She wasn't going to let it happen again.

A wedge of moon lit the night sky on a clear night. Bluish haze settled on everything like a fine powder glowing in the dark.

Mike Draper, outfitted in his Kevlar vest and FBI windbreaker, raised night-vision binoculars to his face and watched the warehouse at the end of the deserted street. The hot and muggy air clung to his skin like a second layer. Sweat trickled down his temple and from his armpits under his clothes. His gear was a necessity of the job, and he'd grown used to the weight and the heat it generated.

Earlier, he had received a report on the truck connected to the alleged kidnapping of Rebecca

Montgomery. It had been spotted driving into the underground parking beneath the warehouse. The driver had either keyed a code or punched an automated opener to lift the heavy door to the delivery bay. He hadn't witnessed the event himself, but the SAPD cops tailing the truck had.

Draper scanned the perimeter once more, listening to the muted crackle of radio chatter. He had his own FBI Hostage Rescue Team in place and working with the SAPD's tactical team. The HRT officers had been briefed on the mission and provided the available intelligence on their target. Draper would oversee the tactical plan as the commander. He gave his officers their assignments and their respective areas of responsibility within the op. No man would leave his AOR unless Draper ordered it.

His men were geared up with ten-millimeter Heckler & Koch MP5s, night-vision goggles, explosive charges to blow obstacles, and plenty of flashbangs for the element of surprise on entry. Draper had plenty of probable cause to enter the premises with weapons drawn. He believed the men inside were armed and dangerous, with one or more hostages. Probable cause wasn't an issue, and no warrant would be required given this scenario.

The stage was set for "Breach, Bang, and Clear." Now, he waited. This was his jurisdiction. His case. His responsibility. And his ass was on the line if it blew up in his face.

The warehouse under surveillance looked no different from any of the other dilapidated shit holes in this section of town. Anyone driving by wouldn't notice it. But one thing really chapped his skinny white ass. He'd been in the area before, weeks ago, on a lead from Diego. That time, it had been a deserted factory only blocks away. Sources reported activity in the old textile district regarding young girls. Repeat appearances of the same girls, all in the company of older men, clued the tipsters. In this dump of a neighborhood, such activity would stand out. The tips fit what Diego had fed to Draper. So close, but so very wrong.

"Fuck me over once," he muttered under his breath, vowing tonight would be different. "But not twice."

"SAPD Tactical is waiting for the word, sir." Murphy walked up behind him, with Lieutenant Arturo Santiago at his side. The ranking officer for the SAPD looked like the calm before the storm.

Draper caught the look of anxiety on Murphy's face. Guilt can eat a man alive if he let it undermine him. Draper didn't believe in guilt. Santiago, on the other hand, glared at him like a man with something to say. After Murphy left, and he was alone with the lieutenant, Draper was the first to speak.

"I expected to see your chief. Where is he?"

"He's on his way. ETA seven minutes. And he's not a happy man."

"Whether your chief is here or not, this is my op. I'm not jumping the gun. Rebecca's a trained police officer. She knows how this'll play out." He turned his back on Santiago.

"Then maybe she should clue me in, 'cause I didn't get the memo." Santiago stepped in front of him with eyes narrowed and voice raised. "If there's a chance in hell she's in there, Rebecca's being held against her will. I believe a crime has been committed on one of my detectives, Draper. Hell, we've even got probable cause with the suspicious activity in and out of condemned property this time of night. I might even be convinced I smell a meth lab from here. And if those missing girls are in there, the tactical units can treat this like a hostage rescue and do their jobs. That should be enough for you."

"Except Cavanaugh is the focus of my investigation, and because of those girls, it's my jurisdiction. I'm calling the shots here. And I say we wait to get him." Draper matched Santiago's tone. "The bastard left the restaurant in his limo. He's coming here."

Draper lied . . . or rather overstated his argument. His men were still tailing the limousine, and the warehouse seemed an unlikely destination given the direction in which it headed. But it was still too early to make the call, not with a man as cagey as Cavanaugh.

"But you don't know that, not for sure," the lieutenant replied. "He could be heading home or grabbing a nice wedge of pie at Denny's for all you know. I think you got a bad dose of wishful thinking, and no amount of penicillin will make it go away. In fact, this whole investigation has got you messed up. You're obsessed with this guy."

"And your men are so filled with guilt over what happened to Rebecca, you'd rather blow my case to cover up your department's embarrassment. Admit it. Your guys blew her surveillance. Now back off, Lieutenant."

Santiago pulled back and began to pace, his jaw tense. He wasn't done. The man wiped his brow and adjusted his SAPD ball cap. Turning on Draper for round two, he stepped in close and lowered his voice so the other men wouldn't hear.

"Let's examine this situation with some objectivity, if you can muster it." Santiago exercised his right to sarcasm. "In actuality, you have no idea who these men are, the ones that took Rebecca. They may not even be linked to Hunter Cavanaugh. But for the sake of argument, let's make that wild ass leap in logic." The police lieutenant adjusted his Kevlar vest, hoisting it at the collar. "You know what Cavanaugh does with these young women. What do you think is going on right now with Rebecca? You think after those bastards gang-rape her, she'll really give a rat's ass about your letter-perfect bust of Cavanaugh?"

The lieutenant seethed with anger and sarcasm, a side of Santiago Draper hadn't seen before tonight. Despite the man having a legitimate point, Draper stared him down out of habit. But he couldn't allow himself to think about what he said. Plenty of times he ordered good men to do their duty only to see some carried away in body bags. And he delivered the bad news to their families. Being a lieutenant, Santiago must have had his share of the same.

Any skirmish worth fighting had its casualties. Someone had to weigh the good with the bad and make the hard decisions. This time, it was his call. Next time, it might be someone else at the helm with him fitted for a body bag. Either way, he wouldn't shirk his duty.

"I don't know what's happening in there any more than you do." Draper refused to justify his judgment call.

He had said all he intended to say, but Arturo Santiago hadn't.

"That's the point, Draper. You're satisfied with that answer. I'm not." The lieutenant gritted his teeth and took a step back. "How do you live with that ego? You're a user, Draper. And I figured something else out, too. You and Cavanaugh have a lot in common."

Staring at the lieutenant's back as he walked away, Draper swallowed and clenched his jaw. Santiago's words resonated deep in his craw. He would have thought more about the lieutenant's take on the situation, except a dark sedan rolled down the street. A Mercedes, from what he saw. It turned onto the warehouse property. He shifted focus and dismissed Santiago from his mind.

"Who the hell is this?" he muttered under his breath, holding the binoculars to his eyes. Barking into his com switch, he ordered, "I want to know who that is. Anybody catch a good look, report in."

Draper wanted it to be Cavanaugh, but the man had left the restaurant in a limousine, not a Mercedes. His men still followed the luxury vehicle. He didn't like surprises.

"Damn it."

With men waiting on his order, Draper reminded himself of two vital things. He didn't do guilt, and he had made his decision. He hit the switch to his com set.

"Tac team leaders? No one moves without my order. I repeat. Wait for my order."

CHAPTER 16

Becca strained against the duct tape that bound her hands and body to the metal railing. Her heart hammered in her chest as she worked the tape with her weight.

Matt Brogan kept an eye on her, but his real focus was Danielle. Under the stark light overhead, Dani looked washed-out. And so afraid. She lay sprawled on the cement floor, too scared to move. Brogan knelt over her with a knife in his hand.

In the stillness, Danielle's fear echoed off the walls. Every gasp, every shiver made a sound. If others stood in the shadows, Becca couldn't hear them. They watched in cruel silence, witnessing the atrocity without lifting a finger. She had to do something to distract him from her sister.

"Tell me. How did a classy guy like Hunter Cavanaugh get into trafficking and prostitution?" she prompted. "I mean, he's got the money to invest in anything he wants. Why pick something so vile and despicable? It seems like such a bonehead move."

"He saw an opportunity to make real good money,

that's why. That damned Mex Galvan acts so high-and-mighty, but do you think some lame merger with Global Enterprises has made the old man what he is today?" Brogan raised his voice. "No. I'm the one who asked him to step up into something better. I had the connections. He just took my advice. It was all me."

She'd struck a chord. Under the heading of good news, Brogan was talking. But under the header for bad, she could list the same thing. Flexing his jowls the way he was, and admitting to criminal acts, the man had no intention of letting them go. He had too much to lose. But Becca had no choice. She kept working the duct tape, keeping him engaged in conversation.

"Does Cavanaugh come down here often? I mean, who's he gonna trust with an operation this size?"

"Boss man leaves it all up to me. He trusts me to take care of . . . things." As he spoke, Brogan tugged at her sister's grimy T-shirt, a taunting move. "'Cause I know what to do."

"Please . . . no." Danielle trembled, eyes wide in terror. "I'll do whatever you want, but don't hurt me."

"It's not that simple anymore, sweet meat."

In a steady and measured move, Brogan made his first cut.

His knife ripped through her shirt, from the collar down the middle. It hissed—a high-pitched and abrasive sound—like fingernails on a chalkboard. Becca's mind raced with what to say next. Her breath caught in her throat when Brogan trailed the blade down

Dani's breasts. She forced herself to think and remain calm, when all she wanted to do was scream.

"Sounds like Cavanaugh has been playing this whole thing real smart." Her voice cracked.

Brogan looked up and smiled at her. "Yeah, that's what I said before. He's a real smart man. Knows a good thing when he sees it."

"Knows to steer clear of a disaster you mean." Becca set her jaw, watching the look of surprise on his face.

"What are you talking about?" Brogan let Dani go.

"Sounds like Cavanaugh is playing both ends against the middle. He's keeping this thriving enterprise going with you, but washing his hands of it in case the cops knock at his door. I'd say that's a real smart move." She took a gamble Cavanaugh hadn't set foot in this dump. And by the look on Brogan's face, she'd guessed right.

"It's not like that," he argued. "I'm runnin' the show here, but he wouldn't leave me hangin'. I know too much."

"Exactly." She nodded. She had planted the seed of Cavanaugh's betrayal. Now she would test the waters with another approach. "Earlier, you told me an old friend gave you the connection between me and Danielle. I got a pretty good idea who told you. Only she's not much of a friend."

Brogan snapped his head in Becca's direction, seething but curious. "Humor me. Tell me what you think you know."

"More like *who* I know. Sonja Garza," she said. Recognition flashed across Brogan's face. "In fact,

I've met with her on more than one occasion. And she loves talking about you."

"You're lying. Sonja told me she saw you once. And she came to me right after. We met at some roach coach motel off Guadalupe Street. And we did a hell of a lot more than talk. That bitch knows better than to lie to me."

"Maybe she hasn't told you about our little meeting tonight." Becca definitely had his attention now. "She told me about you raping her at the pool house years ago. And about you buying your girlfriend Isabel Marquez an expensive gold necklace back then."

Brogan grimaced, then started to laugh. His intense curiosity vanished. *What the hell had just happened?*

"You don't know jack shit. Sonja always wanted a piece of me. I never had to rape her to get it neither. And I don't know nothin' 'bout that other girl . . . what's her name. Sonja knew her, not me."

"But you got Isabel the necklace, the heart with diamonds on it. Sonja said so." Becca tried to recapture the moment, but she'd lost Brogan. She tugged harder at the duct tape, panic setting in. She couldn't budge it. "I met with her tonight in the Cielo Vista cinema parking lot. She said you might've killed Isabel seven years ago."

"You got some imagination, lady. But you don't have all the facts. One of my guys tailed you to that theater, but he got spooked and took off when you turned the tables on him. So that much might be true." His voice low and threatening; Brogan was ready to blow. "But Sonja knows I'd kill her if she told lies about me. Hell, I'm not taking credit for that dead bitch. Sonja knows what happened. And buying some bimbo an expensive necklace is not my thing. I get plenty of the *Big O* right here. And what my bitches don't gimme, I take. I don't need to pay for it with jewelry. Shit."

He wasn't buying any of her story. Brogan's face knotted in a sneer. "You're playing me for some kinda fool. But I got a better idea. From here on out, every time you open your fuckin' mouth, I'm gonna cut off a piece of your sister and feed it to you. Now let me see what kind of a rise I can get out of *you*."

Brogan fondled Danielle's breasts and squeezed too tight. She cried out in pain, but the sound of her cry only fueled his lust. He lowered his lips to her nipple, sucking and biting until her sister couldn't stand it any more.

"Please . . . don't," Dani wailed.

Seconds bled into hours for Becca as she struggled against her restraints, helpless and unable to speak. But when she looked up, something caught her eye. Danielle had turned her head toward Becca, even as Brogan fed on her fear. New tears streaked her rawboned face, but Becca saw something more. In a show of submission, Dani collapsed under Brogan's weight, submitting to his degradation one final time. And with her surrender, she fixed her precious eyes on Becca—eyes brimming with all the love she held in her heart.

Her baby sister mouthed the words—*I love you*—in silence. Danielle knew she would die. And Becca could only watch it happen.

*   *   *

Diego recognized the seedy neighborhood, making him more anxious. Sometime back, he and Draper had raided an old textile factory nearby, thinking Cavanaugh had his girls stashed in it. At the time, he believed it to be another waste of energy and manpower. Not so much now.

As their Mercedes pulled up to a loading ramp and a subterranean parking garage entrance, the driver hit a code into a keypad. The heavy door rattled as it lifted. With the noise and Cavanaugh's distraction, Diego peered out the rear window. He searched for any signs of Draper but saw nothing. If the fed had gotten his message, he should have stormed the garage with the door open like this.

Why hadn't Draper gotten his message, damn it? There should have been enough time, but now things were looking bleak. It was probably too late. Cavanaugh had screwed him over with the FBI surveillance. The man switched cars, sending the higher-profile stretch limo on its way with two other passengers on board, no doubt with the FBI on its tail. And Cavanaugh had taken the less conspicuous Mercedes of Brogan's. They had planned it from the beginning.

When Diego saw the switch going down, he pretended it didn't matter. But inside, his brain struggled for another way to alert Draper.

As he slid into the backseat of the Mercedes, with Cavanaugh giving last-minute instructions to one of Brogan's men, Diego had palmed his small cell phone out of his pocket. He shot a quick glance to its display as he held it close to his thigh, away from Cavanaugh's sight. With the cell muted, Diego thumbed 9–1–1 and hit send without a sound. But as the call went through, he slid the phone into the seat pocket next to him. No time for him to pass on a direct message—too dangerous.

A dispatcher would get the call and have to respond, whether he remained on the line or not. And with the GPS feature the FBI had installed on the phone, someone would eventually contact Draper and track his exact location. It wasn't much of a plan, but he had run out of options, especially after one of Cavanaugh's men held him at gunpoint from the front seat at the switch site, demanding his .45-caliber Colt.

Now with no gun, the sheath of knives strapped to his leg was all he had left. Diego stared into the dismal shadows of the garage up ahead. He was about to enter one of Cavanaugh's strongholds.

"You surprise me, Diego." Cavanaugh's voice caught him off guard. He hadn't spoken since the switch. "You didn't ask one question about the switch in cars. Why is that?"

Before he answered, Diego remembered another phone call not so long ago. The recollection came to him not out of nostalgia, but from the harsh reality of his present situation. His "death wish" conversation with Cavanaugh. He didn't really know why he thought of it. Or perhaps he did. *One of these days, I might surprise you and grant your death wish, Diego,* the man had said. How prophetic, he thought.

Diego hadn't resisted at the switch site for one reason only. If he had a chance to discover the location of the missing girls, he had to take his shot—despite the odds. He knew he'd be outnumbered. And if this was his day to die, he would refuse to go quietly . . . or alone. He'd have his sights set on the man sitting next to him. Diego stared at Cavanaugh now, anger not part of the equation.

"Weren't we just talking about trust, Hunter?" In a deliberate move, he used the man's first name. After all, death made all men equal. "It seems one of us was listening . . . and the other scheming."

"I will miss our little chats, Diego." Cavanaugh smiled, a genuine show of humor in his eyes.

"So will I," Diego lied. He felt no such affection for the man.

Yet from here on out, subterfuge would no longer be necessary. Neither man would make the pretense of civility. Every remark would matter . . . and every word would be the truth. The warehouse door rumbled closed behind them with such finality, it devoured the moonlight and belched its foul air. But worst of all, it robbed Diego of his life with Rebecca.

"How long are you gonna wait for Cavanaugh? Do the bodies have to pile up outside the door for you to reconsider this so-called strategy of yours?" Lieutenant Santiago had his hands on his hips and glared at Draper. The moon cast its light on half his face, the rest in shadow.

"Look, I've already had a long talk with your chief. He's doesn't like the situation, but . . ." Before Draper finished, his cell phone vibrated. He answered the call. "Draper. You better have good news."

Santiago watched his reaction with interest.

"We're outside the Cavanaugh estate. The limousine dropped two men off and split. What now?" The voice of Special Agent Russo.

"Did you get a good look at the men? Was it Hunter Cavanaugh and Diego Galvan?"

"We haven't been able to confirm that, sir." Embarrassment crept into Russo's tone. "It might've been them. We couldn't get closer with the security they have on the grounds and at the gate. But with binoculars, we might—"

Draper interrupted him. "I don't want you to risk getting spotted. Cavanaugh's men are armed, and they'd be within their rights to shoot first and ask questions later if you tried to infiltrate the place." He shut his eyes tight and heaved a sigh. The look on Santiago's face didn't help. "Stay at the estate and out of sight. Report any activity. Draper out."

After he ended the call, Santiago cocked his head to say, "What? Don't your men have x-ray vision, or was the limo made of lead?"

The lieutenant took his cheap shot, but Draper had it coming. "You've made your point."

"Not yet I haven't," the lieutenant insisted. "We still gotta figure out a way into that damned warehouse, one that won't get my detective and those girls killed if they're in there."

"My HRT Unit found a way in the main level, stealth mode, but the stairwells to the garage have been sealed off. A recent addition, by the way," he offered.

"Sealed off?" Santiago asked. "What kind of a renovation concept is that for a condemned building? If they've done work like that, it's likely Cavanaugh or Matt Brogan are behind it . . . and hunkered down below ground."

"That's what I was thinking." He nodded. "We'll have to blow the doors to gain access. Maybe first we'll need a little diversion out front to distract the bastards inside."

Santiago grinned. "Now you're talking, Draper. I haven't seen a problem yet that couldn't be solved with a little well-placed C–4."

"Remind me not to go hunting with you." His cell phone buzzed again. "Draper."

He listened to the voice on the other end of the line, his jaw dropped and eyes narrowed. Draper gave his instructions and ended the call.

"You're not gonna believe this." He fixed his eyes on Santiago. "Dispatch got a 9–1–1 call coming from a phone I gave Diego Galvan, my inside informant. No one on the line, but it's still open. The cell's got GPS tracking on it."

Santiago scrunched his face in question, not grasping if this was good news or bad.

"Dispatch tracked the signal to this location." Draper's heart ramped up a notch. "Galvan is inside that damned warehouse, sending up GPS flares. And I bet Cavanaugh is standing right next to him. This is going down . . . now."

CHAPTER 17

Only a matter of time. Brogan had a knife at Danielle's throat. Becca's sister strained to avoid the blade, chin high and veins jutting from her neck. The bastard trailed the weapon down her body, hovering over major arteries. One deep slice, and she would bleed out in minutes. And Becca would be forced to watch it happen. He had stripped off most of Dani's clothing, leaving tattered remnants to hang from her limbs.

Now, the tip of his blade creased her sister's breast, so sharp it cut a thin white line that erupted in beads of blood and dribbled down her rib cage. Dani gasped and gritted her teeth against the pain.

Becca rocked and tugged against the duct tape holding her down, not caring if Brogan saw. Her eyes stung with tears, and bile stirred hot in her belly, making her nauseous again. All she wanted was to talk to her sister for the last time. To tell Dani all the things she had dreamt about saying if she had a second chance. But if she did, Brogan would make Danielle's death excruciating. She knew it. And the pain of that knowledge ripped her apart.

Brogan locked eyes on Becca and a slow sneer spread across his face. He was only getting started. She saw it in his eyes as he unzipped his pants.

Killing Danielle wasn't going to be enough.

"Such a despicable animal. I see you are well represented, Hunter. You should be very proud." A man's voice with a Hispanic accent came from deep in the shadows, accompanied by the heavy echo of footsteps.

Becca peered into the dark, looking for the man who dared to speak against Brogan. Although her face twisted with a rage from deep in her soul, she dared to hope someone would intervene for Dani's sake. Behind Becca and all around, people lurked in the shadows and whispered. She sensed a stirring of urgency. At her back, the weight of their eyes closed in. Even Brogan raised his ugly head and squinted into the murky shadows.

When the man with the mystery voice stepped into the light, a flood of emotion swept over her. *Diego . . . Oh my God!* Dressed in an elegant suit, he didn't belong to this squalid and depraved world. And seeing him reminded her that another life existed beyond this hell. The promise of a future.

But Diego wasn't alone. Hunter Cavanaugh stepped from the dark and stood at his side. The privileged man grimaced with obvious disdain as he looked around, repulsed by the world Brogan thrived in. The interruption diffused Brogan's fury, and he scrambled off the floor, zipping his pants up.

In an uncontrollable show of relief, Becca let her body go slack. She collapsed against her restraints, drained and exhausted. *Maybe the nightmare would be over.*

Yet when reality struck, Becca knew this couldn't be true. Diego stood next to Cavanaugh as a free man. But two men hemmed him in, only waiting for Cavanaugh to give the order to restrain him. He would suffer their same fate, and her heart sank with a deep and pervasive regret. Earlier, Brogan told her Cavanaugh knew about Diego's visits to her and assumed he was talking to the local cops. And her interference with the blackmail attempt on Diego had gotten him noticed by the wrong man. The rich bastard and his obscene disciple had won.

Before she knew it, the words were out of her mouth. "I'm so sorry, Diego. I didn't mean for this to happen."

At the sound of her voice, Diego jerked his head to the right. His beautiful Rebecca. Duct tape bound her to a railing. And her eyes pleaded for him to help, tears shimmering down her face.

"What . . . what's going on here?" he questioned. "Why is she—?"

He looked for an answer in Cavanaugh's face, but the man only smirked, a sickening reminder of his twisted nature. Finally recognizing the scene for what it was, Diego shifted his eyes from Rebecca to the young girl near Brogan. When he saw the face of the blonde, he knew it had to be Danielle. He recognized her from Draper's files.

Oh my God, this can't be! Danielle is alive!

His mind grappled with the shock, but another realization hit with a powerful jolt. Brogan had set this up. Rebecca and Danielle. And Cavanaugh had known about it. *His big surprise.* Brogan's phone calls. The whole fucking dinner had been orchestrated for this vile finale. While they ate, Rebecca had been subjected to a living hell . . . with Danielle only feet away. It all came in a rush. His heart hammered, and his throat wedged tight and choked off his air.

Brogan's torture of these two women spiraled him into a seething rage. Diego shook with it. He felt an angry fist clutch at his heart, threatening to rip it from his chest. Something snapped inside him.

"You pathetic coward!" he yelled.

Diego raced for Brogan. He grabbed him by the scruff of his neck. And with all his weight behind it, he pounded his fist into the man's gut, over and over. Even with Brogan being the heavier man, Diego lifted him off the ground with every punch. Adrenaline fueled his frenzy.

Voices in the dark shouted garbled words he couldn't understand. The mass of bodies closed in, the circle of light growing smaller. Suffocating and oppressive.

"Aarrgghh . . . aahhh." Brogan grunted and moaned. "Get him . . . off!"

No amount of punishment would ever be enough. For Rebecca. For Danielle. For every one of the missing girls. Their faces raced through his brain at a fevered pace. Diego couldn't stop. He battered the man, out of control. The injustice. The years stolen from him because these men bartered with human life as if it meant nothing. Blind rage had taken over. And a dark side of Diego's soul emerged, a side Cavanaugh had fostered.

"That's enough." Cavanaugh bellowed. "Pull him off."

Diego shoved Brogan against a wall. When his fist connected with the bastard's face, hands tugged at his arms. A man shoved into his rib cage with a dropped shoulder to back him off. Two men grappled him into submission, but Diego fixed his eyes on Brogan . . . nothing else.

"It took . . . you long . . . enough." Brogan glared at Cavanaugh, panting.

"Quite frankly, I had hoped you would rebound, Mr. Brogan." The man knew how to twist the knife. No one's ego was sacred. "And the viciousness of Diego's attack, I found it . . . astounding."

Diego glared at Cavanaugh, his body shaking, still in the throes of his brutality.

Brogan hunched over and spat blood on the floor, heaving with hands on his knees. The aftermath of his beating still echoed through the chamber. But the angry voices had trailed off, waiting for what would come. When Brogan rose, his face swollen and battered, he scowled at Diego with a new scale of hatred.

"I'm gonna—" He spat again and wiped his mouth with a sleeve—"take pleasure . . . in killing you . . . real slow, Mex."

"Big talk . . . for such a small insignificant man." Diego wrestled against the men who held him. His rage smoldered, a sustained burn unappeased.

Cavanaugh intervened. The stark light overhead cast shadows across the features of his aristocratic face, giving him a deathlike pallor. A macabre master of ceremonies.

"As you know, Diego, I do not tolerate disloyalty. Clearly, you are working with the police. You know Detective Montgomery quite well." Cavanaugh gestured with a wave of his hand, pointing to Rebecca. "I can only assume your fascination with her would not be in the best interest of Mr. Rivera or myself. So consider what comes next your severance package. Mr. Brogan, he is yours as I promised."

Brogan stood and flexed his shoulders. He torqued his head to one side and popped his neck. Slowly, he walked toward Diego. The men grasping his arms reinforced their grip. Diego steeled himself for the beating, his stomach taut.

"You won't get away with this," he argued, glancing over at Cavanaugh. "Joe Rivera won't stand for it."

"Now there, you are wrong. As Mr. Rivera's new business partner, I am only protecting his interests along with my own." Cavanaugh beamed. "You see—"

Brogan interrupted the man's gloat by taking his first punch. He rammed his fist into Diego's gut, doubling him over. But the men yanked him back up.

"Uurrgh." Diego grimaced and taunted his abuser through gritted teeth, "Is that all you've got?"

Brogan fumed, his eyes dark and menacing. He stepped to one side and pounded Diego's rib cage, each blow aimed to break bones.

"No, please . . . let him go," Rebecca screamed. He heard her sweet voice through the haze.

Cavanaugh continued, as if he were at a cocktail party speaking about the weather. "Well, yes, I'm afraid that's going to leave a mark."

Oblivious and smiling, Cavanaugh walked around Brogan as he pummeled Diego with beefy fists, over and over.

"As I was saying, I've planted some very incriminating evidence on a computer at the estate . . . and in your quarters. When your employer finds out about it, he will be grateful to me for heading off a disaster."

"Rivera won't . . ." Diego forced the words from his mouth. ". . . he won't believe you."

Brogan planted a fist to his jaw, jolting his head back. He saw stars, tasted blood. A warm stream dripped down his chin.

"Of course he will, my dear boy. I've thought of everything." Cavanaugh caught Brogan's eye. Without a word, he stopped the man's assault with a glare. For the time being, Diego had his reprieve. He slumped in the grasp of the two men, his legs wobbly from the vicious beating.

Cavanaugh carried on. "You see, this despicable trafficking business will appear to be all your idea. And you've done splendidly so far, financially speaking. A rather lucrative account has been set up under your name in Switzerland. The Swiss Credit Bank in Zurich. All confidential, of course, but the paper trail will lead back to you. And with the rush on setting it up, the police might assume you intended to leave the country in a hurry. Imagine that."

"But the police . . ." Diego shook his head to clear the fog. His throat parched. "Rebecca . . ."

"The police will figure you've been feeding them bad information only to protect yourself. Can you imagine their embarrassment? And, of course, this brave detective over here will try to stop you, getting killed in the process. But not before killing you first. A nice tidy package for the police to uncover. Case open, case closed."

Diego pushed himself to stand. He raised his chin, mustering a defiance he had to fake. "Very clever. Local cops . . . might buy that. But Rivera?"

Cavanaugh grinned and shook his head. "Mr. Rivera will want to make it up to me, for strapping our new enterprise with such a miscreant. Game, set, match, Mr. Galvan. Rather clever, don't you think?"

"It would be . . . except for . . . a couple of minor points." Diego gulped air into his burning lungs. He licked the blood off his swollen lip.

Cavanaugh furrowed his brow in question. "Such as?"

Brogan shrugged with a snort. And from the corner of his eye, Diego saw Rebecca stand at attention. During the brawl, Danielle had crawled to her sister. Now she clutched at Rebecca's clothes, her eyes wide and fixed on the unfolding drama.

Diego had nothing left to lose. Unlike the old saying, the truth would not set him free. But it would give him great satisfaction to know he had removed the smug look from Cavanaugh's face with surgical precision. He chose his next words carefully.

"My interest in the local police is purely . . . personal." He glanced to Rebecca and summoned a painful smile. "But the FBI is . . . another matter entirely."

"What?" Cavanaugh's jaw dropped, the look on

his face priceless and worth all the pain Diego had endured. "You can't be . . ."

While the man staggered with that bit of news, Diego hit him with a combination punch. "And Joe Rivera is not just . . . my employer. He's my father. And I assure you, he would not question my loyalty . . . in this lifetime . . . or any other."

"Oh my . . . God." The old bastard stumbled backward. He glared at Brogan, who only shrugged and stammered, "I d-didn't know, b-boss. I swear."

The men holding Diego loosened their grip. He pretended not to notice but tensed his body to move.

"Let me k-kill him for you, b-boss. I can . . ." Brogan hadn't recovered, but his mouth shifted into autopilot.

"Haven't you done enough, Brogan? Give me some time . . . to think." Cavanaugh ran a hand through his hair, his skin taking on the ashen color of his hair. He paced in and out of the light. "I just have to . . ."

Diego saw it in the man's face. Cavanaugh knew his scheme had backfired. His only prayer for survival would be if the FBI got to him first. Rivera would not be as generous. Even if Cavanaugh walked out of here alive, he was a dead man.

Suddenly, an explosion ripped through the cavernous space. One . . . two . . . three loud booms. Each blast shredded the stagnant air with a percussive shock wave.

"Mooove . . . move . . . Mooove!" Voices bellowed, a distant assault on a level above. Another one sounded closer. They came from nowhere and everywhere.

At the threshold of the garage tunnel to the right, several metal canisters clattered across the cement floor. Diego saw them, but had no time to react. In seconds, each one detonated. A brilliant flash of light. And a deafening blast buffeted his body with a violent pulse and left him dazed. The roar rang in his ears, leaving him deaf.

"Aaahhh." Diego covered his face, too late, and toppled to the floor. His head ached from the jarring concussion. Stars pierced the darkness and spun out of control, a blinding assault. Diego couldn't see. His night vision was gone.

Even in his stupor, he knew what had happened. Police tactical teams used a diversionary device called a flashbang. A fuel-air explosive, the device reacts with oxygen to produce an acoustic pulse and a brilliant flash of light. Anyone within range is dazed, seeing stars and unable to hear.

What followed the diversion played out before his eyes like a horror film in silent mode. Shadowy figures seethed through the maze, ghostlike silhouettes. Hard to tell the feds from Brogan's men. Flashlight beams strafed the walls, creating an eerie strobe effect. Bleary-eyed, he could only watch. Both of Brogan's men clung to him. They fired their weapons into the crowd, not taking aim. Maybe they figured to use him as a human shield.

Diego's ears popped from the repercussion of the explosions, in and out. Angry voices were muffled. He couldn't hear the words. Another series of blinding lights tore through the darkness, sudden bursts of white. Diego staggered with the second assault, his equilibrium shaken. He thought the men holding him had gone, but he felt their grip again. Their faces shaken, the men were unsure what to do.

Shots rang out as Brogan's men recovered one by one and scrambled for cover, firing their weapons. In a flash of recognition, Diego spotted Cavanaugh's white hair across a ramp. The man's face was twisted in panic, and Brogan rushed to his side. Cavanaugh yelled something to Brogan, but Diego only heard the incessant ringing in his ears. A steady numbing hum.

Thud ... thwack ... zing. Bullets smacked against the wall behind him. Diego ducked.

"Stay right ... stay right ... Move!" A man dressed in tactical gear shouted to his team. Stacked one behind the other, Draper's men moved as one unit, with weapons aimed and ready. They pressed their advantage, superior numbers and better equipment. But Brogan's men opened fire. Mass confusion and the surge of another standoff.

Diego wanted to shout and urge the feds to take down Cavanaugh and Brogan. Without a head, the snake would wither and die. But Brogan's men shoved him against a wall and forced him to move down another ramp, away from the fight. Diego craned his neck, looking for Rebecca on the level he had left behind.

The captive girls screamed and huddled together in the dark, staying low. The last time he had seen Danielle, she was clinging to Rebecca. Her eyes brimmed with tears and insane fear. But now, the girl cowered in a corner, hands over her head. Close to hysteria. The sharp staccato of bullets covered up her screams.

Now or never. His chance to make a move. Diego shoved into one of the men holding him and knocked the man backward. In the dark, he heard the man's head crack on the cement. Turning, he jammed the heel of his hand into the solar plexus of the other, punching the wind from his lungs. The man doubled over, and Diego finished him with an elbow to the back of his skull. He was out for the count.

Finally free, Diego took a gun from the unconscious man sprawled at his feet and checked his ammunition. He had half a clip. The other guy was nearly empty. He grimaced at his luck.

To help Rebecca and Danielle, he had to go back the way he had come. He shrugged out of his suit jacket, yanked off his tie, and tucked the gun at the small of his back. Crouched at the top of the ramp, he retrieved a knife from the sheath strapped to his leg and waited to make his move for Rebecca, to set her free.

"*Ay Dios mio.*" He sighed, still hearing gunfire. Without thinking, Diego tapped the knife tip shoulder to shoulder, head to heart, making a quick sign of the cross. With a grimace, he hoped God would not be too offended by his irreverent use of the blade. "Sorry. Don't forget, it's the thought that counts."

He forced his legs to work, creeping along the wall, hunkered down low. The smell of cordite hung heavy in the air. Diego felt his way in the dark and almost stumbled over a dead body, one of Brogan's guys. The man's chest was soaked in sticky blood. Diego didn't have to check for a pulse. He wiped his hands on his pants, but the smell lingered. Copper-sweet blood and excrement made for a powerful brew, hard to forget.

More gunfire erupted, a short burst from what remained of Brogan's men. Bullets ricocheted and blasted a hail of cement shards off the walls. He ducked the flying debris. Members of the tactical teams were already herding the girls to safety, one by one, shielding them with their bodies. A slow but effective process. In the dark and under fire, it was difficult to tell friend from foe.

Up ahead, Diego spotted Cavanaugh. Draper's men were gaining an advantage—a fact not missed by the man with ashen hair. He saw it in his eyes and knew Cavanaugh would bail like a rat abandoning a sinking ship. With jaw clenched, Diego fixed his eyes on the man and pulled his gun, ready to close in. But the cold-hearted son of a bitch hadn't missed his intentions. Reloading his weapon and pocketing another clip, Cavanaugh yelled to Brogan. The two men split up.

Where the hell are they going? Cavanaugh headed down a long, dark corridor, away from the strike force. And Brogan dissolved into the shadows in the opposite direction. A handful of his men retreated with him, and the gunfire on the ramp stopped.

"Damn it!" Diego cursed.

He wanted to follow, but as he looked over his shoulder, Diego stopped cold. On the fringe of light, Rebecca caught his eye and held it. A single tear rolled down her cheek, a contrast to the fragile and brave smile on her face. Vulnerable and yet so very strong.

In that instant, she stole his breath, reminding him of their first kiss. Even amidst the fading clamor of Draper's invasion, he stood spellbound and unable to move. If they lived through this day, Diego knew he'd always remember the significance—the moment he realized he loved Rebecca Montgomery.

"Are you . . . okay?" he asked, unsure he had spoken at all. When she nodded, he made himself move.

Diego wedged the gun at his back and headed for her with knife in hand. He cut away the duct tape, and as he freed her arms, Rebecca ran her fingers over his face and down his throat. To make sure he was real. An intimate and endearing touch.

"I'm so sorry," she cried. "I didn't mean to drag you into this."

When she was free, Diego pulled her to him. With the woman he loved cradled safe in his arms, he knew what it felt like to be a drowning man thrown a lifeline.

"No more regrets, Rebecca. It's time to move on with our lives . . . with our future. Cavanaugh has taken too much from both of us. I refuse to give him any more." He cupped her face with a hand and kissed the tears from her cheeks. "And you have your second chance with Danielle now. An unbelievable gift."

At the mention of her sister's name, Rebecca searched the floor for her sister. She peered through the shadows, but found nothing. She pulled from his arms, desperation etched deep on her face.

"Where is she? Oh my God, she was right here? Dani's gone," she cried.

"Maybe she was taken with the rest," he speculated. But even as he said the words, he didn't believe it.

"Come on. I've got to find her." Rebecca grabbed his hand and turned. But when he didn't follow, she stopped. "What's wrong?"

"You find Danielle. She's probably safe and sound already."

"You're going after him, aren't you?" She squeezed his hand, horrified expectation on her face. "Let Draper handle this. Please. Come help me find Dani."

Diego wanted nothing more. But if Danielle wasn't with the other girls, Cavanaugh had her. And he wouldn't rob Rebecca of hope or put her through the torture of watching her sister be threatened again. He had no time left. He had to move now.

With his eyes fixed on Rebecca, Diego shook his head and let go of her hand.

"I gotta do this." He winced and swallowed, putting on a show of certainty he didn't feel. "Go, find your sister. And know you've been blessed with a second chance."

Diego turned and walked into the shadows. When he was sure she could no longer see him, he looked back. Rebecca hadn't left. She stood at the crossroad of indecision, still watching him go. Even as a feeling of dread crept into his heart, he wanted to remember how she looked, standing under the light.

But most of all, he prayed he wasn't right about Danielle.

CHAPTER 18

Brogan knew that Cavanaugh blamed him. The man had grabbed the flashlight and walked up front in silence, not caring if he and his men kept up. Boss man's behavior made him look bad in front of McPhee and Ellis. Who was the one installed the coded hatch at the lowest level of the damned garage, a sure way out if things got hairy? Not many people knew about the old tunnel system, some historical piece of crap forgotten a long time ago. A little bribe money to a city engineer, and he had hit pay dirt. All he needed to do was remove a section of wall in this garage to connect to it and he looked like a genius . . . except to Cavanaugh right now.

But grabbing a hostage would be his ace in the hole . . . especially the cop's sister.

For such a skinny little thing, the blond chick squirmed in his arms and weighed a ton. He still had his hand over her mouth, but after the brawl with the Mex, his muscles ached, and he felt a sharp pang in his side, maybe a broken rib. It hurt like a mother. But did the little bitch appreciate his aches and pains? *Hell, no.*

Women!

"You're gonna fuckin' walk now," he hissed in her ear. "But if I hear a whine or snivel, I'll slit your throat and make a ashtray outta your head. You understand me?"

She whimpered, but stopped struggling.

"I said, do you understand, bitch?" he spat. "I ain't no mind reader."

The girl nodded, a fierce shake of her head. The fear in her eyes told him she believed what he said. Dumb broad! Sure he'd slit her throat, but a damned ashtray? *Un-fucking-believable!*

Brogan stood her on her feet and grabbed her by the hair, keeping her close. From the corner of his eye, he caught McPhee mocking him. The asshole pretended to puff on an invisible cigarette and flicked ashes on top of the girl's head when she wasn't looking. Ellis grinned. The bastards! Brogan glared at his men, but they only shrugged and scrunched their faces in silence.

"Up here to the right, boss. That far wall." Brogan pointed with his free hand, but Cavanaugh never turned around. Boy, was he pissed!

"The key code. I presume you have it, or will this be another pathetic hunt for the Holy Grail?"

The code. Boss man wanted the key code for the passageway. Brogan was sure he heard that part right. But with the echo in this dump, the rest sounded garbled. Cavanaugh said something about a hunt for quail. Fine time to be thinking of birds and such. These educated types never made sense to him. Most of the time, he ignored the hell out of them. A good policy . . . like now. He gave Cavanaugh the code. But if the man wanted to go hunting, he'd be doing it on his own.

"And have you thought of transportation away from here? Or will we be thumbing it?" Cavanaugh laid on the sarcasm.

"No, I got us a car. It's locked, but the key is in a magnetic box fixed inside the left back wheel well. It's parked inside the other buildin'. An old tunnel connects to it. Pretty good, huh?"

"Yes. I see you've thought of absolutely everything. How could I have ever doubted you?"

Okay, Brogan knew that tone. He stopped and shoved the girl into Ellis's chest. "Look, we're gonna . . ."

"Sshh. I thought I heard something," McPhee whispered, pointing a finger behind them.

Quiet like this, the hollow sound played tricks on your head. Four men and a scrawny girl made their share of noise, but when they stopped, McPhee heard something. It could be just another echo or . . .

Brogan felt a presence more than heard one. He grabbed the light from Cavanaugh's hand and doused it. And he wrestled the girl from Ellis and clamped a hand over her mouth.

"No sounds unless I tell you to . . . or I kill whoever is out there, then you next," he whispered to the girl. And to his men, "We're goin' fishin', boys. Spread out. And watch your cross fire. If I end up with a ricochet bullet in my head, I'm gonna be real pissed. Now move!"

Brogan pulled the handgun from his belt and

yanked the girl tight to his chest. *Damn it!* He was having a really crappy day!

Diego had made up some ground, but the sounds of footsteps he followed suddenly stopped. Had they gotten to their destination? And where the hell was that, exactly? This section of the old garage was a maze. Going deeper into it made no sense.

He didn't have a flashlight, fearing it would only act as a beacon to give his location. Diego relied on his night vision and the noise he trailed, but now the footsteps had stopped. He was dead in the water. Should he move and risk making a sound or stay put until they got going again?

"Aarghh. Aahhh." The shriek of a girl rebounded up the ramp. "Please . . . ummphh." The last part faded into a hiss like a whisper in a well.

Diego's heart clenched in his chest. He pressed his back to a wall and moved toward the sound, using a hand to guide him in the dark. His other held the gun. As he made his way, he assessed the situation in his mind.

For starters, he'd pay big bucks for running shoes and toss these custom-made Italian loafers. *No offense, Raffaello.* But he didn't dare slip them off and ditch them. No telling what surprises he might find on the floor in this section of the garage.

His fingers felt a corner. He stopped and edged closer for a look. But before he got near enough, a faint light shone from below. He ducked and held his breath. The light cast a dim glow into the section of ramp where he crouched. The beam shifted, jerky then steady, manipulating the elongated shadows like ebony marionettes. Diego would have stayed put, but hearing a crying woman played havoc on his protective instincts.

It had to be Danielle. Even if it wasn't, he had no choice but to check it out. He inched his way to the corner and cocked his head left for a look.

Danielle stared up the ramp, catching his movement. A flashlight lay on the cement near her feet, the source of the light. It rocked in place like she'd kicked it. Her hands were tied to a section of pipe, the rest of her body sprawled on the floor. A gag stuffed in her mouth. When she saw him, she yanked at the pipe in a panic. She pulled at the bindings on her hands and let out a muffled scream. Maybe the poor girl thought he was one of them and would hurt her.

To be safe, Diego peered through the thin fringe of light into the shadows. No sign of Brogan or Cavanaugh. And a door to the far right was ajar. *Damn it!* They had escaped. Would Draper know about this exit? He stood and stepped quietly down the ramp, gripping his gun in a two-fisted grip. With his back to a wall, he searched for movement as he made his way toward her, eyes alert. He pointed his gun into the shadows at every point he was vulnerable from attack, searching for Cavanaugh and Brogan. Behind old crates and discarded oil barrels. The nooks and crannies in this section were pitch-black. It was like staring into a bottomless vat of crude oil. But nothing.

In his mind, it made sense that they were gone. Cavanaugh would want a head start to leave the country and find a safe haven with no extradition. But Brogan was unpredictable.

As he got closer, Danielle appeared even more agitated. Poor little thing. It broke his heart. She had survived so much. No child should have to know such a hell existed, and yet she had endured it. A casualty, her innocence and sense of safety had been shattered, never to be restored.

When he got close enough, Diego held up his hand to calm her.

"Shhh. I'm here to help," he whispered as he knelt by her. Setting the gun on the floor next to him, he retrieved one of his knives strapped to his leg. "I am a friend of your sister Rebecca."

"Oh, I'd say you and her sister are much more than friends." Brogan's voice came from behind him. "More like two fuckin' dogs in heat. The bitch and the mongrel."

Diego stopped cold, holding his breath. *Shit!* Without making a move, he shifted his eyes down to his gun. Could he grab it and turn fast enough? But another sound to his left complicated everything. A crunch of dirt underfoot. Someone else in the room. Cavanaugh? Diego couldn't hit two targets from a crouch with his back turned. He swallowed, his throat parched with tension.

Stooped by Danielle, Diego stayed put. He gambled Brogan wouldn't shoot him in the back. The bastard would want to see the look on his face as he died. So predictable . . . so very Brogan.

"Remember what I said a while back about the actions of a wise man? A smart man turns and walks

away. Why are you still here, Brogan? Feds are crawling all over the building. Before long, they'll have this
entire sector of the city under lockdown. I thought
you and Hunter were smarter than that."

"We are. That's why we have three guns pointed at
your head," Brogan gloated.

Three? Diego shut his eyes and took a deep breath.
He glanced down at Danielle. Even with the gag in
her mouth, her eyes said it all. His chance of saving
her had blown up in his face. And she knew it. *What
now?*

"Stand with your hands raised, but don't turn
around," Brogan ordered. Diego heard noise behind
him, coming from other parts of the room. When
he did as he was told, Brogan added a new wrinkle.
"Now turn around . . . real slow. And kick your gun
to one of my guys . . . nice and easy."

Diego palmed the knife in his hand and turned
around. With his foot, he slid the gun to the nearest
man. Cavanaugh stood next to the open hatch on the
left. He had probably been hiding in the shadows on
the other side of the door. When Diego locked his
gaze on the man, Cavanaugh couldn't resist a smug
remark.

"Glad you gave us one last shot at you, so to speak.
Very considerate."

Two of Brogan's men stood opposite each other,
with one stepping out from behind a group of barrels. Straight ahead, Brogan emerged from a niche in
a wall. The one flashlight on the floor kept them in
shadows.

Now all eyes were on his gun, but it wouldn't

take them long to see he had something wedged in his hand. Diego wanted to keep Brogan talking, but windy old Cavanaugh was his best chance.

"Leave this sickly girl, Hunter. She'll only slow you down. Take me instead," he offered.

"Now why would I do that, Diego?" Cavanaugh stepped closer.

"You might get away from here. Although with time ticking, you're losing any advantage you may have. But this girl won't keep Rivera off your ass. Not like I would."

Cavanaugh considered his point. He narrowed his eyes and pondered the notion. Brogan sneered, no doubt loving the idea of a slow torture when the bastard had more time. The other two men looked at each other, questioning the rationale of switching a weak girl for a man who could defend himself. But it wouldn't be their call.

"You have always impressed me with your eloquence and logical thinking," Cavanaugh stepped closer, near the edge of the light. "But I've got one problem with your proposition."

Diego shifted his gaze to Cavanaugh. "What's that?"

"Quite frankly, I'd prefer to know you're dead. And as for your old man, screw him. Your riddled body will serve as notice. Our merger is . . . terminated." He turned and headed for the open hatch door. "Mr. Brogan? Fire when ready . . . and put that sniveling girl out of her misery. Mr. McPhee? You're with me. Three guns are a bit . . . overkill, don't you think?" Cavanaugh stepped through the doorway, with

McPhee on his heels, and bellowed over his shoulder, "Mr. Brogan? You and Ellis join me on the other side of this tunnel. Don't dawdle. You know how I hate to wait."

Cavanaugh disappeared into the dark and never looked back. *The coward!* Now Diego settled his eyes on Brogan . . . the last face he would ever see.

Diego lowered his arms and crossed them over his chest, the knife in his grip.

"Hey, no one said you could move," Brogan protested.

"What are you going to do? Shoot me?" Diego took a deep breath. "You wouldn't deny a man his dignity, would you?"

"The way I'm gonna leave your bodies? Dignity will be the last thing you'll have."

With Brogan's snide comment, the other man grimaced and shrugged. "Come on, Matt. We don't have time for this. You know the old man ain't gonna wait for us. We gotta go."

Brogan clenched his teeth and shot a nasty glare at his man. "Ellis is right. Rude and an asshole, but he's got a point. We got a ride to catch. Believe me, I wish we had more time."

Brogan sneered and raised his gun. Diego tensed his body. No time left. He stepped in front of Danielle and gripped the knife, ready to move when . . .

"FREEZE! Lower your weapons."

Rebecca stood at the top of the ramp, gun in hand, locked and loaded with a double-fisted grip. And she had never looked more beautiful!

Brogan refused to budge and never lost sight of his target. He held his ground. His gun aimed at Diego, center mass. "I ain't movin', lady. Looks like we got a Mexican standoff here. But since I'm such a soft-hearted guy, I'm gonna give you a choice. Cavanaugh wants the Mex dead, so I got my orders. But as far as your sister goes, I'm leavin' that up to you. What's it gonna be?" He chuckled, his focus on Diego. "I kill the Mex, and we part company. Your sister goes home with you. You play this any other way, and your precious sister is the first to go." To his man, he ordered, "You hear that, Ellis? The Mex can't protect the girl from both of us. She's your new target."

His man shifted his aim to Danielle. Things had gone from bad to worse. Becca hesitated, her eyes on Diego. He stood with such confidence, arms crossed and defiant. And Danielle sat rigid against the wall, strangely quiet and cowering in Diego's shadow. Becca gritted her teeth. No way Brogan would get his way.

But when she looked back at Diego, he returned her stare and shrugged. "Sounds like a deal you shouldn't refuse, Rebecca."

It all happened so fast, Becca didn't see it coming. Diego flung an arm. Something left his hand. A loud heavy thump! Brogan was still smiling when the blade hit. He cried out and sputtered, staggering back with a knife jutting from his chest, to the hilt. He gaped down at it in disbelief like he'd sprung a new appendage.

Danielle cried out, the pitiable sound of her muffled scream gripped Becca, wrenching her gut with fear for her sister. Shocked by what happened, the other man gaped at Brogan and hesitated long enough for her to react.

"Gun down . . . Now! Or you're dead," she cried out.

The man named Ellis didn't lower his gun. She knew the twitchy aggressive look. He wouldn't be arrested. The bastard was only waiting for his chance. Becca rushed down the ramp to throw Ellis off and take him out of the equation. But Brogan reeled, still on his feet. A macabre and bloodied puppet.

Becca kept her options open. She stood within a yard of Ellis, his back to her. The man watched her from the corner of his eye, waiting for her to make a mistake. She gripped her weapon, her palms slick with sweat. Her eyes shifted to watch Brogan and Diego. But Ellis turned his head, a subtle flinch to keep her honest. She countered as he did, a deadly game of chicken.

Why hadn't Diego moved?

In reflex, Brogan stumbled forward and raised his arm, ready to fire. A look of shock forged on his face. Diego had a slim chance. He might have rushed him, gotten to the bastard before he fired his gun. But he chose to cover Dani—defenseless—shielding her sister with his body.

Oh my God! Becca's heart pounded, and her chest heaved. *Damn it!* Diego was going to die. Brogan aimed his gun just as Ellis dropped his shoulder to turn. Becca had no choice. She had to move. She yanked Ellis by the collar and jerked him back, keeping the man off-balance and in front of her. Using his body as a shield, she pointed her gun at Brogan.

It's going down. Move . . . MOVE! Brogan caught the sudden movement and turned his weapon on Becca. He fired. A deafening sound. Again and again. Ellis bucked in her hand as the bullets hit his chest. His convulsing body had become a liability, too heavy to hold up. She shoved him aside and took aim. Becca looked down Brogan's gun barrel, with him in her sights.

Take the shot! Take it!

Draper's com unit crackled to life. "Sir, we're investigating a report of gunfire. On a lower level. No telling how many rounds fired."

He recognized the voice of his HRT leader Martinez, and asked, "Could it be our guys?"

"We're still verifying our head count, sir. But I sent a team to check out the disturbance."

"Anyone see Diego Galvan or Detective Rebecca Montgomery?" Draper asked.

"Nothing so far, sir. But we're still accounting for the dead. Will keep you posted. Out."

Dead? The word gripped him, hard. And he thought he didn't do guilt.

Draper caught the eye of Lieutenant Santiago, standing a few yards away. The man heard the last report and looked worried. And he had to admit, his stomach had been knotted from the beginning. He had taken liberties with the lives of two people still unaccounted for, and he knew it. And Draper had coerced Joe Rivera to gain an inside informer, but he'd gotten much more in Diego Galvan. He couldn't have expected any better from an agent. If anything happened to him, it would hurt like he had lost one of his own.

"Damn it." He torqued his jaw and peered through the mass of bodies going in and out of the scene. Each face got a second look. But so far, nothing.

The operation shed its harried pace and settled into wrap-up mode with plenty for him to oversee. Spiraling lights, from emergency vehicles and police squad cars, streamed across the night sky and robbed the heavens of its stars. Urgent voices of medical crews and law enforcement personnel muted into background chatter in his mind. Yet when he needed to respond to his com unit, he picked up on every word. Filtered hearing from controlled chaos, he liked to call it.

And of course, an operation this size attracted the media, another reason for superior hearing filtration. He managed to rope off the news crews a couple of blocks away. Their camera lights might attract the wrong attention if one of the gunmen escaped. Keeping them at a distance had its benefits for now. When he was ready, there would be a press conference. Now, he had other priorities.

Up until a few minutes ago, he believed the underground facility had been secured. The wounded and dead were being carted out, and EMT units worked on the injured. The new gunfire added complications, but nothing his men couldn't handle. Thus far, all of the casualties had been Cavanaugh's men. His team had sustained injuries, but nothing life-threatening.

Best of all, every one of the abducted girls had been rescued . . . and then some. A greater head count

than he had expected. The girls had been malnour-
ished, dehydrated, and in need of medical attention.
But overall, the operation had been a success.

When Draper saw the hostages brought out one by
one, he fought a gnarl in his throat the size of Rhode
Island. Cavanaugh had been kidnapping young kids
from Mexico and bringing them into the United
States. He probably promised them work or simply
took them like he had before, knowing the missing
girls' parents would have no recourse across international borders.

Nineteen girls in all, ranging in ages from ten to
twenty-two.

As a father, it gripped him in the worst way, hitting
too close to home. No parent should have to endure
such a nightmare. Daughters were precious gifts. He
had been blessed with four. When he was a young
father, he had yearned for a son to pass on his name,
his futile and self-indulgent attempt at immortality.
Time and experience changed his view.

For him, a bond between father and child tran-
scended gender, in theory. But the connection between a father and daughter had its own unique
miracles. Seeing love reflected in his daughters' eyes,
and knowing it was meant for only him, had fulfilled
him in ways he hadn't expected.

But with this tragedy, Draper imagined the horri-
fying ruin of these young lives. Gazing into the eyes
of a broken child—*your broken child*—would have
torn him in two. And bastards like Cavanaugh deserved hell on earth and beyond for their sins.

"Hey, Mike. You're gonna want to see this." Lieutenant Santiago punched him in the arm and pointed. Two patrol cars pulled up with lights flashing in silent mode. Draper walked with him to the vehicles and looked in the backseats. Each squad car held a single man.

"Well, I'll be damned. Who the hell is that guy?" Draper didn't recognize the muscle man in the second car. "And how did we score the top dog? I thought he might have slipped through our net or not been here at all."

Draper bent down and glared at the man he'd been pursuing. Hunter Cavanaugh had never looked so good, handcuffed and riding in the back of a squad car. And the man sitting in the other vehicle looked scared enough to be a talker.

"The other guy's name is Stan McPhee. He's got a list of priors that should have him willing to talk. We thought it would be a good idea to keep them separated. I smell plea bargain for testimony," Santiago replied. "But under the heading of living right, you're not going to believe the stroke of luck we got with Cavanaugh."

"Oh this I've got to hear. I could use some good news."

"Seems one of our tactical teams secured a staging area in a condemned textile factory behind our target building. It gave us a good view of the back side of the facility." Santiago grinned.

And he talked loud enough for Cavanaugh to hear from inside the squad car. The old man rolled his eyes and slunk down into the seat, his jaw clenched as the lieutenant continued.

"One of our guys found an abandoned vehicle inside . . . a rather pricey Lexus. Only it's clean as a whistle and not lookin' so abandoned. In the course of carrying out their duties, the team staked out the car and waited. What started out as a fishing expedition landed us a whopper. The son of a bitch walked right into us. Didn't even put up much of a fight."

"How did he get over there?" Draper asked.

"Turns out these old buildings had tunnels under 'em. Most had been walled in as the owners took over the property. But there's evidence of new work done to install a coded hatchway at the facility where we nabbed Cavanaugh and McPhee. I bet we'll be able to trace who did the work and get them talking." Before Draper had to ask, the lieutenant added, "We sent a team to investigate the one Cavanaugh came waltzing out of. Murphy will report when he has something."

Draper shifted his gaze to Cavanaugh, staring through the side window. He opened the back door to the squad car and leaned in to get a better look at the man.

"Here's something I bet you'll agree with. You've had better days, right?" Draper glared, not expecting an answer. "What happened to Detective Rebecca Montgomery?"

Cavanaugh shifted in his seat and turned away. Draper thought the man would hang tough with the silent treatment, but the bastard wanted to twist the knife.

"Tragic really. I saw her gunned down by one of your own men. When you find her body, an autopsy will prove my point."

Draper took a deep breath and tried one more time. "Where's Diego Galvan?"

"The last time I saw him, he was breathing. Although you notice I used past tense. You see, I believe Diego suffered from an allergic reaction. A case of severe lead poisoning . . . with extreme prejudice. Don't bet on him walking out of there alive. You'd lose."

Something snapped inside him. Draper had no intention of being the object of Cavanaugh's amusement.

"Go ahead and have your fun, you cocky son of a bitch!" He leaned into the squad car, and whispered, "If Galvan is dead, so are you. And I don't have to pull the trigger. His father will get to your ass even if I can't touch you. I'll personally deliver my version of the case details to Rivera."

The smugness left Cavanaugh's face as fear slithered under the surface of his cool veneer. And Draper was only getting started.

"But there's one thing I *can* control. The system will be taking care of your room and board for a long time, but I'm personally goin' to see to your accommodations. Some lifer named Bruno will be salivatin' over your lily-white ass. Whoever said size didn't matter never met Bruno." Draper leaned closer, venom in his voice. "Every time he bends you over, think of me. 'Cause I'll be the one sticking it to you. In this lifetime, it's only a fraction of what you owe those girls."

To the cop behind the wheel, he said, "Get him out of my sight." Draper slammed the door on Cavanaugh, his heart hammering and stoked by red-hot anger as the patrol cars drove away.

He pictured Diego dead, and Draper's gut snarled. He couldn't catch his breath, his frustration and anxiety mounting. When he turned around, Santiago opened his mouth to say something, but Draper didn't want to talk about it. He didn't want to be consoled. And he sure as hell didn't want to be reminded of his decision to delay the rescue mission.

He walked back toward the old building . . . and waited. With a renewed fixation, Mike Draper searched the faces of everyone coming and going out of the warehouse.

But a man with a familiar gait caught his eye. He carried a teenage girl in his arms. And a woman walked alongside him. Draper couldn't confirm their identities for sure—something blurred his eyes—but he knew enough to call Santiago over.

"Hey, Arturo. Now *I've* got something you ought to see."

The lieutenant rushed over, his eyes following where Draper pointed. The man squinted into the distance until he recognized his detective, Rebecca Montgomery. Then his face lit up like a friggin' Christmas tree.

When he looked back at Draper, the lieutenant did a double take and nudged him with a shoulder. "Allergies. My eyes water this time of year, too. Mainly when I go all gooey inside like a marshmallow. And with my skin color . . . I look like damned S'mores."

Draper rolled his eyes and wiped a hand over his face, glaring at the man. "You say anything about this, and I swear . . ."

"Noooo. These lips are sealed." With a raised eyebrow, Santiago added, "Who would believe me anyway?"

"Damned straight."

Becca squinted into the floodlights, holding up a hand to shield her eyes. With cops and med techs rushing everywhere, she zeroed in on the ambulance units and headed for them.

When she stepped out of the darkness and into the light, reality hit hard. She was a changed woman. Nothing would be the same again. And even though her body was racked with pain, her heart soared as she walked beside Diego, who held Danielle in his arms. Second chances had that kind of effect on a woman. She drew in a deep breath, remembering how she had felt hours before—convinced none of them would make it out alive. She'd also learned a thing or two about hope.

Becca followed Diego to an ambulance. He carried her sister as if she were made of glass. And he kept whispering reassurances in Dani's ear. Becca only caught a few. His Hispanic accent sounded like a lovely melody that lingered in your heart long after it stopped playing.

"It's over. And you're safe, honey. Such a brave girl," he murmured. "Rebecca never gave up on you, Danielle. She never lost hope of finding you."

"Momma?" she whimpered, a tiny voice meant only for him. Dani clung to his neck, burrowing into his chest to hide her face from all the noise and commotion. He lowered his head to hers and held her close.

"Momma will see you at the hospital," he promised. "Your sister and I will pick her up on our way over, sweet girl."

When they got to the ambulance, Diego lowered Danielle onto a gurney and covered her with warm blankets head to toe. EMTs wanted to step in right away, but he waved them off to give Becca a moment with her sister.

Diego managed a smile when he looked over his shoulder at her, his face battered and bruised under the lights. Becca mouthed the words, 'Thank you', knowing it would never be enough. She cradled Dani's face in her hands and kissed her forehead, drinking in the feel and smell of her skin.

"I'm gonna take care of you for a while, little sister. For as long as you let me," she whispered. Danielle nodded, a tear rolling down her cheek as she clutched her hand.

Becca turned to the lieutenant, squeezing his arm in gratitude. And as tears filled her eyes, she held her chin high and looked at Mike Draper.

"Mr. Draper? I'd like you to meet a survivor. Danielle Montgomery. My sister."

CHAPTER 19

Becca jolted awake—her heart pumping adrenaline through her system—the cruelest of wake-up calls. Danielle's hospital room came into focus, along with the cramped chair she had fallen asleep in, but little else. Caught in the twilight between dreams and rational thought, her brain replayed what happened, when she had killed for the first time. She shut her eyes tight and steadied her breathing, but the hospital room faded from her senses. And Becca couldn't stop her mind from summoning the dark account of last night.

Drifting through murky shadows, she was alone again in the dark. Only the steady thud of her heart kept her company. Her memory of the stale oppressive air in the garage overpowered the medicinal hospital odor, merging time and place as if she were back there . . . facing Brogan.

It had all happened so fast at the time. But now, it replayed over and over in gut-wrenching slow motion. Every detail etched into her brain and branded her memory with crippling permanence. Becca saw his face again. She even smelled him.

The nine-millimeter Glock kicked in her hands, twice. Two rounds, center mass. Even now, she felt it. Her fingers tingled, and numbness radiated through her arms. Shots rang out, and the eerie echo punished her eardrums with a nasty piercing ring.

After the bullets hit his chest, Brogan staggered back and dropped to his knees, his chin sagging to his chest. In a last-ditch effort, he raised his head and glared at her, the old fire of contempt still burning in his eyes. She held her breath, waiting for him to take his last gasp. Fear gripped her heart like an icy fist, as if he'd get up one more time and finish the job he had started.

But eventually, his face went slack, and the flicker of life died in his eyes. And so had Matt Brogan. He slumped to the floor, his skull cracking on the cement with a sickening thud. For a long time, she couldn't move, couldn't speak. Her eyes burned. She couldn't close them. Rooted in place, Becca watched the blood spread across his chest and seep onto the cement in a dark thick pool. Diego rushed to her side, and she had been vaguely aware of his arms around her, but she couldn't take her eyes off . . . *him*.

Now, Becca held back tears and forced the nightmare from her mind. She pressed cold, trembling hands to her face as if she could wipe it all away. The trauma of her close call with death had been the culmination of an exhausting siege to her psyche that had started with Danielle's abduction. She understood the consequences of the ordeal, but living through it was another story.

A faint sound poked at the edges of her awareness. And a light pierced the dark. Slowly, she opened her eyes. The hospital room came back into focus. And she heard it again.

"Are you okay?" A whisper.

She turned toward the hospital bed and saw her sister.

"Becca. You okay?" Dani asked again.

She got up from her chair and stretched her back, walking toward the bed with a show of nonchalance she didn't feel. Becca still couldn't believe it. Dani was really here.

Bruises mottled her sister's body, and the dark circles beneath her eyes made her pale skin look gray and pasty under the dimmed hospital lights. Yet the most startling change was in her eyes. The natural twinkle of youthful innocence had been stripped away. Haunted eyes stared back, made old before their time. The stark change in Danielle broke her heart.

But Becca had another chance to do something about it and redeem herself with her family. Near the window, Momma lay curled up on a cot, fast asleep, the most content she'd seen her face in a very long time. Seeing her family together again, Becca wanted to pinch herself, to make sure she was really awake.

"Go back to sleep. It's still early." She smiled and stroked her sister's hair, leaning over to kiss her forehead.

"You've been crying." Dani reached a hand to her cheek.

Becca hadn't realized her tears showed on the outside. She wiped her face and took a deep breath. The cobwebs of her nightmare had crumbled but lurked under her skin.

"I'm okay, really. Nothing for you to worry about, Dani." Becca reassured her in a hushed tone, but a rush of emotion brought the tears back with a vengeance. "I can't believe . . . you're really here."

Dani's blue eyes pooled and her lips trembled. "Me too."

She knew her sister. Dani couldn't talk about it. Not yet.

"Excuse me. Detective Montgomery?"

Becca turned to see a nurse standing at the doorway. "Yes."

"I have a call for you at the nurse's station," she whispered. "Detective Paul Murphy. He didn't want to disturb your family by ringing the room directly. Would you like the call forwarded here or . . ."

"No, I'll take it out there. I'll be right behind you. Thanks."

Becca turned back to Dani and shrugged. "I've got to take this. I may be gone for a while, but I'll be back real soon, honey. You get some sleep, okay?" With drowsy eyes, Dani lifted a corner of her mouth, a fleeting smile. Becca kissed her sister's cheek and walked out the door.

She knew why Murphy had called so early. Last night, she asked for his help to close the Marquez case. Since it had been reassigned to him, Becca proposed they team up. But the paperwork would show it was all Murphy. A fair trade. In her mind, it didn't matter who got credit for the collar. Finding Isabel's killer had always been her greatest priority.

And with the morning papers no doubt carrying the story of the warehouse siege, time would be critical. She didn't want her suspect to *rabbit* out of town. When she got to the station, the nurse gestured for her to take the white phone on the counter.

"Murphy? It's Becca."

"We've got your suspect Mirandized and in custody. Interrogation room number 3. No one in or out, like you said. We'll be ready when you are."

"No lawyer?"

"Not so far."

"Okay, I'm on my way."

A fine line. It would come down to how well she walked one. Becca had nothing more than circumstantial evidence in her bag of tricks for a seven-year-old murder investigation. A necklace of dubious ownership found with the bones, contradictory interviews between potential suspects, and a dead man's version of the truth. She needed an undeniable confession that would hold up in court. Everything by the book. And yet, she'd have to pull out all the stops to manipulate her suspect into admitting to murder. A tough sell.

She opened the door to a room adjacent to interrogation room number 3. In the dark stood Paul Murphy in a rumpled suit that looked like he'd slept in it. He probably had. The pale light coming through the two-way mirror in the next room outlined his silhouette. He glanced over as she entered, then shifted his focus back to the woman sitting at the interrogation table. Sonja Garza.

"Hey, Becca. We took her cigarettes and lighter, told her about the ban on smoking in the building. That pissed her off. She's been stewing for almost an hour. Apparently, she's not a morning person either."

"An early-morning house call from the SAPD would tend to ruin your day."

It looked like Sonja had thrown on whatever lay crumpled on her floor. Or maybe she'd slept in her wrinkled white T-shirt and threw on jeans and an unzipped hooded sweat jacket to get out the door with an impatient Murphy. Either way, the dingy T-shirt made her skin appear washed-out under the fluorescent lights. And without her usual dark-eyed makeup, she lost five years. Becca pictured the girl she'd been in high school.

But most of all, Sonja lacked her usual edge. She picked at the chipped nail polish on her hands, looking bored. A complete contradiction to the fidgety nervous behavior she tried to hide. Jaw flinching, anxious eyes unable to stay focused for long. And without her smokes, Becca imagined Sonja's skin crawled with the ants of her nicotine addiction.

"She looks pretty ripe. How do you wanna play this?"

"Sonja and I have a rapport from the times I've interviewed her. But she's lied to me, thinks she can do it again. I'm gonna nail her this time." Becca shifted her gaze to Murphy. "I need this interrogation to go off without a hitch, Paul. I've got less than zero on evidence, circumstantial at best. The DA will want more. I need a confession, and it's got to be solid."

"How are we gonna get it?"

She liked hearing Murphy use the word "we." Considering she had wanted to rearrange his face once, and he'd probably had similar sentiments, they had come a long way.

"Matt Brogan is going to help."

"The dead guy?" Murphy stared at her as if she'd lost her mind. Maybe she had.

"Yeah. I have no intention of resurrecting the bastard, but he's going to make a brief comeback. Brogan'll play his part in nailing Sonja one last time. And I suspect he'd appreciate the irony."

Becca explained her game plan. Armed with little more than a heaping mound of horse hockey and nerve to match, she walked into the interrogation room with Murphy.

"Well, it's about time. I've been waitin' over an hour." Sonja's eyes flared, her jaw tight.

"Yeah, sorry about that. But I'm sure we'll be able to wrap this up pretty quick with your cooperation." Becca sat across from Sonja and pointed a hand toward Murphy. "I'm sure you've met . . ."

"Yeah, yeah. Detective Muscle for Brains. Cooperation on what?"

Murphy glared at the woman and stood with hands in his pants pockets. He liked to move around the room, forcing her to watch him.

"We have a few questions for you, regarding Isabel

Marquez. Detective Murphy has read you your rights. Do you want an attorney present during this interview?"

Sonja sagged into her chair, her eyes looking from Becca to Murphy. "I got nothin' to hide. No, I don't need no lawyer. Let's get this over with."

It always amazed Becca how frequently suspects waived their rights to an attorney to appear as if they had nothing to hide. Nothing like cop shows on TV. Becca had counted on Sonja's doing exactly that. And she didn't disappoint. In a show of apathy, the woman pulled at a strand of her hair and inspected it for split ends. No doubt a poor substitute for a cigarette.

All interrogation room interviews were videotaped and recorded to document the process and the treatment of the suspect. Special permission from the detainee was not required. Becca aimed to record irrefutable evidence to be used in court by the district attorney and avoid the pitfalls of making a contribution for the defense.

After she asked Sonja a few questions to establish her relationship with the dead girl for the record, Becca hit her with the first nail in her coffin. She knew Sonja would lie straight up, the start of her slippery slope.

"When was the last time you saw Matt Brogan?"

The shocked and indignant expression on Sonja's face told Becca she had struck a chord. She gave her the opportunity to tell the truth, knowing the woman would choose a different path. Lying had become far too easy for Sonja, a weakness Becca hoped to capitalize on.

"You mean the guy that raped me?" She flung both hands in the air and shook her head, a display of exasperation. "Do you think I got him on my speed dial? I can't pinpoint the exact date, but the night he raped me would be close enough, wouldn't it?"

"So approximately seven years ago. Is that correct?" Becca leaned on the table, forcing Sonja to meet her eyes.

"Yeah."

"And you haven't seen him since that night?"

"No, thank God. Like I told you before, people with money don't exactly travel in my social circle. Why? I thought this was about Isabel."

Murphy walked behind Becca and caught Sonja's attention, a distraction from the woman's question. She returned his glare, her outward hostility toward him showing, the man who stole her smokes and woke her too damned early. Now he slouched against the wall with the two-way mirror, playing his head game . . . and loving it.

"And you also said Isabel Marquez tried to recruit you into prostitution, to work for Matt Brogan. But you turned her down because you couldn't go through with it. Is that an accurate statement?"

"Yeah, sure." She fidgeted in her seat and heaved a dramatic sigh, latching her eyes on to Murphy. "What did you do with my smokes, man? I better get 'em back. They cost money."

"Smoking is banned in the building. We wouldn't want you to break any laws while you're here." He slathered on the sarcasm.

Sonja rolled her eyes and sank into her chair,

ignoring him again. Becca knew how tough a job *that* was.

"Look, I already told you all this," the young woman said.

"Yes, you did. And you also told me Isabel arranged for you to attend a party at the Cavanaugh estate around that same time. Can you tell me about it?"

Sonja regurgitated the same story she had told Becca before, nearly verbatim.

"So Matt Brogan insisted Isabel set you up. He raped you and allowed others at the party to do the same. Is that true?"

"Yeah, Isabel set me up all right. And she left me there . . . with them."

"And even though you believed you were drugged, you remember enough of the incident to make this claim."

"You don't forget somethin' like this, lady. I still get nightmares."

"Why do you think she did it?"

"Because of Brogan. He's a mean son of a bitch. When he wants somethin', he gets it."

"And he wanted you." Becca didn't bother to attach a question to her statement, knowing Sonja couldn't resist elaborating.

"Yeah, he wanted me all right. He wanted what he couldn't have otherwise. Guys like that don't take no for an answer. I found out the hard way."

"How did Isabel feel about Brogan's interest in you? Did she ever act jealous?"

Sonja raised her voice and clenched her fists on the table until her knuckles went white.

"*She hated it!* The bastard *never* got enough. For him, an innocent young girl had a target on her back. Fair game and open season year-round. Isabel despised him for it, but she was too weak to say no and walk away. For whatever reason, she needed him like an addict needs a fix. Running with a guy like that? She was bound to get into trouble."

A glimpse of personal truth. Becca knew with the right question, centered on Sonja's feelings for Brogan, the woman might project her own emotion onto Isabel, a coy game. She liked to dangle a bit of truth in front of Becca, her pattern of lying.

"And he was the one who bought her the expensive gold necklace, the one with a pendant shaped like a heart with diamonds on it. Isabel told you Brogan bought it for her, right?"

"Yeah, she did. She bragged about it in fact. Tried to tell me if I worked for him, I could have the same things, like it would be enough." Sonja leaned her elbows onto the table, her eyes fixed on Becca. "You know, you should really be talking to Brogan about all this. But you promised to keep my name out of it. He'd kill me if he knew. You won't tell him, will you?"

"No, he won't be hearing it from me." Becca raised an eyebrow and crossed her arms. Behind her, Murphy cleared his throat and shuffled his feet.

"'Cause I think the son of a bitch killed Isabel and dumped the body where no one would find it. She knew too much. I don't know how or where he did it, but I got a gut feeling he's behind it." Sonja narrowed her eyes. "Hey, why all the questions about Matt Brogan? Sounds like you believe me. He's a sick, twisted guy."

"No more twisted than a woman who arranges a rendezvous with the bastard who raped her seven years ago. A little mattress mambo at a fleabag motel off Guadalupe Street sounds like more than just talk. It sounds like a history of lies and cover-ups."

Sonja's eyes grew wide, and her mouth opened. Her face twitched with a nervous tic of her lips.

Murphy turned a chair around next to Sonja, and straddled it, his elbows on the backrest. "Maybe you got a different definition of hard feelings. Sounds real cozy to me."

"You see where I'm coming from, Sonja?" Becca gestured with her hands. "Matt Brogan is hard to shut up once he gets going, especially when he's got a different version of the truth. And you lying to Murphy and me is proof enough you're hiding something. You've already lied about how well you knew the man who allegedly raped you. Hell, for all we know you've got him on your Christmas card list. That makes no sense if what you said is true. He didn't rape you."

"He told you that?"

"And a lot more. Care to revise any of your previous statements?" Becca asked.

"Matt's here? God, is he pissed?"

"He's been better." Becca cocked her head to one side.

A panicked look spread across Sonja's face. "If he knows I said anythin', he'll kill me."

"You should have thought about that before you lied to me . . . and implicated him."

Implying a dead guy was alive and kicking wouldn't

play too well with the church crowd. But police used all sorts of tactics to get a confession, part of the fine line Becca walked. This session would be recorded and used in court. If the defense screamed foul, they would be opening a nasty can of worms about Sonja's relationship to Brogan, allowing the prosecution to pick at an old festering wound in front of a jury. It wouldn't be worth the risk.

Sonja raked fingers through her hair, then clasped her hands to the back of her neck. She looked deep in thought, considering her options and taking a stroll through her maze of lies. The woman released her grip and let her arms land on the table with a thump.

"You lied about the necklace, too." Becca rocked forward on the edge of her seat and watched the color drain from Sonja's face. "Brogan said so. And considering he's the one who allegedly bought the thing according to you, that's another strike against your version of reality. The guy's got a pretty healthy ego, but with your track record of lying, I'd say he's the odds-on favorite to pull ahead in the stretch. And as for him raping you? He said he never needed to. You were all over him."

"The rape happened. I swear."

For the first time, a tear rolled down Sonja's cheek. Before yesterday, Becca might have believed she'd been capable of remorse, but not today.

"Oh, Matt had plenty to say about the rape."

"He told you?" Sonja asked, shock on her face. She winced and wrapped her arms over her chest and rocked back and forth. After a long moment, she opened up. "He forced me to get Isabel to the party. You don't know what he's like."

"You knew Isabel would be raped. You could've said no."

"Not to Brogan." Her eyes glazed over. "Isabel *was* the party. Him and his friends were waiting for us to get there . . . Isabel to get there. I slipped something into her drink, thinking it would make it easier for her to take it. And maybe she wouldn't know I had anything to do with what happened. But Brogan screwed that up, too. He kept her after the party . . . for his men. No drugs."

More tears, but Becca got the feeling these tasted bitter with regret, more from getting caught than any real remorse.

"He made me watch, you know." Sonja grimaced, and her lips trembled. "Matt, the guys at the party, and his men after . . . the bastard made me watch it all. I thought I loved him once, but you don't love a guy like him. He's a user."

Becca had a sudden appreciation for Sonja and Brogan's mutual attraction. But her heart ached for Isabel Marquez, the innocent girl caught in the middle. Her only fault was being a poor judge of character. And despite Rudy and Victor's efforts to protect their sister, the brothers couldn't be everywhere at once. At some point, they had to let go and hope Isabel would be safe and make the right choices. But that didn't happen. And Becca had a taste of how they must have felt after their worst imaginings had been trumped by the reality of her murder.

"What did she do? Threaten to go to the cops?"

"Not at first. I almost convinced her to forget it. I told her no one would believe her against rich guys like that. And she had no real proof it even happened. So much time had passed, but I guess it ate away at her. 'Cause after the argument she had with her brother Rudy, things changed."

"So you killed her."

Sonja shut her eyes tight and drew a frazzled breath. "It's just that . . . Isabel was gonna ruin everything. I couldn't let that happen." Silence. She clenched her teeth and stared off into space.

"Isabel was going to tell the police about her rape. Tell me what happened?"

"After her brother left the theater, she started talking about what happened at that fuckin' party. Right in the open. The workers took off after all the shouting, but anyone coulda heard her if they walked back in. She didn't care. Her brother Rudy got her all upset. Isabel never told him what happened, but she thought if she told the cops, it would be like confession and wipe her slate clean somehow. God would forgive her. She could be so stupid like that."

Becca tightened her jaw after Sonja called Isabel stupid for wanting to do the right thing, trivializing rape as if it were a silly parking ticket. But she needed to keep her talking and resisted the urge to let her own emotions show.

"She was going to blow the whistle, and you couldn't let her do that."

"Exactly. I had no choice. I kept thinkin' about how I'd be arrested and do jail time. Even if I could live with that, Matt would've been arrested, with his party guests dragged into it. A big mess. He had a lot more at stake. Just like now, I'd be better off in jail, away from him. And it sounds like he's headin' the same direction. Good for me."

So she was protecting Brogan? *Yeah, right*, Becca thought. And oh what a difference seven years makes. Now she couldn't care less if he's put in jail. Sonja's smoke and mirrors were completely transparent now. How could she have been so blind to her lies? Becca resisted the urge to glance at Murphy. If Sonja had found out about Brogan being dead, this interrogation would have been over before it began.

"Tell me what happened," Becca prompted.

Sonja heaved a sigh, her eyes engrossed in her memory. "I stood in her way, shoving her. But she wouldn't back down. When Isabel slapped me, I lost it. The bitch! She didn't care what would happen to me. I grabbed the first thing I found. Some kind of hammer. And I hit her over the head with it. There was so much blood."

She cried. Her sobs echoed in the room until a lumbering silence took over. Becca narrowed her eyes and caught Murphy's eye. He gave a slight nod, letting her know he thought the same as she did. Becca had gotten what she wanted—a solid confession— but it left her empty knowing Isabel's life had meant so little to Sonja Garza. A pawn in her sex play with Matt Brogan.

Becca kept her composure and moved on. "What did you do then?"

Sonja wiped her cheeks with a sleeve of her sweat jacket, choking on her words. "I panicked. Didn't know what to do. I shut all the doors and locked them, so no one would come in. The blood . . . I couldn't . . . I called Matt using my cell . . . and waited."

Just when Becca thought there would be no more twists to Sonja's story, the woman zinged a curve-ball over home plate. But Becca couldn't afford to react. If Brogan were alive and partial to talking, he would've mentioned something as trivial as dispos-ing of a corpse.

Only Isabel hadn't been dead after Sonja struck her. She had been alive. Unconscious, but alive. Sonja waited for Brogan while Isabel's heart beat in her chest, a faint pulse. The outcome would have been the same, but the callousness of the crime made her sick. Becca fought the knot wedged in her throat.

"Tell me *your* version of the story."

Sonja shrugged with depraved indifference. "I can't believe I had to convince that son of a bitch to help me. I would have done much more for him."

More than murder? Becca shook with anger, but held it in. Finally, Sonja looked up and raised her chin.

"You'll find Isabel buried in the old theater, to the right of the stage behind a brick wall. She's been there all along. Brogan bricked the body in the wall with the cement and equipment left behind. And he had Cavanaugh suspend the renovation for a while, to make sure no one would notice the smell and the finished wall. From what Matt said, he never told Cavanaugh what happened, but the old man did him a favor, no questions asked."

Out of the blue, Sonja laughed, a coldhearted

hollow sound. "Matt dumped me after that. Threatened me with a knife to stay away. But knowin' what I did and where the body was buried had been his insurance I'd do what he said. Since he helped me, guess the insurance worked both ways."

Becca couldn't hide her reaction this time. Sonja confessed to killing a friend and reduced the murder to nothing more than a catalyst to a breakup with her boyfriend. Unbelievable!

"Sonja Garza. You're under arrest for the murder of Isabel Marquez. In your own handwriting, I want you to make a statement, telling what happened to Isabel. Then sign and date it." She shoved a notepad across the table, along with a pen.

Becca would wait until she had a written confession and a signature before telling her Isabel had been alive when Brogan bricked the girl in the wall. For most people, that knowledge would make a difference on the guilt barometer. But in this case, Becca suspected the news would have little significance, no more concern than a fender-bender in a rental car.

Sonja wrote a few lines and stopped. She looked up at Becca and asked, "Can I have a cigarette now?"

The cold dead eyes of a killer stared back. No remorse in sight.

CHAPTER 20

TWO WEEKS LATER

This time, Becca had taken a real vacation, taking the first steps to mend her soul. Danielle spent a couple of days in the hospital but was eager to come home. Momma insisted both her girls live under one roof for a while. How could Becca refuse? The gesture touched her heart, along with her mother's willingness to join her and Danielle in therapy.

Dani wouldn't be alone on her road to recovery.

And today, another milestone had been realized. A bittersweet one. Isabel Marquez had come home, too. Over a week ago, a positive ID had been made using the family's DNA, and the bones had been released for burial. Although today's memorial had been a private affair, only a few close friends and family, Diego had pulled strings to make the day solemn for the Marquez family. And in his mind, only one church would do.

On Main Plaza in downtown San Antonio, the San Fernando Cathedral had the honor of being the first parish in Texas, its construction completed in 1755. The historic site was the crown jewel of the Old Spanish Missions, with an elaborate stone façade, ornate stained glass, an impressive pipe organ, and a hand-carved stone baptismal font. Pope John Paul had blessed the church with one of his visits. And politicians, ambassadors, and governors had become a part of the cathedral's distinctive history.

Diego had insisted Isabel deserved nothing less. And he spared no expense, paying for all the arrangements of the tasteful service.

Angelic voices of a small choir heralded the passing of a life cut short. Incense and the aroma of flowers filled the air, along with a sense of relief that the Marquez girl would finally be put to rest. A moving and solemn memorial service, no less extraordinary than Isabel's brief life.

Now, the meager funeral procession pulled into the San Fernando Cemetery on Castroville Road, not far from the Marquez home. Across a piercing blue sky, faint wisps of clouds graced the horizon. And the sun reflected off the glittery offerings left at other grave markers. To honor the dead, tinsel and baubles danced and fluttered in the breeze. A sea of loving mementos, the striking image never failed to touch Becca. Whole families often spent Sunday afternoons at the cemetery, bringing small children and picnic lunches—a celebration of the lives that came before. Here, the dearly departed were never truly forgotten.

Becca parked on the edge of grass and got out of

her car. Danielle and Momma had come along, sensing the importance of this day for Becca. Her mother
and sister clung to each other now, standing under
the dark green awning. And Isabel's shiny copper
casket was covered in lilies and white blush roses.
Innocence lost. On one side of the grave, a solemn-
faced Mariachi quartet waited to strike the first note,
another part of the culture Becca had grown to respect. Diego hadn't forgotten a single detail.

He stood at her side, holding her hand. And as Father
Victor Marquez began a graveside tribute to his sister,
Isabel, Becca leaned her head against Diego's shoulder.
He drew her close, a welcomed intimacy. And she
took advantage of his warmth. She nuzzled her arms
around his waist with eyes shut tight, fighting back a
sudden rush of tears. As Becca breathed in the heady
aroma of flowers, the rich smell of overturned earth,
and Diego's subtle cologne on the breeze, a wave of
peace swept over her. A fragile stillness.

It would take time for her to feel worthy of happiness. But now she had hope the day would come.

"It was a beautiful service, Father Victor." Becca
made a point to speak to the priest in private, away
from the crowd hovering near Isabel's grave.

"Diego Galvan had much more to do with that," the
cleric insisted. "My mother will never forget this day.
Isabel's life honored at the San Fernando Cathedral?
You have no idea what it meant to her . . . and to Rudy
and me. We can never repay Diego's generosity."

"And he wouldn't expect anything in return. I have
gotten to know his . . . quiet ways."

Father Victor smiled, warm and genuine. "Yes, I can see that."

When she returned his gesture with heat coloring her cheeks, the priest added, "You have a look of contentment about you. I can see it in your eyes. Different from the woman who came to my family's home a lifetime ago."

"Not many people get a chance to do things over again." Becca gazed over her shoulder at Danielle and her mother, talking to Diego in the warm sun. "I've been blessed."

"Yes, I read about your sister in the newspaper. Just like our Isabel finally coming home, you experienced a miracle of your own."

"Yes . . . a miracle." She hadn't thought of it that way until now. "An amazing blessing."

It puzzled Becca to hear that Father Victor considered the return of Isabel's body to be a miracle for his family. She supposed time and dashed hopes had convinced him that his sister would not walk through their front door. His mother would never embrace her daughter again. His brother Rudy would not experience the privilege of asking a sister's forgiveness. And he would not play the part of older brother to guide her, protect her . . . save her. Isabel's burial and the peace of mind of his family were all Victor had left.

Perhaps miracles were still miracles, no matter what the size.

"You were at the Imperial Theatre the morning after the fire. Weren't you, Father?" she asked, squinting into the sun. The arson part of her investigation still remained open.

Her question, out of the blue, surprised him. But a look of resignation on his face told her she would hear the truth . . . finally. How could he bend it standing next to Isabel's grave? After all, his sister had been the reason for the priest's subterfuge. He had no more reason to lie now . . . *except one.*

"Yes, I was." He looked away and took a deep breath, waiting for her to go on.

"You set the arson fire hoping Isabel would be found. And I'm sorry . . . sorry we couldn't find Isabel without your help. But you had another reason to put up roadblocks whenever I questioned you."

He nodded, his face grimacing with the memory.

"You were protecting Rudy. Weren't you?" She locked eyes with Father Victor. The look of shock on his face wrenched her heart. She shifted her attention to Rudy Marquez, standing among the mourners. The young man looked lost even in a crowd.

"Please don't make me answer that question, Rebecca. I don't want God to hear those words come from my mouth." His lips trembled as a single tear drained down his cheek.

"Please . . . hear me out. I know about the fight Rudy had with Isabel at the theater on the day she went missing. I think you knew about it, too. That's why you thought he needed your protection."

Father Victor shut his eyes tight—his mouth moving in a silent prayer—a priest trapped in his own brand of hell on earth. She had to set things straight.

"Don't worry, Victor. Rudy won't hear about it from me, but he does need your help whether he admits it or not. Your brother will always carry the burden of his guilt . . . because he can't rectify it. Not now." She reached for the cleric's arm and squeezed it. "I'll get a chance to fix things with Danielle and my mother. It's up to me now to make a difference. But Rudy won't ever get that opportunity. He needs you more than he would ever say. Don't let him ride this out alone. I know how that feels."

"I understand. I'll do what I can. I've asked to be relocated to San Antonio, to be with my family. I owe my brother that much. He's a good man, but Isabel's loss has taken a toll on him . . . on us all." A sadness darkened his face. "I still can't believe what happened. Sonja had been Isabel's friend."

"No, Father. She never really was." Becca took a deep breath. "I don't want to ruin today, but you and I should talk about the details of this case before it goes to trial. You'll have to prepare your family for what they may hear. But I want you to know Isabel was a good girl. She tried to do the right thing, and she loved her family very much. Never doubt the Isabel you honored and cherished. She's someone I would have been proud to call a friend."

Father Victor's face softened into a show of relief, a long-awaited release of his burden. His tears were for a different reason now. And as far as the Imperial Theatre arson case went, the priest would not be charged. Becca had only her suspicions and no hard evidence. Not enough to make a case. The Marquez family had suffered enough.

"Thank you, Rebecca. May the Lord bless you on your journey." He raised his hand and made the sign of the cross.

"He already has, Father Victor. But a good word from you can't hurt." She smiled. "Take care of your family. Let them mourn. Help them heal. And I'll call you soon. But first, I'd like you to meet my family."

As she introduced Danielle and her mother to Father Victor, Becca's mind drifted to Sonja. During the course of her investigation, she had always had a blind spot when it came to her. She wanted to believe her lies because to comprehend what really happened was darker than Becca wanted the world to be.

In the end, Sonja confessed because she thought Brogan was alive and would refute her story, big-time. A major finger-pointing session with her coming out on the losing end. And she thought by serving jail time, she might avoid the man's revenge for her betrayal, a strong motivator.

But being dead was a powerful hurdle to overcome, even for Matt Brogan.

When Sonja found out what happened to him, she stuck with her confession, something Becca hadn't expected. She wanted to believe guilt played a mean game of devil's advocate and persuaded the woman to own up to her crime. But Becca had grown far too cynical to buy it. Sonja had been a willing participant in her own destruction. No repentance required. Maybe jail would be a step up to the life she had lived.

And the little gold necklace with the heart? Sonja bought it for herself. She gave the name of the jeweler, and their records were pulled from archives, giving police another piece of the puzzle. It turned out Matt Brogan wasn't the romantic type after all. Imagine that? In the fight with Isabel, the necklace was torn off Sonja's neck. Her CSI guy, Sam Hastings, confirmed the chain had been broken—one of the reasons it wasn't found dangling from the neck of Isabel's skeleton but lying on the ground.

So much of Sonja's story evolved around Matt Brogan, but he was probably only an excuse—an accelerant to her self-immolation. She had made contact with him again, hoping for a spark of what they'd had before. But when she realized that door had been shut for good, she accused him of Isabel's murder to get the monkey off her back once and for all. She thought the police would buy it. After all, Brogan fit the killer mold far better than Sonja, the consummate actress.

But the bastard was dead. He got off light.

Was Sonja a coldhearted killer and pathological liar or a sick, broken girl? It wasn't Becca's place to say. The justice system and court-appointed psychiatrists would determine that. The insanity plea was a tough uphill battle in the state of Texas. All Becca wanted was to set the record straight on the life of Isabel Marquez.

A higher power would sort out the rest.

THE RIVERWALK
DOWNTOWN SAN ANTONIO, 10 P.M.

During the time she stayed with her mother and Dani, Becca let Diego stay at her place. He had to give up his posh digs at the Cavanaugh estate, a hardship he embraced with open arms. Becca hadn't realized how much he hated living there, even when the arrogant Cavanaugh wasn't around. Diego preferred a simpler existence. And living at her small condo on the river was as basic as life got.

Standing in her kitchen, Becca poured Diego a refill on his wine. She had insisted on cooking dinner for him this time. The Chardonnay reflected golden light onto the counter, shimmering from the crackling fire in her hearth. She breathed a sigh and gazed across the room. He looked at home sitting on her sofa, a sight she could get used to.

Dressed in jeans and a soft flannel shirt, he looked comfortable, a new side to him she wanted to know better. His shirt felt warm and inviting to the touch, but not as good as skin on skin. Seeing his handsome face reflecting the warm flicker of the fire stirred her libido.

But first things first. She had a point to make.

"You brought a knife to a gunfight, Diego." Becca handed him the wineglass and scrunched in close, nuzzling into the warmth of his chest. "Next time, you might consider a better plan."

"Next time?" He laughed out loud, a sound Becca would never tire of hearing. But Diego's smile quickly faded, dimples and all. "I don't want to even think about you going through that again."

He stroked her hair, his dark eyes conveying what she knew he held in his heart.

"Look, I get it. You don't want to talk about it," he said, understanding her use of humor as a shield to protect her tender underbelly. "But you took a risk coming after me the way you did, Rebecca."

"I figured if Dani had been rescued by Draper's

guys, then she was already safe. If not, she'd need both of us."

"I like the sound of that. Us."

Even with her eyes mesmerized by the fire, she heard the subtle smile in his voice.

"So do I." Her crooked grin faded, nudged out by the knot in her throat. "And it *did* take the two of us. You risked *your* life to protect Danielle. It scares me to think how close Brogan came to killing her . . . and you. I still have nightmares, but I won't ever forget what you did."

She breathed a sigh and laid her head on his chest, holding him close. Maybe they did need to talk. Closure *was* important.

"No more than you did for me. I had no choice really. If anything would have happened to you or Danielle, living with that pain for the rest of my days . . . would have been no life at all. And I'm done with merely existing in a fog. I have to reclaim my life, take it back."

"Oh yeah, I hear that." Becca rose and looked into Diego's eyes, taking a chance she might get lost in them . . . for days . . . weeks even. But a lingering thought ruined the moment.

"I guess Joe Rivera is eager to get you home." She'd hoped to sound casual. "You've been gone a long time."

"Yeah, he is. I'm leaving the day after tomorrow," he said. Becca couldn't help it. She couldn't hide her shock. The news gripped her heart like a vise. But when Diego saw her strong reaction, he smiled with a tenderness she had grown to love. "Just to pack my things and have a few days with my father. I'll be gone a week, but I'm coming back home . . . to you. My life is here with you, Rebecca."

She replayed his words in her head, over and over, before she understood what he meant. Diego had made a place for her in his future, and she couldn't imagine a life without him in it. The ticking clock in her head unwound, releasing the sense she might wake up tomorrow, and he'd be gone. Diego was coming back . . . to her. And they had all the time in the world.

"And I think I've been waiting for you . . . to begin *living* mine." Her eyes blurred with tears.

Diego pulled her to him, his lips pressed to hers, with the ambrosial taste of Chardonnay on his tongue. She felt the arousal of his body, his hunger for her. Yet he cradled her face in his hands with such gentleness. She never felt so loved . . . so cherished.

When she burrowed into his arms once more, resting her cheek against his shoulder, Becca remembered the first time Diego kissed her. "You know, I started our relationship with blackmail. Who says crime doesn't pay."

She hugged him tight, listening to the deep and soothing rumble of laughter in his chest. Breathing in the seductive smell of his skin, Becca looked out her window. She watched the cypress trees dance under the colorful lights off the Riverwalk, stirred by a winter breeze. She always wanted to remember this moment, when she knew her heart belonged to him.

"I love you, Diego."

He kissed the top of her head and pulled her close.

"What took you so long, sweet Rebecca?"

The following is an excerpt from

NO ONE LEFT TO TELL

Available May 2008

WAREHOUSE DISTRICT
SOUTH CHICAGO

On the trail of money, Mickey Blair sniffed out opportunity like most men chased skirts—one led to the other, but cash never got a headache. The piece of paper fluttered in his hand as a brisk wind caught its frayed edge. He steadied it with spread fingers to read his own scribbling and looked up, squinting against the cold to verify the warehouse number. The place was a pit. He stuffed the crumpled paper into his overcoat. He'd hoped for better arrangements from his potential new client. The e-mail he had received late yesterday was cryptic, but he was confident the job would be simple and the money irresistible. The best kind of incentive. A glance at his Rolex assured him he wasn't late.

With the sun fading into the layers of dark clouds along the horizon, the bite in the air stung his cheeks.

Large, wet flakes accumulated on the ground, defying the swirling gusts. With a sideways glance, he caught sight of his black Mercedes parked to the left. His latest toy. He'd soon have it stored for winter. Time to break out his SUV. His work provided a nice little nest egg. Images of white sand beaches filtered through the cold. The imagined scent of coconut teased his senses. He pictured grains of sand clinging to his dark skin slick from tropical oils. Before long, he'd be set for life.

Killing was a lucrative business.

Safely locked away until he needed it for a job, his custom-made Heckler & Koch sniper rifle had been a good investment. At his age, he had cultivated a dependable, discreet reputation, built up over the years. Mickey enjoyed the best of both worlds—flying below the radar of law enforcement while reaping all the benefits of his deserved notoriety. The art of assassination provided him a life worth living. He loved irony, when it suited him. A smile influenced his swagger as he approached the side entrance to the building. His unfastened overcoat buffeted in the breeze. Instinctively, he felt for his gun, a SIG Sauer secured in its leather holster under his suit jacket.

After a tug at the metal door, he rubbed his palms together to wipe away the rust and dirt, careful not to soil his coat or Armani suit. Once inside, he shortened his breaths to lessen the intake of stale air and surveyed the carcass of the deserted old warehouse. But his next breath morphed into an instinctive gasp when the door slammed shut behind him. He turned and heard a key slip into the lock. The dead bolt slid

into place. And he caught the distinct sound of someone running away. He yanked at the door, the filth of
the cement floor crunching underfoot. Locked.

"What the hell?" he muttered under his breath,
then called out, "This isn't funny, you sick bastard."

Slowly, he gaped over his shoulder into the cavernous space. In the split second his eyes oriented to the
murky and cluttered interior, the lights went out.
Complete darkness. His equilibrium messed up, he
couldn't see his damned hand in front of his face. He
raised his weapon, fingers tensed against the grip.

"If this is some kind of joke, someone's gonna get
shot!" He raised his voice, covering his tension with
attitude. "I don't have time for this."

"Make time." A low voice assumed familiarity. An
echo disguised its origin. "I made time for you."

The sound mutated to a whisper, prickling his skin.

"Do I know you?" Mickey swallowed hard. His eyes
searched the dark for anything at all. No answer. The
man wasn't giving him a chance to locate his hiding
place, providing a target for Mickey's SIG Sauer.

A glimmer toward his left drew his attention.
Heading toward the flicker of light, he felt his way
along a barrier of varying height, stubbing the tips of
his shoes. In no time, he lost his way. He couldn't tell
where he had entered the old building.

Thud! Thwack! Two rounds hit his chest. A burst
of liquid burned his nostrils. Vapor stung his eyes.
Silenced gunfire? His hands reached for the sore
spots under his suit, rubbing the welts. Anger got the
better of him. He returned fire. Pointing his gun into
the dark, he shot twice before thinking. Muzzle flash

blinded him. Fingers pressed against his eyelids, he squeezed his eyes shut and listened to the ricochet.

"Who are you?" he shrieked. Spittle ran down his chin. Feeling like a cat with nine lives, his hostility bristled. If the pellets had been real bullets, he would've been dead. "What kind of game are you playing here?"

The air was stagnating and thick. Sweat trickled from his brow, nearly blinding him with its sting. He leaned against something firm. All he needed was time to think. *God, think!*

"Who the hell are you people?" he shouted. More than one person hid in the dark. Strange animal noises erupted overhead. The muffled sound of laughter mocked his torment, the only reply.

Although he couldn't be certain, it appeared they were herding him through a maze of obstacles. They pounded him with pellets of some kind. The animal calls only got worse—clamoring all around him. Primal instinct kicked in, and panic gripped him hard, squeezing his chest. Remembering to close his eyes, Mickey fired two shots, reminding them he would be dangerous up close.

"There's been a mistake. I was asked to come here. Some guy had a job for me," he cried, trying to reason with his faceless attackers.

What the hell had he done? The irony wasn't missed on him. Normally the predator, now the tables were turned. This time, *he* would be hunted.

Blood boiled under the surface of his skin. He shrugged out of his overcoat and kicked it aside. Tugging at his tie, he pulled it over his head and hurled it into the dark, not caring where it landed. Only a week ago, he'd bought the designer tie, more impressed by its price tag. Now, he didn't give a rat's ass about any of it. His fingers slick with sweat, he yanked at the collar of his shirt. Buttons popped off onto the warehouse floor.

He squinted in every direction. Nothing but blackness. Emptiness magnified the sound of his heart. Another blast from above. Something slapped him hard. It burned the skin of his neck. He winced and shrugged a shoulder. An object stuck to his body, then slid under his collar and down the inside of his shirt. His fingers followed the path, but he gave up trying to find it.

"What the hell—? Jesus. What's *wrong* with you people?"

With these bastards tracking him in the dark, it meant only one thing. He had to find a hole to hide, unsure where that might be. Feeling his way on all fours, Mickey crawled to change positions. His fingers felt along a wall. But he didn't know if he'd be heading for the door or deeper into the maze. One way might be his salvation. The other would be certain death.

Thwack! A round hit above him. On instinct, he covered his head with an arm. *A damned sitting duck!*

No time for doubt. He had to move. Slowly, he stood and picked a direction to run, a hand out in front. He'd trusted his luck for a lifetime. Surely, it wouldn't fail him now.

Thud! An explosion against his temple sent swirls of blinding light through his head. His eyes were on fire—they burned like acid. Chills of shock ran through him. When he slumped to the floor, his gun skittered across the cement, lost in the darkness.

Stunned, he only needed a moment to catch his breath. Only a moment. He pushed against the wall behind him, struggling clumsily to his feet. But a deathlike stillness seized him. A presence eased closer. Slowly, he turned his head, tears rolling down his cheeks. Someone was . . .

An arm gripped his chest, cradling him in the grasp of someone standing behind him. He smelled alcohol on the man's breath.

"You're mine now." The intimate whisper brushed by his ear. It shocked him. The familiarity sounded like it came from the lips of a lover. "Don't fight me."

For an instant, Mickey relaxed long enough to hope—maybe all this had been a mistake. Then he felt a sudden jerk.

Pain . . . searing pain!

Icy steel plunged into his throat, severing cartilage in its wake. A metallic taste filled his mouth. Its warmth sucked into his lungs, drowning him. Powerless to free himself, Mickey resisted the blackness with the only redemption possible. He imagined high tide with him adrift. He struggled for air, bobbing just beneath the ocean surface. The sun and blue sky warped with a swirling eddy. Mercifully, sounds of surf rolling to shore clouded the fear when his body began to convulse. Dizziness and a numbing chill finally seized him. And the pounding of his heart drained his ability to move at all.

Then a muffled gurgle dominated his senses—until there was nothing.

Euphoria swept through him with Blair's last breath. The man's body now hung limp in his arms. With a gloved hand, he reached for the night-vision goggles and tossed them to the floor. He filled his lungs with the coppery aroma of fresh blood. Closing his eyes, he released the body to fall hard to the cement. He'd used the ego of his prey as a weapon against him. His plan worked. Thinking of Mickey Blair lying dead at his feet, only one thing came to mind.

"Death humbles you when nothing else can."

The sound of laughter dotted the dark landscape. His men rose from their positions, one by one. It had been a successful hunt. The contractor on this job would be pleased. With the overhead light crackling to life, shadows ebbed from the grisly tableau.

"Job well done, men." He raised his voice, relishing the attention. He stood amidst his men. Their applause and shouts fueled his adrenaline. "But it ain't over. Let's get this place cleaned up. We got a delivery to make. And we're on a tight schedule."

The following is an excerpt from

NO ONE LIVES FOREVER

Available June 2008

HOTEL PALMA DOURADA
CUIABÁ, BRAZIL

Gripping his nine-millimeter Beretta, Nicholas Charboneau peered through the peephole of the penthouse suite, responding to a soft knock. The red-and-black uniforms of hotel personnel should not have given him any cause for alarm. And yet, the hair at the nape of his neck reacted to a rush of adrenaline. Two men stood by a rolling cart of white linen, covered with food platters and a bottle of Brazilian Merlot with a distinctive label.

Compliments of the house . . . or a Trojan Horse? The bottle of wine told the tale.

A lazy smile curved his lips. At his age, he relied more on wit and cunning, leaving the chest-thumping to younger men. He had no intention of answering the door, making himself vulnerable.

"No way," he scoffed, muttering under his breath. "Nice try, but never would've happened."

"Who is at the door?" The voice of his young body-guard, Jasmine Lee, drew his attention. Towel drying her black hair, she stood near the wet bar dressed only in the white robe of the hotel. "Did you order room service, Nicky?"

He raised his hand and shook his head, silently mouthing the word, "No."

Her body tensed, dark eyes flared in alert.

The sound of shattered glass from across the room broke his concentration. Jasmine darted from his sight, heading toward the noise.

As he rounded the foyer corner, three men dressed in black paramilitary uniforms burst into the room from the balcony, guns raised. Without hesitation, Jasmine tossed her towel toward the nearest man, a distraction. She punched a fist to his solar plexus, doubling the man over. To finish her attacker, she elbowed the back of his head, toppling him to the carpet. Now, she faced another, chin down and fists raised in defiance.

One down. White queen takes black knight's pawn, threatening the rook.

Nicholas's body reacted on pure instinct as chess maneuvers ran through his head, a practice in discipline and control. Adrenaline fueled his anger. He raced across the room, Beretta leveled. Unarmed, she wouldn't stand a chance if they started to shoot. He chose a spot to her far right, forcing the men to split their attack. A tactical maneuver.

Nicholas squared off with the man he'd coerced into

turning his back on Jasmine. His assailant flinched, fear in his eyes as he faced the Beretta. Not wanting to start any gunplay, he backhanded the man across the jaw, knocking him down.

"Arrgh." Wincing in pain, the man writhed on the floor, holding his jaw. Blood dripped through his fingers.

Two down. White knight to king four, checkmate in two moves.

He smelled victory. With Jasmine at his side, he tilted his head and glared at the final man. His gun aimed dead center between the stranger's eyes. "Who sent you? And you better pray I believe you."

"*Mãos ao alto.*" A stern voice came from behind.

Clenching his jaw, Nicholas wavered for an instant. He gripped the Beretta, maintaining what little tactical leverage remained. But he had a feeling all that was about to change. Unwilling to lower his weapon until he knew for certain, he shifted his gaze to catch a reflection in the mirror behind the wet bar.

The seductive country of Brazil had beckoned Nicholas to its borders, the fertile ground of corruption awaiting his influence. Now, the reality of that summons had a face. The room service attendant narrowed his eyes in challenge, matching his stare in the mirror.

Despite the night air coming from the open doors to the balcony, he noticed the man had a bead of sweat at his temple. The droplet lingered on the brink of a sun-weathered crease, one of many lines marking his face.

Nicholas did not speak Portuguese. But since the

uniformed man held a Kalashnikov assault rifle aimed at his head, understanding the native tongue became a moot point. The universal language of the AK–47 made his meaning perfectly clear. Nicholas lowered his weapon, allowing one of the men to take it, then raised his hands in compliance.

He had no option. Given the odds against a semiautomatic rifle in tight quarters, they were severely outnumbered. And one of the men held a gun on Jasmine. *Check. The black bishop had taken his queen out of play.* As in the game of chess, he would voluntarily topple his king to concede, not wanting to risk her life.

Checkmate. Game over. In an instant, everything changed.

Glancing toward Jasmine, Nicholas noticed her dark eyes communicating a clear message. He knew from experience she would fight if he gave her the slightest encouragement. The beautiful woman's unspoken connection to him made words unnecessary. With a subtle shake of his head, Nicholas gave his order.

You and I shall live to fight another day, my love. He would not challenge the inevitable. Whatever the purpose of these intruders, he would soon find out.

"I'm sure there's been some kind of mistake." He glared at the menacing faces of the five men. The two who entered through the front door via a passkey had wheeled in a large portable table. Aroma from the food wafted in the air, making his stomach grind. "The hotel knows never to send me wine made in Brazil."

Insulting the local wine was his calculated attempt to determine whether these men spoke English. The leader's expression remained deadly focused on him. The man held the rifle tight to his shoulder, clenching the weapon in a taut grip. With no reaction to his first offense, he ventured a second for good measure.

"I hope you realize"—Nicholas raised an eyebrow—"there will be no gratuity."

The head honcho had no sense of humor, nor did he apparently speak any English. Nicholas would not be dissuading him with his keen negotiating skills. Without the use of his quick wit, his best weapon would be gone from his arsenal, along with his gun. Nicholas churned his brain, considering his limited options.

The intruder spoke again.

"Você quer tirar sarro de mim, porco americano? Respeite quem aponta a arma na sua cabeça. Você vai saber logo quem esta engarregado ou vai morrer."

The comment had been directed at him. With so few visits to this country, he had picked up very little Portuguese, but he did recognize the term *American Pig,* and the word *morrer* had something to do with death.

All things considered—this was not a good sign.

The man standing before him clearly had Indian blood coursing through his veins with his mocha brown skin, pitch-black hair, flat nose, and high, angular cheekbones. The hotel uniform did little to disguise his raw, primitive intensity. An ancient lineage reflected in his dark eyes. The man looked out of place in this urban setting.

So why was he here—and holding a rifle with deadly determination? Desperation forced men to take chances. Unlike the men in this room, Nicholas was not desperate. At least, not yet. Greed was a familiar vice in his area of the world, but Brazil had refined it to an art.

"I'm sure we can come to some . . . arrangement. If you would allow me to get my wallet, I'll reconsider your gratuity." Carefully, he gestured with his hands, making the universal sign of *payola*.

Encouraged, he watched the headman give a nod, directing one of his followers to act. Nicholas heard a sound behind his back. Maintaining eye contact with the leader, he resisted turning around until . . . He gasped when something pierced his neck, a sharp sting. Pain forced him to wince and shrug a shoulder.

Too late. The damage had been done.

"What have you—?"

Within seconds, the skin at his neck burned. Muscles in his legs tingled. His equilibrium challenged, he felt weightless, and the room swayed. Walls drained their color.

Gravity pulled at him, forcing him to submit to its will. Nicholas dropped to his knees, his arms falling limp by his sides. He no longer had the strength to lift them. From the corner of his eye, he caught a motion.

Jasmine fought for her freedom, a blur of white. Sounds of a struggle distorted in his head, as if filtered through mounds of cotton. Noise deadened to a dull throb—an erratic and faint pulse. A dark shadow eclipsed his line of sight and an arm flung in retaliation. He sensed Jasmine's loss. It spurred him to stay conscious. His concern for her overwhelmed his body's surrender to the drugs injected into his system—drugs flooding him with an unmerciful indifference.

Falling face-first to the carpet, he held one eye open, searching for her. The muffled sound of his breaths came in shallow pants, slowing with each passing second. With his eyesight failing, he sensed Jasmine's dark hair near his face. Her familiar scent penetrated the veil of his stupor. The coppery smell of blood tainted the memory.

Was she—?

The possibility of her lying dead by his side made his heart ache. Dulled outrage compounded his torment. If anything happened to his beloved and loyal bodyguard, the eternal damnation of hell would appear like a day at the spa for the bastard committing the deed.

He vowed this with his last moment of consciousness, before he drifted through a threshold to his own brand of hell.

The foreign woman lay at the feet of Mario Araujo. Blood trailed from her mouth. Drops of deep red marred the luxurious white robe. It had not been necessary.

But time was of the essence if his plan worked at all. With a quick gesture, he ordered his men to move into action.

"Esta na hora de sair da cidade com a nosso premio, camaradas. Vamos sequir conforme a plano. Rapido."

They hoisted the American's body, jamming him into the hidden compartment of the room service cart. Tomorrow, he'd feel the pain of his unceremonious departure from the city. For now, the drugs in his body made him a compliant guest.

As leader of his people, Mario had taken the job of scout. He would not order his men to undertake such a risky job if he wouldn't make the same sacrifice. After all, the idea of kidnapping for profit had been his from the start. So for two years, he worked at the menial job of bellhop under the name of Rodrigo Santo. He'd taken the name and identification of a young boy who had died years ago in his village.

The dead rarely took offense to fraud and were good at keeping secrets.

Mario studied his usual prey at the deluxe hotel and suffered the indignities of the *civilized* world. Normally, he resorted to luring his targets from the hotel by way of an official-looking document from the Interior Ministry of Brazil or a memo from the Prosecutor General's Office. And business had been fruitful.

Then, nearly a year ago, a man made contact with him over the phone.

He remembered the conversation as if it were yesterday. Mario had gotten the call at the hotel, during work hours. The voice on the phone specifically asked for him and threatened to expose his little enterprise. The man claimed to have proof of his involvement, even had times and dates and known accomplices. Mario had listened, sure the police would burst in and make an arrest that instant, hauling him from the hotel in handcuffs. But when that didn't happen, he regained his composure and assessed his situation in a different light.

"What do you want in return?" he had asked.

"In return?"

"Yes. You'd have me arrested if that were your purpose." Mario persisted, hoping he'd guessed right. "What do you want?"

After a long silence, the man began to laugh, an abrasive sound.

"You see? I knew I picked the right man. You and I are going to get along."

To this day, Mario hadn't told anyone of the secret alliance he had made, not wanting to put any of his people at risk. And with his new partner, Mario had no complaints. His enterprise thrived more than before.

So when the man had called about a rich American, Mario listened again. The kidnapping had been ordered and planned in haste, without Mario's usual care. His *associate* had told him the foreigner wouldn't stay long and would be far too cagey to be lured from the hotel, as the others had been. Normally, Mario's instincts would have cautioned him against moving forward with the plan, but two things swayed him.

First, everything had fallen into place without effort, making it too good to pass up. The rich foreigner had been delivered into his hands, yet another generous gift from his anonymous benefactor. But more importantly, his *associate* had shared vital information on the American and his purpose in this country. For Mario, this carried far more weight than any ransom.

Regardless whether he trusted the man, Mario couldn't ignore the compelling intel. Although it would take time, he'd verify what he could, but shortly it wouldn't matter.

His mysterious comrade made a big show of this being their last venture together, even giving him a special encrypted phone to take with him, for emergency contact only. The phone would work where they were going. And the man had made it worth his while with the American, too. Mario would soon return a hero to his beloved home and provide well for his people. Nothing would make him more proud.

Far enough away from the lowland heat, his childhood village had been located at the base of the rocky outcrop known as the Chapada dos Guimarães. Now a distant memory. It had overlooked the flat plain of the Paraguay River and the marshlands of the Pantanal. Mario longed for the misty cool of those folding hills, still vivid in his dreams. Its pillared rock formations were dotted with the ancient caves of his ancestors. And only the hand of God could have graced such stunning waterfalls.

But too many tourists and the far reach of his own government left him torn apart from his memories. Years ago, he had relocated his tribe to a spot deeper in the jungle, far from civilization and its corrupt influence. Yet there were days, resentment swelled in his belly like a virulent cancer. He would compromise no more. After today, maybe he wouldn't have to.

"Até o nosso próximo encontro," Mario said in

a hushed tone. He watched three of his men escape from the balcony, leaving as they had come.

He'd depart with his accomplice, similarly dressed in a hotel uniform. They'd brazenly haul the American to a service elevator. Once in the parking garage, an inconspicuous van awaited the rendezvous with his men. Soon, he would be on his turf, among his own people.

But before Mario left the extravagant hotel suite, he knelt by the side of the Asian-looking woman who had fought so bravely.

"Para o bem do seu amigo, você tem que obedecer as nossas ordens."

He tossed an envelope of the hotel stationery on her chest and lightly tapped the side of her cheek. By the time the beautiful woman warrior awoke, they'd be long gone. And she would know what to do.

He only hoped she also knew how to follow orders.

Searing light blinded her. Jasmine squinted and the effort sent electrified shards of glass into her brain. She felt the left side of her face throb, swollen and hot. Yet the night air in the room prickled her skin. The sensation made her aware of a metallic tang in her mouth. With a brush of her tongue, she found the source of the blood.

Unwilling to move, she lay perfectly still, waiting for the pain to subside. It only dulled and spread through her body like venom. Soon, her eyes concentrated on the elaborate chandelier overhead. Its iridescent prisms swirled rainbow luster . . . until the shimmer stopped dead center, coming into focus.

Oh, God . . . she had been so careless.

"Nicky? What—?"

As she raised up from the carpet, her head nearly exploded. She planted an elbow beneath her weight to keep from collapsing. Nausea churned her stomach. She held back a strand of dark hair and heaved, spitting up pale yellow foam. Her vision dotted with pinpoints of light from the exertion. Signs of a concussion.

Yet Jasmine knew she deserved far worse for her failure.

A dismal ache centered deep within her chest, spreading its heat to her face. She had failed Nicky, allowed him to be taken. For all she knew, he was already dead. She envisioned his handsome face, strangely passive in death. His violet-blue eyes glazed in milky white. The image would be forever branded in memory for her sin of failure.

Love blinded her, made her weak and neglectful. And Nicholas had paid the price. Splaying a hand against the carpet, she lifted her body to a sitting position. Her fingers touched a different texture.

An envelope.

The note inside the hotel envelope provided little information given the many questions looming in her mind. The instructions were brief and to the point. She had ten days to comply. The ransom wired to a Swiss bank account listed in the note—or Nicky would be killed.

Yet with the instructions in English, it left her wondering who was in charge. Did the uniformed man know exactly what Nicky had said in English and only pretended his ignorance? Or had someone else pulled the strings? For these men to kidnap Nicholas Charboneau, ignorance would be the least of their problems. They obviously had no idea the extent of their offense.

Once more, she stared at the note. No organization laid claim to the abduction. And the ransom was far more money than she had access to. She held no special authority over Nicky's affairs. By outward appearance, he was her employer. End of story. Yet her heart could claim so much more. If only she had disclosed her feelings to him. Now she might never get the chance.

For the first time in her life, she felt completely powerless. That was inexcusable.

Her mind began to formulate a strategy. Because of Nicky's reputation, she was not sure how her demand for help would be received. She would direct the attention of the local law enforcement, overseeing the efforts herself. The nearest American Consulate would be contacted tonight. The US State Department tomorrow. Time was of the essence.

Surely she could garner support, even in this uncivilized corner of the world. And if money was required, she knew how to get it.

Christian Delacorte owed her a very big favor. Despite Nicky's orders to the contrary, perhaps it was time for Christian to learn about his rightful connection to Nicholas Charboneau.